BLOOD ON THE VINE

BLOOD ON THE VINE

A NOVEL

J. T. Falco

NEW YORK

This is a work of fiction. All of the names, characters, organizations, places and events portrayed in this novel are either products of the author's imagination or are used fictitiously. Any resemblance to real or actual events, locales, or persons, living or dead, is entirely coincidental.

Copyright © 2025 by Joseph Falco

All rights reserved.

Published in the United States by Crooked Lane Books, an imprint of The Quick Brown Fox & Company LLC.

Crooked Lane Books and its logo are trademarks of The Quick Brown Fox & Company LLC.

Library of Congress Catalog-in-Publication data available upon request.

ISBN (hardcover): 979-8-89242-120-1
ISBN (paperback): 979-8-89242-238-3
ISBN (ebook): 979-8-89242-123-2

Cover design by Meghan Deist

Printed in the United States.

www.crookedlanebooks.com

Crooked Lane Books
34 West 27th St., 10th Floor
New York, NY 10001

First Edition: April 2025

10 9 8 7 6 5 4 3 2 1

To Leigh, obviously.

*"O thou invisible spirit of wine,
if thou hast no name to be known by,
let us call thee devil!"*

—William Shakespeare, *Othello*

Prologue

She didn't know it yet, but she was already dead.
    And as she stumbled through a thicket of gnarled vines, a gooey redness dripping from her hands and abdomen, she was hit with the sudden clarifying thought that she didn't know much at all. Her name, for instance. How she got here. Where she was going. Why she was wearing this ridiculous pink T-shirt, bedazzled with the words "Welcome to the Shit Show"? And why she was in so little pain despite being covered in so much blood?
    Shouldn't this sort of thing hurt more?
    "Screw it," she whispered through gritted teeth. There was no time to stop and gather her bearings. Given how muddled her thoughts were and how cloudy her vision was, she had a sneaking suspicion that no amount of time or stillness would provide answers, and if she stopped—well—then whoever had done this to her would no doubt catch up and finish the job. So, with no other choice, she ran, fast and frantic, her bare feet stumbling over rough patches of dirt and jagged chunks of limestone. Every ounce of energy she could possibly muster was pushing her onward, like a car sucking up its last few drops of fuel as it sputtered toward a gas station that it had no real chance of ever reaching.

Why does everything look the same around here?

Those twisted vines planted in straight, narrow rows stretched out in every direction, a dizzying maze designed with agricultural precision. Under the haunting light of a full October moon, the grape leaves lost their quaint, daytime charm and took on the guise of a cage, a thorny prison in greenish yellow. And the evening fog, so common on these mountainside vineyards, may as well have been a cloud of mustard gas, slowly choking the life out of her as she raced through it in search of salvation.

Suddenly, a figure appeared in the path ahead.

"You shouldn't have run, Katherine."

Katherine. *Was that her name? Why couldn't she remember anything?* But that voice, so eerily calm in contrast to her heaving, desperate breath, struck a familiar chord and sent a series of memories flashing through her addled mind: fire reflecting off a steel tank. An animal disemboweled, its innards being invaded by hungry larvae. A single red grape rolling off a wooden table and landing on the floor with a pathetic, overripe splat. A white handkerchief, monogrammed with the letters "C.R.," wiping the gooey redness from her cheeks and eyes with a tenderness that felt disturbingly wrong, almost like a family member's.

"What did you do to me?" she cried out, paralyzed with frightened indecision as she studied the maze all around her. But no reply came. Instead, the silhouette moved steadily closer.

"Please . . . You don't have to do this. I have money. I mean, my friend Charlotte does. I can call her, and she can get you whatever you want!" But her words floated off into the night, ignored by her silent tormentor.

When the silhouette finally reached her and she dropped to her knees in a hopeless act of self-preservation, a cloud drifted across the moon, swallowing it whole and bathing the vineyard in a sea of darkness.

Then a strange thing happened, unsettling the mysterious captor: Katherine laughed.

Maybe it was the drugs she'd been given, a burst of euphoria as her high intensified. Maybe, as she neared her final moments, she found amusement in the realization that her life couldn't possibly flash before her eyes since, in her current state, she had no such life to remember. Or maybe—just maybe—it was as simple as catching one last glimpse down at her ridiculous pink novelty shirt, smothered in the sticky blood of a painless wound.

"Welcome to the Shit Show" indeed.

1

Sex criminal. Petty thief. Embezzler.

It's a nasty habit, reducing people to what I presume to be their most likely crimes and misdemeanors, but I've always found it oddly soothing. Certainly a better way to pass the time than burying my face in a phone like everyone else in this dump. At least I'm engaged with the rest of humanity. I make eye contact—to a point. I just do it from a distance, with no intention of ever following it up with a "hello" or a "how's it going?" I'm interested in human beings the way marine biologists are interested in eels: as a purely scientific matter, detached and unemotional, because once you get close enough, even the best ones turn out to be covered in slime.

Abuser. Another sex criminal. Securities fraudster.

And this last one's checking me out with all the subtlety of a sucker punch to the face. His hair, high and tight around the sides, giving way to a carefully slicked coiffure, reeks of either venture capital or Champions League soccer. And since I'm perched on a rickety metal stool, nursing my third bottle of Heineken in a San Francisco dive bar, my money's on VC. His open-collar shirt and Patagonia vest are practically the standard-issue uniform for the multimillionaire tech-investor set, and the thought of what guys like him have done to the city—to *my* city—makes me want to hurl my half-priced beer into his smug face.

Oh God, please don't come over here and talk to me. That's the last thing I need after the day I've had . . .

He must have mistaken my cynical glare for an invitation, because now he's giving me a ravenous smile as he slides off his stool and starts in my direction.

Shit.

This city used to be interesting. When I first moved here over twenty years ago, I was in a bad place. I couldn't shake the gloom that clung to me like an emotional parasite, reminding me what had happened, what those people had done to me. To my father. But San Francisco whisked me off my feet and gave me hope again in its eclectic weirdness. The jam bands playing discordant guitar in a cloud of pot smoke at some Haight-Ashbury hole in the wall. The unabashedly campy drag shows and refreshingly affordable art galleries of the Castro. The best chilaquiles on the planet at my favorite Mexican spot in the Mission. This was a city where people weren't ashamed to be themselves and follow their hearts, and for a—let's be honest—*broken* girl of seventeen who was searching for a path forward and a purpose in life, it was like stepping into the Technicolor dreamworld of Oz. No one here lived life in the generic. It was a peninsula of hyper-specificity, where hundreds of thousands of people were able to take whatever pain or difficulty life had handed them and transform it into something beautiful. An urban cocoon that churned out well-balanced butterflies. And at the time, that was exactly what I needed.

But then, the tech money came. Facebook. Google. A company called Salesforce that did something no one seemed capable of explaining but that still earned them enough cash to build the second tallest building west of the Mississippi. And with them, an endless parade of nameless, faceless engineers, programmers, and investors who sucked the life out of my vibrant paradise and sent the rents skyrocketing into the stratosphere. Like locusts, they transformed the landscape as they consumed everything in their path, not content until everyone interesting had been relegated to a far-flung exurb, and each block of the city had become an identical, algorithmically curated strip of salad chains, fitness studios, and coworking spaces. And when the good times ended—when a homelessness crisis that *they* exacerbated turned the city into an urban wasteland peppered with cardboard beds and discarded needles—they hightailed it to Austin or Boulder or some other unsuspecting host, where the cycle would no doubt repeat itself.

Consume, destroy, flee.

And leave people like me to clean up the mess.

Which is why my stomach churns at the sight of this smarmy tech investor sauntering over to my barstool with a glass of small-batch bourbon that he probably heard about from some teenage TikTok influencer who can't even drink.

"Do I know you from somewhere?" he asks with the cool precision of a practiced pickup line.

"Have you ever been arrested by the FBI?" I say without missing a beat, not so subtly lifting the fabric of my untucked gray shirt and flashing the standard-issue Glock 19M holstered at the hip of my black jeans.

"Wh—wh—what?" he stammers, stumbling back in surprise. "Why would I . . . ? Are you serious?"

I give him a shrug, then a subtle nod, just enough to let his imagination run wild.

"No!" he cries out in desperation, clearly wishing he'd tried to flirt with someone else.

"Then we probably haven't met," I tell him without a hint of emotion, turning my eyes back to my beer and ending this poor sucker's dream of a quickie in the bathroom. He stands there for a moment staring at me, completely rigid, struggling to comprehend this abrupt rejection. But I just keep nursing my Heineken, giving him whatever time he needs to process how badly he's just been owned by a *girl*.

The truth is, I've gotten used to moments like this. Overconfident bros with an outdated view of femininity having a hard time accepting my existence as a thirty-nine-year-old woman in law enforcement. (Especially a woman with the kind of curves that used to get me mocked in high school for being "pudgy," but which are apparently much more in vogue these days in a world overflowing with Kardashians and Brazilian butt lifts.) I know their understanding of women like me comes primarily from CBS crime procedurals and bondage fantasies on Pornhub, so it's only natural that there'd be a disconnect as they try to place me in a tangible reality. A glitch in the macho male's matrix. And sure enough, after a few seconds, the bourbon-swilling VC shakes his head and slouches back to his stool, Charlie Brown leaving to the tune of some melancholy piano.

For one peaceful moment, I think the interaction's over. That he'll accept defeat gracefully, and we'll both be able to move on with our lives—or at the very least, with our booze. But then he slams his glass down on the bar in a petulant fit of ego-bruised rage.

"You're a crazy bitch, you know that, right?" he shouts with just enough volume for the entire place to hear. And when I refuse to even look back up and acknowledge his outburst, he mutters something I'd rather not hear anyway—more B-words and C-words and whatever else makes him feel better about his undersized P-word. Then he turns and storms out of the bar.

Or, at least, he *tries* to.

"Pull," I finally yell out after his third failed attempt to push open the door, his hands practically caressing the "Pull" sign with each futile shove. It takes him a beat to recognize his mistake; in the meantime, the rest of the bar is having one hell of a laugh at his expense. I watch him try to play it cool and shoot the other guys a casual grin of acknowledgment, but I know he's embarrassed, and honestly, it gives me an odd sort of thrill. Maybe the Germans were onto something with that whole schadenfreude thing. And as Mr. VC begrudgingly heeds my advice and disappears into the blinding white afternoon sun, I smile for the first time all day.

The moment, unfortunately, is short-lived.

"You know the rules, Lana," says the bartender, a perpetually gloomy fifty-something named Evan who reminds me of that donkey from Winnie the Pooh, only talking when he has something awful to say. Which, if I'm being honest, is one of the main reasons I come to this shithole. Evan may not be much to look at, with a jaw that's two sizes too big for his head and a hairstyle caught in that unfortunate no-man's land between receding and bald, but what he lacks in looks he more than makes up for in his ability to mind his own business. Usually.

"The guy was an asshole," I tell him defensively. "You know he was an asshole."

"Well, that asshole just left without paying for a sixty-dollar glass of bourbon," Evan says. "Because of *you* and that gun I told you I never want to see in here again." But there's no anger in his voice, only disappointment; a hopeless surrender from a man who seems all too used to being kicked around by life and by this changing city.

At first, I have every intention of arguing my way out of this mess, of reminding him of my legal right to carry a service weapon in the state of California, even when I'm off duty, but soon I just start to feel bad for the guy. The deep wellspring of guilt that's driven me most of my life begins to bubble up, wetting down the hotter aspects of my personality: my quick temper, my feisty refusal to be told what to do by anyone who isn't signing my paycheck. And I pull every dollar I have out of my scratched-up, knockoff wallet: four crisp twenties, a ripped ten, and two crumpled ones.

"Here," I tell him, dropping the wad of cash on the bar as I slide off my stool. "It's on me." And before he even has a chance to count it, I'm already across the room, pulling open the front door, just like the sign says.

* * *

The air is hot for an October afternoon, especially for a city known for its wintry summers, where a seventy-degree day can be cause for celebration. But today it's pushing eighty, and the ocean breeze that usually sweeps across the hills is nowhere to be found. Maybe it, too, got sick of the daily indignities of life here and followed the money to Austin or Boulder or God-knows-where-else.

After three Heinekens, my mouth is parched, and my head's starting to pound with the warning shots of impending dehydration, so I know I should be getting home, out of the sun and into a pitcher of cold water. But I'm not ready for that yet. I may not want to talk to people or let anyone in, but I'm also not ready to shut the world out. I need to see faces, even if they're whizzing by on e-bikes or trolleys; I need to hear voices, even if they're in a language I'll never understand.

The fact is, it's just been one of those days.

The kind that starts with a shitty phone call that wakes you up at four in the morning—*"Your informant's dead. We need you in Hayward right now. Bring coffee"*—and by breakfast time you know you won't to be able to eat today, not after seeing a good kid lying in a pool of his own blood, all because he agreed to help you out with a drug-trafficking case. I knew it wasn't my fault, not directly, but when you bear witness to enough of life's brutalities, when the darker side of humanity clouds out the good to the point where you're fumbling blindly through a pitch-black field of corpses and karmic injustice, you can't help but feel a little guilty sometimes. For not being able to stop it. For being the one who lived.

It was the goddamn story of my life.

I walk aimlessly for the next hour, up roads so steep the only way to the top is by switchback, then down the other side at a jog, since there's no way to go any slower without busting a knee. I pass a group of women my age laughing, in yoga pants, mats in hand, on their way to a class together, and I can't help but wonder what that would feel like. To be so at ease with others that friendship isn't just possible, it's effortless. A way to relieve stress rather than cause it. But even the idea of emotional closeness is foreign to me these days, and it has been for years, ever since Jess died and the one friend I ever had was reduced to a name on an empty grave. It's part of the reason I prefer my relationships to be transactional, based on sex or work or the simple exchange of food and beer for money. At least then, with those clearly defined roles, there's no expectation of vulnerability; no small talk, which everyone knows can often lead to some very big places.

As my urban hike continues, I convince myself that I'm heading nowhere in particular, that each left and right are simply turns of happenstance, but soon I find myself standing outside an idyllic blue Victorian home and I realize I've been lying. This whole time I've actually been on autopilot, retracing the steps I first took when I arrived here twenty-two years ago, off the ferry from Vallejo, an emancipated minor dragging a heavy Rollaboard suitcase up Fillmore Street toward a hastily scrawled address on a Post-it.

Because the best way to get over a shitty day is to remind yourself of a worse one. Right?

You really are pathetically obvious sometimes, Lana. Really . . .

Mark and Carolyn Alcott's powder-blue house looks exactly as I remember it, perched on a diagonal, like it's always on the verge of sliding down the hill into the bay, and for a moment, I think about knocking. Their own kids must be in college by now—if they're home, they'd probably be thrilled to have a visitor, even if it *has* been years since my last pop-in. But as I step up onto the trellised porch, its paint cracked by the passage of time, I can't help but think about the inevitable conversation to follow: "How've you been, Lana? How's work? Dating anyone? Have you gone to see your dad lately . . . ?" And I realize at once that I've made a terrible mistake in coming here.

Before I can even stop and think, I'm already two blocks away, at the nearest place with a bar, asking for a Heineken and being told by a young woman dressed like a mime without makeup that they only serve wine. Only, I'm still not with it enough to get up and leave, so I give her a gruff "Sure, whatever" and try to gather my bearings. I have no clue what the restaurant's called, but it seems to serve the Bay Area's usual farm-to-table fare, with yuppie couples all around me eating sprouted broccoli and roasted fennel. Everyone looks so goddamn happy, like they didn't see a dead body this morning, like they didn't just wander halfway across the city to their foster family's house for reasons I'll have to unpack later with my therapist. And a small part of me wants to stand up on my plush white leather stool and shout, "What's your secret? How can anyone be this excited about grilled radicchio?"

But then the bartender returns in her crisp white shirt with red suspenders and sets an open bottle down in front of me, along with an empty Bordeaux glass. "The winemaker's a friend, so we're offering this one on special," she says, pouring a small taste for me to try. "It's a 2022 Wappo Crest cabernet sauvignon from the Calistoga AVA. Really pure blue and black fruits, not too jammy, with some nice minerality from the volcanic soils. I think you'll really dig it."

She smiles pleasantly, waiting for me to reach out and take a sip, but my hands stay firmly planted in my lap, gripped by a paralysis that also keeps me from speaking. *Why did I let her pour me a wine when I know I can't stomach the stuff? And why—of all the bottles in all the bars in all the world—did it have to be a Napa cabernet?* I stare blankly at the bottle's no-nonsense design, a piece of abstract art in yellow and orange that reminds me of salmon leaping from a river, and I wonder what my dad would think of it.

"Did you want to try it?" the bartender asks.

I don't know how to explain the messy truth, and I feel bad telling her no, so I force out an awkward smile. Anything to make this excruciating moment a little less weird for both of us. Still, though, I can't figure out what to say or what to do with my hands, so rather than just act normal, I let my eyes fixate on a single drop of wine that clings to the rim of the glass, as if it's desperate to avoid falling into the ruby red pit below. But before long, the inevitability of time and gravity sends the drop sliding helplessly down the side, and I swear I can hear it scream.

"You sure you're okay?"

"I'm fine," I lie, since the truth is a tale I can barely admit to my therapist, let alone a twenty-three-year-old stranger in red suspenders. I mean, where would I even begin? With the boyfriend I abandoned? With the famous family who betrayed me? With the father who's still locked up in San Quentin, who I've been too much of a coward to even visit these past few years? I know some people find it easy sharing their past and their pain, since it serves as a sort of olive branch in these situations. *"I'm telling you my secrets, so you can trust me with yours."* But personally, that's never been my style. I'm not a sharer. I don't gossip. I move through life with my head down and my eyes averted, hoping to avoid even the most casual of conversations.

So rather than explain myself, I lunge my hand out toward the glass, toss back the wine, and try to shoot the thick, tannic liquid down my throat without having to taste it, as if it were a warm, cheap tequila. But it's not. It's clearly beautifully made and rich with flavor, and my taste buds refuse to let it pass my tongue until they've savored every last drop.

Suddenly I'm sixteen again, seated beside my father at the small, round dinner table in our quaint St. Helena bungalow, his canvases piled high in a corner since there was never enough room to display them in the house. Our twenty-pound brown mutt, Ursula, is barking at squirrels through the bay window. Meanwhile, my dad and I are sloshing cabernet back and forth in our mouths, trying to activate its hidden flavors of cassis and blackberry with a torrent of oxygen, but I've sipped a bit too much and now my cheeks are about to burst. Dad notices, and rather than offer me a spit cup, he mimics me, puffing out his cheeks and widening his eyes, eventually contorting his face so much that I can't help but laugh, and the wine sprays out across the table, splattering his white undershirt with a hundred red polka dots.

The sense memory fades, and I'm back on my stool, where I find myself under the gaze of that wide-eyed bartender, who must be wondering if I'm insane. "What'd you think?" she asks politely, doing her best to make my embarrassingly odd behavior seem perfectly normal.

"To be honest," I say slowly, trying to pull my wayward mind back to the present, "I think I need to get the fuck out of here."

2

The call comes at 9:02 AM, just after my first delirious slap at the snooze button.

"Hey boss," I mutter without having to look at the cracked display of my outdated iPhone, since no one else would dare call me this early.

And sure enough, the perpetually worried, maternal voice of the SAC, Special Agent in Charge Connie Chen, floats back through the speaker. "It's not healthy for a woman your age to sleep this late, Lana."

"I can't help it if I'm a night owl," I say with a guilty glance over at the decimated bag of Smart Pop and empty bottle of Heineken on my nightstand. After my bizarre afternoon of existential bar hopping, I decided to spend the rest of the night as I usually do, with a cold beer, a hastily ripped open bag of popcorn, and the soothing certainty of some old episodes of *Seinfeld*, that misanthropic lullaby from my preteen years that I've binged more times than I can count.

"How much Netflix did you watch?" the SAC asks sharply, her words cutting through my morning brain fog.

"That's not what I was—why would you think I—"

"Lana."

"I—I do other things."

"Name one."

"Work."

"*Besides* work."

My mouth opens with the instinctual desire to fight back, to defend my honor as a functional adult with hobbies and passions and a vibrant social life. But my brain knows better. It's also far too groggy at the moment to come up with a suitable lie, so an awkward silence brings our conversation to a screeching halt.

"Lana," the SAC says in that concerned but slightly disappointed way of hers, "I would never tell an agent of mine how to live. Especially not someone who's as good at the job as you."

"But . . ." I interject with no small amount of sarcasm.

"But there *has* to be more than this. No one, no matter how strong they are, no matter how thick their walls have gotten, can sustain this thing alone."

"What thing?"

"*Life*. And I'm not talking about you settling down and getting married. For God's sake, I've been divorced twice—I know coupling off isn't the answer to all our problems as middle-aged women."

"I am *not* middle-aged!"

"Well, you will be soon," she says matter-of-factly. "Mathematically. But that's not really the point."

"Then why'd you bring it up?"

"Lana, pleeeeaaase," she says, extending her vowels in utter exasperation. "Let me put this in words you'll understand. Beer and popcorn—they might make for a quick and easy dinner. But they're empty calories. You can't live off them forever. Okay? Eventually, you need more. You need something that'll fill you up and make you whole again."

My neck turns slowly toward the predictable remains of last night's dinner, that torn bag of inedible kernels and that empty green bottle, and I let out a defeated sigh. "We're not really talking about beer and popcorn, are we?"

"It's a metaphor."

"Got it."

As the SAC lets me stew in the silence of reluctant self-reflection, I take a moment to examine my surroundings. Not in the half-blind, passive way you interact with your bedroom on a daily basis, casually pulling open drawers and ritualistically raising and lowering blinds, but with the keen, judgmental eye you might use when stepping into a date's apartment, as each dirty dish and stray sock gets tabulated in your mental spreadsheet, helping you decide whether to run, stay for sex, or hold out for breakfast. And it doesn't take me long to realize my boss is onto something.

My dirty clothes overflow from a laundry basket by the door, stained black jeans and sweaty sports bras spewing out as if they're ashamed to be seen in a cracked plastic bin rather than the discreet rattan or wicker hamper preferred by most women my age. Beside it, on the white Ikea dresser with the drawer that won't close right, sits a packet of birth control pills, a prescription pill bottle of Lexapro, a few FBI reports, a waxless former candle, and a framed Polaroid of my childhood dog, Ursula. (What can I say—I've always had a soft spot for misunderstood women.) Otherwise, there's not a photo in sight. Even the background wallpaper on my phone speaks to my solitude; it's a picture of the Earth as seen from the moon, all of humanity reduced to a pale blue dot in a sea of infinite black.

So maybe my life isn't some Instagram wet dream, a humblebragging hodgepodge of kittens and babies and home remodels. In the game of Life—and by that, I mean the literal board game from the 1960s—I would be losing in spectacular fashion. *But screw anyone else's standards of living, right?* I'm healthy-ish. I'm happy enough. I have a rent-controlled apartment in a halfway decent neighborhood. And I have a job that I love with the FBI's San Francisco field office, investigating violent crimes and putting away bad guys.

"Boss, did you call me at nine AM to make me feel bad about myself, or is this about a new case?"

I hear her sigh faintly on the other end before she answers. "I need you to pack a bag. Four, five nights tops. Then meet me at the office. Full briefing's at eleven."

"Where am I going?"

A tense silence fills the air as the SAC weighs whether to tell me. Whatever the answer is, she clearly knows I'm not going to like it, which can only mean one thing.

"It's not up north is it?"

"Just get down here, and we'll talk about it in person."

Then she hangs up, and I already know I'm screwed.

* * *

Two hours later, I'm freshly showered and standing in the SAC's office on the thirteenth floor of the Federal Building, a homey corner unit that used to have romantic views of the bay until a tech company built a forty-one-story tower across the street. The shelves and desk have been artfully decorated with pink and purple orchids, along with framed photos of Chen's three grown children and four grandkids, all of which have been turned toward me like some smiling advertisement for the decorative benefits of procreation: *"If you have unprotected sex, you'll finally have something to put on your desk too!"* But where Connie Chen sees a wellspring of love and affection, I just see more opportunities for future pain. *And she wonders why I have so few second dates...*

Special Agent in Charge Connie Chen stands four feet, eleven inches tall on a good day, and I doubt she's ever sent a scale tipping into three-digit territory. But she is fiercely protective of her agents and her department, with a track record unmatched anywhere at the Bureau, and there's not a man or woman in the San Francisco office who wouldn't take a bullet for her. Which makes it all the more difficult for me to stand in front of her and tell her she's wrong.

"There are six other highly skilled agents in this unit," I insist, even though I know three of them are on a major crimes detail in Oakland and one's on maternity leave. "Can't you send one of them?"

"They're busy."

"Not Portnoy," I remind her.

"Portnoy is barely qualified for desk duty. And he doesn't have your knowledge of the area. No one does."

"But . . ."

"Lana."

". . . I haven't been back to the Valley since high school."

"I know," she says, taking a seat on the edge of her desk. "And I don't mean to diminish what happened to you back then. But two women are dead, and a killer's on the loose. Which is why I need you to swallow your pride, get in your car, and go do what you do best before it happens again. Before we find another body ripped open on the side of a vineyard road."

I stand there for what feels like an eternity, and in the tense silence, I can hear a drop of water fall from my damp hair onto the white tile floor. The SAC must have heard it too, because now she's eyeing me skeptically, no doubt thinking that a real adult would have found time to blow-dry her hair before a meeting that didn't even start until eleven. "Is this because of the Hayward case? Am I being punished?"

"No, Lana. You did nothing wrong."

"I got an innocent kid killed!"

"Do you really think that?"

I shrug, too guilt-ridden to form a response, and I wipe a bit of unwelcome moisture from my right eye.

"Lana, that *kid* was a twenty-one-year-old fentanyl dealer who got high and told someone he shouldn't have told that he was an informant."

"He had a rough life—that doesn't mean he deserved to die."

"No, it doesn't. But you did everything right. You worked that case to the bone, and you protected him every way you could. But sometimes bad shit just happens, and all we can do is move on to the next one."

I feel myself about to cry, if I haven't done so already, and I recoil at the thought of being so exposed in front of another person, especially one who knows me as well as Connie Chen. It's not just the unprofessional display of emotion; it's the inevitable hugs and sympathetic questions that will follow. I don't want her asking me how I'm doing, how I'm feeling, whether I'm still in therapy, what my current dose of Lexapro is, whether I need time off to heal. So, without her noticing, I pinch my left palm with my right thumb and middle finger, digging my jagged, bitten fingernails into the skin with such force that I draw a bit of blood. It's agonizing, but I don't stop. Not until I'm so distracted by the physical pain that I'm no longer thinking about my informant lying in a puddle of blood in a graffiti-stained alley, surrounded by the stray fast-food wrappers and half-crushed beer cans that serve as a sort of cheap urban carpet in neighborhoods like his. And just like that, my eyes dry out and my face hardens.

"Fine," I tell her. "You want me to move on? Let's move on." And before she can say another word, I snatch a thin case file in a manila folder out of her unsuspecting hand, a file I'd no doubt be expected to thicken in the coming days. Paperclipped to the front are the photos of two young women: Pilar Cruz and Katherine

O'Shea. One Latina, one white. Both in their twenties, both dead. And printed in the middle, in the Bureau's standard, no-nonsense font, are three words that send a chill down my spine: "NAPA VALLEY MURDERS."

I guess I'm going home.

3

The drive north gives me plenty of time to sort through the details of the case; better that than let the passing signs and landmarks trigger any unwelcome memories.

On September 7th, a twenty-one-year-old Guatemalan farmworker named Pilar Cruz went missing during one of her night shifts picking grapes at an Oakville vineyard. As with many of the seasonal workers who arrive in the Valley for harvest, she was in the country illegally, so when a cousin reported her disappearance to the County Sheriff's Department, it was met with an apathetic shrug.

Even when her body turned up a day later on the side of the road, next to a dead cat, with lacerations on her wrists and abdomen, a cursory investigation lasting forty-eight hours found no leads and ruled out any suspects. She hadn't been raped, but a toxicology report did show several different drugs in her system, including LSD and a powerful sedative called pentobarbital.

Like most crimes in which the victims are undocumented, this one never would have made its way to my office had it not been for a second murder—this one involving a white girl.

Five days ago, on October 6th, a twenty-seven-year-old named Katherine O'Shea got separated from a bachelorette party. She was visiting wine country, from Dallas with some girlfriends, to celebrate the impending nuptials of a Charlotte Croydon, when she stopped answering her phone and didn't show up to a planned dinner in Yountville. Her friends assumed she went home with a woman they'd met in a tasting room, so they didn't contact the authorities until the next morning. But by then, it was too late. Katherine was found dead at the base of Howell Mountain, with lacerations on her wrists and abdomen and a disemboweled opossum by her side. She hadn't been raped, but a toxicology report did show traces of LSD and pentobarbital.

The similarities between the two murders were uncanny, too precise to be coincidental. And just like that, the Pilar Cruz case was reopened, and an obligatory report was made to the FBI field office in Santa Rosa. Two days later, it found its way to me.

Now, as I merge into the steady flow of tourist traffic on Highway 29, the main artery into the beating heart of wine country, I'm struck by how little I recognize. *Was this part of the Valley always so pockmarked with fast food restaurants and discount motel chains?* I feel like I'm coasting through an endless strip mall of gray concrete slabs and crowded parking lots, a game of brand-name bingo that could just as easily be in Naperville as in Napa. This had always been the poorer side of the Valley, but my memories of it are somehow more romantic than this, even despite how it all ended. The winding creeks and lush mountains; the wooded pathways that felt built for biking; the family-run groceries where everyone knew your name and your usual order. When I close my eyes and think of home, those are the images I see. Not whatever this is.

My dad and I first moved here when I was twelve, just a few months after Mom died. We both needed a change—Santa Fe would always remind us of her, those flowing white dresses she loved to wear around the house, like an angel drifting past the pink adobe walls—and when he sold his first two paintings to Holly Bancroft to use on her wine labels, we took it as a sign. Napa was our second chance, our salvation, our California *Carpathia* tossing out life preservers to our sinking *Titanic* in the New Mexico desert. So we drove northwest and settled into a rented bungalow where I taught myself how to grow up and he taught himself how to grow grapes.

Needless to say, one of us was far more successful than the other.

Over the years, he went from being one of the Valley's favorite label artists to one of its most beloved vineyard managers, helping to grow and harvest the grapes that went into some of the most expensive wines in the world. Meanwhile, I went through puberty without a mother and without any real friends (yet), which was why I spent so much time in nature, losing myself in the woods and streams and hidden trails that seemed to exist just for me. Out there, no one could see that I had bad acne and no idea how to treat it. Deep in the woods, I wasn't the chubby girl getting mocked by her peers at a time when no one had ever heard of terms like "fatphobic" and "body shaming." I was free, and I was alone, and for a long time I loved it.

Of course, that was before I met Jessica Bancroft. Before she took me under her wing and taught me how to count calories and flirt with boys and all sorts of other self-destructive teenage behavior that I soaked up like a sponge. Before I got to know her brother Jonah and learned to appreciate my body in a way I'd never thought was possible. Before we all got caught up in the most high-profile crime to hit Napa in decades. And before my father traded his art-filled bungalow in St. Helena for a grimy holding cell at the Napa County Sheriff's Office.

A sudden terrifying thought rips through my brain. *How did I not think to check this sooner?* And as I pump the brakes far too aggressively, sending my ten-year-old, forest-green Toyota jolting forward on its chassis, I lunge my hand toward the FBI case file on the passenger seat. A pickup truck lays on its horn behind me, and I can hardly blame the driver as he swerves to pass me on the left with an outstretched middle finger.

Shifting my focus back and forth between the file and the road ahead, I finally spot a shoulder wide enough to pull the car over, and immediately turn off the busy highway. Then I scan the police report as fast as my eyes can move, desperately hoping I won't see his name there. *Lead Deputy: David Guzman. Shift Supervisor: Letitia Williams. Sheriff: Angus McKee.*

And just like that, I'm hit with an overwhelming sense of nausea, yesterday's beer violently shaken up by today's trauma. I throw open the car door, and before I even have a chance to unbuckle my seatbelt, I vomit out onto the asphalt, sending bits of stray spittle bouncing back up at me, right onto my last pair of clean jeans.

I really need to quit drinking.

NAPA COUNTY SHERIFF'S DEPARTMENT
BUREAU OF CRIMINAL APPREHENSION

TRANSCRIPT

Interview Date: October 10, 2003
Case #: 2003-271
Interview of: Lana Burrell
Interviewed by: Deputy Sheriff Angus McKee

A.M. You aren't from here originally.
L.B. Is that a question?
A.M. Let's say it is.
L.B. No. I was born in New Mexico. Santa Fe. But we moved here after my mom died and my dad got his first commission.
A.M. How'd she die?
L.B. Don't see how that's relevant.
A.M. Your father is a suspect in a murder investigation. I'd say his wife's death is highly relevant.
L.B. She had fucking breast cancer, all right?
A.M. Don't get testy with me.
L.B. Testy?
A.M. Hostile.
L.B. Fine. I'll smile more next time you ask about my dead mom.

RECORDING STOPPED.
RECORDING RESUMED.

A.M. When did you first meet Jessica Bancroft?
L.B. Freshman year. She was in my homeroom, and our lockers were close. You know, Bancroft, Burrell. So we started talking.

A.M. About what?
L.B. I don't know. Boys, probably.
A.M. Was she dating anyone?
L.B. She was always dating someone. Jessica was . . . she knew how to use her looks to get what she wanted.
A.M. Did that bother you?
L.B. You mean was I jealous?
A.M. Sure.
L.B. No. I mean, maybe a little. But she was my best friend for the next three years.
A.M. There's no rule that says you can't be jealous of your best friend.
L.B. Are you saying I had something to do with what happened? Because I—
A.M. Calm down.
L.B. I loved her.
A.M. I'm sure you did.
L.B. Are we almost done?
A.M. Almost.
L.B. I've been here for hours.
A.M. During that three-year friendship, how often would you say your father interacted with Jessica?
L.B. He would never have done anything to hurt her.
A.M. That wasn't my question.
L.B. I'm done with this shit.
A.M. Lana, sit back down.
L.B. You can't make me do this.
A.M. Sure about that?
L.B. Fine, whatever. I'll keep talking. But first I want a fucking lawyer.

END OF RECORDING.

4

How did I get here?

I rub my eyes and stare out through the bug-splattered windshield of my car at the most stunning tree I've ever seen. Its branches stretch out twice as wide as it is tall, as if it's spent the last fifty years elbowing away any competition.

And who could blame it with a view like this?

The valley oak stands alone at the edge of a small promontory, a lone sentinel looking out over an endless sea of grapevines. It certainly is an ideal place to build a memorial for someone whose body was never found, and as I step out of the car and approach the magnificent tree, I realize why my subconscious brought me here. *How can I possibly find justice for Pilar Cruz and Katherine O'Shea if I don't first confront the original sin? The murder that condemned my father to life in prison over twenty years ago.* And with a sigh of exhaustion, I get out of the car and take a seat on the weather-beaten bench bearing Jessica Bancroft's name.

My best friend went missing on October 7, 2003, the night of her family's annual Crush party, a Valley tradition celebrating the successful haul of another harvest.

I remember because we'd had a fight that afternoon. Not one of our usual teenage tiffs over nothing, but a real, drawn-out, top-of-our-lungs, tear-ducts-on overdrive argument. The kind that leads to romantic breakups and permanently fractured friendships. And this one started the night before, when her mother, the legendary winemaker Holly Bancroft, fired my father, who had not only managed her vineyards for the last three years but had also painted a unique piece of art for every label she sold. To some fans of Golden Eagle's wines, my dad's designs were as much a part of the allure as Holly's rich and jammy cult cabernets, and for a raging narcissist like her, that must have driven her mad. Sharing the spotlight with a mere farmer and artist while she and her "brilliant" wines were supposed to be the center of attention? *Unthinkable!* It's no wonder she sacked him and publicly accused him of starting a fire at the winery that destroyed some of her 2003 vintage (a claim he denies to this day). He'd flown a little too close to the sun in a Valley where the gods didn't take kindly to strivers and imposters, and where the name Bancroft was both feared and revered, somewhere between Yahweh and Voldemort.

    I told all this to Jess, expecting a little sympathy from my so-called best friend, but instead she lashed out with ferocious precision, poking at all my insecurities with her painfully sharp tongue. "I am so sick of your poor farmgirl pity-party bullshit! I get it, Lana! I'm richer than you! My last name is all over this fucking Valley! But that doesn't mean my life is easy, all right? I've got shit going on too! Shit that would ruin both our lives if anyone found out. So will you please quit being such a whiny little bitch all the time?"

    I'd never seen her so worked up. She was like a toddler having a meltdown over nothing, the emotional response wildly outweighing the circumstances. And in retrospect, it's clear there was something else going on that day. Something that probably got her killed. But how could I have known that at the time? All I heard was my best friend calling me a whiny bitch, so I lashed out like any teenager would, saying all the things I'd suppressed over the years for fear of losing the one person who stood between me and social irrelevance.

"Fuck you, Jess!" I remember screaming. "The girls at school only pretend to like you 'cause you're a Bancroft and they want to get invited to your stupid fucking parties, and the guys just put up with you 'cause they all want to fuck you. But no one actually likes you! You're mean and manipulative, and you take whatever you want, with zero concern for how that might affect the people around you. Even your own brother thinks you're awful, and he's biologically programmed to love you. So you know what? Maybe it's a good thing your bitch of a mom fired my dad because now we can stop pretending. We were never actually friends. I was just using you for popularity, and you were just using me as a fucking accessory, dragging around the "help" so people would think you actually had depth and a conscience."

At the time, I remember being surprised that my mouth was even capable of spewing such venom, but clearly I'd learned a lot from Jess over the years. She had a way of finding people's most painful wounds and pressing against them with a few perfectly chosen words, eliciting just enough discomfort to remind you where you stood in the social pecking order. In that way, she was like a mafia don, only more terrifying because she didn't need enforcers with guns and baseball bats to keep people in line; she did it herself with a disdainful look and a cutting remark.

If I'd said those things to Jess at any other time, she would have fought back and won, leaving me in tears and tatters. But something was off that day. She was hiding a secret that I didn't know to look for until it was too late. And according to the police report, I was the second-to-last person to see her alive.

The last, unfortunately, was my father.

I'd sent him over to Jess's house to drop off a box of her things that she'd left at our place: a toothbrush, a spare cell phone charger, some makeup, a few CDs, the sapphire ring with the fleur-de-lis that she was always wearing but that she'd let me borrow a week earlier for a school dance.

It was a stupid symbolic gesture that felt important at the time in my solipsistic teenage mind. And in a way, it *was* important. Because it placed my father at the scene of her disappearance and eventually got him charged with her murder. Meanwhile, instead of sending him back home with all *my* belongings that I'd left at her place, she just gave him a goddamn wine cork. That's it. Sure, the doodle on it was an inside joke between us, a nostalgic callback to the cartoonish TV characters we used to draw on her mother's discarded corks when we were fourteen: Corky the Vampire Slayer, James VanderCork, Corkson Daly. Only instead of the silly caricatures from our youth, this drawing was far simpler: a girl with a frown and a single tear. An obvious reference to her own mental state at the time. But that night, when my father handed me the cork, I was far too upset to consider its true meaning. And before I ever got the chance to ask my friend how she was really doing, Jess was dead.

"What were you really up to?" I whisper out loud, grazing my fingers across the engraved lettering of her name on the faded memorial plaque: *Jessica Anne Bancroft, Beloved Daughter and Sister. 1986–2003.*

"Figured I'd find you here."

The man's voice comes from behind me, quiet and nonthreatening, but I recognize it at once, and my fists clench with instinctual rage. It's a voice I haven't heard since my father's trial, and in all those years I've never forgotten it.

"Hello, Angus," I say as I slowly turn to face him, calling him by a first name I'd never had the authority or audacity to use when I was a terrified seventeen-year-old locked in an interrogation room. But I'm not just an adult now and his peer; as an FBI agent on a special crimes deployment, I outrank him. And with those two simple words, I let him know exactly where he stands in the pecking order.

"*Agent* Burrell," he replies, dripping my title in a sticky sap of cynicism, letting *me* know what he really thinks of my position, as well.

Sheriff Angus McKee has never been the sort of law enforcement officer who feels regret or empathy when putting someone behind bars, no matter how morally gray the case or how questionable the crime. He's someone who savors it like a Wagyu steak, chewing every morsel with complete and utter satisfaction. Each arrest is a feast of pleasure, each conviction a heaping helping of seconds. I don't think it's because he's a sociopath, or even a bully. I think he genuinely believes in a dualistic world where there is good and there is evil. Light and dark. And once he views you a certain way, there's no hope for redemption.

I wonder where I fall on his two-sided scale . . .

Given how he's staring at me through narrow eyes, his jowly, bulldog face bunched up in clenched suspicion, I have a pretty good idea.

He removes his hat, the sandy-brown cowboy style he's always preferred, and runs a hand through his receding gray hair. "You know, when the FBI's invited to join a case, it's customary to start with a visit to local law enforcement. Pay your respects and such." His voice has a slight twang to it that I don't remember being there, more Texas Ranger than cabernet country cop.

"And yet you found me anyway."

"One of my deputies saw you coming in on 29, and when you turned up into Coombsville, I figured this was where you were headed." He looks past me at the tree bearing Jess's plaque and grins with quiet satisfaction. "How *is* your daddy these days?"

I want to slug the bastard right then and there. Knock that smug look off his face and let him feel a smidgen of the pain I've carried with me for two decades because of his rushed, biased police work, charging my father with first-degree murder, based on a weak alibi and circumstantial evidence: Jess's blood in the trunk of his car, her DNA scraped from underneath his fingernails, and some particularly damning testimony from Jess's mother. But I know that's what he wants. There's no better way to get kicked off a case than by assaulting another officer, especially a well-liked local sheriff. And somehow, standing here at Jess's memorial, in a verbal pissing match with the guy who unintentionally motivated me to join the FBI, I know I can't give up on these women. I realize I'll never figure out what really happened to my best friend all those years ago or clear my father's name, but I can at least make sure Pilar Cruz and Katherine O'Shea get the justice they deserve. The justice they'll never get with Angus McKee handling their cases alone. So for their sake, I ignore his provocative question and focus on what brought me back here in the first place. "There isn't much to go on in those police reports for Cruz and O'Shea."

"There is if you know where to look."

"Okay," I ask with obvious skepticism, "so where've you been looking?"

His eyes narrow even further as he studies me more closely, not the broken-down teen he once knew, but the commanding presence with a badge I'd become. "Lana, I need to know you won't let any personal grudges dictate the way you steer this case."

"Just 'cause I don't like you doesn't mean I'm gonna get in the way of you doing your job, Angus. I'm here for these women, not for whatever happened between us."

He shakes his head with a sigh and puts back on his cowboy hat. "I wasn't talking about *that* grudge."

"What do you mean?"

"Cruz and O'Shea. There are only three things their murders have in common: the drugs we found in their system, the dead animals near their bodies, and the fact that they were both last seen alive at Golden Eagle Winery."

The name hits me like a thunderbolt, stunning me into a long, drawn-out silence. *Golden Eagle*, Holly Bancroft's pride and joy. The place where I'd spent so much of my youth—what, with my dad on the payroll and my best friend living on site, not to mention my boyfriend working the vineyards that one magical summer. A thousand questions swirl through my brain, but there's only one I have the presence of mind to ask: "Are Holly or Jonah suspects?"

"Jonah had a falling out with his mom and doesn't work there anymore. Plus he was out of town during the second murder. So no."

A falling out? Interesting . . .

"But Holly?" I ask.

Sheriff McKee scratches his three-day-old stubble, as if the weight of this case and the local politics involved have already unsettled him, causing him to ignore such mundane distractions as shaving. "She's got no motive, no real connection to the deceased, no reason to do anything like this. Far as we can tell, she's just the victim of circumstance. Pilar Cruz *happened* to work her harvest, and we found her a block or so from Golden Eagle. Katherine O'Shea *happened* to visit her tasting room on the day she died. That's it."

"I would hardly call Holly Bancroft a *victim*. She's worth millions, and I'm pretty sure she has the governor on speed dial."

"Which is why I'm gonna say this again, Lana. I need to know you won't let your personal grudges interfere with this case and stir up shit that don't need stirring."

The tone of his voice might be calm and professional, but not every threat has to sound threatening. I know what he's really telling me: The Valley's a small place with big mouths and even bigger egos; and unlike my position, McKee's is an elected one. Every four years he needs to run for office, getting down on his knees and begging for the very votes and dollars that I have the potential to disrupt with my investigation. And if I do anything to jeopardize his next run for sheriff, well, let's just say he'll find a way to make me pay for it.

But Angus McKee has already stolen everything from me. He put my dad in jail for a crime I know he didn't commit. And if that bastard thinks I can be intimidated into doing things *his* way—treating the Valley's rich and powerful with kid gloves—then he is sorely mistaken.

"I'm here to do my job, *Sheriff*," I tell him as I start toward my car, eager to get to work. "Wherever it takes me."

J. T. Falco

An excerpt from
The Sommelier's Guide to California Wines
by Pippa Robinson

The story of the modern Napa Valley begins and ends with one name, that oft-maligned ouroboros of viticulture: Bancroft. Today's casual wine drinkers might be forgiven for associating the Bancrofts with the generic fourteen-dollar fruity reds and buttery whites that have made them their fortune, labels like J.B. Bancroft, Bancroft Home, and Bancroft Family Reserve that line the mid to lower shelves of every wine aisle in America. But that billion-dollar brand is the sole work of second-generation CEO Peter Bancroft, who, in the late 1990s, transformed his father and uncle's original estate into a global empire of modestly priced, entry-level wine. (His cousin, Holly Bancroft, went the other direction, focusing on small plots of organic, biodynamically farmed cabernet to create one of the most sought-after and expensive wines in the country: Golden Eagle.)

But to truly understand this family's influence, you have to go back to 1961, when the Napa Valley was hardly more than forgotten farmland, where a few nineteenth-century wineries like Charles Krug, Inglenook, and Beringer were still producing the sacramental church wines that helped them survive Prohibition.

That's when two brothers with no winemaking experience, James (known as J.B) and Michael Bancroft, decided to invest their modest inheritance in a vineyard in Oakville. Inspired by a trip to Bordeaux in their youth, they ripped out the zinfandel, Riesling, and sémillon that had grown there for a century, and instead planted the largest parcel of cabernet sauvignon in the Valley. Whether it was dumb luck or pure genius, we may never know. But the usually reticent cabernet came alive under the Valley's intense sun and rich, heavy soil, and the modern Napa wine was born.

By their 1968 vintage, Bancroft Family Cellars was already the best-known and one of the top-selling wines in America, and their reserve chardonnay's second-place finish at the Judgment of Paris in 1976 only further cemented their reputation. But like so many feuding brothers from history, J.B. and Michael could never get past the sibling rivalry that haunted them since their youth, and in 1978, they decided to split up the company.

Rumors abound as to what actually drove them to this decision—affairs, financial scandal, even murder—but such idle gossip isn't the concern of these pages. It's the wine that counts, and that's what suffered more than anything over the coming two decades. Together, the Bancroft brothers balanced out each other's worst traits and produced wines that transcended both of their individual talents. But apart, each one fell victim to his own worst impulses, with J.B. (under his eponymous label) becoming known for sweet, almost syrupy blends of grenache, zinfandel, and petit verdot, and Michael (under the label Golden Eagle) trying so hard to replicate his favorite Left Bank Bordeaux that his unusually early harvests resulted in cabernet blends that were thin, vegetal, and hated by critics and the American public alike.

It wasn't until both men died (on the exact same day, one year apart, in 1996 and '97) that their respective children took over and brought some form of redemption to the family name. J.B.'s son, Peter Bancroft, shared his father's passion for lower-priced, more quaffable wines, but he approached it with the marketing and sales savvy of a Stanford MBA, so by 2001, his labels were producing over a million cases each year. Meanwhile, Michael's daughter, Holly Bancroft, coupled her father's obsessive attention to detail with a New World focus on plush, heavily extracted flavors, leading her to produce what many consider the original cult wine: the 1997 Golden Eagle cabernet sauvignon, which today—if you can find it—sells for ten thousand dollars a bottle.

J. T. Falco

As for the family feud that divided the first generation of Bancroft winemakers, well, let's just say some things never change. But at least the second (and now third) generations are focusing on what they do best: crafting the wine that makes Napa Valley such a magical place to live, work, and visit.

5

Golden Eagle Winery is a fortress of imported French limestone, salvaged from three different chateaus in Normandy; the bones of the Old World, bombed out by the Luftwaffe in World War II and reassembled in the New World as a testament to Michael Bancroft's Francophile ambitions. As I step out of my car and take in the afternoon sun cresting over the elegant stone villa and its attendant vineyards, I watch a group of twenty-something tourists posing for photos, arms contorted in impossible angles to snag the perfect selfies. To them, this is a stunning architectural backdrop for a series of joyful posts on Instagram; to me, it's just a bunch of old rocks left behind by the Nazis.

I wonder if Holly will even recognize me.

We never spoke much when I was a teenager, even while I was clinging to her daughter and sleeping with her son. I suppose she was too busy, either tending to the vines with my dad or traveling the world to promote her iconic label. She barely had time for her own children, let alone the village stray. But she did pull me aside once when we were in the courtroom after my father's trial. I thought maybe it was to offer a hug of condolence; after all, I'd not only lost my dad, I'd lost my best friend too. But no. Like her daughter, Holly Bancroft had no sympathy for unworthy strivers. All she did was pull me close, place two firm hands on both my shoulders, and whisper into my ear, "Stay the fuck away from my son."

I broke up with Jonah that same night.

What was I supposed to do? Challenge the most powerful woman in the Valley by declaring my undying love for a boy I'd only been dating for six months? I was a terrified teenager who'd just watched her father get sent to San Quentin on a life sentence. I had no fight left in me, which was why I soon fled to San Francisco and never looked back.

I just wish I had told Jonah why I left. He never did anything to hurt me; he certainly deserved better than a half-hearted breakup over the phone, followed by two decades of complete radio silence. Even his "follow" requests on social media have sat unanswered in my inbox for years, a digital purgatory for the guy I've been too ashamed to accept and too guilty to reject. *I wonder what he's up to these days.* McKee said he'd had a falling out with his mom, a development I find oddly promising. *Maybe I should look him up while I'm here?*

No. Stay focused, Lana. This isn't your chance to casually bump into your high school sweetheart so that you can show off how much more competent and adventurous you've gotten in the bedroom. You're here to find a killer!

And if what Sheriff McKee said is true—both victims last seen at Golden Eagle—then that killer could very well be here at this winery. So, with a deep exhale, I clear my thoughts and gird myself for battle. Then I march through the main archway of reassembled Nazi rock, ready to drop some bombs of my own.

* * *

The tasting room is exactly as I remember it, cathedral ceilings of repurposed wood giving way to massive windows that extend all the way to the floor, offering up idyllic views of the Mayacamas Mountains and the hillside vineyards below. Impeccably tasteful French country sofas and tables fill the room with a kind of rustic elegance that could only work in a place like Napa, home to a unique set of multimillionaires who fancy themselves farmers.

By the bar, a chic crowd of appointment-only visitors in pastel polos sip flights of sauvignon blanc and cabernet sauvignon under the guidance of a bubbly young woman with a head full of blonde ringlets. Her bare arms are covered in the sort of vaguely Eastern mystic tattoos you might find on the streets of Berkeley, and her faded denim overalls are stained with soil on both knees.

Drug dealer, I think, playing my usual game. *Pot when it wasn't legal; now she's moved on to ecstasy and mushrooms.*

How did someone like this slip through the cracks of Holly Bancroft's carefully curated wine country aesthetic? She used to make my father bring a second pair of boots to work on the off chance she needed him to meet her in the tasting room, lest he drag in any mud from the vineyards he'd been tending. And tattoos? I once saw her snap at Jess when she came home from a friend's birthday party with some temporary henna on her shoulder. Has she gotten so distracted by her sprawling wine empire that she's no longer keeping watch over Golden Eagle with her famously keen eagle eye?

There's only one way to find out.

I march up to the bar and tell the buoyant blonde who I am, and a minute later she's leading me through a side door out to the vineyard itself. Along the way, her mouth never stops moving. "Holly's been out all day testing Brix levels. I told her we can't start harvest on a Leaf day, especially during a waning crescent, but old habits die hard, ya know? It's not her fault. She's a perfectionist. And with this heat wave, she's worried about the sugar in the cab, so I said fine, do what you need to do, just don't start picking 'til we talk."

"Interesting," I mumble with complete and utter disinterest.

"You must be here about the girl. From the bachelorette party."

"That's right."

"We usually don't take appointments from groups like that—ya know. *Aah, I'm so drunk! Look at my necklace with all the little plastic dicks on it!* It's really not the vibe we're going for here, and our wine's, like, not cheap. But the bride's dad knows someone who knows someone who knows Holly, or something like that, so she made an exception."

"Did you talk to her when she was here? Katherine O'Shea?"

"Yeah, I already told Sheriff McKee everything—"

"We're conducting separate investigations. So would you mind talking to me after I speak with your boss?"

"Of course. I'll be right out front. You just say the word, Agent . . ."

". . . Burrell."

"I'm Bex. Bex Potter."

We shake hands amicably, and I start to understand why Holly hired her to work the tasting room despite her questionable aesthetic. There's just something inherently likable about this woman. Even when she's rambling about some esoteric aspect of the winemaking process—something I truly couldn't care less about—I find myself drawn in by her friendly eyes and disarming smile. As someone who's been told on more than one occasion that she has "resting bitch face," I can't help but feel a pang of jealousy whenever I meet someone like Bex. How much easier would life be if I had her inherent magnetism? My dad was like that, a natural charmer who made instant friends with everyone he met. But I seem to have inherited my mother's introversion, and that quality's only calcified after all this time holding a badge and a gun that, by design, scare people away.

"There she is," Bex says, pointing out an older platinum-blonde woman hunched over a grape vine with an odd instrument in her hand. And before I have a chance to thank my guide, she disappears back into the building, an oddly quiet exit from such an avid talker. *That was strange,* I think. *Almost like she's avoiding Holly.* But I don't have time to dwell on it, because the woman in the vines has spotted me and she's moving in this direction.

"Is that Lana Burrell?"

Well, I guess she remembers me.

But even more surprising is the warm—dare I say *loving*—hug that Holly wraps me up in as soon as she reaches me. Her strong, toned arms squeeze tight around my back with a sentimental tenderness, and I'm hit with a waft of sweat and soil coming from her damp work clothes after what must have been a long day outside in the heat.

"Oh my God, are you a sight for sore eyes. And look at you! How do you still look so good after all these years? Please tell me there are some kind of secret FBI workouts I should be doing."

Her unbridled joy—not to mention the oddly casual girlspeak that bears no resemblance to the calculating, even cruel demeanor I remember—leaves me stunned into a fumbling semi-silence of "ums" and "wows." For starters, I'm twenty pounds overweight (at least according to the doctor who does our annual physicals at the Bureau) and hardly have the toned physique of someone who might be accused of practicing secret government exercises. I'm also desperately in need of a haircut, with split ends that are probably visible from the Space Station. But beyond that, I've spent the last two decades hating this woman, and I always assumed the feeling was mutual. My instinct tells me that this is all an act, a classic, albeit slightly unexpected form of psychological warfare designed to disarm a prying FBI agent. So I decide to play along with Holly's game and see where it leads.

"It's good to see you too, Holly. And please, the only time I get any exercise is when the elevator breaks in my building, and I have to trudge up two flights of stairs."

"Well, whatever you're doing, it's working," she says with an earnest smile. "Did Bex offer you anything to drink? We're pouring the 2021s today, and the Hilltop Vineyard is just... chef's kiss right now."

"As amazing as that sounds," I lie, "I'm not supposed to drink on duty."

"Right. You're here about the girl."

"*Girls*," I correct her. "Katherine O'Shea *and* Pilar Cruz were both last seen here."

Holly's smile slowly inverts, and her head shakes sympathetically, although I swear I catch a hint of fury flash across her eyes for just a moment, a brief loss of control that she swiftly rectifies. "It's getting hot out here, and I could use some water. Mind if we talk in my office?"

"Of course," I tell her. "Lead the way."

* * *

Five minutes later, I'm seated across from Holly as we sip bottles of ice-cold Topo Chico in a second-floor office I remember well from my teenage years. The room has a grandiosity that I always found arrogant, a one-thousand-square-foot shrine to a queen rather than a functional workplace. It shares the same French country aesthetic as the rest of the villa, with soft, pastel-green chairs and faded white cabinets and tables that are either genuine antiques or designed to look as if they are. And the entirety of two walls consists of floor-to-ceiling windows that let in the most stunning views of the vineyards imaginable as they roll and crest their way right up into the Mayacamas.

It's the opposite wall, though, that really speaks to the Holly Bancroft I knew and feared as a teenager. A metal trellis the length of the room juts out a few inches, creating a strange and shadowy three-dimensional effect. And built into the trellis is an abstract web of frames and shelves, each one displaying an article, plaque, or award bestowed on the woman in front of me. There are the usual glowing reviews and profiles in *Wine Spectator* or *Decanter*. There are the one-hundred-point score announcements from Robert Parker's *Wine Advocate*, including the 1997 cabernet that gave Golden Eagle cult status among connoisseurs and collectors around the world. There's a picture of Holly with her arm around California's photogenic second-term governor, Teddy Mason, an old friend from their days growing up together in the Valley. There are charity awards, keys to cities, coauthored books, trophies shaped like wine bottles and corkscrews—a true "Menagerie of Me" that tells the epic tale of wine's leading lady. But the thing that catches my eye and leaves me breathless is a pencil-drawn sketch of a much younger Holly standing by the window in this very office. The precise lines and soft shadows have a romantic quality, like a portrait of a loved one. Only this wasn't drawn by her milquetoast ex-husband, Greg, whose forgettable last name she wouldn't even allow her children to take. It was done by my father less than a year before his arrest.

I can't believe she still has his art on display after everything that happened . . .

"Should we get started?" she asks with a glimmer of impatience behind her polite smile.

"Yes, but do you mind if I record this?" I place my digital voice recorder on the desk between us before she even has a chance to respond.

"I've got nothing to hide," she says. And I start the recording with the distinct impression that I've just been told a bold-faced lie.

"Tell me about your relationship with Pilar Cruz. When did you first hire her?"

"I wish I could help you there, but the truth is, I have no idea. I don't actually hire individual pickers. We contract the process out to a third-party company."

"Which one?" I ask.

"VFS—Valley Farming Services. They work with the migrant farmers every year to coordinate their travel and accommodations in the Valley."

"Are these workers undocumented?" I watch her cordial smile fade ever so slightly as a glimmer of hostility flashes across her eyes. "Ms. Bancroft, I'm not going to narc on you to some other agency like the INS. That's not my job. I'm here about two murders—nothing else. And I'm just gathering information that might help me solve them."

"I understand. And please, call me Holly. We've known each other far too long to use silly titles, all right?" She waits for me to nod, before continuing: "To be honest, I don't know the immigration status of any of my pickers. I'm sure some of them are documented, but odds are the vast majority aren't. It's the same here as it is on every other farm in America. The reason you can get a sixty-nine-cent apple at Trader Joe's is because the person picking it has no legal protections or minimum-wage guarantees."

"Only your wines hardly sell for sixty-nine cents, do they?"

"No," she says, her brow furrowing. "They don't. Which is why we use VFS. Unlike a lot of these companies who work with migrant labor, they actually do pay quite well. Twenty, sometimes twenty-five dollars an hour. They also provide free health care and dormitory services whenever these workers come to Napa."

I can see that she's fishing for some sort of compliment, as if ensuring that her employees' basic needs are met deserves a humanitarian award, another trophy to hang on her wall of self-importance. But I refuse to give her that. Instead, I hold her gaze disapprovingly and move onto the next question. "So what's the process when you hire someone like Pilar? How does it all work, in layman's terms?"

"Well," she says, "when a vineyard like ours needs temporary help, we make a call. My sauvignon blanc was ready to harvest, so I called them up and a dozen workers were here the next day."

"For how long?"

"We don't grow a ton of whites, so they managed to bring in the whole crop over the course of two, maybe three nights."

"Which was it?" I ask, pressing her for certainty, knowing that any little detail could make the difference between a solved case and a never-ending mystery. "Two or three?"

"Three," she says without hesitation.

"And all the picking happens at night because the cool air helps concentrate the flavor of the grapes . . . right?"

She smiles fondly. "Your dad taught you well, Lana."

I don't return the smile. Realizing her mistake in even mentioning my father, she quickly adds, "It's also for the benefit of the workers. The night harvest, I mean. I can't imagine anything more dangerous than picking grapes on a hot summer day."

"I'm sure Pilar Cruz could," I tell her with an icy glare.

"Hmm?"

"Imagine something more dangerous."

Holly sighs, leans one elbow on the desk, and props her chin up on her hand, as if the weight of these heinous crimes has left her mind too burdened to support itself any longer. "Lana, I'm not stupid. I know you blame me for what happened to your dad, and I know you have no reason to believe me now. But all I can do is share my truth, so that's what I'm going to do." She reaches one hand out across the desk to place it supportively over mine, and for some reason I let her. "I've done a lot of work over the last twenty years, not just on this place, but on myself. The trauma my family's been inflicting on itself for generations, that cycle of abuse and pain that started with my father and his brother—it had to stop. So I started therapy, I went on silent retreats, I did ayahuasca in a Mexican jungle, and I started surrounding myself with better people. People who understand that our lives and our relationships and this soil we till, it's all intertwined with something bigger, something beautiful and universal. And once you grasp that fact, all those petty grievances and childhood traumas just melt away into nothing."

It doesn't take a seasoned FBI agent to see that Holly Bancroft believes every word she's saying. She *has* changed, and it's no doubt that her spiritual journey and people like the bubbly Bex Potter had a lot to do with it. But if there's one thing I've learned about the so-called saved and transformed, it's that finding the light only works when you come from a place of darkness. Whether it's Evangelical Christianity or Islam, Zen Buddhism or New Age healing, a sudden midlife conversion is almost always just a mask. Sometimes the mask fits and leads to a better life; sometimes it falls off and the struggle begins anew. But it's always hiding something beneath its carefully sculpted plastic smile, and often, at least in my line of work, that something is a monster.

What are you hiding, Holly Bancroft, I wonder. You obviously know more about Pilar Cruz than you're letting on . . .

But before I have a chance to press her on this and see where my suspicions lead, the window behind her explodes in a sudden, terrifying burst of glass and a shower of deadly shards comes raining down on both of us.

"Get down!" I scream, moving on instinct as I shut my eyes, kick back my chair, and dive for cover below the desk.

6

The jagged limestone rock on Holly's desk is no bigger than a softball. But it's not the size of the stone that's meant to scare us; it's the handwritten note wrapped around it with two rubber bands:

Vas a pagar por lo que le hiciste a Pilar.

"You're going to pay for what you did to Pilar," I read aloud, drawing on the rudimentary Spanish I picked up going to school in Napa with so many children of farmworkers.

"Let me see that," Holly snaps with an impatient gasp, and she snatches it off the desk before I have a chance to remind her that it's evidence. I watch her read the note over and over again, although what she's looking for, I can't possibly imagine. It's almost as if she *expected* something like this to happen, and now she's trying to find some small clue to validate her preconceived paranoia. Finally, she sets it back down and looks me directly in the eye. "It's not true."

"What?"

"I didn't do anything to this woman. I never even met her."

"That's not what the note says."

"You're going to trust an act of terrorism over a—"

"Vandalism," I correct her.

"Fine!" she snaps, fully letting go of any semblance of Zen. "An act of *vandalism* over someone you've known for twenty-five years? Lana, please. It's *me*!"

"Exactly, Holly. It's *you*." My threat lands with the clarity of a summer sky, and for the first time, I see fear in the eyes of this woman who prides herself on being fearless.

"I think you should go," she says bitterly, choosing her words much more carefully now that the battle lines have been drawn and she sees me for who I really am rather than the girl I once was.

"We still need to talk about Katherine O'Shea."

"Some other time," she says, her eyes narrowing into a threatening sneer that I remember all too well. "I'd hate for my statement to be inadmissible in court because I was in too much shock to think straight."

"Fine," I tell her as I carefully wrap the note and chunk of limestone in a towel so as not to disturb any possible fingerprints. "I'll come back tomorrow. But in the meantime, do you have any security cameras on the property?"

"No," she says, shaking her head. "It's always been a safe place to live. Until now."

And it's not until I'm alone in the hallway that I realize what a strange thing that is to say for a woman whose daughter was allegedly murdered on this very site.

* * *

After calling the Santa Rosa Field Office—I want to make sure an FBI team checks this note for fingerprints rather than Angus McKee's Sheriff's Department, which is inept at best and corrupt at worst—I drop off the evidence in my car and head back inside the tasting room. There's still one more person I need to talk to, and when I enter, she's seated alone in a quiet nook, surrounded by display bottles of Golden Eagle cabernet in varying formats and sizes: magnum, jeroboam, methuselah. *Leave it to the wine industry to give some of their oversize bottles Biblical names, as if they're doing God's work rather than just getting people drunk.*

"Are you okay?" Bex Potter asks with a look of tender sympathy. "Holly just told me about the window."

I offer her a quick nod of thanks but nothing more, not wanting to give the impression that I could be rattled by the mysterious vandal's lazy, primitive threat. "Did you notice anything strange? Anyone who shouldn't have been here?"

"I'm sorry," she says with a solemn head shake, her little blonde ringlets bobbing adorably as she does. "I was busy pouring for some of the guests. Do you think it was her cousin?"

"Whose? Pilar's?"

Bex nods and glances conspiratorially back over her shoulder, as if the walls—and comically large wine bottles—have ears. "I forget his name. Hector, maybe? Jorge? Something with an 'H.' Or a 'J' that sounds like an 'H.' But he was in the harvest crew with her, so I'm sure he'll be easy enough to find."

Knowing how unreliable my memory can be—I'm the kind of person who forgets what I had for breakfast by the time lunch rolls around—I turn on my digital voice recorder and have Bex repeat herself. Then I take a seat across from her and continue the interview.

"I take it Bex isn't your legal name."

"It's Rebecca," she says with the sour revulsion of someone who's spent a long time running from that name—or perhaps just the people who gave it to her.

"Where are you from?"

"Milwaukee."

"And how long have you been with Golden Eagle?"

"Five years next month," she says with a look of pride. "Holly brought me on after the Glass Fire, to help her implement a biodynamic program for the vineyards."

I can't help but grin, the inner skeptic in me unable to even talk about biodynamic farming with a straight face. "You really believe in all that Rudolf Steiner stuff, huh?"

"What do you mean?" she asks, as if I've just questioned whether the sky is blue.

"The horns full of cow shit," I tell her. "The magical days when it's safe to harvest. It all kinda sounds like superstition, not science."

But the mysterious Bex Potter doesn't share in my amusement. I may as well have drawn a cartoon of Muhammed for a devout Muslim. "It's easy to mock a person for having faith, Agent Burrell. It's a lot harder to have it yourself. Because faith takes work. But I've *done* the work, and I've seen what biodynamics can do. For a vineyard and for the people who tend it."

There's an intense devotion in her eyes and her voice that leaves me unsettled. An almost fundamentalist certainty that I've seen lead people down extremely dark paths during my fifteen years at the Bureau. I wait for her to blink, as if her wide eyes are a stoplight in the conversation, and I need them to change before it's safe for me to proceed. But five more seconds pass, and she's still staring at me with unflinching obsession. *Why won't she blink?*

Ten seconds. Fifteen.

Finally, I blurt out a response, unable to take it anymore. "You're right. I'm sorry. My dad worked in vineyards and used to tell me about Steiner before—" I fall silent, furious at myself for revealing personal details to a potential suspect. It's just those eyes and the way she's staring at me, like she has a window into my soul. They leave me so unsettled that I find myself saying things I wouldn't even admit to a close friend . . . if I still had any.

"Before what?" she asks innocently.

But I can't risk going there. Not with this strange young woman who has set off every alarm bell in my gut. She knows more about these murders than she's letting on—I can feel it. The question is, *Did she kill Katherine and Pilar? Or does she just have some idea about who did?* I'm going to have to find a way to earn her trust, but that sort of thing takes time. Right now, all I can do is regain my composure and steer the conversation away from me and back toward her. "Tell me about Katherine O'Shea. Were you working the tasting room while her party was here?"

"I was," she replies matter-of-factly. Then she proceeds to tell me *her* version of what happened on that fateful day.

* * *

An hour later, I'm tucked in the far corner of the closest thing the Valley has to a dive bar: a no-frills burger joint outside St. Helena called the Cooperage. The prices are ridiculous—eight dollars for a bottle of Heineken—but it's dark and smells like cheap frying oil, plus it's not far from my motel, so it feels like the perfect place to calm my nerves and go over Bex Potter's statement.

As I await my order, I scan the faces of the clientele, playing my usual game, slapping hypothetical crimes on people I don't know and never will. There's an overdressed young couple with too much jewelry and clothes that don't quite fit, as if they were bought for someone else: *identity theft, robbery*. There's a farmer in denim overalls and muddy work boots, his bushy gray beard and dirty hands an odd juxtaposition to the glass of chilled white wine in front of him: *on the run for murder*.

Eager to pin a few more crimes on a few more unwitting suspects, I shift in my booth to get a better look at the far side of the bar, which is when I realize I'm not the only one casting curious stares across the room. The guy is grinning at me with a goofy look that I swear makes me think he knows what I've been up to, like he's been inside my twisted head, and now he's telling me he's in on the joke. He has a mop of dark, curly hair, all wild and unkempt in a strangely attractive way. And over his sun-kissed brown skin he wears an oddly casual outfit for a grown-ass man in his mid-thirties: leather Rainbow flip-flops, loose khaki shorts, and a bright blue T-shirt with the logo for some streetwear brand on it.

Drug dealer? No . . . Credit card fraud? Don't think so. I doubt he's ever even whipped it out and taken a piss in public. Who is this guy? And why can't I find anything wrong with him?

All I want to do is keep staring, piercing through his benign outer layer to find something terrible lurking under the surface, some dark malignancy to satisfy my sick obsession with the broken and the damned, where there are no nice people, just monsters in disguise. But he's still smiling at me, and not in a gross way like a dog salivating over a juicy piece of meat. There's an inherent sweetness to his gaze that I can see from here, all the way across an underlit room. *I wonder what his name is, and whether he's the kind of guy who would kiss me first or wait for me to make the first move. The latter, I presume . . .*

But before my thoughts can drift any further, my view's blocked by the approaching bartender, a middle-aged woman with a chain-smoker's wrinkles and a trucker's taste for flannel. Without a word of acknowledgment, she drops a plastic basket of sweet potato fries on my table and immediately turns to leave, even though I ordered regular. I don't bother correcting her, though, as I doubt she'd care enough to fix the mistake. Instead, my eyes are drawn like magnets back toward that mysterious watcher from across the bar; only by the time they get there, he's gone. With a frantic jerk of my neck, I just barely catch a glimpse of his floppy hair disappearing into the men's room, and in another life—or at the very least, at another time—I might have followed him just to see if I was right about his passive approach to a first kiss.

But I'm not that girl anymore—or at least, I'm trying not to be—so I figure it's time to get back to work. I shovel down a few fries dipped in an "aioli" that I know is just Best Foods Mayonnaise, then I pop in my earbuds and listen to the part of my interview with Bex Potter that I can't stop thinking about.

Me: *In the statement Charlotte Croydon gave to the police, she said she wasn't worried about Katherine on the night of her bachelorette party because she seemed to have a connection with a woman here at Golden Eagle.*
Bex: *Okay...*
Me: *In fact, Charlotte assumed they might even be hooking up somewhere. Any idea who that woman could be?*
Bex: *There were quite a few women here that night.*
Me: *Bex, do you ever sleep with women?*
Bex: *Kinda messed up to try and weaponize my sexuality against me.*
Me: *It's a relevant question.*
Bex: *Well, if it's relevant, then no, I don't. I'm not a big labels person, but these days I consider myself straight.*
Me: *So you* have *slept with women.*
Bex: *Yes. But not in a long time. I have a boyfriend.*
Me: *Is it possible Katherine O'Shea may have been interested in you?*
Bex: *If she was, that wasn't my intent.*
Me: *So you do think it's possible.*
Bex: *Look, part of my pay comes from the tips I get in the tasting room. And the more a guest likes you, the more generous they are when it comes time to pay the bill.*
Me: *So you do admit to flirting with her.*

Bex: *I don't even remember which girl she was. They all had the same ridiculous T-shirts on—"Welcome to the Fuck Fest," or something like that. I'm just saying that sometimes in the service industry a little flirty energy goes a long way. That's all.*

As I stew over Bex's version of events, I stop the tape and glance up at the surly bartender. She's playing some mindless game on her phone, ignoring her customers, and all I can think about is how much to dock her tip from the standard twenty percent, given the French fry mix-up. The truth is, I understand where Bex is coming from as a tip-based employee, and I have no right to question her sexuality; but still, I can't help but wonder if she *is* the person from Charlotte Croydon's statement. If I were a queer woman Katherine's age, wine-drunk and lovelorn after a day spent with a blushing bride-to-be, I could absolutely see myself falling for the flirty sommelier with the big eyes and the blonde curls. *But what really happened after Katherine's friends got back on their party bus and left Golden Eagle? Does Bex know more about the murder than she's letting on?*

My questions will have to wait, because a forty-two-year-old man has just entered the bar with what looks to be his wife and two kids. He's staring at me in shock, ignoring his daughter's incessant tugging at the leg of his pants. And as we meet eyes, I only have one all-consuming thought:

I'm not nearly drunk enough to have a run-in with my ex-boyfriend.

J. T. Falco

An Entry From the Diary of Lana Burrell

August 24, 2003

Dear Mom,

I am in love. I know I haven't written to you much lately, and I'm sorry (which I know is dumb since you'll never actually be able to read this), but I still feel bad. We agreed I'd keep writing to you, and I haven't been keeping up my end of the bargain this summer, but at least I have a really good excuse. His name is Jonah, and he's pretty much the best thing that's ever happened to me.

I always knew Jess had an older brother. I saw him in pictures around the house, and she'd mentioned something about him going to UC Davis, but he's been away at school ever since Jess and I became friends. And since he wants to be a winemaker like his mom, he's spent the last two summers in France and Spain, learning from literally the best people in the world. But this summer's different. Mrs. Bancroft wanted to teach him herself, so he's been home for the last sixty days, and we've basically been together for fifty-nine of them.

It all started during finals week. It's like the one time of year I can actually convince Jess to study with me, so we were over at the winery, cramming for Mr. Booth's AP history exam in one of the empty offices, when I got up to use the bathroom. The ladies' room was full, like it always is there, with all the wino tourists peeing like racehorses, so I snuck into the men's room, which is almost always empty. Only this time it wasn't. There was a guy in there *trying to clean a wine stain off this amazing T-shirt from the Strokes' tour last summer, and he clearly had no idea what he was doing since he was using soap and water. So normally I would have been way too embarrassed to stay and talk, seeing as he was (A) a super-hot guy and (B) I was caught red-handed using the wrong bathroom. But I am obsessed with the Strokes. Julian Casablancas is my dream man. Or at least he was until about two minutes later, when I convinced this random bathroom guy to take off his shirt so we could dab it with a mixture of hydrogen peroxide and water, just like you taught me. And that's how I got to see Jonah Bancroft shirtless before I even learned his name. (He has a tattoo on his left side, just three words and a question mark: "Is this it?" And I pretty much fell in love with him the moment I saw it.)*

When we were done, it was super obvious we were into each other. But we were both way too awkward and nervous to exchange numbers or anything. It just felt so . . . adult, I guess. So before I went back to find Jess, I gave him my screen name on AIM. And the next morning, when I logged in before school, he sent me what I thought was the most random message: "I've lost my page again." I literally had no idea what he was talking about, so I typed back, "???" And like a second later, he responds: "I know this is surreal." And I seriously almost had a heart attack. Or maybe it skipped a beat, as people say. I don't know. But I died. Because I knew what he was doing, and I knew exactly what he was going to say next, so I quickly typed it before he got a chance to: "But I'll try my luck with you." Then a few seconds later, he typed a little smiley face—":)"—and asked me to meet him after school at Gott's for burgers.

J. T. Falco

It was genuinely my dream way for a guy to ask me out, using fucking Strokes lyrics (pardon my French), so I was in love before we even had our first date. And before I got the chance to kiss him—which, don't worry, I made him wait for the third date before I did. But that first day at Gott's, you could just tell this wasn't going to be some stupid fling. He understood me in a way no one ever has—not Jess, not Dad, not even you. And I felt like I could really be myself around him, which we all know I haven't been lately at school.

Fast-forward two months, and things couldn't be better if we tried. Which is why we're going to have sex tonight. At our house, while Dad's over at the winery to start harvesting the whites. Which is why I finally remembered to write to you again.

I so fucking wish you were here to talk about this, although if you were, I probably wouldn't have used the F-word just now. But I can't talk to Jess about it—she's been so weird to me ever since I started hanging out with her brother, and I'm pretty sure she'd die if she found out we were about to do the deed. And you know how Dad gets when it comes to me and boys. If he knew what we were about to do, he would literally murder Jonah and turn him into fertilizer for his grapes. But I know you'd know what to say, and you wouldn't be all weird and protective about my body. I've been on the pill for two years for my acne, so no worries there. And he said he's going to wear a condom too, just in case. So it's not the logistics that are bothering me. It's what comes afterward. What if everything changes? What if it's not good, and we don't have that easygoing chemistry anymore because all we can think about is how

weird and awkward it was to wriggle around on top of each other? What if . . . I don't know. Just WHAT IF?
   Ugh. I miss you, Mom. I'll let you know how it goes.

Love,

Lana

7

I gasp for air, struggling to catch my breath as I lean over the side of my car, using it to support my suddenly wobbly limbs. *Did I really just race out the back door of a bar in plain view of Jonah Bancroft—not to mention his ridiculously attractive wife and two perfect children?*

Yes, I remind myself, *I did*. And I'm fairly certain that I knocked over a metal chair in the process, drawing disgruntled looks from everyone in the place, especially the surly, flannel-wearing bartender. But I didn't care. Not in that moment of surreal disorientation as adrenaline and shame mixed together like a cheap cocktail in my mind, overwhelming the senses and sending me stumbling toward the nearest door in search of fresh air and daylight. Was it a juvenile overreaction to a chance encounter? Maybe. But it's an odd thing being confronted by an ex, particularly one associated with adolescence—that time when unchecked hormones cause such heightened emotional stakes that even the smallest moments linger in the memory like massive traumas. That's what adolescence is, really—one mercilessly long trauma that you spend the rest of your life either working through or drowning under—and for me, the sight of Jonah Bancroft triggered a sort of PTSD that I still wasn't ready to deal with. Not in that bar, not in that moment, and definitely not in full view of his family.

Of course he has a family . . .

I make a mental note to schedule time with my therapist as soon as this case is over. Clearly, I've gotten too confident in my coping mechanisms, trusting my daily twenty milligrams of Lexapro to do the work of a weekly talk session. But as the day's events have shown, I'm not there yet. This broken watch may be ticking, but it still can't keep time, especially not while the past continues to remind me of its stubborn presence.

On second thought, maybe I'll call my therapist right now, just to check in. She always said I could reach out in an emergency, and while she probably meant the death of a loved one or something, I'm sure she would make an exception. Especially since I don't have any loved ones to speak of—not really. But when I search my back pocket for my phone, all I feel is the plushy curve of my woefully out-of-shape ass, and I realize what I've done.

Fuck. Me.

In my mad scramble to escape, I'd completely forgotten to scoop my phone up off the table, where it had been propped against a beer bottle while I listened again to Bex Potter's interview. Which leaves me with three possible courses of action.

One: Slouch back inside with my head hanging in shame, retrieve the phone, and look like a total ass in front of Jonah and his family, not to mention the cute mystery man with the floppy hair and unforgettable smile.

Two: Wait until Jonah leaves and hope the shifty bartender hasn't already swiped the phone and stripped it for parts.

Or three: Forget the phone entirely, quit my job, and move to another state, where no one will ever know what a fucking embarrassment I am.

As I discreetly check my reflection in the car window, in preparation for the inevitable choice of option one—*my God, have the bags under my eyes always been this droopy? I look like a stoned basset hound*—I catch a flash of movement bouncing off the glass, a calm walk in faded leather Blundstones, and I know right away that it's him.

When I finally gather my bearings and turn to face Jonah Bancroft, he's standing five feet away from me with a wry grin on his face and my perpetually cracked phone in his outstretched hand. "Not my finest moment," I tell him, shamefully taking the phone and sliding it into my back pocket.

"Yeah," he says with a look of casual irony that I remember painfully well. "I really thought you'd be cooler now—what with the whole FBI thing."

And while I know he's joking, I can't help but feel as if there's an element of truth to his comment. Over the years, I've faced down organized criminals, violent drug dealers, and one genuine serial killer; you would think arresting the Marin County Marksman would add a permanent layer of ice to my veins. But of course life—and human nature—are far more complicated than that, and badass deeds don't necessarily create badass people. So I smile back at Jonah and acknowledge his joke in the safest, least revealing way possible: "I guess some things never change."

"No," he replies wistfully. "Definitely not."

Then we stand there for a moment in the quiet parking lot, taking each other in with deliberate objectification, the sort of blatant physical study that would never be acceptable anymore in the real world. But this *isn't* the real world. It's Napa: a fairytale dreamscape of countryside castles built to cater to people's epicurean fantasies. And he's Jonah. And I'm Lana. And for a few thrilling seconds, we're back in my teenage bedroom, exploring the bumps and curves of each other's naked bodies with trembling lips and curious fingers.

Only we're not kids anymore, and when I look past those sparkling green eyes and that unflappable smile, I see the subtle signs of age all over him. His dark chocolate hair now has a generous sprinkling of sea salt, not just around the ears, but all over his head. And there's a slightly worn look to his face, a bit like the leather on his work boots, still pleasing to the eye but gently warped by long days in the blistering Napa sun. Even his voice has a softer, scratchier quality now that I find oddly soothing, like listening to a favorite song on an old vinyl record, instead of that perfect digital copy you've gotten used to. But nowhere is his transformation into adulthood—and parenthood—more evident than in his wardrobe. Gone are the baggy shorts and graphic tees that defined our blissful summer of 2003; in their place, he wears simple bootcut jeans and an untucked black polo shirt with a single word in red letters emblazoned on the chest: "Coach."

"I thought you hated sports," I say, even though there are a thousand other things I'd rather be asking him.

"What?"

"Your shirt."

"Oh, right," he says with a knowing laugh. "I still do. But after Emma watched the Women's World Cup, she begged to join a soccer team. Only the one her age didn't have a coach, and I genuinely can't say no to that girl, so . . ."

"You became Coach Jonah."

"They actually call me Coach J."

"That is fucking adorable."

He laughs, causing the slightest of dimples to form on his cheeks, just like I remember. "Yeah, well, we'll see how long it lasts. I thought I was signing up for, like, two hours a week, only now we've got these out-of-town tournaments every month. Monterey. Sacramento. Last weekend we were up in Tahoe. And these girls are only seven! They're terrible! I have no idea why we even enter these things."

I see the heartfelt satisfaction and fatherly pride shining in his eyes, hidden behind his mock horror, and I know *exactly* why he does it. "Because you love it, Jonah. You were born for this dad shit, and you know it."

He shrugs coyly, acknowledging the truth without having to say it. "How about you? Any kids? Family? Apartment full of cats?"

"Just me," I tell him, trying not to seem pathetic, as if it were a calculated choice rather than the inevitable outcome of an emotionally stunted adulthood. "I'm on the road a lot for work. My office covers everywhere from Eureka to Monterey, and the nature of what I do—well, it doesn't exactly lend itself to stable relationships."

He warily glances down at the soft bulge of my Glock under my shirt. "I've got to admit, I never saw you going down this road. Law school, maybe. I could totally have seen that. But the FBI? I mean—it's amazing, Lana; don't get me wrong. It's just ... not what I imagined."

I try to respond, but instead a knot wells up in my chest, squeezing my heart and making it difficult to breathe. Part of me knows he's right. Of course he is; he knows me better than anyone. And I can't help but feel as though I've let him down somehow, as if the person I am doesn't live up to the infinite potential of the person I once was. But what Jonah doesn't understand is that I'm not that idealistic, intellectually curious teen anymore. I stopped being her not long after we broke up, when my dad was wrongfully imprisoned and a part of my soul calcified, hardened by hate and the cynical realization that hope and possibility were the exclusive domains of people richer than me, people more powerful than me, people with better connections than me. People like the Bancrofts. Instead, I became the living embodiment of the American Nightmare: a dead mom (*thanks, health-care system*), a jailed dad (*thanks, justice system*), and no way to pay for the liberal arts college I'd hoped to attend (*thanks, education system*). So at some point during that ferry ride across the San Pablo Bay and under the San Rafael Bridge, while I tried not to glance up at the hulking facade of San Quentin State Prison on the western shoreline, I made the conscious decision to become someone else. Someone who would one day carry a badge and a gun and feel a morsel of the power that people like the Bancrofts no doubt felt every time they woke up, even if they didn't realize it. The understanding—even if it was subconscious—that their destiny was within their control, and with the right choices, with enough gumption and tenacity and good old-fashioned hard work, they could have *anything*.

Of course I can't explain any of this to Jonah, not without making him feel guilty for the convoluted circumstances that led me to where I am today: single, childless, and packing heat in a St. Helena parking lot. Because it's not his fault—not directly—and I don't want to make him feel as if there should be an asterisk next to all *his* accomplishments. Especially when I am genuinely happy to see him, even if my face and body language aren't quite confident enough to express it. So I force a pleasant smile and turn the conversation back around on him before he can dig any further into my personal life: "Was that your wife and kids in there?"

He nods, unable to contain his familial pride as his face practically bursts with love at the mere thought of them. "Keri and I have been married ten years now. And Emma and Cole are seven and four."

"Wild," I say, never entirely sure how to respond to people when they gush about their children.

"Very," he says, clocking my discomfort and mercifully checking his paternal impulse to tell me some adorable but meaningless story about them. "But I'll spare you the details. Especially with how busy you must be. You're here about the murders, right?"

I nod, quietly relieved to move past the personal and talk about a more comfortable subject: death. "With all the similarities between the two cases, I was brought in to oversee."

"And by similarities, you mean . . . my mother."

He says it with such icy detachment that I'm instantly reminded of what Sheriff McKee said about Jonah and his mother having a falling out. "So it's true, then. You two aren't working together anymore."

"We don't talk. Period."

"Mind if I ask why?"

"Are you asking as a friend? Or as an FBI agent investigating two murders?"

"Guess it depends. Which one gets me the truth?"

We share a grin, and for a moment, we're just those fumbling teenagers again, searching for the right words to convey emotions that we aren't mature enough to fully understand. But then his smile fades, and he moves in closer with a paranoid glance back over his shoulder. "Lana, I know you're probably really good at what you do, and I'm not saying this out of some bullshit patriarchal need to protect you. But this place—it's not like it was when we were growing up."

"What do you mean?"

"I mean there's more money, which means there are more outsiders trying to get a piece of it. And some of them . . . they can be dangerous."

"Dangerous how?"

He squirms uncomfortably, clearly wanting to tell me more, but he's either too afraid or too compromised to do so.

"Jonah, if you know something about these murders—"

"I don't," he says with an earnest look I remember well and can't help but trust. "But I do know my mom's gotten caught up with certain people who don't necessarily have her best interests at heart."

"What people?"

"*Bad* people." But before he can say another word, his phone buzzes in his pocket, a valve that instantly releases the pressure building in our conversation. He eagerly checks it: "It's Keri," he explains as he types a text back to her. "Cole's been going through some stuff lately, and he can be a lot when we try to eat out."

"Go. Dad duty calls."

He nods appreciatively and starts to leave, when one last urgent thought sends him whirling back around to face me. "Just promise you'll be careful."

"Don't worry. I've handled a lot worse than anything this place can throw at me."

He swallows nervously, and again I see that desperate desire to share some painful secret. "I wish that were true, Lana. I really do."

"Jonah, what aren't you telling me? Who are these *bad people* you're so scared of?"

He falls silent, taking a moment to choose his words with life-affirming precision, as if a single wrong syllable could spell death for him, or me, or possibly both. Finally, he glances back at the bar and lowers his voice to a paranoid whisper. "Have you noticed how many days passed between the two murders?"

"I hadn't really thought about it. A month?"

"Not exactly . . ."

I think for a moment, doing the mental math in my head with the stumbling inefficiency of a B-minus student. "Twenty-eight—no, twenty-nine days."

He nods almost imperceptibly and gives me an odd look, his eyebrows raised with subtle acknowledgment, as if the significance of this number should be evident to anyone hearing it. But of course it's not, and when he turns and hurries back toward the bar, I can't help but feel let down by the one person in the Napa Valley I thought I could trust.

"Is that it?" I call after him, not bothering to hide my disappointment. "Jonah, you've got to give me more than that!" But he doesn't say another word. He just disappears through the front door, eager to rejoin the comfort and certainty of his perfect family while I stand there in the looming dark, knowing things are about to get far more *un*comfortable and *un*certain than I could have possibly imagined.

8

I'm halfway to my motel when I first notice the SUV tailing me.

It's a midnight-blue Ford coated with a layer of late summer dust, the sort of anonymous "everycar" found all over the Valley, and I wouldn't have given it a second thought if it had simply turned on its headlights. But it didn't. And with the last red-orange glimmers of sunset fading to black, it isn't just a safety issue; it's a necessity on these winding, unlit vineyard roads. That's when I know—either this driver behind me is a careless fool who doesn't realize their mistake, or they're trying (and failing) to avoid suspicion by blending into the encroaching darkness. So with my hackles raised and my Quantico-trained muscle memory springing into action, I decide to test my theory.

Gradually, I pump the brakes to slow down to twenty-five miles per hour, only ten below the speed limit, but a pace that feels oddly unnatural on a quiet night like this. Then to fully sell the act, I pretend to use my phone to search for directions, a common occurrence in an area full of buzzed, out-of-town tourists struggling to navigate their way from one tasting room to the next. Most locals would pick up on this cue and impatiently pass me on the left, given the lack of oncoming traffic, but the midnight-blue SUV doesn't do that. No, this shady bastard abruptly slams on its brakes to match my speed and settle in right behind me.

Shit.

My mind races with possibilities, an endless parade of suspects who might be trying to scare me off the case before I can even check into my motel. Chief among them would be one of Angus McKee's cronies at the Napa County Sheriff's Department. It would hardly be the first time a corrupt local cop tried to nudge a federal agent off a case, and McKee has made no secret of his intense dislike for me, an oil-and-water relationship that dates back twenty-two years. But there's also the note-strapped rock that crashed through Holly Bancroft's window. Could whoever have tossed it now be following me, hoping to do the same thing to my windshield? Run me off the road as a means of forcing me out of town? And what about these so-called "bad people" who left Jonah Bancroft so rattled with paranoia? If they're able to scare the scion of the most powerful family in the Valley, then surely they could pay some thug in a beat-up Ford to see to it that I never walk again.

I try to casually glance back through the rearview mirror without straining my neck or making it obvious what I'm doing, but in the darkness, I can only glean the most basic of features from the driver's silhouette. It's clearly a man, although I can't see enough to discern his age. And I get the vague sense from his complexion that he's probably Latino. But that describes thousands of law-abiding Valley residents, and connecting this to that Spanish-language note in Holly's office feels like a leap I'm not yet willing to take. I need to see more—at the very least get a clear look at his license plate—but without some light, I'm not sure how that's going to be possible.

A quarter mile up the road, my motel emerges out of the darkness. The Silverado Inn is a twelve-room, single-story dive whose flickering purple neon sign hearkens back to what I'm sure must have been its 1970s heyday, long before the Valley was overtaken by five-star resorts, Michelin-star chefs, and five-hundred-dollar cabernets. It's exactly the sort of place I've come to expect on a government budget, but can I risk pulling into the lot and showing my tail where I'll be spending the night? If it's the same guy who hurled a chunk of limestone through a second-story window, he's clearly willing to get his hands dirty.

On the other hand, if he's a sheriff's deputy or part of the powerful cabal Jonah hinted at, then it's only a matter of time until they track me down here anyway. And if there's one thing I've learned over fifteen years and hundreds of cases at the Bureau, it's that criminals, no matter how capable of violence, will almost never risk harming a federal agent. Will they threaten us? Sure. Intimidate and bully? Absolutely. But every bad guy worth his salt knows that an injured—or, even worse, dead—agent will inevitably bring the full force and fury of the US government down on them, and that kind of attention isn't just bad for business. It's existential.

As I near the turnoff for the motel, another thought strikes me, the answer to my original problem shining down like a beacon from the heavens. Or at least from the tacky 1970s. And I jerk my wheel hard to the right, pulling into the lot so abruptly that the driver of the midnight-blue Ford doesn't have time to think. All he can do is react, and before I know it, he's swerving into the lot behind me, passing right under that pink neon sign. Within seconds, his face lights up like a frontman taking center stage at a rock concert, and for a moment, I'm able to look right into his cruel, dark eyes and at the strange scar on his left cheek, like he'd been cut open from ear to nose. I also catch a fleeting, but ample glimpse at something far more valuable.

"7PSA246. 7PSA246. 7PSA246." I repeat the license plate number over and over, desperate to keep it from slipping through the holes of my sieve-like memory. "7PSA246."

We both pass out of the sign's neon halo and back into darkness, but when I take another right toward a row of empty parking spaces, the other driver finally reconsiders. With a squeal of tires on the loose gravel, he zips back out onto the main road and quickly disappears from sight.

Whoooooosh.

I feel the air exploding out of my lungs in a torrent of breath that I didn't even realize I'd been holding, and as soon as I throw the car into park, I frantically reach for my phone and pull up the Notes app, my thumbs flying across the screen. *7PSA246*. It's not much, but it's a lead, and along with that threatening note from Holly's office, the only evidence I can trust since it hasn't been gathered and curated by Sheriff Angus McKee. So with a profound sense of relief at this smallest of victories, I slouch back into my seat, crack my neck, and allow myself the slightest of smiles.

"Gotcha, motherfucker."

* * *

Half an hour later, I'm sprawled out on the queen-size bed of my modest, outdated motel room, waiting for an update on that license plate from the SAC. My small suitcase sits unzipped on the stained carpet floor, and save for a toothbrush and some deodorant on the bathroom sink, there's almost no evidence of my residency. To be honest, I've never trusted people who unpack their bags and load their neatly folded clothes into dresser drawers and closets. It's not in the clinical definition of psychopathy, at least according to the DSM-5, but it conveys a level of implied ownership and need for control that I think speaks to larger problems with a person's character. Plus it's just a giant waste of time. I once dated a guy who insisted on unpacking his clothes the moment he arrived in a hotel room—he couldn't even start his vacation until every shirt was neatly hung and every boxer brief was folded with precision. And wouldn't you know it, after two months together, I found out he'd been paying a sex worker to piss on him every Thursday afternoon. Does correlation imply causation? No, of course not. But I can't help but think the traits were somehow linked.

If only I could round up the suspects in the O'Shea and Cruz cases and watch them all check into hotel rooms. *Shit*, I'd have the killer behind bars by bedtime.

The thunderous buzz of my phone on the nightstand shakes my wandering mind back into the present, and I lunge to answer it without bothering to look at the display. "Did you find it?"

"I'm not sure," says a confident male baritone that I can't quite place. "What exactly was I supposed to be looking for?"

I check the phone—it's a random number with a 707 area code, which could place it anywhere in Napa or ten other counties—and I sigh with embarrassment. "Sorry, I was expecting a call from someone at work. Who is this?"

"We've never met, Agent Burrell, but I knew your old man."

Right away, my hackles go up, a junkyard dog who smells an intruder. "And you are . . . ?"

"Peter Bancroft."

That name hits me like a freight train, an empire of power, wealth, and global influence conveyed in just four syllables. This is the man who turned his father's half of the original Bancroft wine business into a multinational conglomerate, gobbling up smaller wineries around the world with the insatiable appetite of a shark, single-minded in its drive to be the biggest fish in the sea. Or, in this case, the biggest wine company the planet has ever seen. No one in the Valley would ever accuse him of making *good* wine—true oenophiles like his cousin, Holly, look down their noses at him and his warehouses full of boxed, jugged, and canned beverages that only loosely meet the traditional definition of wine. But in a society where money talks, Peter Bancroft always has the last word. I once read somewhere that he's the first self-made wine billionaire, which, in an industry famous for bleeding money and losing shirts, is saying something. ("How do you make a small fortune in the wine business?" the old joke goes. "Start with a large one.")

I want to say something, want to play this cool, but I find my throat sealed shut and my tongue too dry to form words. *How the hell did Peter Bancroft get my number?*

As if he can read my mind, he answers the question I was too blindsided to ask. "I hope you don't mind me reaching out like this, but I just had dinner with Sheriff McKee, and he gave me your number. I hear you're running the show now with these murder cases."

"That's right," I manage to tell him, finally finding my voice. "Did you, uh, have some information you wanted to share?"

"About the cases?" he asks, oddly confused by what I assumed was an obvious question.

"That *is* usually why people cold-call the FBI. They typically know something and think it might be useful for our investigation."

"Ohh," he says, catching on. "No. I don't know anything about those girls. In fact, I was in New York on business when the first one was killed. I can have my assistant send you the travel memo, if you'd like."

"That won't be necessary, Mr. Bancroft. You're not a suspect."

"Of course," he says a bit too quickly, as if for a moment there he wondered if he might be. "Just trying to be helpful."

As he regains his composure and I wait there for him to get to the point, a tense silence settles over us, and what started as an innocent call starts to seem more and more dodgy by the second. "So if you didn't have a tip to share," I ask, "why *did* you call?"

"Right, well, let me start by saying I want nothing more than to see whoever did this put behind bars. What happened to those girls was disgusting—*reprehensible*—and if there's ever anything I can do to help with the investigation, you have my number. But..."

Here it comes.

"... we need to make sure we're all being careful about the optics here."

"The optics?" I spit back at him, barely stifling the disdain that's starting to burble up from the pit of my stomach.

"We're a tourism-based economy, Agent Burrell. We aren't just selling people wine. We're selling them a lifestyle. We're selling them paradise. And paradise crumbles as soon as the media gets involved and starts doing what they do, exploiting an unfortunate situation and pointing fingers at the wrong people."

"And by 'wrong people,' I assume you mean your cousin Holly."

"That's not what this is about," he says defensively.

"Did she tell you to call me?"

"Of course not. We're not even all that close these days. What I'm concerned about here is the Napa Valley. I've always seen myself as a bit of an ambassador for this place, and I'm just trying to look out for it. For *everyone* whose lives would be ruined if this thing gets blown out of proportion, and tourists stop coming because they don't feel safe."

"This *thing*," I remind him, "is the brutal murder of two innocent women."

"And as I said, I want nothing more than to find justice for them—"

"I wasn't finished, Mr. Bancroft." My voice slices through his with razor-like precision. "Twenty-two years ago, I saw exactly what happens when people are so concerned with making a case go away that they arrest someone without even considering other suspects."

"Now that's not fair—"

"My father is *still* in jail. And whoever *did* kill your niece is probably still out there. For all we know, he's the same guy who killed Katherine O'Shea and Pilar Cruz. So I'll tell you what I'm *not* going to do. I'm *not* going to rush this case and slap cuffs on someone just so the tourists can feel safer. I'm also not going to let power and influence dictate the truth, and if the facts point somewhere you don't like—at your family, maybe—then so be it. I've got absolutely no qualms about putting a Bancroft behind bars."

I hear his forceful, angry breath on the other end. Clearly, he's not used to being spoken to like this, but I'm not about to apologize or walk back my threats. I'm the one with the badge and the responsibility for those two women, and if I don't stand up for them, then nobody will. So I let him stew in his own silence for as long as he needs. A full ten seconds pass before he finally says a word. "What makes you so sure your father didn't kill Jess?"

"Because I know him."

"Then how do you explain the blood in the trunk of his car?"

"Someone set him up," I say calmly and with a steely self-assurance, repeating the story I've always told myself. "Or they just happened to steal his car when they did it."

"Awfully convenient," he mumbles.

"I was with him all night!"

"You were asleep," he reminds me. "In different rooms. He could have easily slipped out to move the body somewhere."

"There was no body to move," I say with a growl, furious that I'm still having this conversation over twenty years later.

"Fine," Bancroft says, refusing to let up, "then what about the skin fragments under his fingernails? Forensics said it only could have gotten there if he'd scratched her that night."

I feel my fists clenching with rage, with the desire to fight back to defend my dad, like I'm still that teenage girl lashing out in the courtroom, almost charged with contempt. "Have you ever scratched anyone, Peter?"

"Sure," he says smugly, playing along.

"Did they charge *you* for murder because of it?"

He lets out a cynical laugh, the same one I used to get from police officers and local news reporters anytime I tried to stand up for the man who raised me, despite all the evidence stacked against him. "That's a bit of an oversimplification, Agent Burrell," he says, "and I think you know it."

"Yeah, well, I also know my dad better than anyone," I snap with disdain, having long since lost my composure. "And I know what he's capable of."

"Okay," Bancroft says. "But I know Napa. I know what its *residents* are capable of. And if you aren't careful, not even I can protect you."

Click.

The line goes dead, but I can't stop myself from shouting into the phone, my mouth frothing with self-protective rage. "Was that a threat? Did you just fucking threaten me?!" But of course there's no answer. Peter Bancroft is long gone, and I'm left alone in a dreary motel room that suddenly feels a whole lot smaller.

9

Twenty-nine days

I repeat the number over and over as I pace the confines of this wallpapered tiger cage masquerading as a motel room. Of all the secrets Jonah Bancroft couldn't bring himself to divulge—bad people holding private sway over his infamous mother, and more—why would he act as if nothing were more important than the time between the two murders? If it were anyone else, I'd probably dismiss it as the wild ravings of an unreliable witness; the sort of conspiratorial nonsense I hear all the time at work in this age of unhindered social media posts, where the truth has lost any sense of objectivity. But it's Jonah. *My* Jonah. And unless he's suffered some sort of mental breakdown in my two-decade absence, he's the closest thing I have to a trustworthy source here in Napa.

My first thought, most likely because I'm just a day past my own period, is that it has something to do with menstrual cycles. Mine is twenty-eight days long and as regular as a Tokyo train schedule thanks to my birth control, but I know a twenty-nine-day pattern is also quite common. Still, the idea that two women who were almost certainly on different cycles were killed because of their periods in present-day California is straight-up laughable.

No, it must be something else. Something less random and... bodily.

The moon?

I'm fairly certain it's on a twenty-eight- or twenty-nine-day cycle as it waxes and wanes from new moon to full and back again. And it's not just werewolves who lose their shit anytime a full moon pokes its mischievous head through the clouds. There's a legitimate uptick in violent crime on nights when the moon is full. I've seen the data, even if I can't logically explain it. Is it possible that this is what Jonah was suggesting? That a lunar cycle had something to do with the murders? I do a quick search on my phone, my heartbeat quickening as I await the results, and sure enough...

September 7: Full moon.

October 6: Full moon.

With newfound excitement, I scramble through the police reports assembled by Sheriff McKee's staff to confirm the coroner's estimated times of death.

Pilar Cruz: Sometime between ten PM and two AM.

Katherine O'Shea: Sometime between eleven thirty PM and three AM.

"Fucking hell..." The words slip through my lips at a whisper, the shock of this discovery sending my synapses into overdrive. Two women, disconnected in almost every way two women can be, both killed around midnight during subsequent full moons.

And both last seen at Golden Eagle Winery.

Suddenly, the casual ramblings of Holly Bancroft's tasting room assistant, Bex Potter, come roaring back, her seemingly innocent obsession with Leaf days and planting cycles, and her almost fundamentalist faith in biodynamic winemaking. The more I reflect, the more the scattered pieces of this case begin to fuse together in my mind, a puzzle snapping into place, revealing a picture as bizarre as it is fascinating.

A picture I can only see because of my father.

Growing up alone in a cramped house, with a vineyard manager for a dad, we inevitably talked a lot about wine and viticulture, even though I couldn't have cared less about it at the time. But it was his newfound passion, and along with his art, it's what got him through those devastating, isolating years after my mom's death. So I indulged him, for his sake. And when he came home late one night with an article by some French winemaker who had just switched his vineyard over to biodynamic farming, I listened. Half-heartedly, of course, but enough that I still remember the basics, especially since it was far from the last time we talked about it together.

Honestly, I just thought it sounded nuts.

A group of winemakers around the world had recently rediscovered the writings of a dead Austrian philosopher named Rudolf Steiner, a guy once famous for using so-called "scientific methods" to investigate ghosts and clairvoyants. Despite his questionable pedigree, Steiner's biodynamic farming principles had sparked something in the minds of people who'd grown sick of mass-produced, factory-farmed everything—the *Fast Food Nation* generation—so quite a few vineyards took to it with the zeal of a new religion. Certain aspects, like using the dung of live animals to fertilize soil in a chemical-free manner, are hardly controversial. But others, like filling a cow horn with manure and burying it in the field every autumn for reasons I'll never understand, are certifiably bananas.

And then there's the moon. Its twenty-nine-day cycle drives everything behind Steiner's teachings, from when to plant your seeds, to when to irrigate your crops, to when to harvest your fruit. It's why Bex was so upset about Holly Bancroft wanting to pick her cabernet on a "Leaf day." Since people who believe in this stuff adhere to it like gospel and coordinate every aspect of their lives around lunar movements, is it so much of a stretch to think that a particularly unhinged devotee might even *kill* because of it?

I've certainly heard of crazier motives for murder. The Son of Sam was apparently listening to instructions from his talking Labrador retriever, and even my own Marin County Marksman was choosing his targets based on women's Tinder photos. The fact is, when a human mind has snapped loose from its moorings, there's no telling what might push it toward the previously unthinkable. Even, dare I say it, *the moon.*

Which brings me back to Bex Potter. She may have looked innocent enough, with her adorable blonde curls and her infectious smile—and let's face it, a petite twenty-five-year-old in cute denim overalls is hardly how one envisions the brutal killer of two young women—but she's clearly a biodynamic zealot, and she works at the site of both disappearances. Could there be a secret darkness lurking beneath that bubbly exterior?

First thing's first: I need to find out if she's the woman who Katherine O'Shea was flirting with on the night she went missing. So I track down contact information for Charlotte Croydon, the bride-to-be in Katherine's party, and text her my question, along with a photo of Bex that I pull from her LinkedIn page. While I wait for a response, I figure I'll do some research on Bex, see what social media and the FBI database have to say about my new chief suspect, but barely ten seconds pass before my phone lights up with a text from Charlotte: *YES!!!! THAT'S HER!!!* Another text follows a moment later: *Do you think she had something to do with this?*

Yes, Charlotte, I do.

But I can't tell her that—not yet—so I send a polite, noncommittal response and tumble back onto the bed in exhaustion, letting the cheap motel pillows cushion my whirling, swirling head as I work out a plan of attack. First thing tomorrow, I've got to learn everything I can about Rebecca "Bex" Potter. Then I'll start on interviews—anyone who knows her and who might be able to connect her to Pilar Cruz as well as Katherine O'Shea. Was Bex lying when she said she no longer slept with women? Had she and Katherine spent any time together after the bachelorette party left the vineyard? And how closely did she work with migrant farmers like Pilar?

So many questions. So many possibilities. As I stare up at the dusty black ceiling fan, spinning hypnotically against the off-white stucco, I try to imagine the tiny blonde with the golden locks committing such heinous, inhuman acts. Dosing two women with LSD and injecting them with pentobarbital. Bleeding them out at the wrists and then cutting them open across the abdomen. Dragging their bodies and dumping them alongside a couple of disemboweled animals. At first it hardly seems possible, but then I think back to her eyes, those unsettling, unblinking orbs that make her seem capable of anything. And I know I'm onto something. Something big. And with visions of those wide, piercing eyes staring down at me—not unlike the two full moons that watched over the ritualistic murders of Pilar Cruz and Katherine O'Shea—I drift off to sleep.

* * *

Boom. Boom. Boom.

Three sharp knocks jolt me out of a dream. It wasn't a pleasant one—I was in a windowless cell in San Quentin, wondering when my father was going to come visit me—but that hardly makes the sudden, thunderous wakeup call a welcome disturbance. The pounding is so forceful and the motel door so flimsy that it feels like the whole room is shaking, and for a moment, I wonder if I've been roused by a small earthquake. But then a brief pause is followed by two more knocks, just as loud, just as violent, and I finally piece together where I am.

My eyes dart instinctively over to the alarm clock: 6:42 AM. What kind of monster wakes a person up this early? I'm about to march over to the door and unleash hell on my uninvited guest, when I remember the mysterious scarred man in the midnight-blue Ford who tailed me here. What if it's him behind that door, coming to finish whatever business he chickened out on last night? I open the nightstand drawer, where alongside a virginally untouched Gideon Bible, I've hidden my loaded Glock and its holster. With a practiced slide of my finger, I check the safety, then smoothly tuck the gun in the back of my waistband—one of the unexpected benefits of sleeping in the same pair of pants I wore yesterday.

Boom, boom, boom.

I wait for the knocks of my iron-fisted guest to subside before I cautiously approach the door and peer out through the peephole. But what I see standing there leaves me so shaken and perplexed that all I can murmur are four simple words:

"What the actual fuck?"

10

"I am so sorry, hon—I hope I didn't wake you. Warm muffins?"

I'm so confused by the maternal smile and bifocal lenses on the older woman standing before me that all I can do is gawk for what feels like the better part of a minute, my lips curled out like those of a puffer fish or someone doing a bad impression of Mick Jagger.

She lifts the plate of homemade muffins even higher, as if they're some exotic, foreign baked good that needs extra clarification. "Blueberries weren't in season, so I made banana nut. I hope you're not allergic—I didn't even think of that 'til now. Can people be allergic to walnuts, or is that just a peanut thing?"

"I'm not allergic," I manage to say despite having no idea who she is or why the hell she's trying to ply me with baked goods at 6:42 in the morning.

"Oh, thank God!" she says with an overly dramatic sigh of relief. "What a waste of time *that* would have been. Ya know, I got up at four thirty to make these for you?" She inches the plate even higher, slathering her muffins with an extra dollop of guilt, until I finally give in and take one. "Of course I'm always up that early these days. Ever since the kids left home, I just love waking up before sunrise. It's like I roll out of bed and I'm on vacation at some five-star resort, only it doesn't cost me a nickel, and I'm the one cooking breakfast." She transfers the plate to her left hand and extends her right in a professional manner. "Sheriff's Deputy Essie Leroux."

I absent-mindedly shake her hand, still trying to fight through the morning brain fog to piece together exactly what's happening. "Did McKee send you?"

"No," she says. "I mean yes, he did assign me to be your right-hand man, so to speak. But he didn't specifically send me to your motel room with a plate full of breakfast treats, if that's what you're asking. That part was my idea." Her eyes drift down to the unbitten muffin in my hand. "You're not one of those gluten-free types, are you?"

"No," I assure her, and I take a small bite to appease those probing, maternal eyes, leering at me from behind her unabashedly outdated tortoiseshell glasses. As I chew the muffin, I try to get a better sense of Deputy Essie Leroux, who looks nothing like any law enforcement official I've ever seen. Her uniform is as to be expected: black boots, olive-green slacks, short-sleeve khaki button-down, black duty belt stocked with her radio, service weapon, and baton. But it's everything else that jumps out as an odd personality mismatch, a sixty-year-old librarian cosplaying a cop, rather than the real deal.

Her hair is an unnatural auburn with dissonant streaks of gray where her natural roots are colliding with what I can only assume was a do-it-yourself dye job. It's done up in a bun, no doubt to stay out of the way while she's on patrol, but there's so much of the stuff that it's spilling out every which way. And her jewelry—well, to be honest, I'm surprised McKee even lets her report for duty with so many dangly baubles and chunky bracelets hanging from her lobes, wrists, and neck. She sounds like a wind chime in a hurricane every time she moves.

"Jesus Christ!" The words leap from my mouth before I've even swallowed my first bite of muffin.

"Not bad, eh?" Leroux says with a knowing wink, a gesture that would get a guy punched but that she somehow manages to pull off in a sweet, endearing way.

"This is the best thing I've ever tasted," I tell her, and I mean it. It's way too early in the morning for flattery and bullshit, and I'm already devouring a much larger bite of banana-nut muffin while I wave the deputy into my cramped room. "Are you running point on the two cases?"

"Not quite."

"But you've been working on the Cruz murder since the beginning, right?"

"No," she says, and I watch her face scrunch up with embarrassment.

"I'm confused."

"Have another muffin."

But I set the plate down on my bed before she can distract me with another mouth-watering treat. "Deputy Leroux . . . how long have you been on the Cruz and O'Shea cases?"

"Technically? Since seven o'clock last night—"

"Jesus Christ . . ."

"*But* I've been assisting Angus and the boys on it from the start, so I know all the pertinent details."

"What do you mean by *assisting*?"

"Okay—full disclosure," she says, taking a nervous breath. "I'm a bit of a late bloomer."

"Go on . . ."

I watch her sit on the edge of my unmade bed, as if her story is such a doozy that her legs can't even support the weight of it. "For the first part of my life," she says, "I was really just a mom. Frank made good money driving delivery trucks for the big wineries, so

I stayed home 'til all the kids went off to college. But then Frank had a heart attack and couldn't drive much anymore, and I needed something to keep us going. Only I wasn't about to be one of those old hags bagging groceries at the Albertson's. I wanted to do something that mattered. Something that touched people's lives in a meaningful way. And I am just the biggest fan of *Law & Order—*"

"You joined the police academy in your fifties because you liked a cop show?"

"Yes, ma'am," she says without a hint of irony. "As you can imagine, I was a bit of an outlier—what with all the boys in their twenties with the buzz cuts and the biceps. But I passed all the tests, same as everyone else. Can still run an eight-minute mile, thank you very much. And I joined the Sheriff's Department just shy of my sixtieth birthday."

"How long ago was that?" I ask.

"About four months."

"Jesus Christ . . ."

"You say that a lot, don't you?"

I consider apologizing, since she's about as sweet as the banana-nut muffin I just polished off, but it wouldn't be my style, so I give her a shrug and mumble something unintelligible.

"It's fine," she says with a wave of her hand. "I get it. I've mostly been on desk duty since I started, but I've been begging the sheriff to put me on a case to help me get my sea legs. Nothing major, just a carjacking or a break-in maybe. I would've even settled for a routine noise violation. So you can imagine my surprise when he called last night and asked me to be the department's liaison to the FBI on the two big murders! I swear to G-O-D, I just about shit myself. Don't worry, though—I didn't. I may be an old bitch, but I still have excellent bowel control."

As I stand there trying not to think about this oversharing older woman and her apparently reliable bowels, my fists clench in fury, and I begin to burn with a singular rage against Sheriff Angus McKee. I know exactly what he's doing. When I'm on a job, it's customary for the local PD to assign me one of their own. Some mid-level uniformed cop who knows the case well enough and can get me what I need while also keeping me out of their lead detectives' hair. It's both a courtesy to me and a convenience for them; this person often saves the local sheriff or lieutenant from having to deal with my incessant questions or requests for evidence, so it's in everyone's best interest to make this relationship work.

But never—not in all my years—have I been handed someone like Deputy Essie Leroux, a geriatric amateur in need of a babysitter. McKee is obviously doing this to slow me down and keep me from meddling in two highly sensitive cases that could become political minefields. The more distracted I am by Deputy Essie and her mouthwatering muffins, the more likely his team is to make an arrest without my involvement. And given his motives, his desperation to make these cases go away before the next election, he'll probably find a way to pin it on the easiest target. A migrant farmworker, maybe. Someone with no resources and a bad public defender. But there's no way in hell I'm letting him do that—not again.

"Deputy Leroux, I'm sure you're good at what you do, and I know I'll probably regret saying this, but I'm not someone who works well with others. Never have been."

"You seem nice enough to me."

"I'm like one of those cuddly dogs you can't bring to parks. They're fine at home, but as soon as you put them around other dogs, they turn into vicious killers."

She eyes me skeptically, and I can see her wheels turning. She's clearly no fool despite my initial impressions, and she knows precisely what I'm doing. I hold my breath and wait for her to lash out, to accuse me of ageism and sexism, and I won't be able to say a word in response because I know she'll be right. But instead, she gives me a polite smile. "Suit yourself," she says, popping up off the bed and retreating toward the door without a fuss. "You can keep the plate. I've got plenty at home."

I'm about to shut the door behind her and try to get another hour of sleep when I see her stop abruptly at the edge of the sidewalk. "Or..." she says, her back still turned, "you *could* return the plate *after* I tell you everything I dug up on Peter Bancroft."

"Peter?" I ask, his weaselly voice still echoing through my brain after that strange call last night. "What does he have to do with any of this?"

She slowly turns to face me, her eyes shining mischievously as a cryptic smile stretches across her face. "I'll show you."

* * *

After a short drive, I'm standing in a detached garage on Leroux's property in Rutherford, realizing that I've sorely misjudged this bizarre woman.

Behind a beat-up, rust-colored El Camino with a missing engine, and right next to an old gardening shelf full of seeds and trowels, she's hung a corkboard that's so new it still has the price tag on it: $19.99 from Walmart. Tacked onto the board with careful consideration are a hodgepodge of photos, newspaper clippings, and financial statements all connected to Peter Bancroft and his J.B. Bancroft wine empire. Truth be told, I've been with the FBI for fifteen years and have never actually seen anyone put together a murder board like this. I think most of my colleagues would probably laugh if they saw one in person. But for the *Law & Order* fan turned sheriff's deputy, who's just become my new favorite Napa Valley resident, it makes perfect sense. And I've got to say, I kind of love it.

"When did you do this?" I ask, stunned by the impressive display. "I thought you were just put on the case last night."

"Well, the thing is, Agent Burrell, I wasn't entirely honest with you earlier."

"How so?"

"I know who you are." She sees my eyes narrow with paranoid anger and starts to backpedal, explaining herself before I can lash out. "I mean, I know who your father is and what the Bancrofts did to him. My husband, Frank, he actually used to play softball with your dad, one of those silly beer leagues—"

"Bad News Beers," I say, fondly recalling the screen-printed T-shirt he used to wear to games, something I thought I'd long since forgotten.

"That's right. It damn near killed Frank when he heard about the arrest. Said your dad was one of the sweetest guys he ever knew."

"Well, that's really nice of him, Deputy, but what does that have to do with Peter Bancroft?"

"Ahh, right. You'll have to forgive me. Frank always complains I have this annoying habit of telling stories in a circle instead of a straight line."

"Take your time."

"All right," she says, taking a breath to chart her path forward before she continues. "You see, we have this little plot of vines in our backyard—you probably saw them on the way in. It's not much, enough for maybe a barrel every year, but these are some really special grapes we're dealing with. You see, our property, it bumps right up against one of the most famous vineyards in Napa: Eu Topos. Ever hear of it? No? Well, it means "the good place" in Greek, or something like that. Actually, maybe it's "good vibes." Do you think the Greeks had a word for "vibes"?"

I can feel my patience wearing thin, but for her sake, and the sake of my case, I try to stifle my frustration and give her the time she needs. "I have no idea, Deputy."

"Oh, will you please stop calling me that?" she says in a scolding tone. "It's Essie. It's always been Essie."

"Sure."

"Anyway, whatever it means, a single ton of grapes from that plot of land sells for around fifty thousand dollars."

"And what does a normal ton of grapes sell for?" I ask, utterly clueless about wine country economics.

"About eight grand in Napa. Maybe a quarter of that in Sonoma. And just a couple hundred bucks down in the Central Valley."

"Jesus Christ..."

"There you go again," she says.

"Sorry. Force of habit."

"I'm not complaining," she says with a naughty grin, like we're in on some secret together. "Not much of a church girl myself. I was just pointing it out."

I force a smile and try to nudge her onward, intent on keeping this hopelessly circular speaker from veering off course. "You were saying..."

"Right," she says eagerly, as if she'd gotten lost and just remembered where she was. "Well, if you look at the old deeds and historical registers for the area, our yard was a part of the original Eu Topos Vineyard, way back in the 1860s. So our grapes, they're as much Eu Topos as the ones growing on the other side of that fence. Same slope, same soil composition, same drainage. Which is why Frank decided to pay a friend to make some wine out of it. Not much, mind you. Like I said, it's only one barrel. But when the first bottles were ready, around eight years ago, we sold a few of 'em at auction under the name Eu Topos Vineyard. Forty bucks a pop, just to help cover expenses. And do you know how much money we made on wine that year?"

"How much?"

"Twelve hundred dollars," she says, and then repeats it more slowly, for effect: "Twelve. Hundred. Dollars. And yet we were sued for copyright infringement by the billionaire who owns the land on the other side of that fence. I'll give you two guesses who that was."

"Peter fucking Bancroft."

"Not sure about the middle name, but yes, that's the guy. Poor Frank, he was so torn up about the whole thing—the lawyer fees, the arbitration, the threats—he ended up having a heart attack. A bad one. And he hasn't been the same since. All over a measly twelve hundred bucks and a name we had every right to use, if you know your history."

Leroux falls silent, lamenting what's become of her husband, and as her eyes drift across the corkboard, they burn with an impassioned rage that startles me. Grudges like this can be dangerous. I know better than anyone the psychological toll that such enmity can take on a person. It can slowly drive you mad and lead you to see things that aren't really there; so police uniform or not, whatever this woman tells me about Peter Bancroft, I'll have to take with a grain of salt (as tempting as it might be to drag Napa's First Family through the mud). Still, there's something about her that I can't help but trust . . .

"I'm sorry about your husband," I tell her with as much sympathy as I can muster. "And believe me, I want to see that family go down more than anyone. But how exactly is Peter connected to the murders? He already told me he was out of town when Pilar Cruz was killed, and I can't imagine he had a connection to some Texan's bachelorette party."

Leroux's eyes burn with intensity, her voice lowering to a growl as she pulls me in close. "Just 'cause he didn't hold the knife doesn't mean there's no blood on his hands. Understand?"

"Why then?" I ask. "Evidence aside, what motive would a billionaire have to kill two random, innocent women a month apart?"

"Oldest motive in the world," Leroux says with a grim expression, her voice deathly serious. *"Money."*

IN THE SUPERIOR COURT OF NAPA COUNTY, CALIFORNIA
CIVIL, ESTATES, & FAMILY LAW DIVISION

PETER BANCROFT, Plaintiff, 17CI 04183-01
v.
HOLLY BANCROFT, Defendant
Judge Presiding, Hon. Abigail R. Cox

Procedural Background

On March 4, 2022, the Plaintiff filed a suit against the Defendant alleging mismanagement of the family's Conservation Easement on Property known as Redwood Vale, the grounds for which were laid out in a filing and recorded with the County of Napa on December 2, 1978. Plaintiff wishes to remove Defendant from the Easement under California Civil Code 815.3, subsection a), which requires an Easement to be held by a tax-exempt nonprofit organization in good standing under Section 501(c) (3) of the Internal Revenue Code. Plaintiff argues that Defendant's unusual use of the Redwood Vale property negates her 501(c) (3) standing, thus making her an unfit conservator of the Easement in question.

Conservation Easement History

Per Section 815 of the California Civil Code: *The Legislature finds and declares that the preservation of land in its natural, scenic, agricultural, historical, forested, or open-space condition is among the most important environmental assets of California. The Legislature further finds and declares it to be the public policy and in the public interest of this state to encourage the voluntary conveyance of Conservation Easements to qualified nonprofit organizations.*

Following this declaration, Plaintiff's father, James B. Bancroft, and Defendant's father, Michael Bancroft, entered into a Conservation Easement with the state to protect the use of their jointly owned properties. These included several vineyards not pertinent to this case, as well as a woodland preserve known as Redwood Vale. Per the terms of the Easement, Grantees agreed to voluntarily restrict the use of their land to agricultural purposes, including farming, grazing, ranching, and the production and sale of wines, but specifically excluding commercial logging in any form. Other exclusions included the development of any new commercial or residential structures not related to the aforementioned agricultural uses.

Under California law, the Easement is tied to the property itself, not the deed holder(s), and thus cannot be altered following a sale or inherited transfer of the land. Per the terms of this specific Easement, however, Grantees agreed that an alteration would be possible with a unanimous vote of the two shareholders, Michael Bancroft and James B. Bancroft. Following the deaths of both original Grantees, those voting shares passed on to their respective heirs, the Defendant and Plaintiff.

Plaintiff wishes to alter the terms of the Easement to allow for commercial development on the Redwood Vale property, but Defendant has denied that request on numerous occasions.

"Unusual Use"

Plaintiff's argument in favor of removing Defendant from the Easement relies on a claim of "unusual use" of the property, thus making her an unfit trustee of a 501(c) (3) organization. According to the Plaintiff, such unusual use was as follows:

Beginning on ████████, Defendant and a group of associates known collectively as the ████ ██████ are alleged to have ██████ ██████████████ ████████ █████████

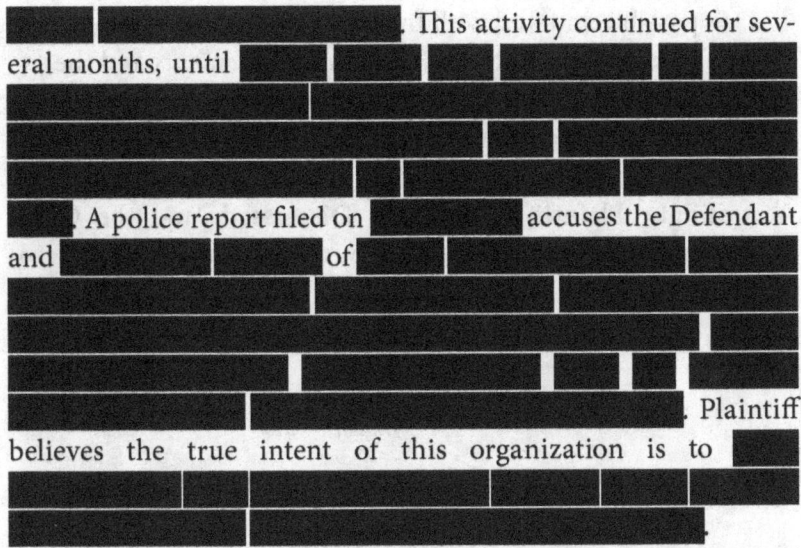

███████████████████████████. This activity continued for several months, until ████████████████████████████████.

████. A police report filed on ████████ accuses the Defendant and ████████████ of ██. Plaintiff believes the true intent of this organization is to ██.

Defendant denies said use of the Redwood Vale property, as well as the Plaintiff's characterization of her behavior as "unusual" or a commercial enterprise that would jeopardize her 501(c) (3) status.

Conclusion

Based on the foregoing discussion, the Court finds as follows:

1) The terms of the Conservation Easement dated December 2, 1978, are clear and binding, and the Plaintiff has not shown cause to alter said terms.
2) Section 501(c) (3) of the Internal Revenue Code grants substantial leeway to the range of organizations that fall under its terms, and Plaintiff has not shown that Defendant's activities would jeopardize her tax-exempt status.
3) Historically, this Court and others have made it a point to preserve Conservation Easements whenever

possible and find with the party who wished to do so, in keeping with the spirit of those Easements and the original law establishing them passed by the California State Legislature.

Accordingly, Plaintiff's lawsuit is **Dismissed,** and the Court hereby orders Plaintiff to cover all court costs and legal fees associated with this suit for Defendant.

Entered

Abigail R. Cox

_____

Judge Abigail R. Cox
Napa County Superior Court
Civil, Estates, & Family Division

Date: January 19, 2022

11

We take two cars to Peter Bancroft's office in downtown Napa rather than share a ride. I've told Leroux that I have to make a few private calls to the San Francisco office, but the truth is, I just desperately need forty-five minutes of peace and quiet. The woman may bake a mean muffin and build an impressive murder board, but she's physically incapable of a silent moment between two people. I imagine it's driven by the same post-parental loneliness that sent her to the police academy after her three kids left home; like many ex-truck drivers who spent their life on the road, her husband, Frank, doesn't sound like much of a talker. So as I crawl down Highway 29 in the usual tourist traffic, I use this silent reprieve to try and make sense of everything Leroux told me about the Bancrofts.

The feud between Peter and Holly started four years ago when he showed her his plans to build the biggest family-friendly resort in Northern California. As he saw it, the Bancroft Family Wine Ranch was going to be his version of Disneyland. Equal parts wine country day spa and farmland fun park, it would offer something for everyone and drive tourism to Napa from the same middle-market consumers who tended to buy his lower-priced, entry-level wines. But it wasn't just Holly's elitist sensibilities that turned her off to the idea (even though her brand *was* more suited to the sort of high-end tourist who didn't mind shelling out fifteen hundred dollars a night to stay at Auberge du Soleil and a thousand dollars for the tasting menu at The French Laundry). What rankled Holly more than anything was that his plans would require breaking the Conservation Easement on Redwood Vale that their fathers had put into place four decades earlier in an effort to protect the land in perpetuity. As an ardent environmentalist and a newly devout practitioner of biodynamic farming, Holly refused to let him pave over their family's paradise and turn it into a parking lot—not to mention a hotel and theme park—so he sued her, multiple times apparently, and failed on each occasion.

None of this is all that surprising given what I know about Peter and Holly Bancroft, and their family certainly has a history of feuds dating back to their fathers, J.B. and Michael. The bigger question is what to think of Leroux's theory: that Peter had those two women killed as a way to frame Holly for murder and get her removed from the family's Conservation Easement. On the one hand, given the Deputy's grudge against Peter, it's easy to see this as an unsubstantiated conspiracy theory based on nothing more than her own desire to see him fry. But on the other hand, it *does* have a sort of insane logic to it. If Holly were arrested and it could be proven that her crimes were somehow connected to Redwood Vale, then this might give Peter the legal grounds necessary to claim she's an unfit caretaker of the land. Get her booted from the Easement and give him carte blanche to build his dream resort. And with that in mind, I can't stop thinking about our unprompted phone call from last night. If Peter really has nothing to hide, then why would he try and muscle his way into my case like that?

I grip the steering wheel tighter as my impending meeting with Peter Bancroft leaves me tense with anticipation. I've never questioned a billionaire before, let alone accused one of a double homicide. This could definitely get interesting...

* * *

The J.B. Bancroft building in Napa is mainly remarkable for how unremarkable it is. The biggest wine company in the world, responsible for millions of cases across dozens of brands, with around two billion dollars in annual revenue, is based out of a nondescript, four-story brick building next to a Bank of America and across the street from a Chevron station. It's as generically corporate and unpretentious as a headquarters can get, with neither the Francophile majesty of the vineyards it owns or the tech campus whimsy of the Bay Area start-ups it competes with for talent. Even the lobby is oddly stark and austere, with not so much as a mention of the wine labels in the company's portfolio, as if the marketing executives and accountants who pass through here five days a week are too ashamed to admit their association with the cheap jugged wines of Bancroft Home or the sugary canned concoctions of Bancroft Spritz.

As I move through the cubicle-filled fourth floor, all I can think is how painfully boring it must be to work here.

That's when I spot Peter Bancroft waving me over from the open doorway of his spacious corner office, grinning with that unctuous smile I recall from the headshot that runs with most of his media appearances.

I look around for Leroux—she must be running late with all that traffic—so I smile politely at my host and consider him carefully as I move to join him. What strikes me at first is that he's far shorter than I imagined. Something about his booming voice on the phone gave me the impression of someone well over six feet tall, the sort of commanding presence who projects strength and power by entering a room and immediately looking down on everyone else in it. But Peter Bancroft is at least two inches shorter than me, and he weighs less too. There's almost something sickly about his thin frame, and I can tell right away that he never touches the wine he peddles. That's the taut face and trim figure of a teetotaling health nut—maybe even a vegan—which tells me two things about Bancroft. He's patient and calculating, making for a dangerous adversary in an investigation like this. But he's also someone who thinks about his own mortality and fears for it enough to adopt an ascetic diet and lifestyle, and that's someone who *can* be reasoned with when push comes to shove. He's wearing a bespoke gray suit, carefully tailored to fit his wiry frame, but he's gone tie-less, and his top two buttons are undone, the only thing in this bland, structured office that might be described as remotely casual. As for his hair, it's thick and wavy, belying his sixty years of age; it's also as inky black as his cousin Holly's is platinum blonde, as if even their heads couldn't get along and had decided to go off in opposite directions.

"Thanks for coming," he says, shaking my hand firmly as I follow him into his private suite. "I know it can be a pain to get down here on a weekend, but I had a few other meetings I couldn't cancel."

"Traffic wasn't great," I tell him with a bitterness that lets him know I'm in no mood for any bullshit. "I think my colleague from the Sheriff's Department must have gotten stuck in it somewhere."

He unleashes a heavy sigh and his eyes lower to the floor, as if he's debating whether to tell me something. Then he plops down into one of the two matching Eames chairs on the front side of his massive mahogany desk. "Look, I wasn't going to tell you this, Agent Burrell, but you seem like someone I can trust, seeing as how you aren't caught up in all the politics of this place."

"Tell me what . . . ?"

He sighs again, this time for show, like he regrets what he's about to say. "I had security stop Deputy Leroux in the lobby and hold her there until you and I have had a chance to chat."

"What?" I shout impulsively, appalled at the very idea of a private citizen detaining a law enforcement official, even one as admittedly distracting as Leroux. "Are you familiar with the term 'obstruction of justice'?"

"Honestly," he says with the calm self-assurance of true power, "she probably doesn't even know she's being detained. My security guard trained with her at the police academy, and I told him to chat her up for a few minutes. It's completely innocent. I just wanted enough time for you and me to talk without my ... *legal* history with the deputy getting in the way of the truth."

"You mean the fact that you sued her and her husband over twelve hundred dollars in homemade wine?"

He bites down on his lower lip, stifling his obvious frustration, and I swear I can see a little blood where he's pressed too hard. "Agent Burrell, I'm not going to demean you by mansplaining the virtues of American copyright law to a distinguished FBI agent. But let me put it this way: just because you build your house on a piece of land where there *used* to be a McDonald's doesn't mean you can start selling Big Macs out of your kitchen. Understand?"

I nod, begrudgingly accepting his corporate logic, which I have to admit, makes sense.

"Now I feel terrible about her husband's heart attack—I really do—but I'm not the one who served him three eggs and four strips of bacon every morning for the last thirty years. So if you'll put my personal issues with the deputy aside, I'd like to talk to you about these murders."

He gestures toward the empty Eames chair across from him, and I instantly regret agreeing to meet on his turf rather than at a police interrogation room. Bancroft is clearly a master strategist and a clever thinker—how else could he have built a billion-dollar empire out of a few run-down vineyards and a brand name that was twenty years past its prime? And he's orchestrated this meeting to a T, causing me to doubt Leroux while also arranging the seating to make me feel like his equal. Unlike Holly, who spoke with me from a position of power behind her imposing desk, Peter wants me to feel at ease in this chair right alongside him; but it's all a ruse, of course. He's in total charge of the narrative, and there's nothing I can do about it.

Well, maybe there is one *thing . . .*

I give Bancroft a smile while making a show of unlatching my holster, then I set my loaded Glock down on the coffee table between us, a deadly reminder that power comes in many forms. Only then do I take a seat. "All right," I say, leaning back into the uncomfortable Eames chair that probably cost more than my used car. "Let's hear it."

"Well, for starters," Bancroft says, "my cousin isn't well. You must have seen it when you spoke with her. She's not the same woman she was when you were younger—the titan who single-handedly caused the price of high-end cab to quadruple in this Valley. The fact is, a part of her died inside when she lost Jess, and she's spent the last two decades searching for something to fill that void. Affairs, religion, CrossFit, psychedelics. She's done it all, and nothing took—not until she fell in with this new group of hers."

"Who are they?" I ask.

"Well, there's who they *pretend* to be, and there's who they *really* are."

"What do you mean?"

"On the surface, they're just a bunch of eccentric agricultural types and artists. People who consult with wineries about biodynamic farming and preach the gospel according to Rudolf Steiner."

"Like Bex Potter, from the Golden Eagle tasting room."

Bancroft nods, his lip twitching as he sneers in derision. "That one's had her hooks in my cousin longer than anyone. I wouldn't be surprised if she's in Holly's last will and testament at this point."

"So if that's who they are on the surface, then who are they *really*?"

He leans in conspiratorially, his voice dropping to a low whisper, much like Jonah Bancroft's did during our brief encounter in St. Helena. "They're a cult."

I want to laugh, but his utter earnestness prevents me. This man is simply too smart, too rich, and too busy to waste either of our afternoons with fantastical exaggerations and local hearsay. What he's telling me is the truth—or at least his perception of it—and I owe it to Pilar Cruz and Katherine O'Shea to give him the benefit of the doubt and see where this strange story leads. "I get it, Peter. The whole biodynamic thing weirds me out too, but a group of people who are passionate about something, no matter how strange, doesn't make them a cult."

"I assume you've seen the unsealed court records from my lawsuit against Holly?"

"I have," I tell him.

"Then aren't you curious why the details about her activities at Redwood Vale were redacted before the records were made public?"

"It's definitely unusual," I have to admit.

"One of the many benefits of being in a cult with members of the county judiciary and key figures in state politics."

I can feel the hairs on my forearms rising with alarm, sent skyward by the tingle of a thousand invisible pinpricks. "That's a very big accusation."

"I'm aware," he says, totally unfazed by the stakes of the political conspiracy he's suggesting.

"So then what *was* she doing at Redwood Vale that was so bad it had to be redacted from the court documents?"

"I could tell you," he says. "Or you could go up there yourself tonight and see firsthand." And before I have a chance to respond, he slides an unassuming brass key onto the table and leaves it beside my gun. I promptly pick it up and give it a once-over, surprised to see that so many mysteries could be unlocked by a generic Schlage house key with the toothless warning, "Do Not Duplicate."

"Wait until midnight," Bancroft says. "Then drive to the end of Las Posadas Road, near the top of Howell Mountain. That key will open a service gate at the back of the property. No one else uses it, so you shouldn't have a problem getting in. Just make your way through the redwoods, and you'll see lights on at the main house. That's where they'll be."

"And then what?"

"Then you'll see what I'm talking about."

I examine the key once more before tucking it into my pants pocket. Then I reach out for my service weapon and slide it safely back into its holster. "How do I know you're not just using me to bring down your cousin so you can finally build Wine Country Disneyland?"

"Oh, that's *exactly* what I'm doing, Agent Burrell," he says, stunning me with his forthrightness. "I'd love nothing more than for you to solve this case and get Holly out of my way. But that's not all this is. I was telling you the truth on the phone last night. My father built this Valley into what it is today, and I see it as my birthright to protect it. To maintain the Napa dream that brings four million visitors a year to this place. So please, go out there and take a look around. If you don't see anything strange, then all you'll have wasted is a good night's sleep."

"Fine," I tell him, oddly convinced by his cohesive narrative. "I'll do it. But there's one thing I need to know."

"Anything," he says.

"Are they dangerous?"

Bancroft's eyes lock onto mine, and he holds me there in his intense gaze for what feels like an eternity. "They drugged and murdered two innocent women. Bled them out like cattle and left their bodies for the vultures. So yeah, Agent Burrell, I'd say they're pretty goddamn dangerous. Wouldn't you?"

12

A voicemail from the SAC is waiting on my phone when I leave Peter Bancroft's private suite.

There were no usable fingerprints on the note or the rock from Holly's office, but she did get a hit on that license plate number I sent—the midnight-blue Ford that tailed me back to my motel—and she spent the morning gathering as much information as she could. Turns out the SUV is registered to a company called Valley Farming Services, the very same VFS that Holly Bancroft used to staff her harvest with migrant farmers, and the outfit that employed Pilar Cruz right up until her death. According to my boss, the Ford is one of fifty-three vehicles owned by the company, most of which are used to ferry farmworkers from their temporary lodgings in Napa to whatever vineyard they're harvesting on a given day. That means there's almost no oversight of these cars, and any one of a thousand part-time workers could have been driving the Ford last night. As far as leads go, it's hardly promising, but it reminds me that there's still so much I don't know about the two women who were killed. With all these Bancrofts coming out of the woodwork, I've been too distracted by Napa's flamboyant upstairs to dig deeper into its victimized downstairs, and that'll have to change.

Soon.

First, I have an allegedly murderous cult to investigate.

Before I take a trip out to Redwood Vale, though, there's someone I need to talk to. Someone who might be able to shed more light onto what Peter Bancroft so cryptically danced around in his office. And as I descend four floors in the elevator of the J.B. Bancroft building, I fire off a quick text to a phone number I've never had the strength to delete: *Hey Jonah, it's Lana. Do you have time this afternoon to talk? It's a work thing.*

While I wait for the elevator doors to open, I stand there rereading my text, wondering if I sounded too brusque and impersonal. Should I have started with something more casual— an inside joke from our high school days, or at least a recognition of how awkward our run-in was yesterday?

No. Two women are dead, and I'm reaching out to a potential lead—the fact that I happen to have given him my first blow job some twenty years ago is hardly relevant. Still, I suppose I could have greased the wheels with a bit more charm . . .

It really was great seeing you, I type. *You looked good.*

Nope. Delete that last part. Then I send the edited text before I have a chance to second-guess myself, before I can send anything too desperate or thirsty or just plain unprofessional, and right on cue the elevator doors slide open. Deputy Leroux is standing there with her usual bemused smile, waiting to go upstairs, clueless as to why she was just stalled in the lobby by an old friend from the police academy. She starts to tell me about her "surprise" encounter, but I stop her halfway through another circular story and let her know we have everything we need from Peter Bancroft. Not the part about the cult—something tells me I need to go out to Redwood Vale alone tonight, and the less I share with the Sheriff's Department, the better. Especially if, as Bancroft said, the local authorities really are caught up in whatever Holly's doing out there.

But I let Leroux know that she was spot on about one thing: Bancroft is definitely trying to pin these murders on his cousin. Of course that doesn't mean he was actually behind the killings. As far as we know, he's just conveniently using them to get the Conservation Easement lifted at Redwood Vale—but he certainly remains a person of interest in our case.

In the meantime, I suggest we divide and conquer. "Given my history with the Bancrofts, I'll keep poking around there to see what else I can find. Meanwhile, you run down this new lead on the midnight-blue Ford. It's probably better if I don't show my face at VFS anyway, since I was the one being tailed."

"Roger that," says Leroux. "Want me to talk to the cousin while I'm down there? The one who called in Pilar Cruz's disappearance?"

"Great idea," I tell her. "Find out everything you can about her. Where she's lived, what her hobbies were, who she'd been sleeping with. You never know what might turn out to be relevant."

With that settled, we go our separate ways, Leroux driving a few miles south toward the VFS offices while I start the long trek north on Highway 29, hoping against hope that Jonah will answer my text.

* * *

My phone buzzes right as I'm passing the historic vineyards in the heart of Rutherford: names like Inglenook and Beaulieu that are as closely intertwined with the Valley's past as Bancroft. Sure enough, it's a text from Jonah: *How about a drink after dinner? Keri's taking the kids to her mom's tonight, so I have the place to myself.*

I'd love that, I text back at the next stoplight, relieved to be having this conversation through a technology that hides my unavoidable schoolgirl blushing. *What time?*

How's 8? he responds half a second later.
Perfect.

* * *

I have three hours before my meetup with Jonah, so after a brief but scalding shower at the Silverado Inn, I wrap myself in the two scratchy towels I've been provided and hop into bed with my laptop. Before I ask him more about the twenty-nine days between killings—and certainly before I go trudging into the woods at midnight in search of a cult—I need to brush up on my Rudolf Steiner. I still don't know exactly what's driving Holly Bancroft, Bex Potter, and whoever else I'll find at Redwood Vale, but it somehow seems connected to the father of biodynamics.

So I start with a basic Google search and a bit of Wikipedia. Then I tumble even further down the online rabbit hole, until two hours have passed and I've devoured everything I can find about the mysterious Austrian mystic.

Steiner was born in 1861, the son of a telegraph operator, and from his earliest days, he was intensely drawn to the spiritual world. At the age of nine, he claimed to have been visited by the apparition of an aunt who begged for his help; she died that same night in a far-off town, something he never could have known when he had his supernatural encounter.

Throughout his academic career at the Vienna Institute of Technology and the University of Rostock, where he received his doctorate in philosophy, he grew obsessed with finding ways to link the spiritual world with the scientific, a synthesis he'd eventually call "spiritual science." At times, he managed to harness those ideas into positive developments across a multitude of disciplines. As an amateur architect, he launched an entirely new style of building with an ecological focus that influenced many prominent architects in Europe and North America. As an educator, he founded the Waldorf school system, which still teaches tens of thousands of students in over sixty countries to this day. As an economic thinker, he inspired the modern-day concept of social enterprise, in which businesses sacrifice some profit for the sake of the common good and the environment. And of course with his biodynamic agriculture, he created the very idea of organic farming.

But that was only one side of this incredibly complex man. Through his religious teachings, deeply grounded in Christianity, he preached a kind of gnostic spiritualism in which contact with Christ was possible through meditation and vision quests, and Christlike reincarnation was possible for anyone who followed Steiner's path. He was so devout in his unique form of Christianity, however, that he questioned the very existence of Judaism and promoted several conspiracy theories about the Jews, most notably their alleged involvement in causing World War I. It should come as no surprise, then, that some of Steiner's biggest fans in the 1930s were Nazis, including the chief of the Gestapo, Heinrich Müller.

Whether Steiner was a Nazi himself remains an open question ...

Beyond that, many of his more mystic beliefs have been lost to time, most likely by his own design, as he was deeply secretive about his more controversial teachings. What we do know is that he claimed to be clairvoyant, with a supernatural ability to perceive future events that he offered to teach many of his closest disciples. He was also a noted believer in the myths of Atlantis and Lemuria, the two so-called "lost continents" that were thought to be the cradles of human civilization, and through his meditative practices, he claimed to be able to experience many of his past "earth lives" in each of those places.

On top of all that, I'm pretty sure he founded a cult.

Details are scarce, even in the darkest corners of the Web, but in the early twentieth century, he was briefly a member of an occultist sect known as the Order of the Oriental Templars that was at one point led by Aleister Crowley, a man whose so-called "sex magick" would one day become infamous across the world. But at a certain point, Steiner had a falling out with the group's leadership, and from 1906 to 1914, he led a secretive lodge *within* the Order known as the Mysteria Mystica Aeterna. What they did and what they believed remains an absolute mystery, but if it was too controversial for a guy like Aleister Crowley, whose ritual orgies were the stuff of legend, you can bet it wasn't all on the up-and-up.

I glance over at the outdated motel alarm clock and see that it's already seven forty-five PM. *Shit.* I'm due at Jonah's in fifteen minutes, and I'm still wearing nothing but two damp towels that are starting to smell like sweat. So I scramble out of bed, throw on the only bra in my suitcase that didn't come from the sportswear aisle at Target, and take a wary gaze at my reflection in the full-length mirror.

Fucking hell, do I always look this tired?

I know nothing's going to happen tonight with Jonah. He's happily married and I'm not a homewrecker. But that doesn't change my desperate need to impress him, to make him feel a glimmer of that passion we used to have for each other as kids. Does that make me a hopeless flirt and a terrible person? Maybe. But I never claimed to be a saint. *And at least I'm not in a murderous wine-growing cult.* With a sigh of self-loathing, I dig a makeup kit out of my suitcase and set about making myself somewhat presentable.

* * *

I arrive at a modest house in St. Helena that bears none of the usual Bancroft family opulence, and my first impulse is to double-check the address, since it never even occurred to me that Jonah might not share in his mother's and uncle's wealth and lifestyle. It's a cute two-story with pale yellow aluminum siding and white trim, and a farm-style porch that wraps around the front and side of the home. Two bright red Adirondack chairs sit side by side on the porch, next to pots of blooming lavender, and I can almost picture Jonah and his wife lounging there, basking in the simplicity of the life they've built together—a blissful, carefree, unpretentious, very *un-Bancroft* life.

Something burns deep inside me, and I frankly don't have the emotional maturity to tell what it is. Jealousy? *Probably.* Regret? *Maybe.* Loneliness, triggered by the realization that I'll never have the need to buy two matching chairs like that? *How the hell should I know?*

Rather than dwell on it—soul searching has never really been my strong suit—I scramble up onto the porch and ring the bell, and before I'm even able to take my finger off the button, the door flies open, and Jonah's greeting me with a warm hug that I didn't even realize I needed. But now that I've had time to process our reunion, I'm able to really sink into his strong arms and let myself enjoy the moment, just two old friends who will always have a soft spot for each other, no matter where our divergent lives happen to take us.

"Since when do you wear cologne?" I ask when I catch a musky whiff of leather and pine.

"Keri buys it for me," he says with a hint of embarrassment. "Do you like it?"

"Not really."

"Neither do I. But it makes her happy."

We stand there for a moment in silence, him on one side of the doorjamb, me on the other, both feeling a certain danger in our next move, as if crossing that threshold would represent some unspoken moral failing on our part.

"She doesn't know you're coming over," he says guiltily.

"Oh."

"Not because she'd get upset or anything. She's not, like, jealous of other women."

"Then why didn't you tell her?" I ask, fighting through the lump that's forming in my throat, giving my voice a kind of bashful, schoolgirl cadence that I hardly recognize.

"Honestly," he says, struggling to find the right words, "I don't know. It just happened. We were talking as she was leaving with the kids, and I had a chance to tell her, but I didn't, and now I feel like an asshole when we should really just be having a good time catching up." He squirms uncomfortably, his moral center thrown off balance, and I can see how nervous I'm making him. Part of me wants to turn around and go back to my motel, if only to spare him the guilt trip of my presence. But I remind myself that this isn't about me, and it's not about us. Two women are dead, and the least we can do is act like adults instead of a couple of immature teenagers who can't stop thinking about how they used to have sex.

I look around the property, and I notice a wooden picnic table in the back of the gravel driveway. Four crisscrossing strands of darkened twinkle lights hang above it, creating what I imagine is a lovely outdoor dining room on cool summer nights. "Do those lights work?" I ask him. He nods with uncertainty, and I confidently take him by the elbow, which really is the safest appendage to touch in a situation like this. "Then let's stay outside tonight. Keep things professional. All right?"

He smiles with relief, all the awkward tension gone from his face. "Deal."

* * *

For almost two hours, we never say a word about the Cruz and O'Shea cases. We just laugh and reminisce and swap stories while we sip sparkling water under the twinkle lights. I tell him about my rise through the ranks of the FBI, and some of my more high-profile cases, and when he prods me, I even share a few embarrassing stories from my pathetically inconsistent dating life. Then he takes me through what he's been up to over the last two decades.

After college, Jonah spent his twenties apprenticing under a Who's Who of the wine world: Aubert de Villaine of France's Domaine de la Romanée-Conti; Elisabetta Geppetti of Italy's Fattoria Le Pupille; Peter Sisseck of Spain's Dominio de Pingus. He worked harvests in New Zealand, studied barrel-making in France, and learned water management from grape farmers in Lebanon's Bekaa Valley. Then he came back home to put those skills to use with his mother, hoping to be the third generation of Bancrofts to lead the Golden Eagle label, and for a few years things went smoothly. Holly was increasingly distracted by her new hobbies outside the vineyards—her yoga retreats in Costa Rica, her ayahuasca trips in Mexico—so Jonah had free reign to take his family's label into a new era, bringing more subtlety and complexity to a cabernet sauvignon that had always appealed to the Robert Parker crowd: the wealthier, older wine drinkers who still yearned for the plushy, overly extracted fruit bombs of the late '90s. And with the 2017, 2018, and 2019 vintages, Jonah brought new, younger fans and plenty of accolades to Golden Eagle.

Or at least, that's how Jonah explains it.

As he takes me through his work at the vineyard and casually mentions some of the acclaim his wines have received, I'm reminded of certain things that used to bother me about my high school sweetheart. Something happens long after a breakup, where, thanks to the mind's preference for simple narratives and clean-cut memories, an ex either becomes a saint or a psychopath.

All their jagged nuances—either positive or negative, depending on which direction you've chosen to go in memorializing them—are washed away by the smoothing sands of time, and their inevitable grayness is rewritten as either black or white. With Jonah, I've somehow decided to only remember the good parts: the fuzzy feelings of first love, my awkward but still satisfying early encounters with sex, the concerts and campouts that highlighted our one spectacular summer together. But now I'm realizing, he was hardly perfect.

More than anything, Jonah could be childishly arrogant. Because of his elite upbringing and his family legacy, he always acted as if his success as a winemaker was predetermined. Even at twenty, when he was nothing more than a B+ viticulture student at UC Davis, he would tell me all about the labels he'd launch one day and the exciting new blends and techniques he'd pioneer. At the time, seventeen and smitten by an older guy with above-average abs and a collegiate vocabulary, I found these musings unbelievably romantic, as if he were telling me *our* plans for *our* future. But I soon came to realize that my name and my role never actually factored into his fantasies. It was always about Jonah, much like it was always about Jess, or it was always about Holly, or—I can now add—it's always about Peter. Part of being a Bancroft means buying into the inherent power of that name; not just the expectation of success, but the *guarantee* of it. And other people are either obstacles or tools on the path to achieving it.

The truth is, I don't begrudge Jonah this one (admittedly annoying) shortcoming. It's not his fault he was raised by a narcissist; some of Holly's less desirable qualities were bound to rub off on her son and protégé. And in fact, as I hear bits of that old entitlement slip out while he's talking, I'm actually kind of *relieved*. Somewhere deep in my subconscious, it knocks Jonah off that pedestal where he's lived for over twenty years, rent- and fault-free, and in its place, there's just . . . a guy. Sure, he's a guy I used to love, and who I'll probably always fantasize about—just a little. But the pressure of having to perform in front of him and try to be something I'm not is gone. I can just relax and enjoy the company of an old friend and, more importantly, a potential source in my investigation.

After the high point of his story, his massively successful 2019 vintage, Jonah's demeanor changes entirely as he tells me about his lowest moment: the Glass Fire in the fall of 2020, and with it, the total destruction of his family's most important vineyard, including many vines that had been growing since Holly's father first planted them in the 1960s. According to Jonah, that month of smoke-filled devastation brought about a permanent change in his mother. What had been a slow, somewhat amusing descent into New Age teachings and drug-influenced therapy went into overdrive, and the woman Jonah had always known and loved was gone. She'd divorced his father, Greg, without so much as a warning or a fair explanation, and had fallen in with a new group of friends whom she'd met on some of her retreats. When Jonah tried to talk to her about this, when he pushed her to get help and give up some control over the label, she'd instead cut him off entirely and fired him from Golden Eagle. So rather than fight her, he decided to move on completely and join a new company that had just been started by a friend. Since then, they've quietly released their first few vintages, and he hasn't spoken a single word to his estranged mother.

As he sits there in the near-dark, his face dappled with soft light from overhead, I can see how deeply wounded this rift has left him. Whether he'll admit it or not, he feels abandoned by a woman he grew up worshiping, so much so that he blindly followed her into the family business with the expectation that he'd get to carry on her mantle one day. The crown prince who always just wanted the approval of a cold and unloving queen. A part of me wants to change the subject and spare him any more agony, but the other part of me knows that's not possible. If Holly Bancroft really is caught up in these murders, like her cousin Peter intimated, then Jonah could be my best chance at proving how and why.

I let the soothing sound of evening crickets wash over us while I choose my next words carefully, then I lean in closer and get right to the heart of it. "Jonah, I'm not going to force you to tell me anything you don't want to. But here's what I know, and if you want to add anything to it, that's entirely up to you. Okay?" I wait for him to nod, no matter how reluctantly, before continuing.

"So I know these murders happened at midnight on subsequent full moons, twenty-nine days apart, just like you said. And I know it probably has something to do with these Rudolf Steiner–loving zealots your mom's been hanging out with. People like Bex Potter, who was seen flirting with the second victim on the day she died. I also know your uncle thinks Holly's part of some kind of cult, and they use the family's property up at Redwood Vale to do God-knows-what. But beyond that, I don't know a damn thing about who they are, what they do, or whether they're actually capable of murder."

He nods along quietly as I lay out my admittedly flimsy case, and when I fall silent, his eyes drift up toward the sky, as if he might find answers in the stars. I wait patiently while he sits there on his side of the picnic table, thinking about what to say—how much he can reveal to an FBI agent, even if she is his former girlfriend. Then without ever making eye contact, he starts talking; whether it's to me or the heavens, I'm honestly not sure.

"I know people like to romanticize what we do here," he says quietly and with evident sadness in his voice. "A bunch of artists and farmers plucking grapes and sipping wine in their castles. But this business is grueling. And to dominate it, to reach the top of that greasy pole, you need to be ruthless. I've seen my mother spread horrible lies about a competing label just to get their bottles removed from one wine list in one restaurant, purely so she'd have the most expensive Napa cab on it. When a certain critic only gave her top wine ninety-four points in 2011, she threatened to blacklist him from some of the biggest industry events of the year; by the time his score was published, it was suddenly a ninety-seven. And when Jess went missing, when it looked like your dad might have something to do with it, I saw her corner him down in the barrel room and press a corkscrew to his temple, demanding answers."

"*What?*"

Jonah nods, dead serious, and finally looks me in the eye. "I actually think she would have killed him if I hadn't walked in and stopped it."

"He never told me that," I whisper in shock.

"We'll never know why our parents do what they do, or did what they did," he says with a hopeless shrug. "But I can tell you this much. Holly Bancroft is, and always has been, capable of murder. It's just a fact. Now I have no idea what she's been up to these last few years, and I don't know a thing about what really happened to those girls, but I'm telling you as a friend—as her son—that she *is* a killer. Even if she's never killed anyone."

A gust of cool October air sends a rattle through the old oaks and sycamores lining Jonah's property, and I feel an ominous shiver run down my spine and arms. There's something so broken and bereft about the way he describes his mother—the same mother he once idolized—that for a moment, a terrifying thought crosses my mind. Could Jonah have been so betrayed by Holly that *he* would commit two murders to try and frame her?

No. Lana, now you're just being ridiculous.

Sure, it's been years since Jonah and I spent quality time together, and he's hardly a saint, given his occasional bouts of

Bancroft-style entitlement, but he truly is the gentlest, sweetest man I've ever known. And besides, he was four hours away in Lake Tahoe, coaching a soccer tournament, when Katherine O'Shea was killed. The distance alone is enough to exonerate him, and I quickly shake off that fleeting glimmer of suspicion. *Of course* he's upset about the recent changes in his mother's behavior and her questionable new social circle. He has every right to be.

Then another wild idea hits me, and I can't help but ask him. "You don't think Holly had something to do with what happened to Jess . . . do you?"

He looks at me with an intensity that suggests he's absolutely considered this possibility over the years. "I don't know. Before she disappeared, did she say anything to you? Anything that might explain . . . you know . . ."

I shake my head. "We had the worst fight of our lives that day, so we weren't really in a place to talk. The last thing she ever said to me was *'Go fuck yourself, Burrell.'*" I smile fondly, recalling her unique way with words. "I think she felt bad about it, though. A few hours later she sent my dad home with this dumb wine cork as a way of telling me she was sorry . . ."

"A wine cork?"

"It was an inside joke. When we were younger, we used to draw on them, turn them into these little characters that we'd play around with. Just a silly, thirteen-year-old-girl thing. Honestly, I have no idea why she'd choose that day—of all days—to draw one for me after so many years. But after she disappeared, I couldn't bring myself to throw it out. Still can't. It's like this weird tangible memory of our very teenage friendship."

Jonah watches me reminisce, and I can tell he understands exactly what I'm saying. We both knew how flawed a person Jess was, and yet we'll both love her dearly for the rest of our lives. Like many people, her complexity was simply a part of her charm, even if she could be a bit cruel. And I still laugh sometimes thinking about all the nights we spent together, her instigating wild adventures while I desperately tried to talk her out of them. I can see that Jonah wants to talk more about his sister—as do I, if I'm being honest—but before he can say anything else, his wife's car pulls into the driveway, cutting our conversation short with a beam of headlights and a loud crunch of gravel.

"I should go," I tell him, already pushing myself up from the picnic table.

He nods in agreement. "It's been real, Burrell. Please don't be a stranger while you're up here. I forgot how much I missed talking to you."

"Right back at you, Bancroft."

We smile, deeply nostalgic but mutually content with all the life choices that have led us here to opposite sides of a picnic table. Then, before I have to share an awkward encounter with his no doubt lovely wife, I leave behind the warm glow of the overhead lights and hurry off into the darkness, alone.

13

What are you supposed to wear to a midnight stakeout of a murder cult?

I've obviously been on my share of FBI raids—drug busts and the like—but something about tonight's activity feels more illicit. I just can't fathom the idea of showing up to Redwood Vale in my standard-issue windbreaker with those bold yellow letters on the back announcing me as a Fed.

I'll bring my badge, of course, and you'd better believe my Glock will be by my side, just in case, but a black hoodie and dark jeans somehow feels more appropriate for the skulking I plan on doing. So as the digital clock changes over from 11:29 to 11:30, I slip on the outfit, pull my hair back tight, and take one last deep breath to calm my buzzing nerves.

Here we go.

* * *

Halfway to my destination, as I wind my way through the dark, narrow roads leading up Howell Mountain, my phone rings. I figure it must be Peter Bancroft since no one else knows I'm working this late, but I'm surprised to see Connie Chen's name appear on the display.

"Kinda late for a work call, don't you think?" I say into the car's Bluetooth speaker.

"Couldn't sleep," she replies. "And I figured you'd be up watching TV in whatever shithole motel room we booked you."

I laugh on cue, preferring not to let the SAC know my plans for the evening. If she found out, she'd insist on backup, and that's the last thing I need given my history with the local Sheriff's Department. "You know me. Popcorn, Heineken, and Netflix."

"So how's the investigation going? Any new leads?"

"Some interesting ideas, but nothing solid yet."

"All right. It's still early." There's a long pause while I check Google Maps for my next turn, during which Chen gets to the real reason she called, as I knew she would eventually. "What about you? Everything okay?"

I shoot a guilty glance at my reflection in the rearview mirror, the dark eyeliner and contour I may or may not have put on a few hours earlier for Jonah's benefit. "Why wouldn't it be?"

"Lana, come on." She sighs, seeing right through me despite not being able to see me at all. "I know that place is nothing but baggage for you. Have you run into anyone from the old days?"

As I struggle with what to tell her, the goddamn Bancroft family saga that's hijacked my investigation and turned it into a wine country telenovela, I notice another road up ahead and hang a sharp left onto Las Posadas. Just a minute away now. "I should really get to bed, Boss—"

"Lana, this isn't an interrogation. I'm just ... I'm genuinely worried about you, and if you need anything, if you want to talk ... I'm always here. Okay?"

I let her words float there in the air, and a big part of me wants to grab onto that life raft and spill my guts out to the SAC. A therapy session with someone who isn't paid to listen to me unload my problems—imagine that. But then I see the "Dead

End" sign up ahead, and any emotional momentum I've built up with Chen is lost. There are far too many questions that still need answering, and it's already eight minutes 'til midnight. I can't waste another moment on Connie Chen's maternal worrying, no matter how thoughtful it might be. "Thanks, Boss," I tell her brusquely, "but I've really gotta go."

"All right," she says with another sigh. "We'll talk in a few days. Goodnight, Lana."

"Goodnight." And I hang up the phone before she has a chance to reconsider.

With no one in sight—there's not even a light visible through the trees surrounding me—I decide to park along the side of the road, up against a thick row of bushes. Then I grab Peter Bancroft's key and hurry over to a barely noticeable gate in the chain-link fence. "No Trespassing," reads one sign on it. Another warns me that "These Premises Are Under Video Surveillance." But it's rusted over and at least two decades old; I'll take my chances that no one's actually monitoring the site. I press the key into the lock—it fits perfectly—and within seconds, I'm slipping inside and quietly shutting the metal gate behind me.

After a brief stroll on a gravel path, I make my way into an untamed forest. The ground is thick with weeds and shrubs, the kind with tedious little burrs that I know I'll have to spend the morning picking off my socks and shoelaces. No trail of any sort seems to have been cut into this portion of the woods, so I push my way through the brush in search of some sign of human life. Anything that might point me toward the unusual activity hinted at by Peter Bancroft.

Soon I'm surrounded on all sides by some of the oldest, tallest redwoods I've ever seen, hundreds of them fanning out in every direction. And when I look up, I find myself dwarfed by their impossibly tall trunks, thick towers of dark wood that leave me disoriented; sylvan skyscrapers, as if the whole world has flipped upside down and I'm walking on a black sky.

The experience leaves me dizzy, and I resolve to keep my eyes lowered so that I don't pass out; it's not as if a moon or stars are visible anyway on this cloudy autumn night.

This goes on for several minutes, my legs kicking away broken sticks and my arms pushing aside sappy branches, until I finally land on a dirt path. It stretches off in two directions—north and south (I think)—but I have no clue which one might lead me toward the main house that Bancroft spoke of. I still can't hear anything but crickets and the occasional barn owl, and there don't seem to be any footprints. But then I look up and let out an audible gasp when I see what's been carved into one of the redwoods:

I recognize the glyph immediately from my afternoon of fervent googling. It was created by the sixteenth-century alchemist John Dee and later adopted by Rudolf Steiner as the symbol for his secret Order, the Mystica Aeterna. For the life of me, I can't remember what it means—it may be that no one actually knows—but it's the first clear piece of evidence I've seen that Steiner's ancient cult really *does* have something to do with Holly Bancroft's mysterious group of friends. Could they have reopened the Mystica Aeterna a century after it shut down in Europe? And if they have, what does that even mean, practically speaking? A thousand questions swirl through my head, but one thing is suddenly quite clear: I've got to head north since that's the way the glyph is facing.

After another five minutes of walking—this time, thankfully without the burrs and brambles—I begin to hear music in the distance. First, it's nothing more than the soft pulsing beat of a steady bass; then, as I draw closer to the source, I can hear additional layers. The rhythmic hum of an electronic dance music track, and some trancelike female vocals. The farther I walk, the louder the music gets, until finally I come over a small crest and spot the farmhouse.

Two stories tall and modestly sized, it looks to be at least half a century old, if not more, with faded clapboard siding and a wraparound porch that makes me think of the Midwest. It's the kind of rustic home you'd find in a Kansas cornfield rather than the California redwoods; or perhaps it was simply built before California had developed its own unique architectural style. The curtains are all drawn shut, but they're thin enough to give a sense of the strange light pulsing within, soft purples, pinks, and deep blues flashing with no discernible pattern. Laser lights, perhaps? Coupled with the music, I get the sense that some sort of rave is going on inside.

I can't see anyone outside the house—the porch is definitely empty—so I'm about to continue onward when I hear the loud crunching of heavy footsteps on a bed of fallen leaves. Instinctively, I duck behind the nearest redwood, with a trunk thick enough to hide six people, let alone just me. Then two voices ring out clearly in the night air.

"Marie, come on, you're being ridiculous," shouts the first one, a man in his twenties or thirties.

"How am I being ridiculous?" replies the woman, no doubt named Marie and about the same age as her companion. "I'm the only normal person here!"

"You said you wanted to give it a try."

"I said I would watch. One time. I didn't say I'd do . . . whatever *that* was."

"Then you shouldn't have worn the goat!"

"You *told* me to wear the goat!"

"Fine, so what? You want to go home already?"

"Yes!"

"But we *just* got here!"

"Who the fuck cares, Chris? I'm uncomfortable, and I don't like this, and I want to leave right now, so please give me the keys, 'cause there is no way I'm letting you drive after whatever the hell you just took in there."

"It hasn't even hit me yet."

"Not the point."

"What if I want to stay?"

"Seriously?"

"Yeah."

A tense silence hangs over the unseen duo, but I don't need eyes on them to imagine their body language. The woman, feeling betrayed by what I'm guessing is a newish boyfriend, can't decide whether to cry or slap him. The real question, though, is what was he pressuring her to do that made her so uncomfortable? And how the hell does someone "wear" a goat?

"Just give me the keys, Chris." I hear the distinct jingling of a set of keys as Chris hands them to Marie. "How are you getting home?"

"I'll figure it out," he says.

"Fine. Have a great night, asshole." Then I hear her footsteps crunching across the leaves as she storms off in the other direction. I hold still, waiting for Chris to move, but he stands there in silence for what feels like an eternity. He mutters something to himself—I can't make out what—and then he finally trudges back toward the house.

What the hell was that all about? I certainly never expected to walk into the middle of a domestic melodrama, but now I want nothing more than to find this Marie and ask her what happened. Given her feelings about whatever's going on inside that farmhouse, she sounds like she'd be an ideal source of information. Unfortunately, by the time Chris clears the area, she's long gone, and any hope of finding her in the darkness is pretty much nil. So I step out from behind the tree and start toward the house, knowing my best hope is to get a look inside myself.

I only make it about twenty feet when I nearly step on the mask.

It's a sturdy piece of black plastic in the shape of a goat head, with small holes for eyes and a mouth and a black elastic band meant for holding it on a person's head. It looks like a cross between a Gothic masquerade mask and a creepy Halloween costume. But given what I just heard between Chris and Marie, this clearly belonged to her. As I gaze into the empty eyes of the startlingly strange goat, I get a sinking feeling in the pit of my stomach. There's something so... *not right*... about it. A cruel asymmetry to the animal that makes me think of some barbaric, pagan ritual. *What the hell are these people up to?*

With a newfound urgency, I start toward the house at a faster clip. I'd been wondering how I would get a sense of what's going on inside given the tightly drawn curtains, but thanks to Marie, I have my answer, so I slip the goat mask over my head to hide my face from anyone who might recognize me. A minute later, I'm striding up the steps of the front porch, expecting to find some sort of bouncer or security guard, but instead, there's no one staffing the entrance.

Interesting, I think. *Hardly the sign of a nefarious murder cult.* So I push open the unlocked door and step inside, naively reassuring myself, *How bad can it be?*

* * *

My first thought upon moving through the foyer and glancing into a few rooms is that I'm wildly overdressed. Not in terms of formality; just in terms of actual layers of fabric. Most of the revelers in the farmhouse are in nothing but their underwear—an assortment of boxer briefs and shorts for the men, sexy lingerie on most of the women. A few women are topless, and at least one's completely naked save for her abstract black leopard mask. And when a shriveled penis makes its way down the stairs and passes directly through my eye line, I realize so too are some of the men.

Thankfully, I do notice a few people in pants and even a handful of shirts, so I decide to take off my black hoodie and hang it on one of the empty hooks by the front door. At least in a T-shirt and jeans, I won't look too ridiculously out of place in this den of flimsy fabrics and exposed flesh.

On the lone table in the foyer, I find four identical wicker baskets, each with a different pile of masks inside. A goat, a leopard, a bull, and a snake, all with similarly odd features and all made from the same sturdy black plastic. As I look around more carefully, I realize that all four of these animals are well represented among the crowd—or should I say *herd*. The men seem to prefer the bulls, although I do notice a few male goats as well. The women seem to have on an equal assortment of all four creatures. *Perhaps it's a signal,* I think. *Your choice of animal must let everyone else know your sexual appetites . . .*

My curiosity piqued, I move deeper into the house to try and get a better sense of the place. The decor is woefully outdated, bad floral wallpaper from the 1980s, with cheap, mass-produced artwork from Thomas Kinkade and Norman Rockwell on the walls. And the furniture looks equally shabby. But with the lights off and everything illuminated by gently flashing laser projections, the place manages to feel oddly modern, like a louche nightclub with an intentionally kitsch aesthetic. The music, as well, is strangely soothing. It's not the kind of oppressive EDM with the overly dramatic beat drops you might expect to hear at a Las Vegas nightclub. It's softer, more transporting, with an ethereal quality that makes you feel like you're on drugs even when the most mind-altering substance you've had all day is a cup of Folgers.

In the first room I pass, a group of nearly naked masked revelers are laughing and dancing, some as couples and others swaying gently by themselves. I see a few of them passing around small gummies, which I'm guessing aren't just some children's candy. Edible mushrooms or LSD, most likely. Two men in their underwear are kissing feverishly in a corner, their matching goat masks flipped over onto the backs of their heads, and I can't help but notice how much older one of them is than the other.

In the next room, another group, mostly snakes and women in bull masks, sit around a dining table, drinking red wine from clear plastic cups. A few of the snakes are dressed like me in plain T-shirts and comfortable jeans, but most are in their underwear, making for an odd scene in such a formal dining room, with old-school china cabinets and a crystal chandelier. They seem to be whispering intently about something, and I debate joining their conversation to learn more, but I decide to come back after I've seen the rest of the house.

In the kitchen, I find more half-naked dancers swaying to the music, as well as bowls full of multicolored gummies sitting out on the Formica countertop. I grab a few of them—a red, a blue, a green—and pocket them for analysis later, even though I'm pretty sure they're nothing too nefarious.

I glance out the window onto the back porch, where I see a few more people enjoying themselves. Some dancing, some laughing, a bit of casual kissing with masks askew, but nothing you wouldn't find at an above-average high school party.

I'm beginning to think I've been hopelessly led astray—maybe these people aren't as evil as Jonah and Peter claimed—when I turn a corner into a dark hallway and walk straight into Holly Bancroft having the early stages of a screaming orgasm.

14

A black leopard mask obscures most of Holly's face, but I'd recognize her platinum-blonde hair and trim but powerful figure anywhere. She's wearing a pastel purple bra with boosting underwire that gives her an oddly perky-breasted look for a woman in her sixties. Below that, she has on nothing but a simple black skirt, although I can't tell how low it hangs, seeing as it's currently being used as a kind of privacy curtain for the man performing oral sex on her. As for him, he's completely naked—even his bull mask has been taken off, for obvious reasons—and I'm surprised by how toned and young his body appears to be. I can't tell for sure, given where his face is buried at the moment, but I can't imagine he's more than thirty years old.

I watch in paralyzed shock as Holly arches her back in pleasure, inverting her elbows to press her upside-down palms back against the wall behind her. She lets out a cry of drug-induced delight—maybe MDMA was also on tonight's menu—and her neck turns in my direction. For a moment, I think I'm caught. She stares straight at me through the round holes of her mask, and I swear she knows it's me despite the plastic goat face obscuring my more obvious features. But then she turns the other way and arches her back some more to fully enjoy the man's tongue work, either not realizing who I am or simply too caught up in the thralls of pleasure to give a shit.

With a sigh of relief, I bolt back down the main hallway, eager to forget what I've just witnessed. *Did she recognize me?* It certainly seemed like it, but there was something so deliriously glazed over about her eyes that I think she may have reacted that way to anyone. Regardless, I decide I've seen enough. I've read plenty of literature about murderous cults, especially during my early FBI training at Quantico, and there's a big difference between group-led ritual killings and comparatively innocent midnight orgies. So I start briskly toward the exit, head down, trying to avoid seeing anymore floppy body parts or cringe-inducing hookups, when I notice something else that stops me in my tracks. I don't know how I missed it on the way in, but the same strange glyph from the tree outside—the one I saw in an online forum about Rudolf Steiner's Mystica Aeterna—has been painted in white on an otherwise unassuming brown door. I look around, but no one seems to be watching, given how absorbed they all are in the hypnotic lights and pulsing music, so I quickly push open the door and slip inside.

The immediate drop of an unfinished wooden staircase catches me by surprise. I'm not used to seeing basements in California—again, this house feels like it fell out of the sky and landed here, delivered by a tornado from a black-and-white Kansas cornfield. But the warm orange glow of a light farther downstairs is enough to help me gather my bearings. I lunge out to grab the railing, and once I steady myself, I creep down a few more stairs, trying not to let the creak of the old, unsettled wood give away my presence.

"Is it ready?" I hear someone whisper in the darkness below. Then a few other voices start to chime in, all in the same hushed tone. "Hold still," one of them says. "Put this in your mouth," adds another. "Are you sure?" says a third. "Just bite down," comes the reply.

Everything's at a low, conspiratorial whisper, making it hard to tell how many people are down here, but there's one voice in particular that I'd recognize anywhere. "It's time," says Bex Potter with a steely assertiveness that cuts through all the other mumbling. "Let's start the rite."

I creep down two more stairs and lower myself to a squat so that I can bend forward and see around the staircase wall.

At the center of the empty unfinished basement, on a bare concrete floor, there's a naked man lying face up. He's about twenty-five, rail thin, with long black hair—Japanese American, if I had to guess—and he has some sort of rubber gag in his mouth. Surrounding him are the first fully dressed people I've seen since my arrival; hooded burgundy robes cover just about every inch of their bodies. From under one such hood, I spot the distinctive wide eyes and blonde ringlets of Bex Potter. She's holding what appears to be a cattle brand with an end shaped like Steiner's symbol, glowing bright red thanks to a woodburning stove nearby.

Holy shit, are they going to brand him?

My initial impulse is to pull out my gun and intervene, but I have to stop myself. Whatever's about to happen, it's clearly not what Katherine O'Shea and Pilar Cruz went through; neither of them were branded, and there's not even a full moon tonight. Which means that this is something else, some sort of initiation, perhaps, so I hold still and start to record video on my iPhone, with no idea what sort of horror film I'm about to capture.

Within seconds, the four people in robes begin to speak in turn, finishing each other's sentences in what I can only assume is a practiced ritual they've repeated many times.

"I call upon loud-roaring and reveling Dionysus, primeval, double-natured, thrice-born, Bacchic lord.

"*Bearer of the vine,*
Thee I invoke to bless these rites divine.
Bassarian god of universal might,
Whom swords and blood and sacred rage delight.
In heaven rejoicing, mad, loud-sounding god,
Furious inspirer, bearer of the rod.
Come mighty Bacchus to these rites inclined,
And bless thy supplicants with rejoicing mind."

Three of them step back, and Bex comes forward with the burning metal brand to complete the ritual alone.

"With single purpose, we follow Him. Under sun and over soil, we serve Him. Bound by blood, we honor Him. By fire and stone, we become Him."

Then, without warning, she plunges the brand down hard on the naked young man, burning him just above his groin, where his pubic hair looks to have been shaved for the occasion. He screams out in agony through the rubber gag, which I now realize is meant to prevent him from biting off his own tongue. But Bex never relents. The more he screams, the harder she presses down, and I can smell his sizzling flesh from twenty feet away. It takes everything in me not to vomit, but Bex looks completely unfazed, like it's nothing, like she does this sort of thing twice a week.

Finally, she removes the metal brand and her three hooded colleagues race in with creams, towels, and bandages. As they do, I try to get a better view of the symbol burned into the man's skin, but when I put my weight down on the next step, it lets out a resounding creak.

Fuuuuuuck.

Four robed heads turn simultaneously in my direction, but I don't wait to make eye contact. Before any of them can say a word, I'm scrambling back up the stairs, pocketing my phone, and hurrying down the main hallway. Within seconds, I'm grabbing my hoodie, bursting through the front door, and racing into the woods so that I can duck behind the nearest redwood tree. That's when I finally take off my mask and suck in the cool night air, gasping for breath.

Who are these people? And what the fuck did I just see in there?

At the moment, I have no idea what to think. I just know that I need to get out of Redwood Vale before someone else notices me or, worse, recognizes me. So I take one last glance back at the pulsing, flashing farmhouse, even more confused than I was this morning, and then I race off into the woods toward my car, burrs and brambles be damned.

15

Monday arrives, and I haven't slept a wink. The misfiring synapses in my brain are crying out for a jolt of caffeine, but the same thoughts that kept me up all night are now preventing me from rolling out of bed and seeking out some coffee. All I can do is stare up at the ceiling fan, reliving what I saw, trying to make some sense of it. Strange occult symbols all over the Bancrofts' wooded property. Holly hosting masked orgies, complete with gummy psilocybin and MDMA. Bex Potter branding a naked man in the basement while chanting something about Greek gods.

Jonah was right when I first spoke with him two days ago: This is *definitely* not the Napa I knew growing up.

I must have watched the recording from the basement a dozen times already and can practically recite Bex's portion of the ceremony by heart. At some point last night, when I realized sleep was futile, I typed everything she and her hooded companions said into an AI chatbot to see if it recognized any of it. And while there were no exact matches—even artificial intelligence doesn't have access to Rudolf Steiner's most carefully guarded secrets—portions of it seemed to come from the *Orphic Hymns*, a collection of poems and rituals from an Ancient Greek mystery cult.

From what I could gather, over two thousand years ago, across Ancient Greece and the Roman Empire, there were numerous cults that pledged their loyalty to Dionysus (also known as Bacchus), the god of winemaking, fertility, and ritual madness. At certain times of the year, especially the autumn grape harvest, these cults would gather for what amounted to drug-induced orgies, complete with music, dance, and ceremonial sex that would sometimes last for days on end. Wine spiked with opium was the drink of choice, and in their hallucinatory state, these revelers would pay tribute to their favorite god, shouting out esoteric chants like the one I heard in that basement, until they allegedly reached a higher plane of existence, becoming bestial and one with nature.

It would all sound utterly insane if it weren't so eerily similar to what I'd witnessed at Redwood Vale. As if a bunch of Tesla-driving, cabernet-swilling, Hoka-wearing winemakers had stumbled on some three-thousand-year-old secret, causing them to act like Nero or Julius Caesar or whichever one hosted all the violent orgies.

Goddammit, I should have packed some Advil. My head's starting to throb after a long, sleepless night, but there's no sense in trying to go back to bed now. I have far too many mysteries to unpack, and I realize for the first time that I can't possibly do this alone. At the very least, I need a sounding board, someone who knows the area and the players involved, and my thumb reluctantly scrolls through my phone for Essie Leroux's name. Until now, I'd avoided sharing too much with her, worried that she was nothing more than an information sieve, constantly leaking key details to her boss, Angus McKee. But there's something about her honest eyes and genuine demeanor as well as her relentlessly positive outlook on life—and on our case—that I desperately want to trust. So I banish whatever skepticism remains in my heart and press firmly on the call button, each monotonous ring of the phone sending a painful rattle through my unrested skull.

* * *

"Don't just stare at me like that," I tell her. "Say something."

But Essie Leroux can't seem to find the words. We're seated next to each other at the countertop bar of a kitschy old diner in Calistoga called Café Sarafornia, where hungover tourists are slowly starting to trickle in. She hasn't touched her biscuits and gravy; I shovel down berry pancakes like someone who spent the night sprinting through the woods, trying to hide from a half-naked murder cult.

Finally, she looks me in the eye, ready to discuss everything I've just told her about Holly, Bex, and Redwood Vale. "You really watched her get cunnilingus?"

"For fuck's sake, Essie!"

"What?"

"Is that really the part of the story you're stuck on?"

"It's just unusual for a woman Holly's age!" she says. "And I'm telling you that as a woman who is *exactly* her age." She lowers her chin to shoot me a disappointed look over her bifocals that I presume has something to do with the state of her own sex life, or lack thereof.

"Fine," I tell her, eager to keep the conversation moving before I have to find out what goes on in her own bedroom. "But what about everything else? The branding? The occult behavior? And let's not forget—Charlotte Croydon identified Bex Potter as the woman Katherine O'Shea was flirting with on the night she died."

"It's a lot to take in," Leroux admits. "Even without the cunnilingus."

"Can you stop saying 'cunnilingus'?"

"Honey, I'm sixty-one years old. I'm not gonna call it rug-munching—"

"*Jesus Christ, Essie!*"

"All right, all right, I'll stop," she says. "But I do think, in general, you're onto something. Miss Potter certainly has all the makings of a primary suspect."

"Agreed. But for now, can you keep this between us? When I was talking to Peter Bancroft, I got the sense that there are certain people in the Sheriff's Department who might be caught up in this, and I don't want it getting out until we know more."

Leroux's face stiffens at the suggestion of corruption among her colleagues, and for a moment I worry I've made an error in judgment. "Well," she says, "I hardly think we should be taking the word of a scumbag billionaire over the men and women in uniform."

"That's fair," I tell her, cautiously trying to walk back my statement. "And I'm not saying I believe him. But I've known Angus McKee for a long time, and I'm—well—I'm just not sure he can always be trusted."

She nods, placated by my explanation, and takes a small bite off her gravy-smothered plate. "That's actually not a bad transition into what I found out yesterday."

"About McKee?"

"No," she says, washing her food down with a sip of black coffee. "About your father."

The fork drops from my hand and clatters onto my nearly empty plate of pancakes. A dozen prying eyes turn in my direction, so I smile and wave awkwardly, apologizing for the noise. Then I lean in closer to Leroux to find out more.

"I went down to VFS to follow up on that car that tailed you home the other night," she says. "Nice people over there. Very forthright. I talked to the owner, a guy named Miguel Ordoñez— or maybe it was Ortiz—I honestly don't remember. But I described to him the man you saw: Latino, twenties to forties, with a scar from his ear to his lip. And he knew right away who I was talking about."

"He did?"

"Yessiree," she says. "And don't worry—this one I wrote down." She checks something on a small notepad, then looks back up at me. "Carlos Ruiz. Ring a bell?"

"No," I tell her, shaking my head in disappointment.

"Well," she continues, "VFS hired him as a part-time driver two months ago as a condition of his parole. They have some kind of agreement with the prison system, helping guys find work when they get out. It's actually kinda nice."

"So he started working there just before Pilar Cruz was killed."

"That's right."

"Awfully convenient," I say, seeing the dots of the case finally begin to connect.

"Sure is," says Leroux.

"So what was he in prison for?"

"Sexual assault," she tells me, no longer needing to check her notepad. "Tried to force himself on a student at Napa Valley College. But that's not the interesting part."

"Okay..."

"What's interesting," Leroux says, "is that for a three-month period, back in 2020, he was your father's cellmate at San Quentin."

Her words land on me like an anvil, crushing every other thought I've had over the last few days. All my wild theories about Dionysian sex cults—gone. Every piece of evidence linking the deaths of two murdered women—forgotten. This unexpected connection to my dad consumes me and leaves me breathless, to the point that Leroux has to place a concerned palm on my forearm.

"You all right, hon?" she asks tenderly. I nod, even though I'm clearly not. "I made a call down to the warden, but he doesn't remember much about Ruiz. Apparently, he was only at the prison those three months, then the state transferred him up to Folsom for the remainder of his sentence."

"That's unusual . . ."

"Highly."

"The warden didn't say why?" I ask.

"He didn't know," says Leroux with an ominous stare. "The call came from the higher-ups in Sacramento."

I stew over this strange coincidence for a moment while I push my last few bits of pancake around with a fork; it doesn't take long for me to realize it's almost certainly *not* a coincidence. Larger forces are at play here. The question is, *How does it all connect?*

"What about Pilar Cruz's cousin?" I ask. "Did you manage to talk to him?"

"Sure did."

"And?"

"See for yourself," she says, placing her own digital voice recorder on the counter in front of me. "Or, I guess I should say, 'hear' for yourself. I recorded the conversation."

"You know you could have just emailed me the file."

"Huh?"

"These audio files—they're not that big. You didn't have to bring your whole device."

She stares at me like I'm speaking a foreign tongue. "Hon, do I look like someone who knows how to email off a—whatever one of these is?"

"Fine," I say with a sigh as I snatch the device from her. "I'll take care of it. Was there anything particularly interesting, though?"

"He told one heckuva story about crossing the border with Pilar last year. Gripping stuff. Really makes you think about how good we all have it, being born where we were. But as far as why she might have been killed—nothing new."

"Did you ask if she ever slept with women?"

"To try and connect her to O'Shea—yeah. I brought it up. The guy acted like I'd just called his cousin the Wicked Witch of the West Coast."

"Catholic?"

Leroux nods. "He had one of those crucifix tattoos on his chest. Not sure what the pope would think of that, but whatever floats your boat, right? Really, though, I got the sense it wasn't about JC so much as it was a kind of machismo thing. Don't think he liked the fact that I was bringing up his lady cousin's sex life."

"So he seemed overly protective?"

"I know what you're getting at," she says. "Some kind of old-school honor killing? But I don't think he's the type. It was more posturing than anything. He felt like he was supposed to defend her honor, being the closest thing she had to a big brother in this country, but he wouldn't take it any further than that."

"All right. Thanks for talking to him. I'll give the tape a listen on my drive down."

"Down where?" she asks.

I take a long sip from a mug of coffee that I've sweetened and creamed until it practically tastes like Ben & Jerry's. While Leroux has been rambling about her dead-end interview with Cruz's cousin, I've made up my mind to do something I should have done ages ago. There's only one person who might be able to connect all the scattered dots of this case for me, and I've been too scared and heartbroken to go visit him for the last few years. But my father spent three months locked in a cell with the guy who tailed me on my first night back in Napa. He also knows more about Rudolf Steiner and biodynamic farming than I could ever learn on the internet, having tried his hand at it that final year at Golden Eagle before Jessica Bancroft disappeared, so he might have insights into whatever it was I saw last night. Plus, the truth is, coming back up here, being around these people and these places again, it reminds me how much I miss him. So finally, I set down my mug and look up at Leroux's prying eyes.

"To San Quentin," I tell her. "I'm going to see my dad."

J. T. Falco

CRIMINAL DISTRICT COURT
COUNTY OF NAPA
STATE OF CALIFORNIA

STATE OF CALIFORNIA
v. No.2003-271
CLIFFORD LEE BURRELL

Testimony and Notes of Evidence, taken in the above case, before the **HON. WILLIAM HOFSTETTER**, Judge, presiding on the 10th day of December 2003.

APPEARANCES:

    REPRESENTING THE STATE OF CALIFORNIA:
    ABIGAIL COX, ESQ., ASSISTANT DISTRICT ATTORNEY
    REPRESENTING THE DEFENDANT:
    PAUL LOWENSTEIN, ESQ.

The Court: This is the matter of the State Versus Clifford Lee Burrell.

Mr. Lowenstein: Yes. Mr. Burrell is present in court and ready for trial.

The Court: Very well. The Prosecution can call its first witness.

Ms. Cox: The State calls Holly Margaux Bancroft.

HOLLY MARGAUX BANCROFT,
after having been first duly sworn, did testify as follows:

—Direct Examination—

Ms. Cox: Could you please state your name for the record?

Ms. Bancroft: Holly Margaux Bancroft.

Ms. Cox: And Ms. Bancroft, how are you employed?

Ms. Bancroft: I'm the owner and head winemaker at Golden Eagle Winery.

Ms. Cox: And when did you first hire the Defendant?

Ms. Bancroft: As my label artist, six years ago. But I brought him on full-time to help manage my vineyards three years ago.

Ms. Cox: And you and your family live on the same property where you and Mr. Burrell worked together?

Ms. Bancroft: That's right.

Ms. Cox: So did that mean he had much contact with your daughter, Jessica?

Ms. Bancroft: Yes. Quite a bit.

Ms. Cox: In what way?

Ms. Bancroft: We'd all have meals together sometimes. And she'd often be hanging around the vineyards while he was working.

Ms. Cox: Seems unusual to let your teenage daughter hang around with a forty-four-year-old man.

Ms. Bancroft: She was best friends with his daughter, so I didn't think much of it at the time.

Ms. Cox: His daughter, Lana Burrell?

Ms. Bancroft: That's right.

Ms. Cox: And did you ever see the Defendant alone with your daughter?

Ms. Bancroft: Yes.

Ms. Cox: When?

Ms. Bancroft: I'd noticed it happening more frequently lately, starting this past spring. I found them talking a lot in the vineyards.

Ms. Cox: About what?

Ms. Bancroft: I don't know. Never asked.

Ms. Cox: And is that all it was between them? Just talking?

Ms. Bancroft: No.

Ms. Cox: What else was there?

Ms. Bancroft: Well, that October, the day before she ... before she disappeared ... we had a fire break out in the barn where we do our fermentation. No one was hurt, but the entire crop of sauvignon blanc was destroyed since it was in the tanks at the time.

Ms. Cox: Sounds like a pretty big financial hit.

Ms. Bancroft: Around a million dollars. But we were insured. The real tragedy was that it was the first wine I ever let my son make with me. He took it pretty hard.

Ms. Cox: I'm sorry to hear that. And what did the Defendant and your daughter have to do with it?

Ms. Bancroft: Well, they were the only two people in the barn when it happened. So afterward, I asked Jess what they were doing together.

Ms. Cox: And?

Ms. Bancroft: She started crying hysterically. More than I'd ever seen from her. I mean, she was a tough girl. She wasn't... she wasn't the kind of girl who got overly emotional about things. So I knew something had to be wrong, but when I pushed her on it, she shut down and wouldn't tell me a thing. It was like she was... scared.

Ms. Cox: Of the Defendant?

Ms. Bancroft: Yes.

Ms. Cox: Any idea why?

Ms. Bancroft: I have my suspicions, but no. I never got answers from either of them.

Ms. Cox: What did you do about it?

Ms. Bancroft: The only thing I could do to protect my daughter. I fired him.

Ms. Cox: The Defendant, Clifford Burrell.

Ms. Bancroft: That's right.

Ms. Cox: And what was the date you fired him?

Ms. Bancroft: October 7, 2003.

Ms. Cox: The same day your daughter went missing.

Ms. Bancroft: That's right.

—End Direct Examination—

Ms. Cox: No further questions, Your Honor.

16

The drive from Napa Valley to San Quentin State Prison is less than an hour, but it feels like a lifetime, even without traffic. I spend most of the trip drowning in guilt and regret, trying to decide how to explain my four-year absence, but there are no words that are up to the task. The truth is, I don't know the answer myself. It just kind of... happened. Inertia rather than intent. And that just makes me feel like an even bigger asshole.

At first, in the years after his conviction, I made a point of visiting my father every weekend. The drive from my temporary new home in San Francisco wasn't a long one, and my broken teenage heart desperately craved those brief encounters with the only living family member I had left. We'd talk about school, my plans for college, any boys I might have a passing crush on post-Jonah—anything *other* than the crime that had ruined our lives and the cuts or bruises I'd occasionally spot on his hands and face. It was our unspoken rule: during those thirty-minute visits, we'd pretend to be as normal as possible, even though we obviously knew we were anything but.

As the years passed, though, my visits became less and less frequent. Once a week became once a month; once a month became once a quarter and then once a year. I can't exactly explain why this happened. It wasn't a conscious decision. I just think the charade we were engaged in, a never-ending father–daughter dance on hot coals, became too painful to sustain. Especially as I grew older and got caught up in the hectic self-importance of my twenties. My aimless college years at San José State. My hard-charging FBI training at Quantico. My all-encompassing first few years at the Bureau, when I bounced from field office to field office in search of a good fit. Not to mention my wayward love life, which largely consisted of bad first dates and good one-night stands, plus a couple epic multi-month mistakes.

By the time I entered my mid-thirties and my visits had been replaced by perfunctory emails and monthly phone calls, I'd become too embarrassed to go back and see him. The guilt and fear of having to explain my absence extended that absence even further, creating a vicious cycle of shame and regret that I saw no conceivable way out of. But the murders of Pilar Cruz and Katherine O'Shea, as well as the strange appearance of my dad's ex-cellmate, have changed all that. They're exactly the kick in the ass I've needed to get over myself and my baggage and go see the man who had only ever been a good and loving father.

So in the end, I decide that the best story to tell is the true one; I'll just need to hope he forgives me long enough to hear it.

With that settled, I spend the rest of the drive listening to Leroux's interview with Pilar's cousin, Hector Cruz. The deputy's questions are long-winded and circular, as expected, and Cruz's English is choppy at best, making for a tedious discussion full of repetition and misunderstandings. But there is one part of the conversation that causes my ears to perk up, and I raise the volume to make sure I don't miss any pertinent details.

Leroux: Did anything strange happen during the three nights you were picking at Golden Eagle?
Cruz: Sí. On the third night, there was a big fight.
Leroux: Who was involved?
Cruz: Pilar and Señora Bancroft.
Leroux: What? Why wasn't this in your initial statement to the police?
Cruz: I try, but the Sheriff—he not like it when I say her name.
Leroux: Ms. Bancroft.
Cruz: Sí.
Leroux: Okay. So what were they fighting about?
Cruz: Pilar was new. Only third time picking. She not want to crush the grapes, so she take her time. Very slow. And Señora Bancroft got super mad. Yelling about, uh . . . azúcar.
Leroux: Sugar.
Cruz: Sí. Sugar.
Leroux: And who else saw this fight?
Cruz: Just me. And one of the drivers from the company.
Leroux: Do you remember his name?
Cruz: No. I'm sorry.

I play back this portion of the tape twice, just to make sure I don't miss anything. An argument between Holly and Pilar, particularly one that Sheriff McKee tried to bury, is certainly a juicy lead. I'll have to push Holly on it next time I see her. She'll never admit to things escalating beyond a few choice words, but it'll be interesting to see how she reacts when I bring it up, especially since she told me she'd never spoken to Pilar. As I've learned over the years, the best interrogations are often about what's *not* being said rather than what is.

Even more curious is Cruz's mention of a driver from VFS. I want to call Leroux and scream at her for not asking if the man had a scar across his face, but I have to remind myself that, despite her age, she's only been a cop for four months, and this is technically her first case. It'll be easy enough to follow up on later, but the possibility leaves me even more curious about the man who tailed me home in the midnight-blue Ford. If he was there on the night Pilar went missing, could he be a bigger part of this puzzle than I'd thought?

There's one person who might know the answer: the man I once knew better than anyone else in the world. I just hope he's not so mad at me for abandoning him in San Quentin that he refuses to say a word.

* * *

One of the many benefits of the badge is that the warden agrees to set me up with my own room. The last thing I need, given the recent distance between my father and me, is the added barrier of a thick polycarbonate window. And there is no way in hell I'm doing this in a crowded common area where teary-eyed wives and confused children pay their weekly visits a few feet away, just a whirlwind of raw human emotion that I'll never be able to match; that'll make me seem like a sociopath in comparison. No, what I need is privacy and the absolute certainty that no one else is listening in on our conversation. Otherwise, I'm not sure I'll be able to do this. So while a guard goes and collects my father, I anxiously pace the concrete box where I'm about to have the world's most awkward family reunion.

After a few minutes, I hear a click and a loud digital buzz; then the door opens, and an old man in an orange jumpsuit, whom I barely recognize, steps inside. We stare at each other in silence from across the room while a pudgy guard dutifully removes a set of handcuffs. Then the guard leaves, that buzzer sounds again, and the door locks us in with an ominous click.

I don't know why I'm so surprised to see my father with gray hair, glasses, and a wrinkled face. He's in his mid-sixties, and it's not like they offer Lasik and Botox in state prison. But the man they took away two decades ago was so charismatic and handsome—the kind of guy who had no shortage of interested women after my mother died—that I struggle to rectify that memory with the senior citizen standing before me now. He's put on some weight since my last visit, but nothing too dramatic, just the gentle paunch of a healthy appetite and a sedentary lifestyle. He's also grown a beard and mustache that he keeps gray and fairly long—not Santa Claus territory by any means, but the sort of facial hair you might expect to find on the seat of a Harley-Davidson. I actually quite like it.

I try to get a sense of what he's thinking under that bushy 'stache and behind those thick glasses, but the eyes and mouth are completely foreign to me. Whatever he's had to do to survive in this awful place has left him hardened and noticeably less expressive, but I can hardly fault him for that. My smile hasn't been the same since his arrest either.

"Hi," I finally manage to say, and I pull out one of the two metal chairs for him. "Do you want to—I don't know—do you want to sit down?"

"I was actually thinking a hug might be nice."

The tears begin to pour down my face the moment he says it, and I move so quickly across the room that it almost feels like I'm floating. We embrace as if not a single minute has passed since my last visit four years ago, and I bury my head in the same chest that comforted me when my mother died and when I struggled to make friends at school. I'd forgotten how good it feels to have family. To love someone without condition and to be able to say that without words, simply by holding each other tight. And I realize there's no need to explain why it took me so long to do this. He understands. He gets it. And I'd much rather find out what he's been up to lately than waste our time dwelling on my own failures.

We spend the next two hours talking. He wants to know everything, and so do I, so we go back and forth swapping stories, not just about our time apart, but also our time together: memories from my childhood that leave us both laughing and crying, that delicious emotional cocktail that only family can stir together. I know he's faced more challenges in prison than I can possibly imagine, but I can tell he wants to spare me the worst of it, so I don't push him. Instead we focus on some of the lighter moments, like the genuine friendships he's made and the college courses in philosophy and theology that he's taken online. Only after we've exhausted every possible personal topic and he reminds me that it's getting late do I dare risk losing the magic between us by bringing up the murders. But it had to happen eventually, and as I tell him about Pilar Cruz and Katherine O'Shea, he leans in with a morbid curiosity.

"This doesn't have something to do with Jess, does it?" he asks. "I assume that's why you're here . . ."

"Actually, no, that's not why I came. Do you remember a cellmate you had four or five years ago—a guy named Carlos Ruiz?"

His face goes cold, and I know instantly that it wasn't a good relationship. Something clearly happened between them that still has my dad on edge. "What about him?"

"Well, two nights ago, he tailed me back to my motel—"

"What?"

"It's all right—he didn't try anything. He just seemed to want to know where I was staying." I watch my father's hands clench with a barely restrained rage on the metal table. "Do you have any idea why he would do that?"

"You know he tried to rape a nineteen-year-old girl."

"I know. But this wasn't a sexual thing. It was more like... surveillance." When I say this, a cloud of worry overtakes my father's face, as if he now understands what Ruiz was up to. "What is it?" I ask.

"Our first night locked up together, as soon as the lights went out, he started asking about Jess. Said he recognized me from CNN and knew all about the case, so he was just asking as a fan. Like I was some reality TV star, or something. But night after night, it wouldn't stop. He was obsessed with her and what kind of relationship we had. He was always asking if I was... if I was having sex with her. And whenever I'd deny it, he'd give me this laugh, like we were in on some sick joke together. Eventually, I couldn't take it anymore. I'm not proud of this, but—well—I beat the living shit out of him. Hit him so hard in the side of the skull, my fists were bleeding. But I couldn't keep listening to him talk about her like that. As if I were some... predator... like *him*. I had to do something to make it stop."

I try to picture this gentle old man in front of me hurting someone, but I can't make the mental leap. It's all too surreal. "The scar on his face. Was that... you?"

My father nods, filled with regret and not an ounce of pride.

"Then what happened?"

"I had to do some time in solitary. Two weeks, I think. And when I got out, he was gone. They told me he transferred to some other prison, but honestly I didn't care. I was just so relieved to never have to see him again. Although it sounds like he wasn't done with me after all."

A terrifying thought crosses my mind for the first time. "You think him tailing me had nothing to do with the murders at all? It was about getting revenge for what you did to him in here?"

I can tell that this is *exactly* what he thinks, but he's trying not to frighten me. "I'm not sure," he says. "But just in case, is there anyone working with you up there who can—you know—*be there* if something happens."

I think about telling him the truth, that our FBI field office doesn't have the budget or the manpower to spare a second agent on a case like this one, but I don't want to scare him. Even in an orange jumpsuit, he'll always be my father, trying to protect me.

"There's a sheriff's deputy I've been working with," I tell him.

"Do you trust him to have your back?"

"Sure," I say, figuring he'll rest easier if I don't correct the gender pronoun or describe just how *not* helpful Essie Leroux would be if I were attacked by an ex-con. "But I can also handle myself, Dad. Especially now that I know he's out there."

"You carry?" he asks.

"Always."

"Good," he says—never mind the fact that he was passionately anti-gun during my youth. Circumstances have changed, and so have we.

"Dad . . . did you ever get a sense why this guy was so curious about Jess? The superfan thing kinda feels like bullshit, especially since he transferred out as soon as he realized he wasn't going to get anything from you."

"I've definitely thought about it," he says. "Like, was he sent in here by the Bancrofts?"

"Exactly."

He lets out a deep, cleansing exhale, as if he has to purify his lungs every time he even hears that toxic last name. "It's not inconceivable given the money they have. The influence. But there's something about it that just doesn't add up."

"What's that?"

"If it *was* the Bancrofts, you'd think they'd want Ruiz to find out the one thing they never managed to learn in court. But he never asked me."

"Asked you what?"

"What I did with the body."

He says it with such cold objectivity that I find myself unable to speak. He's right, of course—that's exactly why Holly would put a guy like that in a cell with my father—but the way he utters the words is so emotionally detached and unlike the man I used to know that I'm left trembling on my side of the table. Is he saying that he *did* kill Jess? Or is that just how a convicted felon learns to speak about a crime in prison, even if he didn't actually commit it?

I'm genuinely not sure how to follow that up, and luckily I don't have to. A loud buzz interrupts our tense silence, the door clicks, and the pudgy guard returns with a set of handcuffs.

"Sorry," he says, oddly deferential of my FBI badge. "I gotta get him back in his cell before rounds."

"Of course," I tell him, and I leap to my feet, eager to escape this concrete bunker. The place was small and dank to begin with, but now, with my cluttered mind asking questions it shouldn't be asking, it feels downright claustrophobic.

I shuffle my way around the guard, trying to get out of there without looking back at my dad, because if I do, I'm afraid I might cry. And even if I don't, I might feel things I don't want to feel, the kind of emotions I've been drowning with booze for the better part of the last twenty years. But the old man is too quick for me, and he slips around the guard to wrap me up in another hug. Of course, I have a much harder time with this one, and I know he can sense it.

"Have a safe drive," he says as he reluctantly releases me. "And keep an eye out."

"You too," I tell him with lowered eyes, too scared to meet his and feel that awful punch to the gut. "I'll see ya soon." Then I hurry out the door and into the hallway, desperate to breathe real air and put San Quentin far, far behind me.

17

I need a drink more than I ever have, like I'm going to scream if I don't do something about this awful feeling, this tremble that won't go away, so I pull into the first bar I see in St. Helena, even if there *is* a corkscrew standing in for the letter "T" in its logo.

Needless to say, the drive back to Napa Valley hasn't been a pleasant one. With the sun all but down and the sky dissolving into blackness, every car on the road became a potential threat, a menace on wheels that was just waiting for the right moment to send me spinning into a ditch. I couldn't see the faces of any other drivers, didn't know if any of them had that awful scar running across their cheek—my dad's handiwork—so my paranoia got the better of me. Behind each pair of headlights, I thought I saw Carlos Ruiz. Anytime a car tailed me for more than a mile, I abruptly pulled over and let it pass. I had to admit, the fact that this man might have a personal vendetta against my father and want to take it out on me was far more unsettling than if I thought he had killed Pilar or Katherine. Murderers I can handle; they tend to have clear motives and repetitive behaviors that allow them to be tracked down and arrested. But a violent stalker whose endgame remains a mystery? That shit's too unpredictable for my taste.

Now I glance suspiciously over both shoulders as I hurry from my car to the front entrance of The Saint, whose bougie wine cellar vibe is hardly my style. But beggars can't be choosers, not when they're this thirsty, not when their whole body is vibrating like a guitar string that the universe won't stop plucking, won't just leave the hell alone. So I plop my tired ass down into the only empty seat at the bar and promptly ask for a bottle of Heineken, only to be told, once again, that they don't serve beer. *Of course.*

"It literally says 'Wine Bar' in the window," says the bored bartender in head-to-toe faded blue denim, the sort of thing we called a "Canadian tuxedo" growing up, but which Gen Z seems intent on making us wear again. Not that I ever will. I've got about ten pairs of the same black jeans and about a dozen matching gray shirts that I plan on wearing until the day I die, fashion trends be damned, because I'm a creature of habit. There's safety in repetition, comfort in known quantities, like the reassuring taste of a Heineken when the rest of my life seems to be spiraling out of control. Only here I am, halfway to a panic attack, just trying to feel safe, and some smug, twenty-something stranger in a jean jacket that I swear I owned in first grade is telling me I've got no choice but to adapt to her way of doing things.

"What about a vodka tonic?" I ask, trying to stay calm.

"*Wine bar,*" she repeats slowly, with smug self-satisfaction.

"Fine," I sigh, my impatience winning out over my obstinance, and I begrudgingly grab the list of wines by the glass. I'm about to point to the cheapest thing on the menu—anything with alcohol will do—when I notice a familiar label halfway down. "I'll have a glass of the Wappo Crest cab."

"Oh," says the bartender with a strange little gasp of surprise, as if she too expected me to choose the cheapest thing on the menu. "Good choice."

"Thanks," I mutter, not because I mean it, but because it requires less effort than lifting up my hand and flipping her off for being so patronizing.

"You know, one of the winemakers is actually here tonight."

"Great," I tell her, not impressed in the slightest. This town has winemakers crawling out of the woodwork; of course there's one here tonight. There's probably one here *every* night.

But for some reason she's unfazed by my blatant lack of interest, and she points out a table in the back corner, tucked into a darker part of the bar designed to resemble a wine cave. "Right there, see the guy closest to us? That's Caleb Roche. He comes in here all the time."

I turn to look, mainly just to appease my new friend in denim, maybe get her to shut up and pour faster, but when I see the man in question, I nearly fall backward off my stool. *It's him!* The same floppy-haired goofball, the guy with the sun-kissed skin, magnetic smile, and bizarrely out-of-place shorts and flip-flops, with whom I had a staring match at that dive bar two days ago. Right now, he seems to be holding court with a few friends, all of them laughing about something, and I can't bring myself to turn away. There's just something about his carefree face that I can't get enough of, that I just want to grab onto and—

"Do you want me to introduce you?" asks the bartender, interrupting my runaway train of a dirty mind and handing me a generous glass of the Wappo Crest cab. Not just any wine, but *his* wine.

"No," I say awkwardly, with a bit too much nervous energy. "That's all right."

"Suit yourself." And she thankfully wanders off to go bother another customer.

Alone now, I clutch the stem of my glass and stare down into the gorgeous garnet liquid inside, so intrigued by it now that I know who made it, even if I still don't know the first thing about him. And this time, when I take a sip, there are no transportive sense memories that leave me spastic and antisocial. On the contrary, the drink relaxes me to the core, temporarily ridding me of my concerns about my father's ex-cellmate, and I find myself overcome with a confidence that I barely recognize. Before I know it, I'm striding across the room with my glass of wine and pulling up a chair beside the floppy-haired winemaker whose smile does something to me that I can't even explain. That makes me feel like someone else, someone hopeful and carefree, at least when I'm watching him.

"Hi," I say when he finally turns away from his friends and notices me there, leeching onto his table without an invite. "You probably don't recognize me, but—"

"Sweet potato fries!" he says with a knowing smile.

"What?"

"You ordered regular fries, I ordered sweet potato, but Carla messed up the order, like always. I was gonna say something, but by the time I noticed, you already seemed to be enjoying yours, and I didn't want to interrupt."

I let out a laugh, a real one without pretense, the sort of thing I don't do much anymore, and before long, he's laughing with me. I don't say anything, not right away, even though I should. But the truth is, I just want to lose myself for a moment in his honest brown eyes. I can tell right away that he's not my type—*nice* is hardly an adjective I'd use to describe any of the men I've slept with over the last two decades—but after the weekend I've had, it's a quality I'm desperate to be around. Someone who doesn't know a thing about my past, someone who can't possibly be a suspect in my murder investigation. Someone... normal. So I tuck the faces of Katherine O'Shea, Pilar Cruz, and even Jessica

Bancroft into a compartment deep within my mind and lock them away, if only for one night.

"I'm Lana, by the way."

"Caleb," he replies, giving me a gentle handshake with his rough, calloused fingers and palm. "I can see you have good taste in wine."

I shoot him a coy look and hold my glass up higher into the light. "How can you tell it's yours?"

"I could answer that," he says, "but I'd just end up sounding like a pretentious asshole talking about color and clarity and all sorts of other somm-speak that'll probably just scare you off. Only, I don't want you to leave yet . . ."

"That right?" I ask, giving him the flirtiest grin I can manage.

"Yup," he says, staring me right in the eyes, a look I never want to end.

"Well, that's only 'cause you don't know me yet. And 'cause I haven't told you that I usually hate wine."

His big brown eyes narrow and he moves in closer, like he's peering into my soul. "You don't hate wine."

"Yeah, I do."

"You're drinking it right now."

"It's all they serve."

"No," he says with absolute certainty. "What you hate is what you *think* wine is, not what's in that glass. What you hate is what these corporate behemoths like J.B. Bancroft have spent the last thirty years filling our grocery stores with. All that cheap, overly processed plonk with names like Slutty Syrah and Pop-Drop Purple Juice—"

"Okay," I interrupt with a laugh, "there is *no way* anyone sells a wine called Pop-Drop Purple Juice."

"You don't know that."

"It's an objectively terrible name."

"Exactly my point!" he says with a burst of boyish excitement that I'll admit I find adorably attractive, especially when he pushes a few stray curls out of his eyes. "It's no wonder people like you *think* you don't like wine. You're being sold marketing campaigns and branding instead of the stuff that really matters."

"Which is . . . ?"

"The soil. The mineral composition. The cool summer nights of a south-facing slope. The art of a perfectly timed harvest." His eyes are so eager and his demeanor so earnest, I can't help but hang on his every word. "Here," he says, gently nudging my glass of wine up closer to my lips. "Just indulge me for a minute. Take a sip, let it rest on your tongue, and then tell me how it makes you feel."

"Alright," I tell him, and I hold his eyes in mine as I do exactly as he said. The lightly chilled cabernet washes over my taste buds, and I'm hit with an explosion of flavor, elegant fruits and toasted cedar in perfect balance. "There's some blackberry—"

"No," he stops me, placing a strong hand on my thigh that sends a quiver through my entire body. "Don't tell me how it tastes. Tell me how it makes you *feel*."

I manage to nod my head, when really all I'm thinking about is that touch, his fingers pressing into the flesh of my leg with just the right amount of pressure—not tender, not creepy, but sexy. And I take another sip, this time closing my eyes, letting the wine transport me back to my youth. Only it's not my dad I think about this time, but Jonah, getting drunk on wine with him during that dreamlike summer, using it to lower our inhibitions, an appetizer to a main course of trembling teenage sex.

Finally I open my eyes and give Caleb a smile. "I can't answer that," I tell him.

"Why not?"

"Because you'll think I'm some kind of pervert."

He lets out a buoyant laugh. "Alright," he says, "now I've *definitely* got to know."

"Fine," I say with a coy grin, making my intentions known. "Your wine makes me feel sexy, like I'm a horny seventeen-year-old and anything's possible."

He stares at me for a moment, dumbstruck, then leaps up from his chair like the place is on fire.

"Where are you going?" I ask as he hurries away from me.

"To the bar," he says. "We're gonna need a whole bottle."

* * *

We spend the rest of the night tucked into a private corner table, just the two of us, no distractions.

I learn that he grew up farther north, up in Lake County, a quiet backwater region known more for its pot farms and wildfires than anything else these days. But he came to Napa seven years ago to take over a plot of land that had been in his family for centuries, long before even the earliest German vintners, like Charles Krug and the Beringers, showed up in the Valley in the 1800s. That's because Caleb is twenty-five percent Wappo on his mother's side, part of an indigenous tribe that once had a village on the site of this very wine bar until the arrival of Mexican colonists and German settlers sent them scattering across the region. Somehow, despite all the property turnover in Napa as its land became some of the most expensive in the world, his family managed to hold on to a few hillside acres outside Calistoga. And when his uncle died, Caleb decided to replant the farm with cabernet vines and try his hand at the Valley's signature business—hence the name Wappo Crest.

There's something so pure and inspiring about Caleb's story: the underdog following his dream and honoring his heritage, fearlessly taking on the multimillionaires who own most of Napa's land and who would probably offer a boatload of money to take over his. He's the kind of guy you can't help but root for; the fact that he's adorably attractive doesn't hurt either. And as he talks, my conscious mind becomes singularly obsessed with one question:

When's the last time I shaved my legs?

Did I do it three days ago—that morning before I spoke with Connie Chen at our office in San Francisco? Honestly, I can't remember. I was so rushed and a bit hungover that day. If not then, it may have been well over a week, which definitely puts me on the fuzzy side of socially acceptable. Although, judging by Caleb's general aesthetic and overall vibe, I wouldn't be surprised if he's been with a few women who are adamant anti-shavers—legs, armpits, you name it.

"Does your boyfriend ever tag along when you're out of town on a job like this?" he asks. And as he says it, every muscle in my body tenses with the realization that my night is about to get a *whole lot* more interesting, because, for reasons I don't understand but am certainly thankful for, this perfect guy is as into me as I am into him.

"I don't have a boyfriend," I tell him. "Although I think you probably already knew that."

He shrugs and smiles coyly, then leans in closer from his chair. "Girlfriend?"

I shake my head.

"Interesting," he says.

"Why is that interesting?"

"Because. I'm interested."

Yes, I think. It's definitely been a week since I shaved my legs. But honestly, who the hell cares?

* * *

My motel is closer than his place, so we take separate cars in the hopes that I can straighten up before he gets there. But when I pull into the lot of the Silverado Inn, he's already standing outside my room, waiting with horny anticipation.

Rather than let my slovenly habits put a damper on things, I leave the lights off when we enter and promptly begin kissing him, keeping his focus on me and not the dirty underwear and burr-covered socks scattered across the floor after my night at Redwood Vale. I pull him down to the bed, never letting his lips leave mine, and we kiss for another minute before I even remember to kick off my shoes.

Our clothing comes off in fits and starts rather than in one fell swoop. Our footwear and socks are followed by more kissing, this time up and down the length of my neck, and a brief nibble of my extra-ticklish left earlobe. We lose our shirts, and I kiss his bare chest, playing with his nipple with my tongue, hoping he'll soon do the same to me. He clearly gets the message, because, after a bit of fumbling with my bra, his tongue gives both my nipples exactly the attention they needed.

Eager to take things to the next level, I tug at his jeans until they're down around his ankles and promptly cup my hand around the hardening bulge in his floral-print boxer briefs. "Take those off," I tell him forcefully. "Now." And he obliges without a word.

* * *

Twenty minutes later, I roll off Caleb in a state of absolute, post-orgasmic bliss, with just the right amount of sweat dampening my skin. We lie there together, side by side, breathing deeply, and after a few long, meditative exhales, I reach over for my phone. "What kind of music do you like?"

"Is it cool if we just lie here in silence for a little?"

"No," I say, surprising him.

"Uh, why not?"

"Well, I need to go pee so I don't get a UTI, but I have this thing where I can't go if I know someone's listening, and these walls are super thin, so for the sake of my urinary tract, what kinda music do you like?" He sees the earnest look on my face and starts laughing, as if I've just told him the funniest joke in the world. "I'm not kidding."

"I can see that."

"So what music do you want?"

"Surprise me," he says through his last few chuckles. Just to mess with him, I decide to blast a particularly bad ABBA track, then I hurry into the bathroom and empty my bladder to the saccharine sounds of seventies Swedish pop.

On the way out, I resist the urge to check the mirror—I know I'll be disappointed with my naked reflection, and I want to feel good about myself for just a little bit longer. But I forget to turn off the bathroom light behind me, so when I leave, there's a harsh glow illuminating the cheap carpet all around the bed and by the front door. What I see there stops me in my tracks and sends me scurrying over to the stack of police reports that I've carelessly dumped on an armchair in the corner of the room.

"Everything okay?"

I glance back over my shoulder at Caleb, who's sitting up in bed with his shirt still off and a sheet pulled up to his waist. His look of utter confusion reminds me how silly I must seem, squatting over a stack of paperwork, butt-ass naked. But I'm too distracted to bother with a full explanation, so all I say is, "There's red dirt on the floor."

"Ohh . . . kay," he says with the slow cadence of someone trying to get through to a mental patient. But I really don't care—not right now, with another piece of the puzzle falling into place—and I finally find what I'm looking for. On the third page of the Sheriff Department's report on Katherine O'Shea's death, the coroner has written: *Red dirt with flecks of quartz found beneath the fingernails on both hands suggests that the victim was dragged somewhere while still alive.*

I set down the report and hurry back over to the door, where I find the sneakers that I wore on my midnight hike through Redwood Vale. Along with some stray burrs still clinging to the laces, the treads underneath are caked with the same red soil that's now sprinkled all over the room. An idea hits me, and I pounce back into bed with the increasingly concerned naked man, whose sheet is now pulled all the way up to his chest.

"You're kinda freakin' me out a little," he says.

But I wave him off and slide under the sheet so that my nakedness isn't a distraction. "You know a lot about the soils around here, right? Composition, terroir, all that shit."

"Yeah . . ."

"How common is bright red soil?"

"Is this for your murder case?"

"I can't tell you that."

"So it is."

"Yes, all right? Now just look at this and tell me what I need to know." I place a chunk of congealed red dirt into his unsuspecting hand and turn on the bedside lamp to give him a better view. He studies it for a moment, sifting through it with his finger, looking for clues that would mean nothing to almost anyone else in the world.

"This is volcanic, probably from a mountain on the north end of the Valley. But see these little specks of crystal? Back home we call these Lake County Diamonds. It's just quartz, but they can be a lot bigger up there thanks to the more recent eruptions, so as kids we'd always dig them up and collect them, not realizing they were pretty much worthless."

"And how common are they in Napa Valley?"

"Not common at all. The volcanic activity here stopped three million years ago, so most of the quartz has washed away into the alluvial fans. You'll still see red soil on some of the hillsides, but I've never seen it with this much quartz."

"So this is unusual."

"Very."

"Which means she was there . . ."

"What?" he asks, but I'm already hopping out of bed in search of my underwear. *Where the hell did I throw it?*

"Lana, do you want to talk about what's going on right now?"

"You should leave."

"For real?"

"Yes." I find my underwear and quickly slide it on, then grab the nearest shirt, not even bothering to sniff it to make sure it came from the clean pile.

"I was kind of thinking we could do that again—"

"The sex?"

"Yes, Lana. The sex."

"We can't have sex again," I explain. "Not when I'm onto something like this. I won't be able to focus and I'll have to fake the whole thing, and that's not fair to you because you're actually pretty good at . . . the sex. So for the sake of . . . whatever this is . . . I think you should go."

He considers me for a moment but seems to appreciate my

honesty, because he nods and begins to put on his clothes. "You're an odd one," he says, sliding on his boxer briefs, "but I like it."

I wait for him to finish, enjoying one last glance at his butt before he pulls his shorts over it, then I watch as he circles the bed and places something on the dresser by the front door. "I know business cards are obnoxiously formal and not my thing at all, but my partner insisted we get them, so here we are. My number's the one on the left, if you decide you want to call. No pressure, though."

"I will," I tell him with the most genuine smile I can muster.

"I'll believe it when I see it," he says, smiling back. Then he slips out into the night, leaving me alone to consider my next move.

18

The thick eyebrows under the brim of Angus McKee's cowboy hat furrow up in consternation. He's watching my video of the basement branding ceremony for the third time, his attitude shifting from disbelieving to disturbed, to disgruntled at the inevitable shitstorm to follow.

When it finishes, he takes off his hat, wipes the sweat from his brow, and finally looks me in the eye, not exactly pleased with my hard-earned discovery. "If this was obtained without a search warrant, I'm not—"

"I didn't need one," I tell him, prepared for this pushback. "I was invited onto the property by its co-owner, Peter Bancroft. He even gave me a key."

Sheriff McKee considers this some more, realizing I've backed him into a corner from which there's only one way out. He reclines into his tall leather desk chair in his otherwise unadorned office in the Napa County Sheriff's Department, all wood-paneled walls and metal filing cabinets, like it was decorated in 1980 and they never had the budget to bring it into the digital age. "Fine," he mutters. "I'll have a deputy track down Potter. We're not arresting her, but we'll hold her for questioning."

"I want to talk to her alone."

"You'll talk to her with *me*," he says definitively, never mind my rank and Bureau badge. "But you can lead. I'll just be there to protect our asses in case this thing ever goes to trial."

I think about this for a few seconds, then nod accordingly. I didn't have to bring this to McKee; there was nothing stopping me from hauling in Bex Potter myself and grilling her about her involvement in the murders. But my visit to San Quentin made me realize how dangerously alone I am up here. If this Carlos Ruiz really is after me because of what my father did to him in prison, then the time may come when I'll need the backing of local law enforcement. Better to win them over now in peacetime so they answer my call in war. So I've decided to use what I learned about Bex and the soil at Redwood Vale as a sort of olive branch with the sheriff; thus far, it seems to be working.

He picks up his cell phone and promptly dials a saved number. "Hey. I need you to go to Golden Eagle and pick up a woman named Rebecca Potter. Goes by Bex. Don't cause a fuss; go before the tasting room opens. But tell her we need her down here for questioning in the O'Shea case." He and the deputy on the other end discuss a few more logistics, then he hangs up the phone and gives me a look that I've never seen before, something vaguely resembling respect.

"What?" I ask him.

"Good job," he says. Then he puts on his hat and begins shuffling the paperwork stacked neatly on his computer-free desk, clearly wanting me to leave but not knowing how to ask. I decide to quit while I'm ahead, so I exit without another word and hurry off in search of some cheap police station coffee.

* * *

One hour and two heavily sweetened Keurig cups later, I'm seated beside McKee in a cramped interrogation room half the size of the one in San Quentin. There's a panel of one-way glass on my left side, which I know Leroux is probably eagerly watching us through, like one of her favorite *Law & Order* episodes come to life. But otherwise the walls, floor, and ceiling are all the same monotone gray concrete. The only splash of color in the place comes from the peculiar woman seated across from me, with her wide blue eyes and her vibrant yellow hair. As she waits for one of us to speak, Bex Potter drums her fingers on the bare metal table, and I can't help but notice the soil caked into her fingernails. It's deep brown, like raw cocoa powder.

"Do you know why you're here?" I ask.

"The deputy said it was about Katherine O'Shea," she says flatly, without betraying any hint of emotion.

"So what do you think we're going to ask you?"

"I have no idea, Agent Burrell." She smiles sweetly. "Why don't you tell me?"

"All right. We have two dead women who were last seen at the vineyard where you work, but for the sake of this conversation, I'm just going to focus on the second one: Katherine O'Shea. According to her friend, Charlotte Croydon, you spent most of the visit flirting with Katherine. Charlotte identified you in a photo and said she thought her friend was going to spend the night with you. Then the next morning, Katherine O'Shea turned up dead. In the coroner's report, he mentioned an unusual red soil with flecks of quartz under Katherine's fingernails, as if someone had dragged her through the dirt while she was clinging for dear life. It turns out this is a highly unusual soil type here in Napa, but it *can* be found at a place called Redwood Vale, which is owned by the Bancroft family and where you were seen as recently as Sunday night."

For the first time, I notice a flash of anxiety pass across Bex Potter's otherwise calm face. Her hand trembles ever so slightly, and I start to hear her foot tapping on the cement floor. "Seen by who?"

"Me."

She stares directly into my eyes with that same unblinking intensity from our first encounter. I can tell she's trying to discern whether I'm lying, so I stare right back at her, eyes wide, refusing to blink first.

"I think I want a lawyer," she says.

"We can do that," I tell her. "But while we wait, can I show you something?"

McKee abruptly puts out a hand to stop me from turning my phone toward Bex. "Not 'til the lawyer gets here."

"I just want to give her a sneak preview. Something to stew on while we wait."

"Bad idea," McKee says.

"What is it?" Bex asks, increasingly on edge.

"I can show you . . . *if* you want to hold off on the whole lawyer thing."

"No!" McKee shouts with an angry slap of the table that brings our conversation to a screeching halt. "We're doing this by the book. No mistakes. Potter, you can get your phone back from the Deputy in the hall. He'll help you find a lawyer if you don't already have one."

Then the sheriff springs to his feet and leads Bex to the door before I can say another word.

* * *

I find Leroux waiting for me in the break room with another mug from the Keurig. "A crap load of cream and sugar," she says, "just the way you like it." I give her a thankful smile and take the mug, letting the warmth from it emanate through my body, soothing me after that brief but tense interrogation. "Angus was right, you know, making you wait for the lawyer."

"I know."

"Then why'd you push her to watch the video?"

"I wasn't going to play it," I explain. "I just wanted to see if she'd blurt anything out before I did. She was definitely about to crack."

Leroux shakes her head sympathetically. "If you ask me, that walnut's been cracked for a *long* time."

"Can't argue there." I take another sip of perfectly sweetened coffee. "Makes you wonder how a girl her age ends up like that."

"I was thinking the same thing," Leroux says. "So I poked around this morning, made a few calls, even had one of the younger deputies do some digging online."

"Find anything?"

She nods. "Rebecca Potter was diagnosed with leukemia when she was sixteen."

"What?"

Another nod from Leroux, and as I struggle to process this new information about my chief suspect, she continues with her story. "Poor thing spent the next two years in and out of hospitals getting chemo, radiation—the whole nine yards. Apparently she needed a bone marrow transplant, but no one in her family was a match, so it looked like she might die until some anonymous donor turned up and saved her life."

"Jesus Christ . . ."

"Amen to that. But it certainly explains the whole biodynamic obsession. Cancer survivors tend to stick to a pretty clean lifestyle afterward. All organic, that sort of thing. You can see how she'd be attracted to an idea like that."

I nod, impressed with Leroux's discovery and analysis, and I try to rectify the story with the peculiar young woman I've gotten to know. A near-death experience during adolescence can absolutely have lifelong impacts on a person's psyche. Of course many people channel that trauma into something positive, a more carpe diem approach to cancer survival. But I can absolutely see the potential for a darker turn as well. Feeling so weak and helpless during her formative years could have easily given Bex a twisted need to feel powerful, which might explain the ruthless way in which she branded that man two nights ago. But would it push her so far as to actually commit serial murder? It's a stretch, but an intriguing one.

"Do you know if she's in remission?" I ask.

"As far as I could tell. But her medical records are confidential."

"Right. Well, I hope you don't expect me to go easier on her now because of this."

Leroux smiles, accustomed by now to my mordant personality. "Wouldn't dream of it, Boss."

* * *

By one PM, a sharply dressed lawyer arrives at the station in a black Mercedes S-Class. She apologizes for being late—traffic from San Francisco is always brutal on a weekday—and I know right away that this must be Holly Bancroft's personal attorney, on loan to her favorite vineyard employee.

Veena Kapur is in her fifties, with short black hair, black-framed designer glasses, and the calm self-assurance of a long-time partner at a white shoe firm. Her power comes from her composure; this isn't a woman who feels the need to prove herself or her credentials. From the moment she walks into the interrogation room, McKee and I both know we're in the presence of a lawyer who could destroy our careers if we make one wrong move, so we cautiously ease our way back into the discussion. We exchange a few pleasantries, then recap the Cruz and O'Shea murders as well as everything we've talked about so far with her client. Finally, I'm able to steer the conversation back toward Redwood Vale and the video on my phone.

"Did you get a search warrant for the property?" the lawyer asks with the same no-nonsense tone she uses for everything, as if life is a courtroom and everyone's a witness just waiting to be badgered.

"I had the owner's permission to be there."

"I'm assuming you mean Peter Bancroft."

"That's right."

"He hasn't used that property in decades."

"Doesn't matter," I say calmly and with a forced confidence, trying not to let her get under my skin. "He's on the deed and he gave me a key to come and go as I please, so I was well within my legal right to be there."

"To *be* there," says Kapur. "Not to film my client without her consent at a time when she had the reasonable expectation of privacy under California Penal Code 632."

"Which would be true," I fire back, "if she weren't committing a crime. But given that I saw what I believed to be a crime in progress, I knew 632 wouldn't apply."

The lawyer strains for another legal path forward, opening her mouth as if to continue our verbal fencing match, but she knows she's been beaten and begrudgingly slouches back into her chair beside Bex. "What crime?"

"Let's just watch the video, shall we?"

Kapur looks over at Bex, who nods her reluctant approval. Then both women fall silent as I play the shaky, two-minute masterpiece that I recorded from the basement stairs. All the while, I keep a close watch on both their eyes: the lawyer seems visibly disturbed, but her client never flinches. In fact, she almost seems to enjoy this sick little movie. When the recording ends, I ask if they'd like to see it again, but Kapur quickly declines my offer.

"I need a moment to talk to my client alone," she says.

"Of course," McKee tells her. "There's a private room next door."

* * *

Thirty minutes later, the four of us are back in our respective seats, only the balance of power has clearly shifted in my direction. If I were a better person, I'd accept this gracefully—nobody likes a gloater—but I can be a real child sometimes, especially around arrogant lawyers who practically wear their Harvard degrees around their necks like jewelry, and I give Kapur my best shit-eating grin.

"My client doesn't deny that she's the one in the video," she says.

"Thank you."

"*But,*" Kapur goes on, "she disputes the notion that any sort of crime was being committed. Everything you saw was fully consensual. In fact, the man on the floor was her boyfriend, and she's willing to give you his name so that he can attest to her innocence."

"Her *boyfriend*?" I shout out, incredulous, my cocky smile now somewhere on the floor with the base of my jaw.

"That's right."

"Fine," I say, trying to stay calm and in control. "But first we still have some more questions for Miss Potter."

"She's willing to answer them, but I *will* step in if anything feels like it's overstepping her Fourth or Fifth Amendment rights."

"Sure," I tell her, stifling a petulant eye roll and shifting my gaze over to Bex. "So why don't we start with that mark you branded into your boyfriend's dick."

"Excuse me!" snaps the lawyer.

"Come on, Lana," groans McKee.

"Fine," I mutter. "His *pubic area*. Is that better?" When none of the adults in the room object, I turn back to Bex. "What does it mean?"

"It's just an old symbol invented by some alchemist back in the 1500s."

"John Dee," I say with unwavering confidence.

Her eyebrows rise up in surprise. "You've done your homework."

"Which is why I'm not asking what it *used* to mean, Bex. I want to know what it means to *you* and why you burned it into your boyfriend's skin with an eight-hundred-degree cattle prod."

She looks cautiously at her attorney, who leans over and whispers something into her ear. Bex pauses, thinking about the advice, then seems to choose her words with extreme care. "I'm part of an organization whose membership and activities are a secret to anyone *not* in the organization. All I can say without breaking my vow is that we've never done anything illegal."

"What about drugs?"

"Okay, *besides* drugs."

"Have you been branded too?"

Without hesitation, Bex rises up from her chair, folds down her waistband, and shows me the top half inch of a brand. This one's much older, though, and the skin has fully healed, just a pale pink reminder rather than a red-hot wound. "Now, if you have any more questions about the girls who were killed, I'd be happy to answer them, but I won't say another word about this brand or my organization."

Her obstinate answers leave me on edge, feeling disrespected by someone who doesn't seem to be taking me or my investigation seriously. It's a common problem, a sad reality in a world that's so deeply misogynistic that even apparent feminists like

Bex are far more intimidated by men with badges than women. But that doesn't mean I have to like it or that I'll ever get used to the double standard.

"Okay," I grumble, leaning in and lowering my voice, "then explain to me how Katherine O'Shea got soil from Redwood Vale under her fingernails."

"The fingernail part I couldn't tell you," says Bex. "But she was at Redwood Vale because I invited her."

I share a wide-eyed look with McKee; he's as surprised as I am that Bex just admitted to this. "Why'd you lie about it last time we spoke?"

"Because I was scared shitless, Agent Burrell."

"Of what?"

"Of *you*. I knew the truth wouldn't look good, and I didn't want you making assumptions."

My impulse, of course, is to crack a big, toothy smile and maybe ask McKee for a high five, let the whole table know how good it feels to be feared by a suspect, especially when I thought she wasn't taking me seriously. But obviously this wouldn't help the situation; if I did that, *no one* would take me seriously. So I bite down hard on my lower lip, trying to suppress my grin with my two front teeth and twist it into a sneer. "Okay," I tell her, half grinning, half smirking, "then why don't you tell us the full story so there's nothing left to assume."

Bex takes a deep breath, and as she works up the courage to admit the truth, her lawyer places a supportive hand over hers, silently reminding her that she's protected by the best attorney money can buy. "The bride you talked to was right. Katherine *was* flirting with me, but I swear I didn't flirt back. I was just being extra nice because I could see how miserable she was. I mean, you can imagine what it's like with a big group of girls like that at a bachelorette party—they're loud and drunk, and there's always some queen-bee maid of honor bossing the others around, making them do things they would never do in the real world. Apparently, Katherine was more of a childhood friend, and the rest of the girls were from the same sorority at the University of Texas, so she didn't really know any of them and was having an awful time. She was also the only queer one in the group, and the others were doing that very Southern thing where they'd smile politely to her face while talking shit behind her back. I honestly just felt terrible for the girl, so I told her about a party we were having that night up at the Vale."

"I thought it was a top secret, members-only thing."

"Sometimes," she says. "It really depends on the event. But this was a full moon party, and we like to open those up to a few select guests who are—shall we say—open-minded, so I figured it couldn't hurt to bring her. Like I said, she *really* needed to get away from that bachelorette party."

"And did you have sex with her?"

"No. We kissed a little, but she's genuinely not my type. Plus, like I said, I have a boyfriend. And I wasn't really feeling it that night, which is why I went home early."

"What time was that?"

"Around ten thirty."

Kapur adds: "She has video footage from the Ring camera outside her front door showing her entering her apartment at 10:54 PM, *well* before the victim's estimated time of death. We're happy to email that to you when we're done here."

I feel the case against my top suspect slipping away, and I hesitate before responding. Sheriff McKee must notice my internal struggle, because he kindly steps in on my behalf. "We'll want to see footage from the *whole* night to prove she never left."

"Of course," Kapur says.

"And are there any other exits to the home?"

"It's a third-story apartment, Sheriff," says the lawyer, "so unless you think my client jumped out a window and fell thirty-five feet to the ground, then no."

The two women across from me smile with the quiet confidence of the utterly victorious. They know I have nothing on Bex, and I know it too. But I hate being wrong almost as much as I hate Napa, so I grasp at whatever straws remain and hope for the best. "When you left at ten thirty, did you take Katherine with you, or did you leave her at the party?"

"She wanted to stay, so I said goodbye, and that's the last I saw of her."

"Fine. We'll take a look at those Ring videos, but before you go, do you have an alibi for the night of September seventh?"

"As a matter of fact, she does," says Kapur as she forwards a quick email on her iPhone. "I just sent you an invoice from the Mayo Clinic in Minnesota. It has all the relevant contact information as well as the dates my client spent there receiving a cycle of intravenous medicine for her leukemia, which recurred earlier in the summer."

"August twelfth through September tenth," Bex says in a surprisingly calm manner, given the gravity of what she went through. "It was a twenty-eight-day cycle of this drug called Blincyto. Which is also why I went home early the night Katherine died. Sometimes I still get hit with fatigue from the treatment, so I went straight to bed."

A devastating silence fills the room, like some toxic air that only I'm affected by. The sheriff seems relieved that he won't have to arrest an associate of Holly Bancroft, and the other two wait patiently, and confidently, for me to accept my inevitable defeat. After a long, painful few seconds that feel more like an hour, I rise up out of my chair. "I'm sorry about the recurrence," I tell Bex, and I mean it too. My mom died of cancer after three years in remission, and I'll always be sympathetic to people who have to go through that sort of thing. "You're free to go."

"Thank you, Agent Burrell," Bex says. "It's been fun." Then she follows Sheriff McKee and her lawyer out of the ten-by-ten box that has just become my very own concrete hell.

19

Sometimes I really wish I smoked cigarettes.

I've been sitting on a bench outside the Sheriff's Department for the better part of an hour with nothing to do but watch the occasional private jet take off at Napa County Airport just a couple blocks away. How nice would it be if I were on one of those right now? Sipping a beer at thirty thousand feet while pumping the same amount of carbon into the atmosphere as twenty poor suckers eating stale pretzels in the back of a Southwest flight? There's something so appealing about being one of those people who manage to live their lives without considering the consequences. The unabashed doers. The fearlessly forward-facing. I bet none of them are on Lexapro, and I'm sure they wouldn't hesitate to bum a Marlboro Light from one of the endless parade of cops who use this area as their smoking patio. But of course when I catch a whiff of their secondhand smoke, all I can think about is my mom on her third round of chemo, bald as the babies in the NICU one floor up, and I'm hit with a wave of crippling nausea. Because I'm not an unabashed doer; I don't face forward into the infinite future. I'm stuck in a past that won't let me go, no matter how hard I try to shake it loose, and I can't even have a cigarette to help ease the burden, if only for a few blissful minutes.

I wonder where the nearest bar is . . .

But when I pull out my phone to check on Google Maps, I notice the time, 2:44 PM, and I stifle the urge to sit in the dark somewhere with an overpriced Heineken—or, God forbid, another glass of wine. There's simply too much to do, and I need to keep a clear head if I'm ever going to crack this case. So I shove the phone back into my pocket; gaze out at the oddly situated vineyard across the street, sandwiched right in between two massive warehouses; and consider the facts.

Bex Potter may be strange, but she's not the killer I'm after. The video from her Ring camera checked out, as did the timing of her monthlong stay at the Mayo Clinic. Which means someone else from her so-called "organization" must have murdered Katherine O'Shea. The drugs in her system were almost certainly administered at the full moon party—these people leave LSD sitting out like bar nuts, and the pentobarbital would have been easy enough to slip her via syringe once she was tripping. Plus the soil samples under her fingernails make it pretty obvious that she was dragged away from the house at Redwood Vale. Clearly, I need to get a forensics team up there to scour the woods for evidence, and it's also time to get a judge involved with searching the farmhouse. Even with Peter Bancroft's permission, I don't want any more highly paid lawyers poking holes in my legal right to be there, so this time I'm getting a search warrant. There's certainly enough evidence to issue one now that we have Bex Potter's testimony.

And what about Carlos Ruiz? How does he fit into all this? He spent three months as my father's cellmate in San Quentin, during which time he wouldn't stop asking about Jessica Bancroft. Then he mysteriously vanished, courtesy of a call from the state capital, and reappeared in Napa several years later, working as a driver at the same company that employed Pilar Cruz when she was murdered.

On top of that, he somehow knew I'd be coming to the Valley to investigate, since he tailed me back to my motel after I'd only been here for eight hours. It's all too intertwined to be coincidental; clearly, he's connected to whatever's going on. But if that's the case, do the Cruz and O'Shea murders have something to do with what happened to Jess? It seems almost unfathomable given how many years have passed since she vanished, but they never did find her body. What if something similar was done to it? What if she was drugged and murdered too, buried somewhere with a slaughtered squirrel? Why else would Ruiz have asked so many questions about her when he was locked up with my dad?

My head starts spinning with possibilities, a silk web of interconnected secrets and lies built up all around me, but no matter how hard I try, I can't see the spider lurking at its center. I need to slow down, take this one step at a time, and focus on Redwood Vale. I can't let my emotional attachment to the Jessica Bancroft case jeopardize the job I was sent here to do. But just as I'm about to head back inside the station, I look up and see a familiar cowboy hat blocking out the afternoon sun.

"You doin' all right?" McKee asks in an oddly sympathetic tone.

"We need to send a forensics team up to Redwood Vale. And I want to get a search warrant before we go back inside that farmhouse."

"Agreed," he says, plopping his tired body down beside me. "Hope you don't mind if I already put in a request for the warrant."

"You did?"

He nods. "Also sent Leroux up that way with forensics twenty minutes ago."

I look over at the sheriff, surprised by his apparent commitment to actual police work, but his world-weary eyes are facing outward, avoiding me. And he keeps them that way as he continues to talk, never once making eye contact. "Lana, I know how you must feel about me, and I'm not gonna try and explain myself, 'cause I know it's too late for all that. But if we're gonna work together and actually get this one right, we're gonna have to trust each other. Now I'm telling you, right here, right now . . . I trust you. I may have had my doubts, but that's why I put Leroux on the case. She was my neighbor for thirty years before she went and got herself a badge, and I trust her more than any man in my department. So when she tells me you've got the stuff, well, I know you've got the stuff. So I'm sorry if I didn't exactly greet you with open arms the other day, but now, if you're willing, I'd love to start fresh, because believe it or not, I really do want to find out who killed these girls."

As his voice trails off, he turns ever so slightly to glance in my direction. I see an earnestness in his eyes that I don't recall being there twenty years ago. "What do you mean *'actually'* get this one right?"

"Hmm?"

"You said we need to work together if we're *actually* gonna get this one right, which kinda makes it sound like you *didn't* get it right last time." He sits there for a moment, rubbing his tongue against his upper teeth as he stews over what to say, and I can tell this isn't a man with a clean conscience. "Do you think my dad was innocent?"

"I honestly don't know," he says sheepishly. "Given the evidence and eyewitness accounts we had, he sure as hell looked guilty. I mean, we found the girl's blood in the trunk of his car. DNA fragments under half his fingernails. And no alibi between the hours of ten PM and six AM. But a guy as smart as your dad—you'd think he'd have known to cover his tracks better if he was gonna move a body like that. At least throw a little bleach in his car."

"That's what I said twenty years ago!"

"I know," he says, filled with genuine remorse. "The more time I had to think about it, the more I started to wonder if *anything* was real in that case. The evidence, the testimony . . ."

"You think someone lied?"

McKee shrugs. "I think Holly Bancroft's story changed enough times over the course of that investigation to suggest she may have been hiding something."

"Then why'd you still charge him?"

"Lana, we were dealing with the high-profile disappearance of a prominent young woman from a very powerful family. And I wasn't sheriff yet. I was just a deputy following orders, like Leroux is now. And at the time, I really did think your father did it. But these days—the more I see from the Bancrofts, what they're capable of—the more I think there was maybe something else going on."

It's a surreal experience, hearing yourself validated by the man you once blamed for nearly all your pain and trauma. McKee's words are like a drug, slowly filling my veins with a heavy dose of profound relief, and now that he's finished, I'm left completely numb. My head feels as if it's floating, drifting carelessly through the clouds, while my feet feel like they weigh a thousand pounds and I'll never be able to move from this bench again. After several deep breaths, I wipe away a tear that I didn't even realize had fallen, and I thank McKee for saying that. Even if nothing comes of it, even if his doubts are unwarranted and my father really *is* guilty, it means so much to hear that I'm not alone in my struggle.

As our conversation ends, he pulls himself to his feet with the achy groan of an over-sixty-year-old back and knees, then offers a hand to pull me up with him. I take it, surprising myself; although perhaps after today I shouldn't be surprised by anything. "Go back to your motel," he says with a firm, paternal kindness. "Take a shower, get some rest, have a hot meal, and let forensics do their thing. By morning I should have a search warrant, so you can start fresh then. All right?"

"I appreciate the concern, Sheriff, but I'm really not a 'sit around and wait' kinda girl." I give him a grateful smile and start past him toward the parking lot.

"Where are you going then?" he shouts.

"To find my stalker . . . before he finds me."

* * *

Over the next several hours, I learn everything there is to know about Carlos Ruiz. I run a background check on the FBI's database. I call in favors with local law enforcement and corrections officers who dealt with him at Folsom and San Quentin. I even call up his mother at her home in Vacaville. But what I learn leaves me more confused than ever about his possible ties to the Bancrofts.

Carlos Ignacio Ruiz was born in Vacaville in the early '90s, and according to his mom, he was a good kid. Always did well in school, wouldn't hurt a fly, and was on his way to a successful career, just like his big brother, an ER doctor in Los Angeles. But around twelve or thirteen, the trouble started. He began acting out in class, and at one point he was suspended for showing his penis to a girl on the school bus. Eventually, his parents found out he'd been molested by their parish priest, and it seemed to have messed with his adolescent mind in a way he never quite recovered from. Sex and power, abuse and affection all got jumbled up in his brain in a way that required extensive therapy—therapy he never got. And Carlos's troubles only worsened from there, reaching a tipping point when, at nineteen, he was arrested for trying to rape a female student at Napa Valley College. He was given a ten-year sentence, most of which was spent at Folsom State Prison, with the exception of those three months bunking with my father in San Quentin. No explanation for his transfer is mentioned anywhere in his record. Two months ago, he was released on good behavior and—per the requirements of his parole—took a part-time job with Valley Farming Services. But he stopped coming to work and disappeared from his apartment three days ago, breaking his parole, which means the US Marshals are looking for him just as avidly as I am.

Nothing about Ruiz's record suggests a connection to any of the Valley's power players, the sort of people who may have pulled strings to get him locked up with my dad in the hopes of learning something about Jess. In between school suspensions and sex crimes, he worked at a Best Buy in Fairfield and an In-N-Out Burger in Vacaville, and as far as I can tell, he never even showed up in Napa until his attempted rape.

But then a name catches my eye on one of his court documents: *Judge Abigail R. Cox.* She presided over his trial and sentencing back in 2017 during a brief stint in the Criminal Division at the Napa County Superior Court. But I know that name from somewhere else—multiple places, actually. Not only was she the assistant district attorney during my father's trial back in 2003; in 2022, she presided as judge over the civil suit Peter Bancroft filed against his cousin. In both cases, she made decisions that clearly benefited Holly Bancroft, even going so far as to redact any public mention of her "unusual activities" at Redwood Vale.

Could Abigail Cox be in the Mystica Aeterna? One of the powerful political figures Peter Bancroft alluded to? And if she is a part of Holly's cult, could she have been the one who connected her to Carlos Ruiz?

J. T. Falco

It's currently 3:43 PM, and according to the receptionist at the Superior Court, Judge Cox likes to dismiss her courtroom for the day at 4:00 PM sharp. I break every speed limit I can on the drive over, somehow managing to call Deputy Leroux on the way without killing any pedestrians, then squeal into the parking lot right at 3:59 PM.

20

The woman who argued the bogus case against my father is a chic fifty-two-year-old with short red hair and a Kundalini yoga class in half an hour, so she asks me to walk with her from her chambers to her car. The studio is up the road in Yountville, and she doesn't want to be late. Of course, Abigail R. Cox has no clue about my unique connection to Clifford Burrell, who she once called a murderous madman in a public courtroom, and simply thinks I'm here on regular FBI business, but I still find her impertinence deeply offensive.

"Remind me what case this is about," she says with an absent-minded glance down at an email on her phone as we shuffle through a private back hallway.

"Well," I tell her, "it's really about a few cases, but I guess we could start with one you tried almost ten years ago. An attempted rape involving a man named Carlos Ruiz."

If she recognizes the name, she does a good job pretending otherwise; such is the benefit of staring at a phone while we walk instead of making eye contact. "Doesn't ring a bell. Is he a suspect in one of your investigations?"

"Not exactly..."

"Okay, then how can I be of service, Agent Burrell?" I can see her patience with me is wearing thin; I find it oddly satisfying.

"Well, in late 2020, he was transferred from Folsom over to San Quentin and placed in a cell along with another man you might recall from your days as a prosecutor: Clifford Burrell."

Her eyes shift with recognition, and for the first time, she slows her gait. "Burrell, as in . . ."

"My father."

"I see."

We stop at the base of a small staircase leading out the back door of the courthouse. Abigail Cox leans against the railing, gripping it like a stress ball as she considers the most legally savvy approach to escaping the trap in which she's found herself. Meanwhile, I wait two stairs above her, allowing me to look down and cast judgment on this judge who is far more accustomed to being in my position, watching the world from an elevated bench.

"Judge Cox, did you use your connections in the state prison system to get Ruiz transferred so that he could ask my father about Jessica Bancroft?"

"That is a ridiculous accusation," she snaps with self-righteous indignation, how dare anyone fling mud on her pristine hands. "Now if you'll excuse me, I've got a class to get to." I watch her shuffle off into the parking lot, resuming her rapid clip from earlier. She simultaneously begins rooting through her bulky designer purse for her car keys.

"I know Holly Bancroft asked you to do it, and as a member of the same *organization*, you must have felt obligated, right?"

She fumbles her keys and drops them on the pavement right outside a black Porsche crossover SUV with vanity plates that read JUDGEABS. She scoops them up without ever looking back at me, then in one fluid motion, she unlocks the car, slips inside, and drives away without bothering to fasten her seatbelt.

Part One down, I think to myself with a satisfied grin from my post on the staircase. Now I just need to hope Leroux got there in time to handle her end of things.

* * *

Ten minutes later, I'm driving north on 29 when a phone call comes in over my Bluetooth speaker.

"Did she call?"

"You were right," says Leroux. "At 4:12 PM, Holly got a call from someone, and she was *not* happy. I couldn't get close enough to hear what she was saying, but there sure was a lot of yelling. Then as soon as she hung up, she made another call. It only lasted about thirty seconds, but she was facing the other way by then so I couldn't get a handle on her mood from where I was standing." I smack the steering wheel with excitement and let out a laugh. "Hey boss, are you sure all this is legal?"

"Did you stay in the parking lot?"

"Yeah."

"Then you didn't do anything wrong, Essie. We can't tap her phone without a search warrant, which we'll never get given how little we have on her at this point. But we don't need to know *what* she said; we just need to know *who* she said it to. And now we've got enough evidence to subpoena her phone records. I'll bet you anything that second call she made was to Carlos Ruiz."

"What about Judge Cox?" she asks. "Can we go after her for this?"

"That's a can of worms we don't need to bother opening. A judge like that can really start to mess with our case and our careers if she feels threatened, so our best bet is to leave her out of it now that we've got everything we need from her."

"If you say so, Boss."

"Good work, Deputy."

Buzzing with excitement, with long-sought answers almost within my grasp, I hang up and promptly call a judge I'm friendly with on the Circuit Court for the Northern District of California. We worked together on my last case, the investigation of a fentanyl network out of Hayward that went bust after my informant was killed, and he owes me a favor. The fact is, I never wanted to put a wire on that kid. He was a sweet guy, but he was too unreliable with his drug habit. He needed help, he needed rehab; what he didn't need was a bunch of federal officers exploiting him and his problems to go after a high-profile target. But it hadn't been my task force to manage—I was just one cog in a much bigger machine—and when I voiced my concerns, it was Judge Mitchell Evans of the Northern District who finally swayed me. I liked Mitch. He wasn't one of these Harvard or Yale guys with Supreme Court ambitions. He went to UCLA, his parents were public school teachers, and I got the sense he was in this for the same reason I was, to restore some semblance of justice to an unjust system. So when he told me it was worth it to bring down the biggest fentanyl distributor in the East Bay, given the hundreds of overdose deaths we'd be stopping, I trusted him. And when my informant slipped up and I saw him in a pool of his own blood that awful morning, Mitch was the first person up the chain to call me and apologize. "This one's on me," he said. "Anything I can do to help, I'm here."

I don't think either of us expected me to be cashing in those chips four days later on an entirely separate case, but a deal's a deal. And after I give him a rough outline of the murder investigation and Holly Bancroft's possible role in it, he agrees to issue the subpoena for her phone records. He's got meetings until seven, but as soon as he's done, he'll file the necessary paperwork, and I should have my records by midday tomorrow.

I check the clock on my dashboard: 4:37 PM. Less than an hour ago, I made the connection between Carlos Ruiz and Abigail Cox. Now I've already got a subpoena in the works for Holly Bancroft's cell phone records, which should formally connect her to Ruiz and point me toward where he's been hiding out. Not bad for about fifty minutes of work.

This calls for a celebration, and I know just the floppy haired, sexually adept winemaker who I'd like to do it with. While I certainly wouldn't admit this to Caleb Roche, the truth is, it's been years since I've had this kind of instant connection with someone. That easygoing rapport which makes a first date feel as natural and safe as a four-hundredth. And the fact that his tongue is proficient at more than just tasting wine doesn't hurt either. I'm also oddly comforted by the knowledge that my stay in Napa Valley has a built-in clock; as soon as the case is over, there's nothing stopping me from disappearing back across the San Francisco Bay, never to be heard from again. Somehow, knowing that I have this escape hatch makes me far more willing to take an emotional risk with him, the sort of reckless leap I wouldn't dare take with just anyone. Even if things fall apart and we realize we're terrible together, all it'll really cost me is the $8.40 toll to cross back over the Golden Gate Bridge.

When I finally get back to my room at the Silverado Inn, I make a beeline toward the dresser where Caleb left his business card earlier this morning. But when I pick it up to look for his number, my heart stops beating. I feel a sharp pain in my chest, and my lungs stop pumping out air; it's the initial stages of a panic attack, but I've had them before and I know how to fight through them, so I pinch the palm on my left hand with my right thumb and middle finger. I dig in as deep as I can with my brittle, half-chewed fingernails until the pain is so intense that it's all my brain can focus on. And just like that, the panic attack stops. My heart resumes beating, my lungs go back to pumping air, and my eyes drift down to the business card that started this whole mess in the first place.

At the top, in embossed black print, are the words "Wappo Crest Winery" and that same abstract salmon logo I admired on the bottle back in San Francisco. At the bottom, along with a business address, there are two names and two phone numbers, both listed as "Proprietors." The first is Caleb Roche.

The second is Jonah Bancroft.

21

This was a huge mistake, I tell myself. But at this point, I can't turn around and run. Someone will see me, and then I'll feel even more foolish than I already do. So I just keep knocking at the unmarked, sheet metal door to this small winemaking facility in a corner of Calistoga that I didn't even know existed. The place looks more like an old moonshiner's shed in the hills of Tennessee than it does a professional business churning out delicious bottles of cabernet sauvignon, but this is where the address on the back of the business card led me. So I knock and knock and knock until finally I hear footsteps inside.

The door slides open with a heavy metal rumble, and I'm soon greeted by the utterly confused face of my high school boyfriend. "Lana?"

"Is Caleb here?"

"Yeah, he's—wait, how do you know Caleb?"

"We had sex fourteen hours ago."

Jonah Bancroft is too startled to respond, so I push right past him and invite myself into Wappo Crest Winery, which looks to be a cross between a hipster microbrewery and an old meatpacking plant. Actually, I'm fairly certain it *was* a slaughterhouse at some point, given the strange hooks hanging down from the ceiling, but it's been converted over to a small crush and fermentation facility by its new owners. All the tanks and machinery have a clean, metallic sparkle that suggests they're relatively new arrivals, at least compared to the rusted sheet metal on the walls and doors. And along one wall, which I presume was the old refrigeration unit for the butchered meat, a wide doorway leads into a cramped alcove filled with wine-stained oak barrels. I find the whole place to be surprisingly creepy, and it doesn't help that the air smells like yeast and spoiled fruit.

I hear Jonah mutter something behind me, but I'm already on the move around one of the tanks and in no mood to ask him to repeat himself. "Caleb?" I call out. "You back there?"

Sure enough, that adorable head of floppy hair pops out from behind a machine and gives me a delighted smile. "Secret Agent Lady!" he shouts, then he hurries over in red-stained gloves and a splattered leather apron. For a moment, I'm taken aback, worried he's been wounded, but then I realize that what's covering his arms and hands isn't blood—it's grape pomace, the thick reddish-purple stew of skins and seeds left over from crush and the initial round of fermentation.

"Why didn't you tell me your business partner was *Jonah*?"

"You two know each other?"

"YES!" Jonah and I shout simultaneously, then he quickly proceeds to ask Caleb and me where we met.

I sigh and rub my eyes with embarrassment, deeply regretting coming here. "At a bar last night in St. Helena."

"And you're already fucking?"

There's a hint of jealousy in Jonah's voice that I can't help but find satisfying, especially since I felt the exact same way when I saw him with a wife and kids a few nights earlier. "We're not *fucking*," I tell him. "We just . . . fucked. Once."

"So far," adds Caleb, giving me a suggestive smile. "But hold up, you're not the girl from high school, are you? The one that broke this poor guy's heart?"

I look over to Jonah, who turns toward Caleb and nods.

"Holy shit," Caleb says as he connects the stories he's heard with the woman he knows. "Now it all makes sense."

"What makes sense?" I ask.

"Why he had to *Eat, Pray, Love* his way around the world after you broke up with him."

"I didn't *Eat, Pray, Love*," Jonah says sheepishly. "I was apprenticing at other vineyards."

"Sure, buddy," Caleb says with a wink. "You keep telling yourself that."

"I'm sorry," I interrupt, "can someone please tell me how you two ended up starting a winery together?"

"Totally," Caleb says. "But first, do you mind if I go wash off? I look like I just delivered a baby animal."

* * *

With Caleb scrubbed clean of all that wine must and pomace, I join the two business partners and—as fate would have it—best friends for a glass of chilled Chablis on their back patio. The views of their small vineyard, looking out over the northernmost point of the Valley, are stunning, especially as the sun begins to set over some golden yellow sycamores to our left. And the saline crispness of the white wine is a perfect complement to the unseasonably warm autumn air, even if I still would have preferred an ice-cold Heineken.

"2020 was an intense year," Jonah says, launching into his story on a grim note. "There was the pandemic, the lockdowns, and then, just when you thought it couldn't get any worse, the Glass Fire hit in late September. Burned almost seventy thousand acres, and even the grapes that didn't burn were hardly usable, so full of smoke taint. I already told you how things were going with my mom. It was just . . . unsustainable. I needed something new. A fresh start. And that's when I ran into *this* guy."

"We'd known each other for a few years," Caleb says, picking up the narrative. "We moved in the same circles, had a lot of the same friends, and I'd just harvested my first crop of cab. But with all the smoke in the air that fall, my wine was undrinkable. It tasted like the water someone had left a bunch of old cigarette butts in, so I knew I couldn't sell it. But I'd sunk everything into that crop. I wasn't going to have enough cash to get me through another vintage unless I brought on a partner who had money, but I didn't want some random investor to leech onto my dream and force me to compromise for the sake of a quick return. I wanted someone who loved the land and the wine just as much as I did. Someone who was in it for the long haul."

"It was fate," Jonah says. "I needed a vineyard, he needed money, and we both needed a friend. We pretty much haven't spent a day apart since."

I look over at them and can't help but smile. It's unusual to see guys their age who so unabashedly love each other that they aren't afraid to be open with their profound friendship. And as I watch them together, it's clear that these two simply aren't encumbered by that awful machismo that often stands in the way of real affection between male friends. It's a beautiful thing to witness, and if anything, it makes me feel better about myself and my taste in men. If I had to fall for two best friends at two different stages in my life, I'm glad it was them, and I decide that I'm not going to let my past with Jonah get in the way of my future with Caleb. *If anything, I kind of want to fuck him even more right now . . .*

But alas, a text message from Essie interrupts my plans for another night of spine-tingling sex.

We found something up at Redwood Vale. Thought you should see it right away. Mind if I text a photo?—Essie

Go ahead, I text back, and a few seconds later, I receive a grainy photograph. There's a bit of Leroux's finger covering the bottom right corner of the frame, but I can still make out the crumpled white handkerchief splattered with what looks to be dark red blood. Monogrammed in one corner are the initials, "C.R."

Lab is going to run the blood and prints tonight. But the C.R. made me think of Carlos Ruiz. Think this is enough to put out an A.P.B.?—Essie

Go for it, I text back, but my mind is elsewhere. In fact, it's about three feet away, where another man with the initials "C.R." is smiling at me over a glass of Chablis.

"I'm sorry," I tell the boys, "but I've got to go. It's a work thing." And I scramble to my feet before the words have even left my mouth.

"I can walk you out," Caleb says.

"No, no—it's all right," I stammer. "You guys, uh, you do your thing. But I'll give you a call tomorrow. I promise." Then I hurry through the nearest door, back into the fermentation room, where I'm hit with the overpowering smell of yeast and rot. The nausea comes on fast and furious, and I know there's no point in fighting it, so I grab onto the nearest trash can and vomit out any hopes I once had of a fun, worry-free night in bed with Caleb Roche.

22

Deputy Leroux greets me as I hop out of my car at the Bancroft's farmhouse, tucked away in Redwood Vale. The place looks markedly different tonight, with so many white forensic tents and vans filling the main driveway, and even the woods have lost their mystery thanks to several blinding searchlights that illuminate the grounds in every direction. "There was only one set of fingerprints on the handkerchief," she says as we shake hands. "They were a match for Katherine O'Shea's."

"And the blood?"

"Lab says they need forty-eight hours to be sure, but they don't actually think it's blood."

"What?"

"Working theory right now is that it's grape must, which is—"

"I know what grape must is, Essie. I actually just saw some."

She looks disappointed, as if she'd had a whole speech prepared, some Merriam-Webster definition that was going to knock my socks off, as she might say. And I immediately feel bad for jumping in like that, for not being a better mentor to my geriatric pupil.

"I'm sorry, I didn't mean to cut you off," I tell her. "I'm just excited."

"Water under the bridge, Boss."

"Have you found anything else?"

"Some scratch marks where we think she dragged her hands through the dirt—"

"What about footprints?" I ask.

"Problem is there's just too many of 'em. We've already found twenty different sets of prints out there, and those are just the human ones. There are also racoons, deer, squirrels . . ."

I desperately want to cut her off, since a rogue squirrel isn't exactly high up on my list of suspects, but she just looks so damn excited, reading off facts from her trusty notebook, my little straight-A student in bifocals. So I bite my tongue, keep on smiling, and wait for her to finish.

". . . rabbits, possums, coyotes, and even one bobcat. Most likely a female."

"Is that right?" I ask, as if this is the most interesting thing I've heard all night.

"Smaller paw prints," she replies, dead serious.

When she finally shuts her notebook, I thank Leroux and send her off to check in with the search party while I make the rounds of the various forensic tents, but there's nothing new to report. I'm about to head off into the woods to join the search when I notice two headlights pulling into the driveway with a strange urgency. My hand instinctively creeps down to the side of my waist, where my Glock hangs from a latched holster, but I soon realize I won't need it. The tan cowboy hat on the driver could only belong to one person, at least in this part of California.

"What is it?" I ask Sheriff McKee as I hurry past the tents to greet him.

"Good news," he says, holding up a carefully folded piece of paper. "We have our warrant."

* * *

The search of the farmhouse takes all night, thanks in large part to the forensic team's insistence that we all wear slippery paper booties over our shoes to avoid contaminating any footprints. I nearly take three or four tumbles, including what would have been one particularly nasty spill on the basement stairs, but in the end we find several interesting pieces of evidence.

There's a cabinet full of mason jars containing the same kind of gummy candies that I managed to swipe a few of two nights earlier. The tests on my three samples actually came back a couple of hours ago—as expected, MDMA, LSD, and psilocybin. But given the questionable legality of my previous search, this new discovery could prove helpful in court, should the need arise. As for the pentobarbital found in the blood of Cruz and O'Shea, that part of the story remains a mystery.

Scattered throughout the house, we find several large knives, any of which could have been used to kill the two victims, given the wide lacerations across their stomachs. All of them are sent in for testing, but one in particular, a long, curved blade known as a cimeter knife, sparks my interest. I find it wrapped in a dish towel, tucked in the back corner of a closet in one of the upstairs bedrooms, and while there's no obvious blood or tissue in evidence, someone clearly went to great lengths to stash it.

Then there's the literature. The basement where I witnessed the strange branding ceremony has been scrubbed clean of any foul play; we can't even find the metal rod Bex Potter used to brand her boyfriend. But an anteroom that's only accessible by pushing aside an old cabinet reveals a bounty of musty tomes and handwritten notebooks. Given what I've learned so far about this strange group, much of the reading material is hardly a surprise. There are the complete works of Rudolf Steiner, including many first editions and writings that I don't recall from my earlier research. There are strange gospel-looking texts by Aleister Crowley and other so-called magic practitioners from the late nineteenth and early twentieth centuries. There are numerous histories of the Greek god Dionysus and the mystery cults that bore his name in the centuries before the Common Era. But one book in particular draws my attention. It's sitting open on a reading table, with all the reverence of a Bible left on a lectern at church. From what I can gather, it's an English reprinting of an old German manifesto, and its title gives me the chills: *The Chymical Wedding of Christian Rosenkreutz*. Of course the name itself means nothing to me, but it's the titular character's initials that leave me on edge: another "C.R."

Carlos Ruiz. Caleb Roche. And now Christian Rosenkreutz. The monogrammed handkerchief could be a reference to any of them, but at least statistically, this new discovery lowers the odds that the man I slept with last night was somehow involved in Katherine O'Shea's murder—so that's got to count for something.

We scour the small library for the better part of an hour, but the things I'd hoped to discover—a list of members, perhaps, or a set of bylaws for the secret club—are nowhere to be found. All in all, the search of the farmhouse proves somewhat disappointing, at least until we get more information back from the lab, and I'm considering calling it a night. After all, it *is* four o'clock in the morning, and I haven't exactly slept well since arriving in the Valley.

As I make my way back upstairs, through the house, and onto the front porch, I notice a flurry of excited activity. Hazmat-suited technicians and uniformed police are running through the woods, all in the same direction. A massive searchlight is being reoriented to get a better look at a new section of the property, and I can hear shouting in the distance. Just like that, all ambitions of a decent night's sleep vanish, and I race through the woods toward the source of the commotion.

A group of cops and forensic analysts have formed a tight circle around something on the ground, all of them eager to get a look at whatever it is that's been discovered. I begin to hear rumblings about human remains, and I push through the crowd to get a look myself. Finally I reach the front, where a spotlight has been pointed down on some freshly overturned dirt beside a particularly thick redwood. In a hole about three feet deep lies a perfectly intact human skeleton, its bones browned and weathered by the passage of time. Of course I know we'll have to wait on DNA testing to find out the truth, but I can feel it in my heart already:

It's Jessica Bancroft. It *has* to be.

23

"You need to reopen Jess's case," I tell McKee once we're back in his drab office at the Napa County Sheriff's Department.

It's six o'clock in the morning, and neither of us has slept a wink. I'm running on nothing but adrenaline and sugary coffee, but I swear that's not the cause of my jitters. I've been trembling with anticipation ever since I saw those bones in the ground at Redwood Vale.

"We don't even know if it's her," McKee says, trying to remain calm.

"Who else could it be?"

"Any number of missing persons—"

"Forensics said it's definitely a woman somewhere between the ages of fourteen and forty. Sounds a helluva lot like Jess to me."

"Lana," Sheriff McKee says, "I want this to be her just as much as you do. Believe me. But you're not being rational right now, and you know it. We need to wait for DNA results before we say a word about this to anyone."

As much as it infuriates me, I know he's right, so I let out a primal groan and give him a begrudging nod. The truth is, I'm not myself right now. Between the lack of sleep, the whole Jonah/

Caleb sex triangle, and the scarred rapist who may very well be trying to kill me, I've been under far more pressure than my mind and body are accustomed to. I need to regroup and get some actual rest; otherwise, I can't trust myself to make reasonable decisions—especially not if that really was Jessica Bancroft in a shallow grave. So I tell the sheriff to keep me in the loop, and then I head back to the Silverado Inn to get some sorely needed shut-eye.

* * *

I sleep for nine straight hours.

When my eyes finally peel open, I forget where I am, and for a few precious moments, I think I'm back in my comfortable queen bed, safely ensconced in my rent-controlled apartment where the name "Bancroft" hasn't been spoken in—well, ever. But then I look up at the motel ceiling fan, dusty black whirling over off-white stucco, and I instantly remember everything. Without bothering to turn my neck, I reach my hand out toward my phone, smoothly pop it off the charger, and place the screen directly over my groggy eyes.

Eight missed calls.

"What the fuck?"

I bolt upright, pressing my back up against the headboard, and unlock the phone to see what the hell I've slept through. Two calls are from Deputy Leroux. Two are from Sheriff McKee. One is from Jonah. One is from Caleb. One is from Peter Bancroft. And one is from Connie Chen.

Eager to start getting answers, I leap out of bed and rip some clothes out of my still-unpacked suitcase, not caring which since they all look the same anyway. I'm starting to run low, having only packed for five days, but that's the least of my worries right now, given all the results we're waiting on from the forensics lab.

So as I hop around the room, trying to tug a pair of dirty black jeans over my thighs, I put my phone on speaker and call the SAC.

She answers on the first ring, never a good sign. "Why are Holly Bancroft's telephone records sitting on my desk?"

"The subpoena went through?"

"Apparently it did," she says, far less enthused than I am at the moment. In fact, she kind of sounds like she wants to reach through the phone and slap me. "Do you mind telling me what the hell's going on, Lana?"

"Sure, just do me a favor first and tell me who Holly called around 4:12 PM yesterday. It should be an outgoing call, around thirty seconds long, right after an incoming call from a judge named Abigail Cox."

I hear a frustrated sigh on the other end of the line, then the soft flutter of freshly printed paper. Connie Chen rarely gets upset with me, but when she does, it manifests as a disappointed silence rather than a verbal rage, and I know by the way she's holding back her response that she's mad about something. But what? It's not like I'm expected to fill her in on every single move and decision I make over the course of an investigation; sometimes I need to be nimble and move quickly to get results, and she knows that. So why the silent treatment?

"Did I do something wrong?"

"Lana," she says quietly and with profound concern, "please tell me you're not looking at Teddy Mason for these killings."

At this, I let out an uncontrolled burst of laughter, too shocked to even pretend to rein it in. "What? No, I'm obviously not targeting the *governor* of California. I'm just trying to establish a connection between Holly and a parolee named Carlos Ruiz."

"Well, I hate to break it to you, but there's no Ruiz in these phone records."

"What?'

"There's no Ruiz on this list."

Suddenly, I feel like a derailed train, wheels spinning, desperately trying to get back on a track that's no longer anywhere in sight. "Then who'd she call yesterday at 4:12?"

"I just told you," my boss says, increasingly exasperated by my apparent confusion. "She called Governor Mason. Now what the hell is going on up there?"

* * *

Even after I spend another twenty minutes talking the SAC through the latest moves in my case, the shock of Mason's name still doesn't wear off. I pace the length of my shabby motel room, navigating around stacks of clothes and discarded bath towels, trying to make sense of this latest wrinkle. My ploy with Judge Cox was supposed to frustrate Holly enough that she'd call Carlos Ruiz and either tell him to back off or give him some other new instructions for how to deal with me. Because the assumption was, if Cox had ordered Ruiz's transfer into my dad's cell as a favor to Holly, then Holly *must* be the one who got him to tail me on Saturday. It's the only scenario that makes any sense. What *doesn't* make sense is being so alarmed by my interest in Ruiz that she'd immediately call the governor of California.

Unless *he's* somehow caught up in all this too.

But how? Sure, Teddy Mason and Holly Bancroft are old friends, having grown up together in prominent Napa Valley wine families, but he's a little too busy leading the biggest state in the country to run around killing random women every time there's a full moon.

Right?

My head hurts just thinking about it, partly from Caleb and Jonah's Chablis, but largely because of the SAC's warning not to follow up on this lead under any circumstance. The political ramifications of tying a sitting governor to a murder investigation are enough to get our entire unit shut down and both of us reassigned to the Anchorage field office. So I temporarily push this strange new connection aside and get back to the long list of phone calls that need returning. Next up: Sheriff Angus McKee.

Like Chen, he answers midway through the first ring, as if he'd been staring at his phone, waiting for me all afternoon. "Looks like you finally got some sleep."

"Right," I tell him absent-mindedly, still stuck on the information about Governor Mason. "What, uh—what did I miss?"

"Do you want the good news or the bad news?"

"I hate it when people say that."

McKee chuckles softly. "All right, well then I'm starting with the bad news."

"Fine."

"That wasn't Jessica Bancroft."

"*What?*"

"The remains we found last night—they aren't hers."

My heart sinks, and I start to feel lightheaded. I take a seat on the edge of the bed, with my jeans still unbuttoned, trying to process what I've just heard. "Lana, I'm sorry," he says. "I know how much you had riding on this—"

"How can they possibly know already? DNA won't come back for at least two more days."

"That's true," McKee says. "We're still waiting on DNA. But they also did carbon dating."

"Why?" I ask dismissively. "That's useless on a body that died so recently."

"It is. Unless that person was born in the 1950s or '60s."

My forensic lessons at Quantico come rattling back through my foggy memory. This is hardly my area of expertise, but I vaguely remember something about the effects of Cold War–era nuclear testing on human remains. "You mean because there was a temporary spike in radioactive carbon molecules in the air when the United States and Russia were doing all those nuclear tests."

"That's right," says McKee, impressed. "I just learned about it a few hours ago, but apparently people whose teeth were forming during that period have double the amount of carbon-14 in their enamel. Then by the 1970s, those numbers dropped back down to normal."

"Jess was born in '86."

"Right," says McKee. "Which is how we were able to rule her out. We still don't know when this woman died, but we do know she'd be in her sixties or seventies if she were alive today."

All my hope of solving Jess's murder and proving my father's innocence comes fizzling out of me like the air from a slowly deflating tire. I didn't realize just how excited I'd been by this possibility until it was taken away from me; now, with it gone for good, I feel that same black cloud overhead that has followed me everywhere since my dad's arrest. It's like Jess has vanished all over again, and my dad is back to square one, starting a brand-new life sentence in some godforsaken prison. *Ugh, I wish I'd never ever even seen that skeleton last night . . .*

"Want to hear the good news?"

At the moment, I don't. The traumatized child in me would much rather wallow in my own depression a little longer, but the medicated adult knows the futility of those impulses, so I rise up off the bed and continue getting dressed. "Sure," I tell the sheriff as I pull one of my usual gray shirts over one of my usual black sports bras.

"The man in your basement video checked into Queen of the Valley Medical Center this morning with third-degree burns and a nasty infection."

"Are you serious?"

"Yup. And once they got his fever down and stabilized him, he told a nurse that he wanted to speak with Special Agent Lana Burrell of the FBI."

McKee falls silent, letting me process this news at my own pace. I know it's good—witnesses don't reach out like this unless they have something big to share—but I'm also wary of getting my hopes up again after last night's carbon-14 fiasco. So I take a few slow, measured breaths while stepping into my boots and sitting back down on the bed to tie them. Only then do I pick up the phone, turn off speaker mode, and talk directly into the receiver:

"I'm on my way."

24

Kaito Yonehana lies fully prone in his hospital bed, unable to crunch his torso up into a seated position. He's wearing a plain white T-shirt folded up over his abdomen and pelvic area, where a massive bandage has been placed over his burnt tissue. According to his doctor, Yonehana came in with a one-hundred-and-three-degree fever, full-blown cellulitis on his pubic wound, and an early case of septic shock that could have killed him if he had waited much longer to seek treatment. They had to perform emergency surgery on the wound to remove all the infected tissue, and it's likely the patient will need skin grafts in the near future. Despite all this, the twenty-five-year-old in front of me seems in oddly good spirits, with a disoriented smile that makes me wonder what drugs are in the IV drip by his side.

"How did you get my name?" I ask after making introductions and getting his permission to record our conversation.

"Bex called to warn me you might be in touch."

"And now here *you* are getting in touch with *me*."

He shrugs and smiles at me through glassy eyes, clearly a bit stoned from whatever the doctors have given him. "Near-death experiences will do that."

"All right, so what did you want to talk about?"

He pauses, glances down at his bandage as he thinks for a few seconds, then looks back up at me. "I don't want anyone to get in trouble, and I'm not pressing charges. That's not what this is about. But I talked to that girl before she died—Katherine O'Shea. She was nice. Sad, maybe. But I liked her, and I feel bad about what happened, so I want to tell you everything I can just in case it helps you figure out who killed her."

"I appreciate that," I say as I sit down on the rolling desk chair beside him. "And I'll make sure no one gets in any trouble unless they were involved in the murders. Okay?"

He nods, then continues: "I first heard about the Mystica Aeterna last harvest. A buddy of mine had just started going to their parties, and he said they were unlike anything you've ever seen. Drugs and sex right out in the open; full-blown orgies; and, like, genuinely hot women who are pretty much down for anything. I thought he was just fucking with me until I finally went to one—and, dude, it was incredible! I've had more sex in the past year than I've had, like, *ever*."

"But there was obviously more to it than that," I remind him, gesturing toward the giant bandage over his belly button.

"Sure," he says. "But I wasn't paying attention to those parts at first. I was just there to fuck girls."

"How noble of you."

"Yeah, well, I paid the price, all right? Doctor said I won't be getting it up for a *very* long time."

I hate to admit it, since hornball young men in their twenties are hardly my favorite demographic, but I kind of feel bad for this guy. He was clearly just a dumb kid caught up in something he couldn't possibly understand, too blinded by the promise of boobs and blow jobs to realize what he was getting himself into, and he almost died because of it.

What the hell is happening to you, Lana? Before this case, I probably would have labeled Kaito a sexual predator and moved on with my life, leaving him to suffer. Now, here I am giving him the benefit of the doubt and thinking about taking it easy on him. *What a difference a week makes...*

"So when did things first take a turn?" I ask.

"You mean when did I realize I was in a cult?"

I nod, and he continues: "Earlier this summer, when I started sleeping with Bex outside of the MA."

"MA?"

"Mystica Aeterna. It's a mouthful, so no one actually calls it that."

"Right."

"She's pretty deep into the whole thing," he explains, "so she started bringing me along to some of the more *spiritual* events. Meditation circles. Vision quests. Book clubs. We'd read passages from Rudolf Steiner and a few other dead mystics and then talk about how it all relates to our lives today, basically connecting the wine industry to some bigger cosmic purpose, or whatever. It was fine. I mean, my parents dragged me to church all the time when I was a kid, so I'm used to people telling me crazy shit. At least in this version I got to go to orgies afterward. And I could tell it really gave Bex purpose after everything she'd been through with the leukemia, so that was cool. But anyway, the biggest celebration of the year was always the Harvest festival. They called it Bacchanalia, and it was like, the drug-fueled orgy to end all drug-fueled orgies. You had to take this drink—pretty sure it was just merlot and roofies, but they called it the blood of Bacchus. And that shit got you *fucked up*. Oh my God, we must have danced in that house for hours, just swaying back and forth to the exact same song over and over and over again. I honestly blacked out for most of it, and I wasn't invited down to the basement for some of the ceremonial stuff, but I know the goal with the diehards like Bex was always to transcend."

"Do you know what they mean by that?"

Yonehana shakes his head. "There are some things you have to be initiated to learn about, and at that point I still wasn't part of the inner circle."

"So is the Bacchanalia what Katherine O'Shea attended?"

"Oh God, no," he says with a laugh, clearly still enjoying his IV drip. "Bex never would have invited an outsider to that. Katherine was just there for one of our usual full moon parties."

"Can you tell me about her?" I ask. "Anything she may have said that night, anyone else you may have seen her with?"

"Like I said, she was cool. Quiet girl, definitely had never been to something like this, but she was down to party. I think she was kinda bummed when she found out Bex and I were a thing, but she didn't, like, get all weird about it. We kept hanging out, and after Bex left, I asked her if she wanted to drop acid."

I let out an audible gasp, genuinely shocked that this unsuspecting young man was behind one of the case's key mysteries. "*You're* the one who gave her the LSD?"

"I didn't know someone was going to kill her later," he says defensively. "I just wanted to show her a good time." But then he has a sudden realization that causes his opiated smile to vanish. "Wait, can I be charged with a crime for that?"

"Technically, yes—"

"Shit."

"—but I don't have to tell the Sheriff's Department since you're a cooperating witness."

"Seriously?" he asks, his eyes still wide with the existential fear that a prison sentence tends to have on people.

I nod, and again I just kind of feel bad for him, so clearly out of his depths, with none of the guile I saw when I spoke to Holly or Bex.

"But Kaito, let's just say it's in your best interest now to keep cooperating. Okay? So tell me what happened after she took the LSD."

"Well, we just kinda laid on the couch, tripping balls for a while—it was really good stuff. But at some point, I must have passed out, 'cause when I came to, she was gone."

"Do you know what time that was?"

"Around one."

Which means Katherine O'Shea was already dead by the time he woke up. I get the sense that I'm not going to learn anything else from Kaito Yonehana, but duty compels me to at least find out if he recognizes Pilar Cruz's photo. As expected, he doesn't, and he's certain she never attended a party at Redwood Vale—although there *was* one during the full moon on September 7th, the night Pilar died. It may not be the straightforward link I would have preferred, but it does mean it's still possible that both of these cases are connected to the Mystica Aeterna.

"Do you know who's in charge of the MA?" I ask him. "I've never heard of a cult without a leader."

"They wouldn't tell me," he says, and I know he's being honest. "Not 'til I was initiated. But I'm pretty sure it's someone big."

"Big?"

"Like, once in a while, there'd be these security guards at the house. Two huge dudes in suits and ties, and you just knew they were packing some kind of heat. So I'm pretty sure they were there for one of the leaders. If not *the* leader."

Only one name crosses my mind after hearing Yonehana's story, and I can't believe I didn't think of it sooner: Governor Teddy Mason. He grew up in the area, from a well-connected family of winemakers, and if he was in charge of the MA, then that would explain Holly's strange call to him yesterday. On top of that, there was Peter Bancroft's warning of powerful figures inside the cult who had helped redact Holly's "unusual activities" from her court records. Is it possible that this thing could go all the way up to the Governor's Mansion in Sacramento?

It's a mouthwatering possibility, the sort of front-page revelation that can makes careers and turn anonymous agents like me into bestselling authors. But I've never been an ambitious person. I don't want a promotion to headquarters in Washington, and I sure as hell don't want to do book tours or CNN interviews. I like my life exactly as it is, thank you very much, so for someone like me who prefers to stay in the background and keep things simple—one pair of pants, one matching shirt, no fuss, no frills—the thought of accusing Governor Mason of a killing spree is a terrifying one. No matter how it goes, whether my suspicions are proven right or wrong, I'm the one who's going to get screwed.

With all of this swirling around in my head, making me dizzy, I turn off my digital voice recorder and rise to my feet. "Thanks for talking to me, Kaito. Really. I promise I'll make sure no one charges you for the LSD."

"Thanks," he says with an appreciative nod from his bed.

"But if you think of anything else, you know where to find me."

We part with amicable smiles, and I leave the hospital through the nearest exit, even though I really need to pee. Ever since my mom died in a place like this, I make it a point of spending as little time as possible in those bleach-smelling hallways.

* * *

Back in my car, I finally have a chance to respond to some of the other missed calls from earlier. I'm not in the mood to deal with Jonah or Caleb, and Peter Bancroft needs to stop assuming his wealth gives him the right to call my personal phone anytime he wants, but I need to check in with Leroux, so I give her a call back over the Bluetooth.

"Where have you *been*?" she says with the same jittery excitement that I recall from her garage when she walked me through her Peter Bancroft murder board.

"I've been in the hospital."

"*What?* Are you okay? What happened?"

"No, no, no," I tell her. "Not as a patient. I had to—wait, you didn't know about Kaito Yonehana?"

"Who?" Essie asks, clearly never having heard the name prior to this.

"I figured that's why you tried to call me earlier," I explain. "What's going on?"

A heavy silence lingers in the air as I pull my car out of the visitor parking lot. I almost make it a full block, and still Leroux hasn't answered me, as if she's been distracted by something. "Essie? Is everything okay?"

Finally, I hear her voice again, only now it's in a low, paranoid murmur, like someone might be listening. "How close are you to the J.B. Bancroft building?"

"Uh, a few minutes away, actually."

"Good," she says, still whispering. "Then you need to get down here right away."

"Why?"

"Because. I know who that body was that we found in the woods last night. She was Peter Bancroft's girlfriend."

The Napa Valley
Register

Friday, September 15, 1978
Police: Search called off for missing Oakville woman
by Jack Conrad

Register Staff

NAPA—The County Sheriff's Department has formally ended its search for Martha Bauman after six weeks. She is now presumed dead, and funeral services will be held this Saturday at St. Helena United Methodist Church.

Bauman, 20, was last seen at a party at the Oakville home of her boyfriend, Peter Bancroft, 18, the son of renowned vintner, James (J.B.) Bancroft. Partygoers described her as highly intoxicated on the night of August 2, and after a public argument with her boyfriend, she left the party alone and on foot around one o'clock in the morning.

After an initial search yielded no results in the 6-mile area between the Bancroft home and Bauman's parents' house on Stockton Street in St. Helena, police began to suspect that she'd been picked up somewhere on Highway 29 while trying to hitchhike. Friends say she didn't own a car and would often hitchhike up and down the Napa Valley, a common practice in the area, but there were no eyewitness accounts on the night in question, and additional evidence proved scarce.

According to the Department of Justice, close to half a million missing person cases are filed each year in the United States, most of which are solved in a matter of days. Those that aren't, however, rarely turn out well.

J. T. Falco

Bauman was a 1977 graduate of St. Helena High School, where she played varsity tennis and wrote for the yearbook. She most recently worked as a secretarial assistant for Michael Bancroft, cochair of the Bancroft Wine Company.

Martha Bauman is survived by her parents, Dean and Doris Bauman, and her older sister, Elizabeth Bauman.

25

I read the article twice in the jam-packed parking garage under Bancroft's office, and I have to admit, Leroux's theory is a solid one. This Bauman girl was the right age when she died, given what we know so far about the bones found at Redwood Vale, and her death bears subtle but eerie resemblances to those of Pilar Cruz, Katherine O'Shea, and even Jessica Bancroft. Not because there was a full moon when she disappeared—it's the first thing I checked, and there wasn't one—but because of her age and her clear link to the Valley's First Family.

Still, there's protocol to follow, and right now Leroux's personal grudge against Peter is getting in the way of her police duty.

"We can't just barge into a meeting upstairs and drag him out for questioning," I calmly tell her. "We still have no idea if those were Martha Bauman's remains, and even if they were, we're never going to be able to prove Peter killed her."

"Of course he killed her!" Leroux shouts, buzzing with anger at the man who sued her husband and left him bedridden after a debilitating heart attack. "It's *always* the boyfriend."

"Essie, there's a right way and a wrong way to do this job, all right? So what do you say we go about it the right way. The article says Bauman had a sister. Let's find out if she's still alive, and if she is, we can send a team out to swab her DNA. Within twenty-four hours, we'll know if those bones belonged to Martha."

"*Then* can we question him?"

"Yes," I tell her. "If it really is Martha Bauman, the Sheriff's Department can reopen her case and talk to anyone involved at the time of her death. Including Peter Bancroft."

Leroux nods, somewhat placated, although I can see her glancing over at the elevator with no small amount of displeasure. I have to remind myself that, despite her age, she's just a baby cop on her first big case. She still thinks police work is the kind of thing that can be done in an action-packed forty-two minutes, like her favorite episodes of *Law & Order*. But as I've learned over the years, more often than not, it's a painful slog. It requires patience and a complete emotional detachment from the people involved; otherwise, you're prone to make the kinds of mistakes that get cases thrown out in court and charges dropped. It's something I've had to remind myself constantly since coming back to Napa, thanks to the baggage I've been dragging around this place like a two-hundred-pound ball and chain.

I carefully explain all this to Leroux, but given her disappointment at pressing "Pause" on Peter Bancroft, I try to add a silver lining to the situation, something to keep her feeling invested in the case. *(Again, who am I, and what have I done with Lana Burrell?)*

"Essie, why don't you head back to the station and take the lead on Martha Bauman. Get in touch with her sister and see if she'll play ball."

"Really?" asks Leroux, overcome with a childlike excitement.

"It's your theory—and a good one too. Go bring it home, Deputy."

Leroux smiles and gives me a thankful nod; then I watch her hurry back to her car, her chunky bracelets and dangly earrings jingling all the way. As she starts to leave, I take a quick look at the traffic on Google Maps: a demoralizing red line stretches all the way from Napa to Calistoga. "Fucking hell," I mutter to myself. It's going to take me all afternoon to get back up to Redwood Vale, where I was hoping to check in on the search, see if they've found anything else now that the sun's up. But I've had to pee for the last hour, and if I don't go now, I'll bust a kidney before I make it all the way up to the Vale. Cursing myself for not just going at the hospital, triggering smells of bleach be damned, I head upstairs to use the bathroom in the lobby.

A few minutes later, I'm feeling much better as I wait for the elevator doors to open and take me back down to the parking garage. But when I finally hear the soft ding of an arriving elevator car, I look up from my phone to see a familiar face giving me a confused smile.

"Agent Burrell," says Peter Bancroft, "you could have just called me back. There was no need to come all the way down here."

I had completely forgotten about my missed call from him, but I decide that's a much better excuse for my presence in his building than the truth about Leroux and her potentially false accusations. "I was in the neighborhood. Mind if I join?"

"Step right in." He makes room for me in the elevator, and we stand there in an awkward silence as the doors slide shut.

"What did you want to talk about?" I ask, hoping he didn't already explain this in the voicemail I didn't bother listening to.

He considers me for a moment, checks the time on his obscenely expensive Jaeger-LeCoultre wristwatch, and reaches out to pull the emergency stop button. Instantly, the elevator jolts to a halt that sends me stumbling back into a wall, and an alarm bell begins to ring at loud, steady intervals.

"What the hell are you doing?" I cry out.

"Making sure we're not interrupted."

"There must be better ways—"

"Listen to me," he says with an anxious edge to his voice. "I know what you found last night. At the Vale."

I can feel my eyes narrowing with annoyance. "That information was supposed to be confidential."

"Yeah, well, it's not anymore. But do you know the story about Martha?"

I nod, surprised that he's bringing her up, and eager to hear where this goes.

"It's her," he says. "I know it is."

"Why do you think that?" I ask, steadying myself on the cold metal railing.

"It *has* to be. Even before she joined a cult, Holly's always been obsessed with Redwood Vale. She and her friends would sneak up there to have parties when we were in high school. Never invited me, of course, but I know what they were up to. I used to watch sometimes from the woods. And I always suspected she and Teddy were the ones who picked up Martha that night. I just had no way to prove it—until now."

My breath gets caught in my throat, and for a moment, I feel dangerously lightheaded. But then a gasp of air comes whooshing out of my mouth, and with my breathing restored, I finally manage to speak. "Teddy," I say. "As in Teddy Mason, the governor of California."

Bancroft nods ominously and starts to explain while the steadily blaring alarm of the elevator continues to cry out for help, as if even it knows that I'm about to step right into a great big pile of political shit.

* * *

Half an hour later, I'm pacing anxiously in McKee's office.

He's seated behind his desk, a look of utter exhaustion on his face; Leroux is in an armchair, her eyes twinkling with excitement; and Special Agent in Charge Connie Chen is on the speaker phone, dialing in from San Francisco. The door is locked and the blinds are drawn shut—no one else in the Department is allowed to know what we're discussing.

"Does he have any proof?" McKee asks after I've laid out every detail of Peter Bancroft's story.

I shake my head, then remember the SAC is on speaker and can't read my body language. "No," I say. "It's just his word against theirs. He already told this to the police back in '78 when Martha first went missing, but it wasn't being treated as a homicide at the time, and he doesn't think they took him seriously."

"So let me get this straight," Chen says through the grainy speaker, another outdated artifact in McKee's time capsule of an office. "The richest man in Napa Valley thinks that Holly Bancroft and the goddamn governor picked up his girlfriend, gave her a fatal overdose of cocaine, and rather than report it to the police, buried her in the woods."

I had the same stupefied reaction when Peter Bancroft first told me his version of the events of 1978, so I try to take the SAC back through the case one detail at a time. "Martha Bauman was two years ahead of Peter in high school, in the same class as Holly and Governor Mason. That's how he first met her, through his cousin, and they all remained friends after they graduated and started jobs or went off to college. But over the summer, when everyone was back home, Peter says Martha started pulling away from him and spending more time with Holly and Mason, who, like a lot of twenty-year-olds in '78, had gotten pretty heavily into cocaine. Peter didn't touch the stuff, and that's apparently what they had a fight about the night she went missing—how he didn't like her using it, and what it did to her personality. So she stormed off out of his parents' house, after which he thinks she was picked up by Holly and Mason."

"But again, he has no proof of any of this," says the sheriff.

"No."

"The police, her parents, *everyone* involved thought she was picked up by a drifter while trying to hitchhike her way back home."

"That's right," I tell him.

"And we still don't even know if those bones belong to Martha—"

Before he's able to finish his thought, Leroux jumps in with the overzealous enthusiasm of a first-time cop on her first big case, her words crashing into one another, victims of her inability to pause or breathe. "I got in touch with her sister, Elizabeth—goes by Liz Calhoun these days. She lives up in Boise now, married, three kids, six grandkids. Super-sweet gal. She works in a dental office part-time, watches the grandkids when she can. Poor thing told me she's spent the last fifty years chasing down leads on the internet, hoping Martha just ran off that summer and changed her name. Even did the whole 23andMe thing, thinking she might stumble onto a match. But of course she never did, and now she's just dying for answers, so she's agreed to submit a sample for DNA testing. Should be on her way to a lab up there as we speak."

McKee and I just nod along, with wary eyes, trying to separate the relevant details from the rest of the chaff in Leroux's rambling monologue. "Nice work," he finally says. "In the meantime, I've got an expert looking at those bones to see if she can determine a cause of death."

"If it really was a drug overdose, we're shit out of luck," I tell him. "You can't run a tox report on skeletal remains that old."

"Good to know."

There's a lull in the conversation, and Chen's voice pipes back up through the speaker. "What do we want to do about the governor?"

"I want to talk to him—" I start.

But before I can get another word out, McKee cuts me off. "Absolutely not."

"I don't have to mention Martha Bauman."

"Then why even bother poking that bear?"

I take a calming breath and raise my palms into the air in a plea for patience. "Okay, don't freak out when I say this, 'cause I don't like it any more than you do, but what I want to ask him is where he was on September seventh and October sixth."

"Of *this* year," McKee mutters, his anger building.

"Obviously."

"Are you out of your goddamn mind, Lana?"

He looks like he might pull that cowboy hat off his head and try to make me eat it, anything to get me to shut up and not jeopardize the career he's spent a lifetime building, but the ever-thoughtful, patient voice of Connie Chen saves me from an argument with the sheriff. "Let's hear her out, Angus. All the facts. *Then* we can tell her she's nuts."

The sheriff sighs begrudgingly and, with fists clenched so tight they're starting to shake, gestures for me to continue.

"We all know the governor has deep ties to the Valley," I explain. "He grew up here, he still owns Barberry Hill Winery and keeps a vacation home on the property, and he's not been shy about his friendship with Holly. She still hosts a few campaign fundraisers for him every year."

"There's one this week," says McKee. "We're providing security for the event."

"There you go," I say. "He's clearly still a presence in the Valley, even if he technically lives in Sacramento. Now, I talked to Kaito

Yonehana earlier—he's the guy who was branded in that video from Sunday night. And he told me the cult's leadership is a closely guarded secret. Only the innermost circle knows who's in charge. But every once in a while, people show up at Redwood Vale with armed security teams, which got me thinking—what if one of them is Mason?"

"I'm gonna say this one more time, Lana, then I'll shut up," says an exasperated McKee. "Are you out of your goddamn mind?"

"He'd hardly be the first politician to have a twisted sex life."

"He's a happily married man."

"So were Bill Clinton, John Edwards, JFK, Elliot Spitzer, Newt Gingrich—"

"Okay, you've made your point—"

"Arnold Schwarzenegger—"

"Lana."

"Fine," I say, relenting, "but let's look at all the information in front of us with purely objective eyes, okay? Holly Bancroft and Teddy Mason are longtime friends. In 1978, they may—or may not—have been involved in the death of a young woman who we just found buried at Redwood Vale. As recently as 2020, Holly joined a biodynamic sex cult called the Mystica Aeterna, which hosts all of its LSD-fueled gatherings at Redwood Vale. On September seventh, Holly had an argument with Pilar Cruz on her property, and a few hours later, she was murdered. When she was found the next day, she had LSD in her system, and she was next to a dead animal. September seventh was also the night of a full moon party at Redwood Vale, where we know LSD was being distributed. On October sixth, Katherine O'Shea was invited to a full moon party at Redwood Vale by Bex Potter. She was given LSD by Kaito Yonehana, and then she vanished. She was found murdered the next day, with soil from Redwood Vale under her fingernails and a dead animal beside her. And we all know cults like this have a long history of animal sacrifice, even if we haven't seen any direct evidence of it yet.

"That's three young women all around the same age, all with drug-related deaths, and all somehow connected to Holly Bancroft or Redwood Vale. Is the evidence circumstantial? Sure. Is there a case there? Maybe not. But then throw in the death of Holly's own daughter in 2003. Sheriff, you said yourself you think Holly may have lied during my father's trial, and Jonah Bancroft told me he saw his mother pressing a corkscrew to my dad's head around the time Jess vanished, threatening to kill him."

"That's all well and good, Lana," says McKee, "but what does any of it have to do with—"

"Do you know who was in Napa for Holly's annual Crush party that day in '03?" I ask, unfazed by the interruption, really rolling now as all the scattered facts of the case come together into one cohesive narrative for the first time. "Teddy Mason. I remember because he was running for mayor of Napa that year, and there were campaign signs all over the place. Now, I don't know if all this is just one big monstrous coincidence, but I'd say there's enough there to at least ask Holly and the governor some questions. And since you said he'll be in town tomorrow anyway, I'm proposing that we use this opportunity to poke around a little and find out if there's anything there."

A weighty silence settles over the room, everyone trying to sift their way through this cavern of evidence, desperately hoping to shine some light on the truth. I obviously can't see how the SAC is taking my proposal, but the sheriff is rubbing the gray stubble on his chin, no doubt contemplating the political consequences of such an action. As for Leroux, she seems disappointed that I've steered the case away from her favorite suspect, Peter Bancroft, but her fangirl interest in a Sacramento-sized scandal has kept her somewhat intrigued by what I've had to say.

Finally, it's Chen's steady voice that breaks through the tension. "I think we should pursue it, but *delicately*. Sheriff?"

"Agreed," he says, and turns to me with a wary look, already regretting what he's about to say. "I'll have my team set aside a secure room at Golden Eagle for you to use before the event. Is there anything else you need?"

I think about it for a moment, relieved to have their support, even if it's half-hearted. "Secrecy. We can't tip Holly and Mason off that this is coming, or they'll have a chance to get their stories straight. I need them both surprised by my questions so that I can look them right in the eye and gauge their reactions before they start lying."

"*If* they have anything to lie about," says McKee. "But I see your point. We'll make sure this stays under wraps, but in return I want you to do something for me. Before we all get carried away with Operation Fuck the Governor, I think you should do some digging into Redwood Vale and what really went on there in the '70s. Who was using it at the time? Who else might have buried a body there? What are we still missing? It's possible nothing will come of it, but if I'm gonna risk my neck having the governor questioned in a murder investigation, I want to make sure we're really onto something first."

I know McKee is just covering his own ass here, and I'm generally not a fan of playing politics, but I do realize I'm putting him in a tenuous position. And he *has* been surprisingly supportive thus far, so I give him a tepid nod. "I'll head down to the *Napa County Register*, see if they have anything in their archives from the '70s that might shine a light on things. Essie, why don't you make some calls to the state commission that granted the Conservation Easement on Redwood Vale. I'd be curious to find out why Michael and J.B. Bancroft asked for it in the first place."

"You got it, Boss," says Leroux, and she's already heading for the door to get to work.

"Deputy, you do realize *I'm* still your boss, right?" McKee tells her on the way out.

Leroux grins and gives me a wink. "Sure, Angus. You keep telling yourself that."

J. T. Falco

An excerpt from
The Courage of Kindness: A Memoir
by Theodore "Teddy" Mason

It wasn't easy being a country boy at Harvard. There I was, surrounded by the spoiled children of New York investment bankers and Boston Brahmins who could trace their lineage all the way back to the Mayflower; the sort of kids who went to boarding schools with fancy names and already had a spot saved for them at their daddy's law firm. All I knew about life was how to trim back a grape vine in the hot summer sun and how to scrub soil out of my jeans after a long day of digging irrigation trenches. People think of Napa Valley as some fancy-pants resort getaway, with spas and rich folk sipping wine with their pinkies in the air, and maybe that's true these days, but back then, growing up where I did, we were all just farmers, no different from the corn farmers of Iowa or the apple growers of New Hampshire. We went to public schools, we went to church on Sundays, and we spent our summers in the vineyards, making three bucks an hour to help produce wine that we were never even allowed to drink. So you can imagine what a culture shock it was for me to suddenly find myself in political science classes with the sons and daughters of ambassadors and CEOs. To be blunt, I hated it (at first).

Every chance I got, I'd buy the cheapest ticket I could find and fly back home to wine country, where I'd disappear into the hillsides with old friends like Holly Bancroft, Bill Wiggins, and Martha Bauman. We were thick as thieves back then, and outcasts anywhere else we tried to live, so we all just kept getting sucked back home by the gravitational pull of the Mayacamas Mountains. As they say, once a farm boy, always a farm boy.

There's just something about those friendships you form in your teenage years that sink deep into your soul and take hold of your *heart. Maybe it's the reminder of simpler times; maybe it's just human nature to crave contact with people who grew up on the same soil as you and understand the cultural forces that built you into who you are. But the bond I shared with that old group was unbreakable no matter where we went in life, which made it all the more tragic when we lost one of our own that second summer back from Harvard.*

We'll never know exactly what happened to Martha Bauman. One day she was there, her usual smiling self, the only one kind enough to laugh at my lame jokes while we all ate ice cream together. The next day she was gone, vanished without a trace. We spent the whole summer searching with the police, fanning out across the vineyards and forests, looking for any sign we could find of our best friend, hoping we might still get to see her alive. But after six weeks, the search was called off, and she was declared dead. The funeral was one of the worst days of my life. To lose someone so near and dear to your heart at such an early age is an impossible task, but I suppose, as my father told me later, it builds character. It teaches you to keep on fighting, and it gives you something to fight for. As for me, I'll never forget Martha Bauman, and I'll never stop fighting to make sure what happened to her never happens again to another young woman in this beautiful country of ours.

26

Like most local newspapers with decent-sized budgets, the *Napa Valley Register* digitized its archives at some point in the early 2000s, so thankfully, I don't have to spend the evening sifting through dusty old boxes of barely legible newsprint. Instead, a flash of my FBI badge gets me into a small office on the second floor of the *Register*'s unassuming headquarters, where an outdated HP desktop computer holds the entire one-hundred-and-sixty-year history of the newspaper on its hard drive. And although everything published before the mid-'90s has been scanned as a full broadsheet rather than as individual articles, I can still do a basic keyword search to help me narrow in on any useful pages. Then I just need to scan each one for the specific article I need.

It sounds simple enough, and it would be—if I weren't investigating the most famous family in the history of the Valley. Not a day went by in the 1970s when the Bancrofts weren't somehow mentioned in the paper; literally thousands of articles pop up in my initial search. So if I'm going to get out of here before tomorrow's meeting with the governor, I'll need to be strategic.

I pay a buck twenty-five for an ice-cold can of Diet Dr. Pepper from the vending machine, a guilty pleasure from my studying days back at Quantico, then I settle into the uncomfortable metal chair I've been given, the kind you might expect to find behind a student's desk in a public high school. First up in the search box: *Martha Bauman*.

Prior to her death, there are about a dozen mentions of Martha in the paper, but every one of them is in the Sports section: brief blurbs about her performance in various high school tennis matches. After she dies, however, she seems to become the cause célèbre of the Napa Valley. Her sudden disappearance is front page news for weeks, with constant updates about the search and the police investigation into her presumed murder at the hands of a drifter. Most of the articles are redundant and not particularly helpful, but I find one that quotes a twenty-year-old Teddy Mason. *"Martha was such a ray of light. She wasn't just my best friend, she was my role model, and I won't stop searching until I find out what happened to her."* It certainly is interesting that he used the past tense only a week into her disappearance, five weeks before she was formally declared dead, as if he knew what had really happened to her. But you can hardly arrest someone for their choice of verb conjugation . . . I think.

Beyond that, there's nothing particularly revelatory about the newspaper's reporting on the Bauman disappearance. It's all essentially how Leroux described it earlier. So I decide to switch gears and try out a new search: *Redwood Vale*.

There are only seven mentions of the Vale throughout the 1970s. The first article, in 1973, describes the Bancroft brothers' purchase of the land from the family who'd owned it for half a century, as well as their plans to plant a vineyard there. *I wonder why they never actually got around to doing it.* My answer comes a few articles later: a piece about a preservationist group suing the Bancrofts to prevent them from clearing any of the redwood trees on the property. There are a few more articles about the dispute over the land, as well as a public announcement from J.B. Bancroft that he and his brother would leave the property intact and forgo their plans for a vineyard.

Then, finally, on September 26, 1978, there's a tiny blurb on page fifteen of an eighteen-page newspaper about a dead body discovered at Redwood Vale.

The body of a woman found two days ago by hikers has been identified as Esmeralda Sanchez, 23, a Mexican native and farmworker. She was discovered by the hikers and their dog on a walk through an area of Howell Mountain known as Redwood Vale. According to police, the woman's cause of death is unknown.

That's it. There's not a single other mention of the body or the woman, Esmeralda Sanchez. As far as I can tell, there was no murder investigation. No one was brought in for questioning. A migrant farmworker from Mexico was found dead, and not a single person in a position of power gave a shit—a far cry from the apparent media frenzy surrounding the earlier disappearance of local white girl Martha Bauman. The uncanny similarity to the current Cruz/O'Shea murder investigations isn't lost on me.
Some things never change...
But if that really was Martha Bauman's corpse last night, that means two different women were killed and left to rot on Redwood Vale within a two-month period in 1978. It's certainly possible that Holly Bancroft and/or Teddy Mason went on some kind of twisted killing spree while they were home from college that summer, but that seems unlikely. And I can't imagine Peter Bancroft's accidental drug overdose theory would apply to two separate women, over a month apart. Something else had to be going on back then...
I decide to switch tactics and go back to a broader search of the Bancrofts, focusing in on the dates surrounding the murders of Martha Bauman and Esmeralda Sanchez. Over that two-month period, there are fifty-one mentions of the Bancrofts. Quite a few of them are in articles about Martha Bauman's disappearance and her

various connections to the family: Peter's girlfriend, Michael's part-time assistant, Holly's best friend. And most of them are bland, irrelevant pieces about the wine industry and the upcoming harvest.

But then everything changes on September 29, 1978. On that day—three days after Esmeralda Sanchez was found at Redwood Vale—J.B. and Michael Bancroft publicly announced that they were dividing the family business in half. The biggest wine brand in Napa was being split in two, with various vineyards and labels being partitioned between the suddenly hostile, competing brothers, and the fact that it was coming on the heels of these two apparent murders feels too connected to be coincidental.

Could they have known more than they were letting on about what happened to Martha Bauman and Esmeralda Sanchez? Was one of them responsible? Or, more likely, was one of their children—or their best friend, Teddy—behind the killings? And did that horrible secret tear apart the most lucrative wine business in the Valley? A million questions rattle around my brain, questions that I know may have died with the two elder Bancroft brothers. But I'm sure now, more than ever, that whatever happened in 1978 is somehow tied to the deaths I'm here to investigate today—and perhaps even to Jess's disappearance twenty-two years ago.

The harsh buzz of my phone on the desk jolts me out of my reverie, and I lunge to answer it without even bothering to flip it over first to check the display. "This is Burrell."

"Hi, Miss Burrell, this is Victor over at ADT Security. Your home alarm's been triggered, and you haven't entered the shut-off code—"

"What?"

"Do you need us to send police over to your address?"

A break-in at my apartment? Now? Right as I'm closing in on the truth?

Someone's getting scared—not to mention desperate—but if that's the case, the last thing I need is some San Francisco beat cop poking around my place before I can get there. I need to keep the apartment pristine so that I can figure out exactly who my intruder was and what they wanted.

"No," I tell the polite voice of Victor at ADT. "It was a mistake. I had a friend pop by to borrow something and forgot to give her my code. Can you turn off the alarm remotely?"

"Of course, doing it now."

"Great."

"Is there anything else we can help you with today?"

"I'm all set. Thanks, Victor."

"Thank you for choosing—"

But I hang up the phone before he can finish his corporate-mandated goodbye, already pulling my laptop out of my bag. Within seconds, I've got an internet browser open and my ADT Security account up on screen. Now I just need to wait for any recent videos to load on the painfully slow Wi-Fi here at the *Register*. As I sit around impatiently watching digital data being transferred at glacial speeds that I didn't even know were legal anymore, all I can think is *Thank God I installed that camera.*

I'm not dumb enough to use a Ring camera like Bex Potter, given how much of that data is made available to local law enforcement, but I did install a tiny security camera just above my front door when I was investigating a particularly dangerous gang a few years ago. They never found out where I lived, so I haven't had any reason to use the account until now, but I still set the alarm out of habit when I know I'll be away for extended periods of time. From what I can recall, the camera is set to record anytime there's motion at my front door. It saves the footage for thirty days before deleting it, and stores each video based on its time code, so whoever just broke into my place should have been caught on camera before the alarm went off.

Finally, after what feels like a lifetime, the videos load on my laptop, and I immediately open the most recent one, motion captured less than five minutes ago. In the high-angle footage, a man wearing a black knit cap and carrying a small bag approaches my door. He has a key to my unit—*how the hell does he have a key to my unit?*—so it doesn't take him long to unlock it and slip inside. At the last second, just before crossing the threshold, he glances up, giving me my first clear view of his face: Sure enough, it's the cold eyes and scarred cheek of Carlos Ruiz.

My mind begins doing backflips as I try to figure out how he managed to get a key to my apartment. As far as I know, there are only three in existence. The first is with the building manager, who I suppose could have had his key swiped without his knowledge, but this seems like a stretch. The second is on the thirteenth floor of the Federal Building in the office that I almost never spend time in anymore; there's no way Ruiz managed to get in there, given all the FBI security. And the third has been in Napa with me this entire time. *Unless* . . .

I grab my phone, Google the Silverado Inn, and then call the number listed. After two rings, I'm on with the front desk, where a woman I recognize as the owner says in a cheery, lilting voice, "Silverado Inn!"

"Hi, this is Lana Burrell—I've been in Room nine since Saturday."

"Yes, Ms. Burrell, what can I do for you tonight?"

"Well, I'm worried I may have had a break-in, and I'm wondering if you have any security cameras facing the door to my room."

"Oh my goodness, I am so sorry, ma'am," she says with an increasingly disingenuous tone, as if bracing for the inevitable accusation to come. "Was something stolen?"

"Yes—I mean, I think so. But I know it wasn't housekeeping, so I'm not calling to blame anyone. I'm just wondering if you have any cameras on the property."

"I hate to say it, but we don't," she says. "Looked into it once, but there's really not much crime up here, so we decided it wasn't worth the cost. Have you talked to the police?"

Realizing she won't be of any help, I try to walk back my concerns and extricate myself from the conversation as quickly as possible. Unfortunately, she won't let me go until I at least agree to accept a free bottle of wine as her personal apology for the trouble, so I lie and tell her I'll pick it up sometime tomorrow. Given the room rate at this place, I have no doubt it'll be terrible—and it certainly won't help explain my mysterious intruder.

Without security footage from the Silverado Inn, I'll never be able to prove my theory, but what I think happened is that Carlos Ruiz waited for me to leave on Sunday and then snuck inside, probably while housekeeping had the door propped open. When I'm traveling, I always like to keep my apartment key in the zipped outer pocket of my suitcase, which means it was in the motel all weekend long and fairly easy to find given my limited belongings. Because of that, it's entirely possible that Ruiz could have made a copy and returned the original key before I was any wiser. *But why? Why go to all that trouble just to get inside my apartment?* A second ADT video shows him hurrying out of my unit two minutes later, no doubt scared off by the blaring alarm that was triggered when he didn't enter the shut-off code within sixty seconds. But what did he manage to do during those two minutes?

As far as I'm concerned, there's only one course of action, only one way to even begin to answer the torrent of questions that are drowning out everything I just learned about the Bancrofts,

Martha Bauman, and Redwood Vale. I need to get back home, and I need to do it *now*.

* * *

I race past a "Speed Limit 55" sign at eighty-six miles per hour, chugging the rest of my Diet Dr. Pepper with my right hand while the left grips the steering wheel impatiently. *What could Ruiz possibly want in my apartment?* Anything case related would have been stored in my work laptop, which hasn't left my side all week. And from what I know about my sex-offending stalker, he's hardly the sort of hacker extraordinaire who could do much damage on my personal laptop. It doesn't make sense unless he wants to hurt me, but if that's his goal, it would have been far easier to attack me in Napa rather than go to all these lengths to steal my San Francisco house key. Something still doesn't add up.

As I'm merging onto the ever-crowded 101 South near Novato, a call comes in over the Bluetooth. It's Deputy Leroux.

"Did you find anything about the Conservation Easement?" I ask, too flustered by recent events to open with a more polite greeting.

"Nothing that jumps out," she says. "It seemed to be the last thing the Bancroft brothers did before they split up the company in '78. But that's not actually why I'm calling."

"Oh?"

"Coroner looked at those bones we found and was able to determine a cause of death."

"So it wasn't drugs . . ."

"No, hon," Leroux says. "She had a skull fracture that's consistent with blunt force trauma. Poor thing probably died from a brain bleed."

There goes Peter Bancroft's theory, I think to myself. Holly and the governor could have certainly still killed his girlfriend, but if they did, it was no accidental overdose. It was an intentional bash to the head. And if they were capable of something so brutal in their early twenties; well, then there's no telling what they might be able to do now, with all that innate evil warped and twisted over the years into something even more perverse.

"Thanks, Essie," I tell my new protégé. "Just hold onto those reports for now, and I'll take a look at them tomorrow."

"Where are you going?" she asks, clearly noticing the background hum of my speeding Toyota, now doing a full ninety miles per hour.

"Back home," I tell her with evident dread in my voice. "Something came up."

* * *

The moment I step inside my apartment, I can feel that it's off balance, contaminated by some unmistakably dark presence, and if I were a superstitious person, I'd already be burning sage.

Beyond those ineffable feelings of discomfort, though, I see that the door to the bathroom is closed, which I never do unless I have company because of how often the rusty locking mechanism gets stuck and won't open. Meanwhile, over at my desk, my personal laptop is open, which again, is never how I leave it when I'm traveling. And there's a single dirty footprint on my beige living room rug that I know right away isn't mine; I wear a women's size six, and this print is at least a men's eleven or twelve.

Ruiz was in here all right, but what the hell did he want?

My first thought is to check my laptop's internet search history, wondering if it was my saved bank account information that he was after. But if he did visit any websites on it, he must have used a private browser, because there's no record of anything unusual. Next, I pull up my personal email. I have no way of knowing if he read anything, but I want to check my Sent and Trash folders to see if my account was used for anything suspicious and he didn't cover his tracks. But again, there's nothing out of the ordinary. Whatever he wanted, I don't think it was digital.

I spend the next half hour scouring the apartment inch by inch, opening drawers and closets, trying to find anything missing or out of place, but there's no sign of any further disturbance. He must have been scared off by the alarm before he was able to find whatever he was after; but still, the fact that a creep like Ruiz was here in my personal space, even for two minutes, gives me the chills. I swear I can still feel his eerie presence, like he's lurking in a corner somewhere, watching me . . .

Which is why I nearly jump out of my skin when, at that exact moment, my phone rings. I see Caleb Roche's name on the display, and my first impulse is to ignore the call. Part of me still can't get over that stained handkerchief with Katherine O'Shea's fingerprints and his initials on it. But I know there are plenty of other explanations for that monogrammed "C.R." My favorite home invader, Carlos Ruiz, for one. And then there was that strange book in the basement at Redwood Vale about a man named Christian Rosenkreutz. At the end of the day, I have no *real* reason to suspect Caleb of any wrongdoing, and I *have* loved every minute I've spent with him. Maybe it's finally time to stop seeing the worst in people—labeling them as sex offenders and abusers based on gut instinct from across the bar—and instead take a chance on a new relationship.

"Hi," I say when I finally answer the phone, already wishing I had thought of a cooler first line.

"You never called me back," he says, not accusatory, but genuinely disappointed.

"Sorry," I tell him, and I mean it. "It's been a long day."

"I can only imagine. Rumor has it they found a body on one of the Bancroft properties."

"Fucking hell, can no one in that police department keep a secret?" The outburst flies out of me before I'm able to check my anger, and I hear Caleb laugh on the other end of the line.

"Sorry," I say, more softly this time. "Not mad at you. Obviously."

"It's all good," he says in his usual carefree demeanor, that relentless optimism I find so foreign and yet so attractive. "Jonah's the one who told me, if that helps. I guess he found out from his uncle. But hey—the reason I'm calling—what are you up to tonight?"

"Oh, well, um, I'm actually back in San Francisco."

"Oh." The disappointment in his voice is palpable, and it gives me a strange sort of thrill knowing that he doesn't just want to talk, he wants to see me. *All* of me.

"I was hoping to stay up in the Valley," I explain, "but I had a break-in, so I had to come back home and make sure nothing was missing."

"Wait—what? Are you okay?"

"Yeah. I mean, I wasn't here when it happened. But it's still a little freaky to know someone was walking around my apartment."

"Jesus, Lana—"

"It's fine."

"It's not fine! I'm coming down right now."

"What?"

"It's not even a two-hour drive."

"Caleb, I don't need you here to protect me—"

"Obviously," he says. "You're a badass secret agent with a gun and a badge and bigger triceps than I have. I know you can protect yourself."

"Then why are you driving two hours to come down here?"

"Because I like you," he says in a tone that's so straightforward and earnest I don't even know how to respond. "Also, I hear post-home-invasion sex is by far the best kind."

The moment he says it, I let out a sorely needed laugh that lowers the last of my protective barriers. It feels good, not just the release of laughter, but the emotional unburdening of it all. The realization that I don't have to go through this thing alone anymore—not if I don't want to—because there's a guy out there who really sees me and who, despite all my faults, wants to be with me. "In that case," I tell him, still grinning from ear to ear, "I'll text you the address."

"See you in two hours," he says, and the line goes dead.

Two hours, I think to myself. *Plenty of time to finally shave my legs.*

27

The sex is even better this time. Home field advantage, maybe. Or perhaps it's just been too long since I've slept with someone who makes me feel more than just titillated or desired. But with Caleb, the experience is about so much more than just sex. It's deeper, more profound; more like an orgasmic manifestation of a hope I didn't even realize I had. And best of all, it gets me to stop thinking about work, if only for a few precious hours. After our third consecutive go at it, we finally—reluctantly—acknowledge how tired we are and begin to get ourselves ready for bed. "Don't take this the wrong way," I tell him as we slip back under the sheets, "but if you try to cuddle with me, I'll kill you."

"Oh really?" he says with a wry, combative grin.

"It's not you," I explain. "It's just, when you sleep alone for twenty years, you kinda get used to your own body heat. Your own pillow technique. Your own position. So for now, is it cool if we don't do the whole big spoon–little spoon thing? That way I can actually get some sleep."

He lets out one of those full-throated belly laughs that made me fall for him that first night in St. Helena, and he gives me an adoring kiss on the lips. "You'd better watch out, Lana Burrell. If you're not careful, this thing between us might actually become a thing."

"I'll take my chances," I tell him. Then I kiss him back, and we curl up on our respective sides of the bed, far enough apart to feel alone but just close enough to feel safe.

I'm pretty sure I spend the whole night smiling.

* * *

When I wake up, Caleb's half of the bed is empty, but I find a yellow Post-it Note stuck to my forehead: *Went out for coffee. Back soon. P.S. You snore like a troll.* I can't help but laugh at his sense of humor, and I spend a few minutes luxuriating in bed. Stretching, moaning, remembering with satisfaction all the things we did to each other. But then I recall why Caleb drove here in the first place, the strange break-in that I still can't properly explain, and I fire off a quick text to Leroux: *Any updates on that APB? I really need to find Ruiz.*

While I await a response—and my coffee delivery—I grab my work laptop off the nightstand and start to do some research in preparation for my meeting with the governor. Unlike most political leaders, Teddy Mason has refused to release his calendar to the public, despite numerous lawsuits from state newspapers who've demanded more transparency. But that unusual penchant for discretion doesn't mean his movements have to remain a complete mystery. Mason loves to see his photo in the press, so the internet's full of articles about his daily comings and goings. I use my FBI account to log into LexisNexis, which is a far more reliable collection of news and legal documents than a simple search engine, and I check for anything that mentions the governor on September 7th, September 8th, October 6th, and October 7th.

An article in the *Sacramento Bee* places Mason in the state capital on the day Pilar Cruz was killed, where he gave a speech to an education nonprofit at three PM. But the next mention of his activity isn't until four PM the following day, when a *San Francisco Chronicle* article notes that Mason had to cancel his planned attendance at a meeting with the city's DA because of a cold.

If that isn't code for a post-full-moon-party hangover, I don't know what is . . .

His October dates are even more suspicious, with a speech at the state legislature on the 6th and a lunch meeting on the 7th at his favorite restaurant in Yountville, just a few miles from Redwood Vale. Which means he most likely spent the night of Katherine O'Shea's murder at his family's Oakville winery, Barberry Hill.

I get a text back from Leroux: *Sorry hon, nothing yet.—Essie*

It's obviously not what I'd been hoping to hear, but Leroux's endearing habit of signing each text message with her name at least manages to give me a chuckle. And to be honest, right now, I'm too wrapped up in my growing case against Holly Bancroft and Governor Mason to give much thought to the strange behavior of Carlos Ruiz. There are simply too many coincidences stacked on top of one another to suggest anything other than Teddy Mason's involvement in the Mystica Aeterna. I *know*, deep in my gut, that he's a part of it; he's probably the whole reason masks were introduced in the first place, given his high-profile face and his presidential ambitions. The question is, *Could he be a serial killer too?*

My thoughts are interrupted by the return of Caleb, who tosses the key he borrowed onto my dresser and shows me a tray holding four to-go coffee cups of varying sizes. "We expecting company?" I ask. "'Cause I should've told you, group sex really isn't my thing . . ."

He sheepishly takes a seat beside me on the edge of the bed. "I didn't want to wake you, but I also had no idea what kind of coffee you drink, or if you're lactose intolerant, or if you're just one of those weird people who actually likes the taste of almond milk. So I got you four options."

I can't help but smile at that perfect answer. "If I didn't have the worst morning breath in history, I would totally make out with you right now." Instead, I give him a quick kiss on the cheek and lunge toward the assortment of coffees, desperate for my daily caffeine kick. "Which one of these is regular milk?" He pulls the largest cup out of the holder and hands it to me, and I point through my open bedroom door, toward a cabinet in the kitchen. "Mind getting me some sugar? It's on the bottom shelf."

"How much?" he asks as he starts across the apartment.

"Just bring all of it," I tell him. With Holly Bancroft and Teddy Mason on the agenda this afternoon, not to mention Carlos Ruiz still in the wind, I have a feeling it's going to be a three-tablespoon kind of day.

* * *

After Caleb and I part ways, I hit the road once more with a new suitcase stuffed full of extra clean clothes. According to Google Maps, there's an accident on the Bay Bridge—*surprise, surprise*—so I decide to take the Golden Gate, which is only a few miles longer and far more scenic than the slog through the East Bay. But it doesn't occur to me until I'm passing a sign for San Quentin that I've chosen a route that takes me directly past my father's prison.

Was this my subconscious all along telling me that I want to see him again? I do feel terrible about the way I dashed out last time, scared to embrace my own dad, and there are still so many questions that need asking, especially given some of the new facts in the case. But I don't want him to feel like I'm just using him to solve a crime. He's not Hannibal Lecter; he's my father. And if I'm going to visit him in jail, I can't just ask him about a bunch of dead women.

An idea hits me, a dumb memory from before Mom died, before everything fell apart and we moved to that goddamn wine country paradise, and I quickly merge right to pull off the freeway at the next exit.

* * *

Half an hour later, I'm back in that same private interview room at San Quentin, watching my dad shovel down spoonfuls of Ben & Jerry's Chunky Monkey ice cream, straight from the pint, just like the three of us used to do whenever we watched a movie together. Back when there were three of us in this tragic excuse for a family. Neither of us mentions Mom while he eats, but we don't have to. She's there with us in every single bite. And while I wish we could just live in this blissful silence all day, the reality is, I have murders to solve and places to be, so when I hear his plastic, prison-issued spoon start to scrape against the bottom of the container, I tell him about the strange cult I've encountered and dive in with my questions.

"I know this is probably a long shot, but with all the reading and studying you've done in here, have you ever heard of a book called *The Chymical Wedding of Christian Rosenkreutz*?"

His eyes glance up from his ice cream, and he sets down his spoon. "I have, actually. How do you know about it?"

"It was sitting out at Holly's place in Redwood Vale, open to this weird symbol that the cult seems to be using as their logo."

"Interesting," he says, scratching his thick beard, taking a moment to think. "It does make sense. Rudolf Steiner was into Rosenkreutz too. Used to give lectures about him, how he thought he was reincarnated as all these key figures from history and how he may have discovered the philosopher's stone."

"As in . . . Harry Potter?"

"No. I mean, yes, technically, but the term comes from the alchemists of the Renaissance, who were obsessed with this idea of transmutation. Turning mundane metals into gold and finding an elixir that would grant eternal life, aka, the philosopher's stone. And oddly enough, *wine* was at the heart of it all."

"Wine?"

He leans closer across the table, his eyes sparkling with excitement, with that endless capacity to learn that sent him from art school to vineyard management to online degrees in philosophy and theology. "Think about it from the perspective of a sixteenth-century mystic. Fermentation is this magical process that somehow turns boring old grapes into alcohol, this delicious elixir that does incredible things to your brain. It's the closest any of them ever got to turning lead into gold."

"And how does Christian Rosenkreutz fit in?"

"Well, no one knows if he's actually real or just a mythic figure, but according to legend, he's the founder of the Rosicrucians. They were these esoteric Christians who were obsessed with alchemy, the holy grail, the secret lineage of Jesus. All that *Da Vinci Code* shit, most of which is just fantasy. But their beliefs were laid out in these three anonymous manifestos published in Germany during the 1600s, the third of which was *The Chymical Wedding of Christian Rosenkreutz*."

"And by *Chymical Wedding*, they were talking about . . . alchemy?"

"In a sense," he says. "But remember, these were also devout Christians, so much of their storytelling was a direct reference to the Bible and the life of Christ. In this case, the Wedding at Cana, in which Jesus turned water into wine, which you might say was the birth of alchemy. It's all part of one big historical pattern that Rudolf Steiner was one of the first people to piece together, starting with the ancient Greeks, whose Cults of Dionysus used wine and sex in their worship. From there, there was Jesus and later the Rosicrucians, who saw fermentation as the key to the philosopher's stone and eternal life. And then you had guys like Steiner and Aleister Crowley, who fused these ideas together, claiming that wine and sex created a sort of ritual magic that would allow people to transcend to a higher plane of existence, a sort of psychological version of immortality or nirvana. So whatever these people are doing up at Redwood Vale, it seems like the next logical step in the journey. Wine, sex, spiritual enlightenment..."

"...and murder." The words drop from my mouth and land on the table like a fist, jolting my father out of his academic trance and reminding us both just how real the stakes are. "In any of those traditions, was there ever a mention of—I can't believe I'm even saying this—human sacrifice?"

He thinks about it, running his index finger across his left eyebrow, over and over, just like he would in the old days when I presented him with a problem. Only back then, it was usually algebra, not alchemy. "The Ancient Greeks almost certainly did," he says, "although animals were a lot more common than people. As for the Rosicrucians and Steiner's Order, if they did, they were smart enough not to tell anyone."

He's not saying it out loud, but I can tell in his wary eyes that he absolutely thinks it's possible, or even likely. And right now, I can't think of any other reason why two unconnected women would be brutally murdered during subsequent full moons. Which really only leaves one question: "Why? If Holly and the others are killing people up there, what do they expect to gain from it? She's already rich, she's already powerful..."

"Besides wine, what's the one thing all those other groups were obsessed with? The Greeks, Jesus and his Disciples, the Rosicrucians, Steiner and Crowley..."

I swallow hard, barely believing I'm about to say what I'm going to say. "Eternal life."

"There you go." He nods. "Now people like you and me, we all know that's a bunch of bullshit, just like we know fermentation isn't magic—it's just microorganisms eating sugar and crapping out booze. But you get a whole group of New Age zealots together and feed them enough LSD, who knows what they might start to believe?"

We sit there for a long time in a heavy silence, thinking about this utterly preposterous, yet shockingly real possibility. Then my thoughts drift over to the remarkable man who helped me piece it all together: Prisoner number 11582182 of the California Department of Corrections and Rehabilitation. My dad. An autodidact with nothing but a high school diploma, who taught himself to paint and became a successful artist; who taught himself farming and became a highly regarded vineyard manager; who spent his two decades in prison immersing himself in history, theology, and philosophy, earning two degrees from UC Berkeley's online program. This man has more potential in his little finger than spoiled rich kids like Teddy Mason and Peter Bancroft have in their whole bodies, and yet they're running the state and a massive corporation while my father is stuck behind bars for the rest of his existence. All because of a damned lie and a justice system that's always been tilted toward the powerful.

"I've been spending a lot of time with Angus McKee these last few days," I tell him.

He slowly takes another spoonful of his now-melted ice cream. "Oh yeah?"

"He didn't come right out and say it, but he seems to think Holly may have lied during your trial." I expect my dad to leap up from his seat in a fit of rage, an outpouring of grief over a wasted life in a grimy cell. But instead, he barely bats an eye and simply nods his head, as if he's known this all along. "Dad, what really happened that day in the barn at Golden Eagle, when you and Jess were alone before the fire started? At trial, Holly said Jess was crying when she found her, like she was terrified of you. But if that's a lie..."

"It was more of an omission than a lie," he says with a Zen-like calmness that I can't even comprehend, given my immature tendency to lash out over the smallest slight. "I *was* alone with Jess in the barn, and she *was* crying and scared that day. But not because of me."

"Who?"

He shakes his head, forlorn. "She wouldn't tell me. She wanted to, I think, but by the time I found her, she'd already started the fire, so she wasn't exactly in a talking mood."

"*Jess* started the fire?" I'd always assumed it had been an accident, some kind of machine going haywire in the fermentation room; it had never occurred to me that it might be arson and that my best friend could have been the culprit.

"She was an absolute mess when I found her. Drunk off wine, high on God-knows-what, screaming and crying and saying she wanted to burn the whole barn to the ground. I tried to get her to tell me what happened, why she was so upset, but all she kept saying was 'Fuck this place. Fuck this place. Fuck this place.' I had to drag her out, kicking and screaming, before the smoke killed her."

This picture of a frantic, disconsolate, unhinged Jessica Bancroft leaves me floored. It's the polar opposite of the self-assured, downright cocky queen bee I'd spent most of high school following obediently, to the point of worship. And yet it does sync up with my last experience with her: that manic fight we had about my dad's firing, during which we vowed never to speak to each other again. "My last name is all over this fucking Valley!" she'd screamed. "But that doesn't mean my life is easy! I've got shit going on too!"

But what was really going on with you, Jess? And why did you never tell me?

A profound sense of disappointment and anger overtakes me as I look my father in the eye. "That's how her DNA got under your fingernails, isn't it? You scratched her when you were pulling her out of the fire."

He shrugs ambivalently, too far removed from these silly details to even give them much thought anymore.

"But if all that's true," I say, "how could Holly possibly have blamed it on you? She must have known Jess started the fire."

"Oh, she knew," my dad says. "Jess flat-out told her she did it. But you know Holly—appearances are everything with her. She couldn't bear the idea of people finding out her precious little girl had snapped, so she started spreading rumors that I started the fire. And when Jess went missing, well, she already had the perfect scapegoat: the disgruntled ex-employee who burned down her barn and made her daughter cry."

A stinging sensation draws my fingers up to my eyes, and I wipe away the salty tears that must have formed during his story. Everything he says, and the way he says it, is so measured and fatalistic—everything happens for a reason, so there's no point in feeling anger or regret about a life predetermined. It all just makes me even more enraged over the events that brought him here—and guilty for my own failure to be there for him in recent years.

"I'm such a shitty daughter."

"You are not a shitty daughter, Lana."

"You deserve so much better than this, and I wasn't even here to support you—"

"Baby," he says, reaching out across the table to take my hand in his, "I don't blame you for any of that. We both did what it took to survive. And the important thing is, *we did*. We're *here* now. And we've still got plenty of time to make things right."

As he grips my hand tight, so full of love and affection, I know that he's talking about us. That *he and I* still have time to make our relationship right. But I'm not my father. I've never been all that Zen, and I don't believe anything in this life is predetermined. I believe in justice and my own ability to execute it. And at this moment, there's only one thing I want to make right: *Holly Bancroft and Teddy Mason need to pay for what they did.*

28

When I arrive at Golden Eagle Winery that afternoon, the place is full of people and abuzz with excitement in preparation for the evening's fundraiser with the governor. Red, white, and blue streamers have been hung across various arbors and archways, giving the old chateau a distinctly French Revolutionary feel, although I suppose the intent was more of an American-style patriotism. Assistants to various important people in both wine and politics flutter about with seating charts and dining menus. A head valet sets up cones while explaining to his team of part-time teenagers how to take keys, distribute tickets, and park cars. And several uniformed state police officers who must be the governor's advance security team inspect the property's perimeter, looking for God-knows-what sort of imagined threat.

I spot Sheriff McKee and Deputy Leroux chatting outside the tasting room, both in uniform, so I head their way while dodging more than a few young political assistants whose phone-glued eyes fail to notice me. "Is everything set up?"

McKee nods. "We told the governor's team to get him here half an hour before they actually need him. That's your window. And Holly knows you have a few follow-up questions, so you'll talk to her first."

"Her office still has a giant hole in it from the rock incident," Leroux adds, "so we couldn't use that. But we put a few chairs and waters in one of the barrel rooms for you. Do you want anything else in there? Snacks, maybe?"

"Snacks?"

"You know, some mixed nuts. Maybe a cheese plate. They've got a great selection—"

"Essie," I say, putting a friendly but instructive hand on her shoulder, "you don't bring snacks to an interrogation."

* * *

As I wait for Holly Bancroft to join me in her private cellar, I'm overwhelmed by the distinctive odor of wood—more specifically, French oak barrels—and I stew with frustration over Leroux's choice of an interrogation room. It's certainly cramped given the racks of wine barrels piled up all around me, and it's always helpful to induce a feeling of claustrophobia when you're questioning someone. Also, the dim lighting makes for a moody if slightly melodramatic ambience that I quite like. But the smell—*Jesus Christ*—it's like I'm trapped in the lumber aisle at Home Depot. I can't believe people actually pay hundreds of dollars to have private dinners in here.

Luckily, my wait isn't long, and soon a wary Holly joins me on one of the two remaining chairs in the room, both of which have been set out by Leroux for the occasion. She takes a bottle of Topo Chico out of an ice-filled bucket without waiting to be offered one, and as she sips, she stares me down with a raw distaste that's a far cry from the warmth she showed me four days earlier.

"No hug this time?" I ask, never bothering to rise up to greet her. But Holly just sits there, sipping her sparkling water with an intensity that would make me laugh if I weren't so furious at her. "Fine. Then if you're sure you don't want a lawyer present, let's get right into it." I place my digital voice recorder on the concrete floor beside me and ask my first question:

"What's the MA?"

"Hmm?" she says innocently while taking another sip.

"The Mystica Aeterna."

"Sorry, I have no idea what you're talking about."

"Holly—"

"That's Ms. Bancroft to *you*, Agent Burrell." The icy threat in her voice is clear. If I go down this road, she has no intention of cooperating. I realize my only hope is to be as unpredictable as possible, to keep her on edge and see if I can get her to break.

"I saw you getting oral sex from a much younger man on Sunday. How was that for you?" No response. "I couldn't see much under that leopard mask you were wearing, but the guy seemed to know what he was doing." No response. "Ms. Bancroft, Bex Potter already told us everything there is to know about your little organization. As did Kaito Yonehana after he almost died thanks to your branding ceremony." No response. "Do you have a brand too?"

She finally looks up at me with a wry grin. "Are you asking me to show you my pussy, Agent Burrell?"

But I refuse to be rattled by her clear attempt at drawing a rise out of me. This is going to be a battle of nerves, and I fully intend on winning. "I'll take that as a yes."

After that, I proceed to tell her everything I know about the MA, from the openly available sex and drugs to the more mystical elements that relate to Rudolf Steiner, Aleister Crowley, and the Rosicrucians, taking some guesses along the way to make it seem as though I'm an expert on the subject. I tell her about Ancient Greek Bacchanalias and the wine-loving alchemists of the 1600s. I talk about Christian Rosenkreutz and Steiner's belief that he could very well be his reincarnated soul. Then, once my authority's been established, I take a massive leap that I hope like hell doesn't backfire.

"Did everyone in the MA get a handkerchief monogrammed with Christian Rosenkreutz's initials? Or was that just a leadership thing? A little inside joke about taking on his mantle?"

I notice a twitch in Holly's eye, a look of surprise that confirms what I'd been hoping: the handkerchief found with Katherine O'Shea *did* come from someone at Redwood Vale (and it has absolutely nothing to do with Caleb Roche, thank God). "Bex really told you about those?" she asks with a mix of disappointment and betrayal. I nod my head, lying my ass off, and wait for her to say more. Finally, she relents: "There were five of them made for the five of us in charge. Like the five points on a pentagram. But it was all just for fun. I know when you frame it the way you just did, it sounds like a cult, but that's not what it is. We don't make anyone do anything they don't want to do. There's no forced sex. There's no—are you a religious person, Lana?" she asks, switching gears all of a sudden.

"So I'm back to being Lana now?" She rolls her eyes at me, and I continue: "No, I'm not religious. Why?"

"I never was either," she says. "Always found it so . . . pedestrian. I think my attitude toward it came from growing up in NorCal in the '70s. We all thought we were so morally superior, preaching free love and peace, while the Phyllis Schlafly types in the middle of the country used their religion to spread hate and mistrust. Atheism, or at least agnosticism, was our way of telling ourselves we were better than them—smarter than them. But do you know what I realized after Jess died? *They* were the smart ones—not us. Because a person *needs* to believe in something. I'm not talking about heaven and hell, or some other fanciful way to explain death when you lose a person you care about. I'm talking about the soul, Lana. *My* soul. It needed a purpose. It needed community. It needed a connection to something bigger, to the universal unknown, to God and the Earth and the past and the future.

"And after menopause I was so *fucking* horny all the time. They don't tell you that—I think it's society's way of desexualizing older women, because God forbid we actually enjoy getting fucked when we can't have kids anymore. But I was *feeling* things, Lana. I was feeling so much for the first time in my life. And Greg, I mean, you know my ex-husband. He's not—well—you know. Sweet guy and all, but he hasn't gone down on me since the Berlin Wall fell. I'm serious, by the way. 1989.

"So when I started going on retreats and experimenting with my body, and with drugs, I also met people, like Bex and a few others, who opened my eyes to things that had been right in front of me the whole time, and it was like . . . getting hit by a lightning bolt. This wine that's all around us—it *is* holy. And again, I don't mean the blood of Christ or anything like that. I mean there's magic in what we do here. For *seven thousand years*, people have been turning plain old grapes into this miracle elixir that brings happiness and fosters community and, depending on your perspective, brings you closer to God or Dionysus or even Jesus, if that's your jam.

"And that's a beautiful thing, Lana. It really is. So a group of us, we decided to celebrate that. And have a little fun—which yes, does mean a certain amount of sexual freedom. And drugs that I'm sure will be legal in the next ten years. But I'm telling you, as one of the people who runs the MA, it's not a cult. It's more of a church for slutty, wine-loving misfits."

When she finally stops talking, I find myself at a loss for words. I'd been so careful to stay in control of the conversation, to steer Holly exactly where I wanted her while keeping her on edge with what I know about her secret activities, but now, all of a sudden, the roles have reversed. Her confession feels so unabashedly honest, so stream of consciousness and free of deception, that I'm left fumbling for a suitable counterattack. Which is quite possibly what she wanted all along. Holly Bancroft didn't get where she is today by naively spilling her guts to anyone who'd listen; she's a master strategist and a ruthless businesswoman. I remind myself what Jonah said about his mother—she's a killer, whether she's actually killed someone or not—and what Sheriff McKee said about her performance on the stand during my father's trial. Was this simply another Oscar-worthy monologue from the Meryl Streep of the Mayacamas? Or was she actually telling the truth?

I honestly don't know anymore...

"What about Governor Mason?" I ask, trying to regain my composure.

"What about him?"

"Is he in the MA? One of the five leaders you mentioned?"

A burst of uncontained laughter nearly causes her to double over in her chair, a startlingly honest reaction that throws me for a loop. "Teddy? Are you kidding me?"

"You *did* call him the other day when you found out I was sniffing around about your connection to Carlos Ruiz."

As soon as I mention that name, her smile fades, her eyes narrow, and she falls silent. I know I've touched a nerve. "Next question."

"Fine. Then why don't you tell me about Martha Bauman."

"What?"

And just like that, I regain control. She clearly hasn't heard about the body we found at Redwood Vale—it's not as if Jonah or Peter Bancroft would share that news with her, given the state of their relationships—and the mention of an almost fifty-year-old missing person's case throws her for a loop. This wasn't something she came prepared to discuss, and I can see her struggling to chart a path forward.

"Martha Bauman," I repeat. "She was one of your best friends in high school, along with Governor Mason. But she went missing in 1978 when you were back from your sophomore year of college."

"I'm sorry, I'm confused. What's your question?"

"Did you and the governor kill her?"

"Are you fucking serious?"

I can see her rage building, the inner turmoil of past traumas or misdeeds manifesting as raw, unbridled anger. But I can't let up. I need to keep attacking, trying to find the right pressure point to make her break. "Does the name Esmeralda Sanchez mean anything to you?"

"No, it doesn't, but—"

"Her body was found at Redwood Vale forty-seven years ago, not long after Martha Bauman went missing." I see a flash of recognition; she may not have remembered the name, but she remembers the circumstances. *What does she know? What is she hiding from me?* "During our search of the Vale two nights ago, we found a body in the woods. Bones, really. They belonged to a young woman around Martha's age, and we're pretty sure she died of a traumatic head injury. Which means someone killed your best friend, Holly. Buried her on your property. Now do you seriously expect me to believe that you and Teddy had nothing to do with it?"

I expect another rage-filled outburst from the ruthless winemaker, but instead she draws inward, lost in some painful memory, and her eyes well up with tears.

"Holly? What are you thinking about right now?"

She wipes her eyes with the back of her sleeve, trying to make it stop, desperate to keep whatever she's feeling from showing on the outside. But some traumas can't be suppressed, no matter how strong or emotionally evolved we think we are, so all I can do is press on. "Not long after these women were killed," I remind her, "your father and uncle had a very public fight and decided to split up their company. Did the murders have something to do with—"

"Fuck you, Lana," she says through bitter tears as she leaps up, kicks over her folding chair, and turns to leave in a huff.

"How many women have to die in this Valley before you start telling the truth, Holly? Huh? This can't go on forever!"

She spins back around like a whirling dervish, her eyes wet with tears. "You don't know what the fuck you're talking about." Then she storms out of the cellar and slams the door behind her, leaving me alone in the dimly lit, sawdust-smelling crypt.

I've clearly touched a raw nerve, but the question is, *With which accusation?*

Patience, I remind myself, *I'll learn soon enough.* The time on my phone reads 4:51 PM. Nine minutes until the governor of California is led in here by Sheriff McKee and Deputy Leroux, clueless that he's being lured into a trap. Of course, it won't be easy extracting the truth from a career politician with a preternatural ability to lie his ass off through a toothy smile, but I don't need Mason to actually admit to anything today. I just need to scare him a little, throw him off his game, and if he *is* a killer, I'll know.

I always do.

29

Governor Theodore Leroy Mason Junior, Napa native and heir to the Barberry Hill Wine Company, started his career in politics at the age of twenty-seven, when he became the youngest congressperson in California history. He served three terms, and at thirty-three, ran for Senate (for the first time) and lost in spectacular fashion. Two years later, when the state's other Senate seat came up for election, he had the audacity to challenge the sitting senator in the Democratic primary, which he lost by forty-seven percent. But Teddy Mason is, if anything, persistent in his ambition, and after a few years in the legal private sector, he plotted his return to politics by winning the race for mayor of Napa in 2003. He served two consecutive terms, then again set his sights on the Senate, only to lose for a third time in 2012, coming in twelve percentage points behind the lieutenant governor. There was a silver lining, though, since a vacancy had just opened up in the lieutenant governor's office, and Mason made no secret of his aspirations for the job. Six years later, when the governor could no longer run because of term limits, then–Lieutenant Governor Mason stepped up as the heir apparent, and in 2018 he won by the skin of his teeth. Now in his second term, he's making a strong play for the White House; hence his continued need for campaign funds from wealthy friends like Holly Bancroft. If he does run for president, he'll be sixty-four years old; not all that impressive given he's been angling for the job since his twenty-seventh birthday.

As he glides across the barrel room with his hand outstretched, seemingly eager to meet me, I'm struck by how unbelievably predictable he looks. Every single chestnut brown hair on his head flows elegantly from one side to the other, a Kennedy-esque coiffeur held together with the sheen of an expensive pomade. His eyes are big and bright, with just the right amount of wrinkles around the edges after a lifetime of smiling for cameras and crowds. And his teeth—*my God, his teeth*—glow with the wattage of a halogen lightbulb. I can only imagine how much money he's spent over the years to keep them so straight and perfectly white. He's handsome, but in an obvious, prefabricated sort of way; a six who bought his way into becoming an eight. And for today's occasion, a fundraiser and dinner among friends at Golden Eagle, he's opted for a casual look: a white button-down shirt and jeans, plus the obligatory charcoal Patagonia vest.

I decide that I hate him before he even opens his mouth to speak.

"You must be Agent Burrell," he says as he firmly grips my hand with both of his, more of an arm wrestle than a traditional handshake.

"You must be the governor."

"My reputation precedes me," he says with a wink. But not the endearing, maternal kind, like when Leroux does it. This is the gross kind of wink. The predatory kind. The kind that makes me want to throw a left hook and end this thing before it even starts.

A reedy, unpleasant voice pipes up from behind Mason, a poorly tuned clarinet following up a smooth tenor sax. I see a balding, bespectacled man in a navy-blue three-piece suit shuffling over to me with a suspicious look on his face. "What exactly is all this about?"

"Agent Burrell, you'll have to excuse Martin here," says the governor. "He's three parts lawyer, one part human being."

"Why don't you both take a seat," I tell them, gesturing toward the two chairs across from mine.

"Is this about money?" Mason asks. "You do know I'm here to raise some, not to give it out—"

"Just so you know, this conversation is going to be recorded."

"I'm sorry—what now?" asks the governor.

"He's not saying a word until you tell us what the hell this is about," adds the lawyer.

I restart my digital voice recorder, place it back on the concrete floor, and give Teddy Mason a look that could boil water. Any preconceived notions he had about me vanish. "Governor Mason, I apologize for not being open about why I needed to speak with you today. But we had to be certain that you and Holly Bancroft weren't able to talk in advance and align your narratives."

"Align our narratives?" repeats the governor, appalled by the presumption. "About what?"

"Two women were killed here over the past two months, and while you are *not* a suspect at the moment, we were hoping you could help us out with our investigation."

The governor shoots a wide-eyed look over at his lawyer, who returns a quick nod that seems to be a prearranged signal between them, and before another word is spoken, they're both rising up out of their seats. "This conversation is over," says the attorney, Martin, as he ushers the governor back toward the door.

"Excuse me?" I call after them. "You can't just walk out of here in the middle of a—"

"Actually he can," says Martin snidely. "He's the governor of the most populous state in America, and in all likelihood, the next president of the United States, so he can pretty much do whatever he wants."

"A lot of women are dead, and your client could help shed light—"

"Not gonna happen, Agent Burrell." Then they storm out of the barrel room and into the hallway, never even glancing back in my direction.

Motherfuckers...

At first, I'm so annoyed at being slighted by these two men that I don't know whether to race after them or hurl my chair across the room. Sure, I knew it was possible that the governor might plead the Fifth or use his position of power to avoid getting his hands dirty in my case, but the utter disregard with which he and his lawyer just treated my investigation leaves me shell-shocked. I didn't even bring up the MA or Mason's possible ties to it, or the mysterious death of Martha Bauman, and still they bolted without a word. Hell, I never actually got the chance to mention the names of *any* of the women who were killed. Obviously, the governor knew where I was headed with my questions; otherwise, he would have at least waited to gather more context before giving that signal to his attorney. And if that's not the behavior of a guilty conscience, I don't know what is.

The question is, *Guilty of what?*

With a deep breath of oaky air, I regain my composure and race off into the hallway after them. Leroux's there waiting for me, jittery with nerves. "What happened?" she asks. "They just stormed off with the sheriff..."

"He knows something," I tell her, quickening my pace with each step.

"What did he say?" she asks, struggling to keep up.

"Nothing."

"Then how do you know? Boss?"

"I just do." And as I step out into a crowded wine reception in full swing, occupying every inch of the capacious tasting room, I see the governor laughing with a group of well-dressed friends and admirers. By the look of him, you'd never know an FBI agent had just questioned him in a murder investigation; in fact, you'd probably assume he just came from a spa, that's how relaxed he appears. The complete and utter impunity of this man makes my blood boil, and all I want to do is march across the room and tell him what I think right to his face, but before I can move another inch, I'm grabbed by a strong hand and pulled forcefully back into a quiet alcove.

Essie Leroux is staring at me with gentle, maternal eyes that belie the firm grip she still has on my arm. "Don't do it, Lana."

"You have no idea what I'm about to do."

"Sweetie, you're all worked up," she says in that caring, coaxing voice of hers, all hot tea and honey. "Probably because of your dad and what these people did to him. And I get that—believe me, I do—but nothing good can possibly come from you marching over there and making an ass of yourself in front of a man who could ruin your career with a snap of his fingers." I try to fight back, but when I open my mouth to argue, there are no words. Leroux nods with complete understanding and continues: "Remember what you told me when my emotions got the best of me and I wanted to accuse Peter Bancroft before we had all the evidence? *'There's a right way and a wrong way to do this job. And I'm telling you right now, you're about to do it the wrong way.'*"

I breathe deep, taking in her words, and look up at those caring brown eyes behind a pair of tortoiseshell bifocals. For some reason, Essie reminds me of my mother. She'd be about the same age if she were alive—maybe a few years older—but still, I can't help but wonder what she would look like. Would she dye her hair like Leroux, or would she let it go a natural gray like her own mother did back in Santa Fe? Would the tedium of daily contact lenses grow so tiresome that she'd switch over to thick glasses like my colleague? I've never actually thought about it before. In my memory, my mom has always been a gaunt, wispy-haired thirty-six-year-old dispensing pearls of wisdom from a hospital bed. What would she tell me now if she were here? If I had to guess, it would probably sound a lot like what Leroux just said, only spicier: *"Pull your shit together, Lana. You're too smart to be such a dumbass."*

The soft traces of a fond smile curl across my face, and I gently peel Leroux's fingers off my forearm. "You're right. Thank you, Essie."

"Any time, Boss."

My eyes drift back across the room over to Governor Mason. He's laughing with a new circle of friends now, giving one of them a congratulatory pat on the back as he casually sips one of the five-hundred-dollar wines Holly Bancroft opened for the occasion. Standing a few feet away is his lawyer, Martin, and two members of his security team from the California State Police, a veritable human force field shielding the governor from anyone who might try to harm him.

But in this country, no one is invincible. If Teddy Mason was involved in a murder—whether it was four decades or two weeks ago—I *will* uncover the truth and bring that sonuvabitch down. I just need to go about it the *right* way, which means gathering more evidence. And it's in that exact moment that I realize my next course of action.

"Deputy," I say as I turn back to my ever-eager colleague, "how would you feel about taking a drive out to Davis?"

30

The University of California, Davis, was founded as the agricultural branch of the prestigious UC system, and over the years it broadened its curriculum to become one of the premiere research universities in the country. But along with its legendary veterinary school, there's one academic branch at Davis that stands head and shoulders above any competing program on the planet: the Department of Viticulture and Enology. Located just forty-five minutes from Napa and seeded with millions of dollars in funding from many of the biggest wine companies in the world, including the J.B. Bancroft Corporation, Davis's wine program has churned out some of the greatest winemakers of all time. And its research labs are truly best in class, responsible for some of the most important innovations in winemaking history.

But I didn't drag Deputy Essie Leroux all the way out here just to bask in the glory of a fabled California institution. I brought her because she had easy access to the evidence locker at the Napa County Sheriff's Department. A locker that contained a monogrammed handkerchief belonging to a leader of the MA, which has Katherine O'Shea's fingerprints on it, as well as the grape must or pomace from the winery where she was most likely killed. And now, courtesy of my father, we're being led into a quiet research lab after-hours by Dr. Zeke Washington, assistant professor of enology and chemistry and a world-renowned expert on grape clones.

"How's your old man holding up?" Washington asks as he flips on some blinding overhead LEDs and boots up a desktop computer system.

"About as well as you could hope," I tell him. "In classic Cliff Burrell fashion, he's already gotten two degrees from Berkeley since he's been in there."

"Let me guess," Washington says, laughing with a high-pitched *hee hee hee*. "Philosophy and theology."

"Nailed it."

"Such a nerd."

Zeke Washington and my dad met around twenty-five years ago when they were both neophytes learning vineyard management from some of the old-timers in Rutherford and Oakville, the guys who could tell you which rootstock would hold up best against phylloxera in a wet year, and which chardonnay clone you should use on an east-facing slope rather than a westerly one. My dad was older at the time, having just decided on a midlife career change, while Zeke was a twenty-five-year-old kid doing field research for his doctorate, but they apparently hit it off like brothers. I even called him Uncle Zeke for a while; that's how often he was hanging around our house in those days, blind tasting cheap Sangiovese and Tempranillo in our kitchen with my dad and a few others who didn't quite fit in with the posh crowd of legacy wine families. I didn't talk to him much back then—I was an angsty teen who didn't exactly share a lot of interests with a geeky wine scientist in his mid-twenties—but I always remembered his laugh. It had this rapid-fire, high-pitched twitter that had no business coming from the mouth of a two-hundred-pound man, and it cracked me up every time he did it.

I'm glad to hear some things haven't changed.

In fact, not much seems to have changed at all with Zeke Washington. He must be around fifty years old now, but he still keeps his shiny bald head shaved right down to the skin. And the neatly trimmed black mustache I used to make fun of when he'd visit us is still there, although maybe a bit bushier than it once was. He also still wears plaid button-downs tucked sloppily into his khaki pants, along with an old pair of white Reeboks that are covered in the dirt of more vineyards than I could possibly imagine.

"So tell me more about this grape must," he says, starting up a shiny cylindrical machine that begins to hum softly like an electric car.

"Honestly, we don't know much. We think it's from a winery in Napa, probably on the northern end of the Valley, but it's hard to say. So what we're hoping we can get from you is something more specific about the grapes in it, something that helps us narrow things down to a specific vineyard."

What I don't tell him is that I have one very specific vineyard in mind: Barberry Hill, the estate owned by Governor Teddy Mason, which just so happens to be half a mile from the spot on Howell Mountain where Katherine O'Shea was found. I'd like Zeke to draw his own conclusions based on nothing but science, rather than let me sway his findings in any particular direction.

He studies the "C.R."-monogrammed handkerchief with gloved hands and narrow eyes. "Give me twenty minutes," he says. "I can run this through my new sequencer and see what kind of grapes we're dealing with. But I'm gonna warn you, it's almost impossible to pinpoint an exact vineyard this way. So many of them use the same clones of the same varietals—it's a real longshot to hope for something so unique that we can say exactly where this was made."

"I understand," I tell him. "But we'll take our chances."

As he places the handkerchief into that strange cylinder, I look over at Leroux and see how utterly baffled she is by the conversation that just took place. That's when I remember that her home-brewed wine project at Eu Topos Vineyard was very much her husband's terrain, and for all I know, her wine knowledge starts and ends with how to use a corkscrew. "Zeke, while we're waiting, do you mind telling us more about these clones and varietals you mentioned? Just so we can put a dumbed-down version in any reports we have to file."

"I'd be happy to," he says. And as steam begins to fill the cylinder behind him, swallowing up the mysterious handkerchief, we move across the lab to take a seat at a cheap plastic folding table that I can only assume Zeke and his fellow scientists use for lunch.

* * *

"With the exception of some rare local hybrids that you'll never find in any mainstream wine store, *Vitis vinifera* is the species of grape used to make every single bottle of wine on the planet," Zeke says with the nerdy excitement of someone who could talk about this stuff all night if we let him. "You can think about it like dogs, if that helps. Every dog you've ever met is a *Canis familiaris*. Great Dane, Chihuahua, golden retriever, you name it; they're all one species. They've just been bred to look and behave differently over the millennia. Well, the same goes for wine grapes. Merlot, chardonnay, pinot noir, malbec, it's all *Vitis vinifera*. But through careful cultivation and a whole bunch of happy accidents over the years, we've wound up with about ten thousand different varieties and cultivars. With me so far?"

Leroux and I nod our heads obediently, and Zeke continues: "Great. Now let's talk clones. Within each cultivar—say, cabernet sauvignon, since that's often what we're working with in Napa—there are hundreds of different known and registered clones out there. Now a clone is a population of vines derived from a single mother vine before any mutations are allowed to occur. Over the last hundred years, we've tracked and monitored these things to such a degree that we now know which clone is the most disease resistant. Which has higher yields. Which has smaller berries and more intense flavors. Which has tighter clusters. Which has stronger tannins. So a lot of wineries actually like to plant several different clones and then blend them in their final product, creating that perfect stew of flavor and texture that suits their palate."

Leroux furrows her brow as she tries to piece together what he's saying. "And that doohickey of yours over there. It won't just tell us what variety of grape is on that handkerchief. It'll tell us which clone of which variety."

"Correct," Zeke says. "Along with some other details that probably won't be as useful. Yeasts and any other additives the winemaker may have used, that sort of thing."

Now it's my turn to jump in for added clarity. "These clones—how common are they? I mean, is every winery in town just using the exact same ones?"

"It depends," he says. "Some are *very* common. You can find cabernet clones six and seven all over California. But then there are some more unusual ones. Like clone fifty-one, which is owned exclusively by Spottswoode Estate."

"So you're saying there's a good chance this could be a total waste of time."

Zeke lets out that high-pitched giggle of his. "Learning about wine is never a waste of time, Lana. But from a murder case standpoint . . . yes. Yes, it could be an absolute waste."

* * *

As luck would have it, our search isn't a waste at all. In fact, it's the furthest thing from it.

"Son of a goddamn bitch," Zeke mutters as he examines the data from his analysis on one of the many computers on his desk.

"What is it?" Leroux asks, about to burst with anticipation after twenty minutes of waiting.

"Clone three hundred sixteen."

"Which means . . . ?"

"I'll tell you in a second."

Zeke slides his wheelie chair over to the end of his desk, where he's loaded some sort of database onto another computer monitor. "Most vineyards register their clone use with the Foundation Plant Services here at Davis."

"Why would they do that?" I ask.

"Disease. Phylloxera outbreaks have ruined enough harvests over the years for us to realize there had to be a better system. So now whenever there's an outbreak, we know which clones are being affected and can prevent it from spreading by replanting with unaffected rootstock."

I only understand about half of what the motor-mouthed enologist just said, but I decide it's not all that important anyway. What matters is that his database can tell us exactly who uses clone three hundred sixteen.

"All right," he says. "There are only three vineyards in the world who registered three hundred sixteen with us last year. One is in the Margaret River region of Australia, so I'm guessing that's not your culprit. But the other two are here in Napa."

"Is one of them Barberry Hill?" I ask, no longer able to contain my eagerness to bust the governor of California, the one person who seems capable of tying together all the mysterious murders that have haunted Napa since long before I was born.

"No," he says.

"What?"

"One is in Coombsville. It's a small producer called Holloway & Hall. The other is even smaller. It's up in Calistoga. A place called Wappo Crest Winery."

I grab onto the wall behind me for support, but I'm not sure if it's going to be enough. Not with my knees wobbling and my head spinning in circles like this. Not now. Because I've finally figured it out. I know who killed these women.

Not just Pilar Cruz and Katherine O'Shea, but Jessica Bancroft too.

31

Deputy Essie Leroux listens patiently to everything I have to say, writing down important information when necessary, eager to ensure that nothing goes wrong with my plan. Then she gets in her squad car in the UC Davis parking lot and flips on her lights and siren. "So it's really not Peter Bancroft," she says glumly through the open window.

"No, Essie. I'm sorry, but it's not."

She shrugs with genuine disappointment, years of personal animus and well-crafted murder boards amounting to nothing, but I know she's not going to let it weigh on her for long. Not tonight. Not when I've just given her the biggest assignment of her admittedly short police career. Once she pulls away, headed north toward Napa, I hurry into my car and promptly check the GPS. It's an hour and twenty minutes to my apartment in San Francisco, which should get me there a little after midnight. But despite the hour, I've never been more awake and alert in my life.

* * *

I park on the street outside my building and look up warily at my dark, second-floor apartment. Before I exit, I log into my ADT Security account to check if anyone has come to the front door, seeing as Carlos Ruiz still has my house key, and the building manager has ignored my request to change the locks. But there's not a single alert from the motion-activated camera.

Thank God . . .

I let out a deep, cleansing exhale, still in shock over what I now know, and hurry inside to get what I've come for.

* * *

I find the wine cork exactly where I left it twenty-some years ago: in a black Converse shoe box full of childhood memories that I could never bring myself to open or throw away. The box is in my bedroom closet, tucked in the back corner, under a stack of six other shoe boxes, all of which contain actual footwear. It's no wonder Carlos Ruiz never found it when he broke in on Sunday.

Now, as I fondle the dusty old cork with the cute frowny face drawn on it, I think back on that night my father brought it home to me from the Bancroft's house. At the time, I was so angry with Jess, so hormonally irrational as only a teenager can be, that I never gave the cork a second thought. I just tossed it in a drawer and forgot all about it until the day post-trial when I had to pack my things and move out. But now that I know what I know—now that I'm being forced to reevaluate every relationship I've ever had—I reexamine the cork with new and wizened eyes.

At first glance, there's nothing out of the ordinary about it besides Jess's little sketch. It's a perfectly average cork from a bottle of Golden Eagle cabernet with the vintage stamped on one end, 1999, and some red wine stains covering about two millimeters on the other side. But upon closer inspection, I notice for the first time that there's a slight hiccup in the font on the letter "N" of Golden, which happens to fall smack dab in the middle of the cork. It's almost as if—yes, it *is* the result of someone cutting the cork in half widthwise and reassembling it to near perfection.

With a mix of excitement and dread, I pull both ends of the cork as hard as I can, and after a few seconds of futile grunting—*POP*—it comes flying apart. Somehow, Jess managed to dig out the center of the cork and replace it with a hollow metal tube that's so sharp at the top, it sealed both halves when they were pressed firmly together. But it's what's inside the tube that interests me most. Wedged into it so tightly that it never moved or made a sound when the cork was shaken, is a blue miniSD memory card with a SanDisk logo. I haven't seen one of these in years, but as luck would have it, I have an old MacBook under my bed with a port that supports the format. So I get down on my hands and knees, reach into the impermeable cloud of dust bunnies that have made their home under my mattress, and hope for the best.

* * *

Ten minutes later, I've finally found a charger that works with my old MacBook and survived the tedious process of waiting for an outdated laptop's hard drive to load. I slide the miniSD card into the corresponding slot, and after a few seconds a single folder pops up on screen. It's labeled "For Lana," and inside, there's only one file. As I feared, it's a video.

My pulse begins to race as I double-click the file and wait for it to load on QuickTime. I have a good idea of what I'm about to see, and yet the encroaching horror of what it will look like and what I'll have to do afterward leaves me in a state of quiet panic.

Breathe, Lana.
You have to watch.
You owe it to her.
You owe it to all of them.

A deep exhale clears out my lungs, and my eyes snap open with purpose. I click "Play."

* * *

Right away, I recognize Jess's bedroom on the third floor of the Bancroft's home, just a short walk from the main winery at Golden Eagle. It was originally built as an attic tucked into the gabled roof, so rather than a typical box shape, the space is really more like one long pyramid. The ceiling slopes downward from a central point so dramatically that you can only stand upright in the middle of the bedroom; by the time you get to the edges, you have to hunch over, making a good portion of the room completely unlivable. I once asked Jess why she chose this strange bedroom in the attic when there was a perfectly normal guest room available one floor below, and in typical Jessica Bancroft fashion, she said, "I like sharp edges, in people *and* in rooms." And that was that.

The camera seems to be hidden somewhere on Jess's dresser, perhaps under a pile of clothes, because there's a bit of fabric obscuring the top-right corner of the frame. But it's pointed directly at her bed, which is centered under the high gable and pushed up against a small window on one end of the room. As usual, the bed has been meticulously made; Jess was the only teenager I ever met who tucked her sheets into hospital corners before leaving for school in the morning. And her four white pillows have been fluffed beautifully atop her wrinkle-free lavender duvet. Just like Jess herself, everything is perfect.

There are twenty-seven seconds of absolute silence at the start of the video. At a certain point, I'm tempted to fast-forward the footage, but before I get a chance, I hear a hushed argument off-camera, followed by a slamming door and the ominous click of a lock. Then Jess slouches across the room and takes a begrudging seat on the edge of her bed. Her eyes are wet with tears, but she's not crying. She seems to be biting down on her lip, suppressing some profound desire to scream or fight or God-knows-what, but instead, she just sits there and waits. Whatever's about to happen, it's clearly not the first time, although I wonder if it was the last.

"Take off your shirt," says a familiar off-camera voice that causes my hands to tremble. I so badly want to close my eyes, but I can't; she wanted me to watch this, so I can't stop now. And with a deadened, hopeless expression, Jess slowly pulls her black V-neck top over her head, then folds it carefully and places it on the floor beside her.

"Your pants," says the voice. And with the same robotic misery, she slides off her skin-tight jeans, folds them neatly, and places them on top of the shirt.

As she sits there on the edge of the bed in a functional gray bra and matching thong, her lifeless eyes drift up toward the gabled ceiling. Then I begin to hear a sharp, staccato breathing and the squishing sounds of lubricant or moisturizer on skin. The man in the room is obviously masturbating. I'm just relieved it's entirely off camera so that I don't have to watch.

"Look at me," says the voice with a quiet, demanding power. Slowly, Jess lowers her eyes from the ceiling to stare directly at the person across from her. I can only imagine what she must have been thinking in that moment: the powerlessness, the anger, the nausea. *Jess, why didn't you tell me sooner?*

Of course, I know why she didn't tell me. Because at the time, I never would have believed her. I was too emotionally compromised, which is obviously why she tried to show me instead.

"Take off your bra," commands the voice. And Jess does as she's told, unhooking her bra with a single practiced hand, revealing the seventeen-year-old breasts that I was so jealous of at the time.

Perfect, perky objects of desire that I wished so badly were on my body and not hers. But now, as they hang there sadly on her chest, drooping helplessly, all I want to do is go back in time and put a blanket over them and apologize for every jealous word I ever said.

The sound of masturbating intensifies. "Panties," the voice says through heaving breaths, and Jess complies without a word, carefully placing her thong atop the rest of her clothes on the floor. Now as she sits there completely naked and exposed, all I can think is . . . *Why? Why isn't she fighting back? Why isn't she saying anything?*

After a full minute of this, the attic floorboards start to creak, and the off-camera voice I've been dreading to see makes his first appearance.

Jonah Bancroft is barefooted, with no pants on and his plaid boxer shorts hanging down below his knees. He's wearing a navy-blue T-shirt that falls just above his waistline, so his pasty, hairless ass is fully visible while he walks toward Jess, still jerking off as he moves.

For the last two hours, ever since the name Wappo Crest appeared on Zeke Washington's computer, I've had a hunch I would see something like this. And yet the sight of Jonah—*my* Jonah—sexually assaulting his own sister—*my* best friend—feels like getting punched in the gut over and over and over again. I want to vomit, but I haven't eaten enough today to make it worthwhile. I want to cry, but I'm too pissed off at myself to allow any tears to fall. I want to scream, but I don't think I could find the voice to do so if I tried.

Jonah. *Fucking Jonah.* He was right there in front of me this entire time, and I was too blinded by the past to see what he was really up to in the present. But now I know, and before the night's over, he's going to be arrested for not one, not two, but *three* brutal murders.

It was the mysterious break-in that pieced it all together for me. Why would Carlos Ruiz go to all that trouble to search my place unless he was looking for something extremely valuable? And then I remembered: on Sunday, I'd told Jonah about the cork I'd gotten from Jess just before she died. He must have known what it meant—maybe he was even the one who'd taught her that trick to hide something in a hollowed-out cork—so he sent Ruiz here to try and find it. Luckily, my alarm scared him off before he had a chance to.

Then there was my father's story about Jess burning down her family's barn back in 2003. "Fuck this place," she had said over and over and over again. And her behavior around that time showed the classic emotional volatility of an abuse victim. But the fact is, she could have burned down any building on the property that day; and if she really wanted to spite her mother, she would have destroyed the chateau that hosted her precious office and tasting room. But she didn't. She went after the barn where the 2003 sauvignon blanc was fermenting: the first vintage ever coproduced by Jonah Bancroft.

And then there's the strange sequence of events in the year 2020 that so profoundly altered the lives of Holly, Jonah, Carlos Ruiz, Caleb Roche, *and* my father. It started with the Glass Fire, which burned sixty-seven thousand acres in Napa and Sonoma Counties and either destroyed or tainted much of that year's vintage.

Something happened during those fires—I don't know what exactly—but for some reason, it motivated Holly to call an old friend of hers, Abigail Cox, and help her get someone in prison to find out the truth about Jess and my father. Maybe some new evidence came to light that made her question the story she'd been telling herself for seventeen years—I don't know—but Cox put her in touch with Carlos Ruiz, who must have exchanged a few months in a cell with my dad for a reduced sentence.

When Ruiz told her once and for all that my dad was innocent, Holly must have realized something about Jonah and confronted him with it, setting off the fight that occurred between them that fall. But rather than report him to the police, for some reason, she simply cut ties with him, banished him from Golden Eagle, and drowned her guilt in the sex, drugs, and sense of higher purpose on offer at the Mystica Aeterna.

I still have *so* many questions: Why, five years later, did Jonah decide to kill two random women and try to pin it on his mother? How did he connect with Ruiz, and why did he have him tail me to my motel that first night in Napa, long before I had said a word about Jess and her wine cork? And what about those human remains we found at Redwood Vale, which belonged to a woman who died well before Jonah was even born?

I'll get my answers soon enough. I dispatched Leroux with a detailed message for Sheriff McKee and instructions to arrest Jonah for three separate murders. They're probably waking him up at his house in St. Helena right now, dragging him out of his perfect life in handcuffs, in full view of his perfect family. And first thing in the morning, I'll question him myself.

But right now, I have to get through this video. I have to understand what really went on between Jess and her brother all those years ago. Why she let him do it, why she never told me, and why he would start a relationship with me while it was happening...

"Open your mouth," he tells her in a quiet but commanding voice.

"Jonah, I really don't want to do this anymore—"

Slap. His open-palmed right hand swings viciously out at her, backhanding her across the face with a violence I can hardly comprehend from the soft-spoken Jonah. A streak of blood drips slowly out of Jess's right nostril, settling just above her full upper lip, but neither of them moves to clean it. They just stand there for a moment, frozen in place.

"Please," she says, still too numb to cry, still too powerless to move. "Jonah. We can stop this. I won't tell anyone. I'll never tell. Just stop, and let's both be done with it."

He seems to think about this for a moment, but the whole time, he continues masturbating. It's like a bestial compulsion he can't control as he stands cruelly over her. "We'll stop when I'm ready to stop." Then he lunges toward her, grabbing her by the neck and pressing her violently back against the bed. He pins her down and chokes her with all his might; then, when a lack of oxygen leaves her no choice but to submit, he begins to penetrate her.

I promptly stop the video and slam my laptop shut. I can't watch anymore. It's too brutal, too dehumanizing, too intensely personal to see another second. How long had he been raping her? How long had she been hiding all that pain, that shame, that inner torment? Part of me knows there's a silver lining here: this tape should be more than enough to get my father released from San Quentin. But I can't think about that right now. All I can think about is my best friend getting raped by my boyfriend—her own brother—while I was clueless to the evil standing right in front of me.

And here I thought I was such a good judge of character. A natural profiler who could eye someone from across a bar and tell if they were an embezzler or a petty thief or a sex criminal. *You naive little child*, I think, wishing I could shout back through time at my teenage self. *The biggest sex criminal of all was the first guy you ever loved.*

Suddenly, another thought hits me. If Jonah had me fooled all this time, then what did his mother know? Holly Bancroft is far from an upstanding citizen, that much is clear, but she couldn't possibly have known the full extent of her children's activities—*right?* No mother could turn a blind eye to such monstrous behavior in her own family, and frankly, no mother deserves to find out about it on the evening news. I don't know why—maybe it's my own protective impulses toward Jess's memory—but I realize that I need to be the one to tell her. Not over the phone, not at a police station, but somewhere quiet, woman to woman, Jess's best friend to Jess's mom. So I fire off a quick text to the number she gave me during our first interview: *We need to talk about Jonah and Jess. In person. Tonight.* Then, not wanting to sound too threatening, I send her one more. *I'm back home in SF, but I can come to you if you prefer.*

As I await Holly's response, still burning with rage over Jonah's abuse and deceit, I hardly notice the soft creak of a floorboard just a few feet behind me. And when I do finally lift my head to face it, I'm too late to stop the needle from plunging into the side of my neck.

As I flail for the now-empty syringe dangling from my body and try to steady myself against a wave of nausea, I see a man towering over me. He's holding a long, narrow knife, and much of his face remains hidden in shadow, but I know who it is before I even see his charming green eyes twinkle through the darkness.

And as I'm overcome with dizziness and my limp body crumples to the floor, I only manage to spit out three hateful words:

"Fuck you, Jonah."

32

When I wake up, my shirt is covered in vomit. I can still taste it in my mouth, that rancid acidity bubbling up in the back of my throat, and I spit what I can onto the floor in front of me. But when I go to wipe my lips, I discover that my hands won't move. They're bound behind me with zip ties that Jonah must have brought with him for this exact purpose. My legs are similarly hog-tied, but I'm otherwise seated comfortably on my living room sofa. Across the apartment, I see my captor standing at the kitchen counter with my laptop open, no doubt watching that awful video Jess tried to show me. He's holding my loaded Glock in his right hand.

"The sheriff already knows everything, Jonah. We can prove Katherine O'Shea was at your winery before she died."

"Then I'll blame it on Caleb. And I know you don't have anything connecting me to the Mexican girl."

"She's Guatemalan."

"Sure," he says with a flippant disregard for the woman he killed. But his eyes never leave the video on my laptop. He stares at the screen with an obsessive focus that I find nearly as disturbing as what I saw on the video itself, as if he's reliving those horrible moments beat by beat.

"Why am I still alive?"

"Honestly? I saw your security camera on the way in, but it was too late. It got my face. So I need you to log into your account and delete that video."

"After which, you'll kill me."

He shrugs, clearly so accustomed to killing at this point that the idea of ending my life has absolutely no effect on his twisted psyche. Never mind the fact that we spent an entire summer sleeping together and sharing what I *thought* were our deepest, darkest secrets.

How fucking wrong I was . . .

I watch him for a moment, his eyes still glued to the laptop screen, and quickly consider my options. I could refuse to comply, but that would only piss him off further, and given what I know about his previous victims, he won't hesitate to cut me with that knife he brought. Personally, I'm not all that interested in being tortured, so I move to the next alternative. I could try to stand up and fight back, but I'll never break free of these zip ties. Especially not with his murder drug of choice, pentobarbital, still coursing through my veins, leaving me nauseous and woozy.

I decide that for now, while I wait for the drug to wear off, my best bet is to stall and keep him talking. Even in the worst-case scenario, I'll at least be able to fill in some of the gaps in this sick family saga.

"Fine," I say with a raspy, vomit-tinged voice. "I'll log in and delete the security tape. But *only* after you answer a few questions."

"What's the point? You're gonna die anyway."

"You killed my best friend and sent my father to prison for life because of it. I'd say you owe me a few answers before you do whatever the fuck it is you're gonna do."

For the first time since I regained consciousness, his eyes shift away from the video to look at me. He considers my offer for an excruciatingly long moment before he shuts the laptop, sets the gun down on the counter, and picks up his knife. He studies it for a moment, smiling devilishly as the kitchen lights bounce off the shiny metal blade. Then he slowly approaches me with it.

"You can have three minutes. Then I want that video deleted."

"Deal."

He takes a seat in the recliner across from me, an old La-Z-Boy that I inherited from a former roommate, and as he leans back and crosses his legs, I imagine how we must look together and almost want to laugh. Take away the zip ties, the pentobarbital, and the glistening murder weapon in his lap, and we're just two old friends swapping stories in the comfort of my living room. I'm even tempted to ask him for a beer from the refrigerator, if only to help wash this awful taste out of my mouth. But I don't. Because we're not friends, and these aren't innocent stories meant to be shared over a Heineken. These are confessions, and I want to look him right in the eye when he delivers them.

"When did you start raping your sister?"

His face curdles with discomfort, and for a moment, I worry I've already lost him. That our tête-à-tête is already on the verge of coming to a swift and violent end. But he takes a calming breath and pulls himself together. "I don't like that word."

"What? *Sister?*"

He smiles cruelly. "I always liked your sense of humor, Lana. Just the right amount of twisted." Then he lifts the knife up to help scratch an itch on his chin, a not-so-veiled threat if there ever was one. "Next question."

"Fine. But at least tell me why you started dating *me* that summer. Was it real, or was it just some sick game you were playing with Jess?"

"Truthfully?"

"You already drugged me and tied me up, Jonah. I can handle a few hurt feelings."

He sighs, looking oddly guilty over what amounts to the least vile of his many offenses. "I was just using you."

"Why?" I ask in a blunt, direct manner, utterly unfazed by a revelation that would have brought me to tears twenty years ago.

"I had just come back from college and wanted to resume our ... activities ... but she wouldn't comply, so I had to teach her a lesson. Show her that I held all the power and could take whatever I wanted from her, including the only real friend she had in the world."

From the moment I saw the video, I figured this might be the case, but it still burns just as much as the zip ties digging into the skin around my wrists and ankles. Of course my perfect first boyfriend was too good to be true. Chubby, awkward, poor, seventeen-year-old Lana Burrell could never have gotten a guy like that—right? A handsome, charming, rich college student who seemed to worship the ground I walked on. And in retrospect, I see now how much he used those adolescent insecurities to drive a wedge between me and Jess. Even if she *had* tried to tell me the truth about what he was doing to her, the abusive monster he really was, I don't think I would have believed her. I was too smitten, too busy living out some sick princess fantasy, and I probably would have just accused her of being jealous. *Ugh, teenage girls . . .*

"Okay," I tell him, pretending I'm not hurt, refusing to give him that slimy satisfaction. "Next question."

"You have two minutes."

"Why'd you kill her?"

I watch him squirm uncomfortably in his chair, chewing on his lip like he's trying to squeeze any last flavor out of a stale piece of gum. The entitled prick isn't used to being confronted over anything; he's used to being praised and propped up for all his mediocre accomplishments, and I can see how hard this is for him. "She snapped," he finally says. "Burned every drop of wine I made that year—my first vintage—and swore she was going to tell our mom everything. Obviously, I couldn't let her do that, so I tried to make a deal with her, but she wasn't listening. She was too far gone. And when she tried to leave, I hit her in the head with a chunk of limestone."

"And then you framed my dad for it."

"No," he says. "That was never the idea. I just needed a car to move her, and his was the closest one. Honestly, it was a total coincidence."

I can tell by the way he says it that he still sees himself as the hero of the story, a good guy who only did what he did because he *had* to, because he deserved the world and *how dare* anyone stand in his way. He didn't rape Jess; he took pleasure in his sister's company. He didn't murder anyone; he removed a few obstacles on his path to success. And a "good guy" like that never would have intentionally framed an innocent man like my dad, at least not in the twisted, tangled narrative that this monster had concocted in his demented mind.

I have to fight every urge in my body not to scream. As much as I want to, as much as I want to keep reminding him how awful he is, how many lives he's ruined, I know I can't do that yet. Not when there's still so much I need to learn.

"Did your mom confront you about Jess in 2020?" I ask. "Is that why you had a falling out?"

"Yes."

"So she's known since then and did nothing."

Jonah's eyes flare with anger. "*She took away my birthright.* Those vineyards at Golden Eagle are the best in Napa. My grandfather knew that, which is why he promised me I'd get to take over one day. And I was doing a fantastic job at it too, while she was off doing yoga and getting fucked by God-knows-who in Costa Rica all those years. I brought that winery into the twenty-first century. But then she decided to write me out of the will. Banished me from the property. And threatened to tell the police about Jess if I ever came back."

"So you joined up with Caleb, but his vineyard wasn't good enough, was it?"

"Do you know how hot it gets at that end of the Valley?" he asks with a smug sneer. "Do you know how much clay is in that soil? It was like trading in a Ferrari for a pair of roller skates and being told to compete in the same race."

"Oh, boo-fucking-hoo, Jonah. You always were an entitled little bitch—"

"She took *everything* from me!" he snaps, practically foaming at the mouth, and for the first time, I truly see the animal within. The feral beast that didn't just rape his own sister, but relished in it.

"Which is why you decided to frame your mother for murder," I say calmly, sticking to the facts. "If you could tie it to her cult, you could argue she wasn't in a clear state of mind when she changed her will, so you could sue to get Golden Eagle back."

He shoots me an impressed grin. "Look at you, Secret Agent Lady—"

"Don't call me that."

"Why? Only *he* gets to?"

"Yes."

Jonah's nostrils flare with rage, and he checks the time on his phone. "One minute."

"Carlos Ruiz. How'd you meet him?"

"During our last epic blowup, my mom told me he was the one who talked to your dad in prison, so when I realized I was going to need help, I tracked him down. Offered to pay him a lot of money if he did me a few favors."

"Like tossing a rock through a window in your mom's office while I was there."

"Among other things..."

"Okay." I nod, one more piece of the puzzle fitting into place. "Pilar and Katherine. How'd you pick them?"

"Honestly," he says with a bizarre directness, as if we're talking about choosing a bottle of wine to drink rather than people to murder, "I was only planning to kill the first one. I figured no one would really miss some immigrant picker without much of a family, and Ruiz told me about the fight she had with my mom, so she seemed perfect. But the fucking cops in this Valley, I swear to God, they're useless. I left breadcrumbs leading straight to Holly, and they completely ignored them. Which is why I realized I'd have to try again, only this time, with a white girl who had just been to one of her parties. And just in case that *still* wasn't enough for Sheriff Fuckface and his merry band of idiots, I used my mom's handkerchief to choke her out and put the murder weapon back in that creepy little sex palace."

"The cimeter knife I found wrapped in a towel."

Jonah nods.

"Were you really coaching your daughter's tournament in Tahoe that weekend?"

He nods again. "Figured it'd make a good alibi, so I slipped out while the girls were asleep."

"That's like a four-hour drive..."

"Three and a half in the middle of the night. Just enough time to do what had to be done and get back before anyone woke up."

"You really thought of everything, huh?"

"Everything but you." He checks his phone once more and lets out a relieved sigh as he rises up from the recliner. "Speaking of which, it's time to erase that security tape." He trudges back into the kitchen and opens my laptop. "What's your ADT password?"

"Capital U-r-s-u-l-a-2-3 exclamation point."

He types it in carefully, making sure each keystroke is correct. Then I see the wrinkles above his eyes bunch up in annoyance. He types it in once more, even more slowly this time, but again he's left without access. "Don't play games with me, Lana."

"I'm not."

"What's the password?"

"I just told you!"

He storms around the kitchen counter and across the room, waving that knife around in his right hand while the laptop is firmly clenched in his left. "I swear to God I'll cut your throat open right now—"

"Great. Go for it. The police will see you in the tape, and you'll be in jail by breakfast."

He lets out a guttural roar of frustration, a lion caged in and unable to kill its prey, and I watch with satisfaction as he starts to pace the living room floor.

"Maybe I got the number wrong. Let me type it in—"

"Fuck you," he snaps.

"What? It's like a muscle memory thing—sometimes you just need to do it yourself."

"You're just gonna get it wrong again, get me locked out of the account for good."

"Okay, then come sit next to me," I tell him. "You can even hold the knife against my throat and watch me as I type."

He narrows his green eyes and stares me down, trying to read my body language for any signs of deception. But I just look right back at him, never breaking eye contact, daring him to make the next move. And finally he does. With an impatient groan, he trudges over to me, plops down on the seat cushion to my left, and places the open laptop on my tightly bound knees. Within seconds, I feel the cool blade of his knife pressed against my throat, the flat side thankfully facing my skin so that I can swallow without accidentally drawing blood.

I look down at the laptop. Then I glance over at him, seeing how the streetlight bounces diabolical shadows on him courtesy of my old Venetian blinds. With a deep breath, I turn back toward the monitor, where the ADT Security window is up with my login name saved. Thanks to my zip-tied wrists, I'm forced to hunt and peck my way across the keyboard, and I feel Jonah's eyes boring into my skull as I type: U-r-s-u-l-a-2-3.

"Can you hold down 'Shift' for me?" I ask, perfectly innocent. "I'm trying to make a question mark, and I can't do it with my hands tied."

He reaches out with his left hand to press shift, lowering the knife from my throat just enough to give me the window that I need—

And I thrust my knees up as violently as I can, launching the laptop into the air, forcing him to choose between grabbing it and swiping at me with the knife. By the time he decides to swing his blade, I've already rolled to my right, where I reach out with my bound hands and just barely manage to grab onto the beaded cord hanging down from the blinds. Jonah lunges at me again, but this time I let him get closer, and as his face dives toward me, I spin away once more and wrap the cord tightly around his neck.

He lets out a roar as he starts to choke, but he won't let go of the knife, and he plunges the blade down into my left thigh. It's the most agonizing thing I've ever experienced. Every nerve in my body explodes with pure, unfiltered pain, and I can't help but scream. But I never loosen my grip on the cord, and as he starts to twist the knife deeper into my quadricep, I squeeze the noose even tighter around his neck.

Blood starts spewing out from the wound in my leg. Before I know it, it's all over both of us and the sofa, a bright red Jackson Pollock painting. But my focus remains on Jonah's face, which is turning from red to blue as the oxygen struggles to make its way into his brain. The sounds coming from both of us are more animal-like than human as we press our weight onto each other, desperately trying to gain leverage.

Suddenly he rips the knife back out of my thigh, and the blade coming out hurts even more than it did going in. More blood spurts out, and an electric spasm shoots from the nerves in my thigh straight to my brain, causing me to slip. Spotting this, Jonah's able to grab the cord with one of his hands and wriggle his way free of my grip. Then he leaps up and kicks me in the face while I'm still on my side, unable to straighten up thanks to my bound extremities. I hear the sound of my nose break the moment he makes impact with his boot, but compared to the agony in my thigh, I barely feel it. Every fiber of my being remains focused on survival, and when he tries to plunge the blood-soaked knife into my exposed back, I slip away just in time. All he manages to stab is the empty seat cushion.

As he struggles to pull the blade free, I grip both of my hands together into one double fist and swing it at Jonah's face like a baseball bat, knocking him sideways and drawing blood from his lip. But he's still on his feet, and now we're staring at each other, no more than three feet apart, separated by a glass coffee table and a twenty-two-year lie. I need to make him pay for what he did. Not just to Jess, not just to my father, but to me too. I'm going to kill this motherfucker even if it's the last thing I do. But just as I'm about to lower my head and charge at Jonah—

BANG!
A single gunshot rings out in the cramped apartment.

Before I can tell who's been hit, I instinctively look up into the kitchen, where Holly Bancroft is standing by the open door, holding my smoking gun. And as I wonder what the hell she's doing here and whether I've just been struck by one of my own bullets, I feel myself tumbling forward. Unable to stop my fall with bound hands and tied ankles, I collapse straight onto the coffee table, shattering it in an explosion of glass.

Everything goes black.

Holly Margaux Bancroft
Golden Eagle Winery
October 17

Dearest Lana,

I've never been good at apologies. It's simply not in my nature to show weakness or to acknowledge a personal failing. But I have failed you. And so rather than risk not being able to tell you these things in person one day, I've decided to write them down in a letter. I hope you don't mind. And I hope you've got plenty of time on your hands because, as usual, I have a lot to say.

To truly understand why I did what I did the other night, you need to go back half a century, so bear with me. All acts of evil have their origins in the past. It doesn't excuse them, and I am not asking for your sympathy. I'm merely trying to give context. *Like wine, people are very much the product of the environment they grew up in. The soil, water, sunlight, and temperature of a vineyard all come together to give a grape its unique flavor; so, too, does the love and trauma of a home provide the character of an individual.*

And in no uncertain terms, my childhood was a traumatic one. Not for lack of resources or opportunity—I know how privileged I was to be a Bancroft—but because of my father. Michael Bancroft was, quite simply, a monster. I don't know how many women he raped during the peak of his power and influence in the late '60s and throughout the '70s, but he was shameless in the way he took advantage of young dreamers who simply wanted access to the industry that he helped build. As for me, he never assaulted me sexually, but he subjected me to a daily torrent of verbal abuse that turned me into the ruthless, cutthroat businesswoman who you had the displeasure of meeting during your teenage years in the Valley.

In August of 1978, I witnessed the depths of my father's depravity firsthand when my best friend at the time, Teddy Mason, dropped me off at home after a night of heavy drinking and, yes, light cocaine use. When I walked inside, I found my father dragging the dead body of my friend, Martha Bauman, into our garage. I don't know what happened. I don't know how he killed her, although given her naked state, I know he must have had sex with her first. But did I scream or run or call the police to report this murder? No. I didn't. I was simply too scared of this incredibly powerful man to do anything but comply with his wishes. And what he wanted me to do was help him bury the body on our property at Redwood Vale. So I did.

It wouldn't be the last time either. The same thing happened a month or two later with a woman whose name I didn't know until you mentioned it the other night: Esmeralda Sanchez. There may have been more too. I honestly don't know. I think my uncle had some idea, though. He never told me directly, but I'm pretty sure it's why they split up the company. J.B. loved his brother too much to turn him in, but he couldn't let his habits drag down the company that he loved just as fiercely.

After I had children, I did everything I could to keep them away from their grandfather. I didn't know what he was capable of, even with his own family. But it pains me to admit that by the mid-'90s, my ambitions as a winemaker overtook my responsibilities as a mother. I was working more, I was traveling, and I let my own drive to succeed cloud the painful memories of my youth. So I'm not sure when it started or how long it lasted, but at a certain point my father began abusing Jonah. He whipped him, beat him, masturbated in front of him, and on at least one occasion, he made him perform oral sex on him.

As for Jess, he never touched her; in fact, he treated her like an absolute princess and promised her the keys to his kingdom, even though she was only seven or eight at the time. Although this wasn't her doing—she certainly never sought out his adoration, and she had no interest whatsoever in the wine business—I know Jonah never forgave her for it.

You're probably wondering when I found out about all this. Well, when he was thirteen, Jonah stole a bottle of wine from our private cellar and drank the entire thing himself. When I found him in his closet, piss drunk, he told me everything like it was some kind of joke. But by the next morning, he'd completely forgotten about our conversation.

Again, did I scream at my father? Did I call the police to report him? No. By that point, I was too afraid to tarnish the Bancroft name with a scandal, especially since I had just taken over the Golden Eagle label. So what did I do? Nothing. Even as I type these words, I hate myself for my inaction, and I can't even explain to you the full cause of it. But when faced with my family and its homegrown evil, I simply shut down and buried my head in the sand. It wouldn't be the last time.

The monster died a year later, and I thought that meant we were free. I thought the worst was behind us. But then Jess disappeared, and I'll admit, I had my suspicions about Jonah. She'd gotten so much worse ever since he came home from college; I could see her mental health spiraling before my eyes, and it seemed eerily timed to his presence in her life. But I couldn't voice these suspicions out loud. I couldn't risk losing my son and my daughter at the same time. So when the police started looking at your father thanks to all that blood in his car and the DNA under his fingernails, I ran with it, never even fathoming that my own son had been the one to shove her lifeless body in that trunk. I told an embellished version of the truth to make it seem as if Cliff were the only possible killer, and I hated myself the moment the words left my mouth.

Obviously, I couldn't tell you any of this at the time, but I did try to protect you from Jonah, just in case. I know it's not a lot, and I should have done so much more—I should have trusted my instincts—but that day in the courtroom when I told you to "stay the fuck away from my son," I wasn't doing it for him. I was doing it for you, Lana. To keep you safe. I know you've probably hated me for it; you probably figured I thought you weren't good enough for him. But that wasn't the case at all. He wasn't good enough for you. He never was.

But of course, the story doesn't end there, does it?

Over the next seventeen years, my guilt began to eat away at me. The emptiness around me created an emptiness inside of me, and I went looking for something with which to fill it. I dabbled in a few local churches, I went on silent retreats, I tried drugs, I began having casual affairs,

I got deep into yoga and meditation. Everything I told you earlier about this part of my life was true. But it was when the Glass Fire hit in 2020 that my past finally came back to haunt me in a way I couldn't ignore. You know part of our vineyard was destroyed by the flames; well, so was my relationship with my son.

Because in the wreckage of an old shed out on the far end of the property, buried under a now-incinerated wooden floor, I found Jess's body. Or at least, what was left of it. Bones, and a sapphire ring in the shape of a fleur-de-lis that my father had given her on her tenth birthday. (I'm sure you remember it; she almost never took it off.)

Part of me had always thought, maybe she just ran away and was living happily on a beach somewhere under a pseudonym. But when I found her there with that ring on, in a shed that only Jonah ever used for some of his more experimental fermentations, I knew it was him. I just knew.

But first I had to make sure. I figured after seventeen years in prison, your dad would have no reason to keep lying; he had a life sentence and no chance for parole. So I had a judge friend of mine put me in touch with an inmate at Folsom Prison who she thought might be willing to help in exchange for an earlier release date. And when he agreed, I got Teddy Mason to pull some strings from the Governor's Mansion to have him placed in a cell with your father at San Quentin. I thought maybe, when pressed, your dad would admit to killing Jess if he had really done so, but after three months together, he never stopped denying it. And when he nearly killed the inmate—that's how upset he was at the accusations—I pulled the plug on my little investigation.

That's when, after seventeen years, I finally confronted Jonah with what he did to my daughter. I wrote him out of my will, I kicked him out of my life, and I told him I never wanted to see his face again. It was the hardest thing I'd ever done, and my guilt and shame and loneliness all mixed together to send me into the worst despair of my life. I'd probably still be there, lost and miserable, if it weren't for the Mystica Aeterna.

I know you think it's a cult, and maybe it is, but I like to think it's exactly what I told you it was the last time we spoke: a church for slutty, wine-loving misfits. Unlike my father and my son, we've never hurt anyone intentionally. I know the branding can look a bit rough at times, but it bonds us in a way that blood never could. We're a surrogate family for people who didn't necessarily have the best biological families, and together we're trying to build something that's bigger and better and more beautiful than any of us. So if you'd like to keep investigating it, or if you want to press charges for anything you saw at Redwood Vale, be my guest. I'm not going to stop you. Although I do want to make it clear that Governor Mason never played a part in any of it. Teddy's far too savvy a political animal to risk dabbling in illicit sex and drugs, even under a mask, and the only reason I called him that day was to warn him about Carlos Ruiz, since he helped me get him placed in your father's cell. (I would hate for there to be any political blowback, since he really was just doing a small favor for an old friend.)

That said, I'll happily send a copy of this letter to Sheriff McKee if you think I ought to be charged as an accomplice in any of the crimes that I was too weak and pathetic to stop or report. The ball is in your court, Lana, and I am entirely in your hands. Because I owe you the life I took away from you all those years ago.

In vino Veritas,

Holly

P.S. For Jonah's sake, I never told the police about Jess's remains, but if you'd ever like to pay her a visit, you should know that I had her moved to her favorite spot in the world, under that old valley oak in Coombsville where we put up her memorial plaque. I'm sure she'd love to hear from you. You were, after all, the best friend she ever had.

33

I wake up with a catheter up my crotch and a pounding headache.

Where am I? And why does everything smell like bleach?

My neck is too stiff to move, but I manage to shift my body just enough to gather my bearings. There's an IV drip flowing straight into my arm, vital monitors beeping softly, a curtained window to my left, and an empty bed to my right. On my bedside table are two bouquets of flowers, a cloth-wrapped gift basket, and three sagging "Get Well Soon!" balloons, all running low on helium. Clearly, I'm in a hospital somewhere, but as for how long I've been here? Well, the depressing balloons would suggest at least two or three days.

The door to the hallway is closed, and the room is otherwise empty, so no one knows I'm awake yet. I could obviously press the red "Call" button by my bedside, and I'm sure I'd be swarmed with an army of medical professionals in blue scrubs. But instead, I decide to savor this surreal moment of peace and quiet, at least for a few minutes.

How did I get here?

I remember flashes of light, translucent faces passing in front of mine like ghosts. I remember voices: Holly Bancroft, Caleb

Roche, the meaningless medical chatter of EMTs and hospital staff. I remember a pain so sharp and overwhelming that I couldn't even keep my eyes open; all of my senses were consumed by that singular source of horrible agony. And then I remember nothing. Just a void of anesthetics and surgical procedures that led me to this moment.

Have I been shot?

My hands, which are still tingling from disuse, start to crawl across my bare skin, feeling for entry wounds under the thin blue hospital gown. My shoulders, my chest, my stomach. But I can't find anything. Just the thick bandage over my left thigh where I remember Jonah stabbing me with a knife.

Blood loss, I remind myself. *That must be why I passed out. They must have had to do a transfusion.*

As my body begins to reawaken, I shift over even more to examine the gifts on my bedside table. The first bouquet, an expensive blend of orchids in a glass vase, is from Peter Bancroft, but he hasn't bothered to leave a proper note. The second, a collection of wildflowers wrapped in paper, is from Caleb: *Nice job, Secret Agent Lady. Call me when you're up. P.S. You even snore when you're in a coma.*

I start to laugh, but immediately regret it. Everything still hurts too much, even with whatever drugs I've been getting from the IV. The balloons are both from the SAC. She's left a sweet note and a suggestion that I take some time off, fully paid, of course. And the gift basket? It's from Deputy Leroux and Sheriff McKee, although I can tell from the handwriting that she just signed his name onto her card. As expected, it's full of homemade muffins: banana nut *and* blueberry.

It feels like I haven't eaten in days, which in this case, may not be hyperbole, so I carefully sit up a bit more to eat one of the muffins. Turns out the blueberry are even more delicious than the banana nut, and I end up inhaling two in a matter of minutes. But when I reach over for one of the three plastic bottles of water on the opposite table, I notice a letter in a red envelope with my name on it. Intrigued, I carefully open it and see that it's been handwritten on the official letterhead of Golden Eagle Winery. Not only that, but it's seven pages long. So I take a sip of water to clear the muffin crumbs from my throat, then lean back into my pillow, eager to read what the woman who seems to have saved my life has to say.

* * *

Eventually, long after the startling revelations in Holly's letter have settled over me, I bite the bullet and press the "Call" button, summoning the inevitable onslaught of nurses and doctors. They tell me that I've been in a medically induced coma for two days, which they had no choice but to do given all the blood loss from my leg. There's severe damage in my quadricep that's going to require extensive physical therapy, but they were able to repair some of the muscle surgically. Otherwise, beyond a few bruised ribs and some small cuts on my face and arms from the glass coffee table, I'm in surprisingly good shape. If all goes according to plan, they expect me to be able to leave the hospital in about three days.

Thus, with nothing but time on my hands, I begin to check in with my various well-wishers, not because I feel obligated to, given all the gifts and cards, but because I *want* to. Because right now, the woman I am doesn't want to hide away in the darkness with some Netflix and Heineken. No, she wants to soak up the love of the people she cares about most in this world. And is it possible that it's just the drugs talking, turning this hopeless introvert inside-out and forcing her to socialize? *Sure.* But I also like to think there's more to it than that. I like to think that maybe—just maybe—Pilar, Katherine, and Jess weren't the only women whose inner mysteries I managed to solve over the past week. And that if Holly Bancroft was right, and people and wine really are both the products of their environment, then maybe this Napa soil has finally turned me into a well-balanced, age-worthy blend, the FBI's very own cult cab.

The first to arrive at my bed is Essie Leroux, who's out of uniform for the first time since I've known her. Instead of her usual olive and brown deputy getup, she races into my room wearing a kitschy red sweater with three dachshunds on it and comfortable black slacks, a much more natural fit for her—shall we say—*unique* personality.

"Oh my God, can I hug you?" she asks before even saying hello.

"Gently," I tell her. "Bruised ribs." And she gives me the most cautious but satisfying hug I think I've ever had, right up there with my dad's embrace in prison. Her sweater smells like mothballs and drug store perfume, but in the moment, it's absolutely perfect, and I breathe it in with a smile.

After the obligatory check-in on my health, including an uncomfortably blunt question about whether or not I've pooped yet—apparently, it's a big deal in these post-surgery situations—I ask her to fill me in on everything that's happened with the investigation. She brought her usual notepad for this exact purpose, and as I close my eyes to give them a rest from the blinding white hospital lights, she runs through her list of bullet points.

According to her statement, Holly Bancroft was already in San Francisco when she received my text messages. Desperate to know what I'd found out about her children, terrified that it might be the secret she'd harbored for the last five years, she texted back that she'd come to me at once. Of course, when I failed to respond, being unconscious at the time and at the mercy of her psychopathic spawn, she called Caleb to get my address. (It turns out they'd become quite close over the years, behind Jonah's back, since Holly liked to check in on her son's well-being without him knowing.) So with my address in hand, she raced across the city to talk to me before I could go public with what I knew. But when she reached my apartment, she heard a struggle inside, then a blood-curdling scream, so she opened the door without knocking and saw Jonah trying to kill me on the sofa. Without hesitating, she grabbed my gun off the countertop, aimed it at her son's leg, and wound up hitting him in the abdomen instead.

He's currently in a recovery room down the hall with an armed police officer seated outside, although the guard hardly sounds necessary. The gunshot ruptured Jonah's liver, and it'll be a long time before he's able to make a run for it—or drink wine again without an organ capable of processing alcohol. Doctors say his surgery was a success, though, and he's expected to make a full recovery, just in time for his court appearance.

The San Francisco PD, who were the first on the scene at my apartment, located my laptop and turned the video of Jonah and Jess over to the FBI, who then shared it with the Napa County Sheriff's Department. The knife he stabbed me with also turned out to be from the same set as the cimeter knife that we found at Redwood Vale, which was indeed the murder weapon used on Katherine O'Shea and Pilar Cruz. As Jonah told me, he had stashed it there in his convoluted scheme to frame his mother and the Mystica Aeterna, but now it's further evidence of his involvement in both murders. He'll be arrested and formally questioned as soon as he's recovered enough to make a legally admissible statement to the police.

"It wasn't just him, though," I tell Leroux. "His grandfather, Michael, he's the one who killed Martha Bauman and Esmeralda Sanchez." I don't show her Holly's letter—much of it is far too personal to put in front of any eyes other than my own—but I explain the events of 1978 as best I can. The murders, Holly's quiet complicity, the fight that caused the breakup of the Bancroft wine business. "I'm pretty sure that's why they put the Conservation Easement on Redwood Vale. They didn't give a shit about protecting the environment. They just didn't want anyone digging up there if they ever sold the place, since there are so many bodies in the dirt."

"Jesus Christ," whispers Leroux in utter shock.

"Pretty sure that's my line."

"Guess you're starting to rub off on me, Boss."

We share a smile, and I know the feeling's mutual. Her innate warmth has changed me in more ways than she could possibly understand.

"Talk to McKee," I tell her. "Let him know we need to excavate that whole property."

"Will do," she says, and she scribbles a reminder down in her trusty notebook.

Then there's the matter of my father. Thanks to the video showing Jonah's brutal rape of his own sister, the prosecutor who tried the original case, now the Honorable Judge Abigail Cox, has agreed to sign off on an immediate release from San Quentin. He should be out in less than a week, once all the paperwork is approved.

As this news washes over me, it's frankly all too surreal to process. Leroux keeps looking at me as if she expects me to burst into tears of joy, but all I feel is a perplexed numbness. Of course, I'm thrilled to know that in a week, I could be eating chilaquiles with my dad in the Mission or taking him for a walk in the fresh air of Golden Gate Park. It's all I've wanted for the last twenty-two years, but my mind seems incapable of wrapping itself around this incredible news. It's all too much, too strange, too wonderful to properly envision, and so instead I just lie there in my hospital bed, staring blankly at the ugly teal walls, waiting to feel something.

"It's okay, hon," Leroux says with a gentle pat to my uninjured right leg. "I know it's a lot to take in right now, but you'll get there."

She stays with me for another hour, and we talk about her disappointment over Peter Bancroft's innocence, as well as her husband's health. Then she gets a call from Sheriff McKee, who needs her back at the station. Needless to say, there's a lot of paperwork that needs filing before they can bring charges against Jonah.

"You're a good cop, Essie," I tell her as she walks out the door of my hospital room. "Thanks for everything."

"Look at you, gettin' all soft on me," she says with a smile.

* * *

My final visitor of the day is the one I'd been the most anxious to see, and he shuffles in with an awkward grimace and his usual pair of Rainbow flip-flops. He stands there by the door for a long, tense moment, just watching me, neither of us saying a word.

Finally, when he realizes that, all things considered, I seem to be in good spirits, he cracks a hint of a smile. "You look like shit."

"Yeah, well, you should see the other guy."

I return Caleb's gallows grin, and he starts toward me slowly, both of us feeling the heavy presence of the third man in our relationship, a name neither of us wants to say because of what it might say about *us*. All the things we knew, or didn't; all the things we *should* have known. It's when he reaches the foot of my bed and places a gentle hand on my sheet-covered shin that I finally have to stop him.

"I want to trust you," I tell him, my voice quavering, barely above a whisper. "But I'm not sure how."

He nods, understanding completely, with none of the prickly self-righteousness I would have gotten if I'd said something like that to Jonah. With Caleb, there's nothing but empathy and patience, along with a face that isn't even capable of dishonesty. It's a face that's too pure for this Valley. "I get it," he says. "How does a guy work with a serial killer for five years and not realize who he is? But can I tell you the truth, Lana?"

"Of course."

"I think Jonah's always been good at making people see what they want to see in him. A human chameleon who we impose all our hopes and dreams on. You wanted the perfect high school boyfriend to sweep you off your feet, and he did. I wanted a partner who shared my ideals about wine and farming, a best friend who I could just be myself with, no pretense, no bullshit, and that's what he was. You see, he didn't actually have a winemaking philosophy of his own, or even a real personality. He was just a cipher who adopted the tastes and interests of the people around him. For a while, that was his mom; eventually, it was me. But when you're around that, when you're with someone who just seems to get you on that deeper level, it's . . ."

". . . intoxicating," I say. And he nods, meeting me in the eye, sharing my particular brand of betrayal. Not just mad at Jonah for his deception, but furious with ourselves for not noticing it, for gazing down at our navels rather than at the monster right in front of us.

"It's not your fault," I tell him as I extend my hand, eager to feel his touch on my skin.

"It's not yours either," he says, letting his fingers overlap with mine.

Then before I can say otherwise, he's giving me a soft, perfectly tender kiss on the lips, brushing some of the ratty, unwashed hair away from my face. He gives me a smile, another kiss, and finally pulls up a doctor's chair from across the room so that he can sit directly by my side.

We talk more about Jonah, of course. All the things we'd both missed or forgiven over the years: the ruthless entitlement, the blood-born arrogance, the subtle signs that he wasn't really the sweet friend, husband, and father he pretended to be. It's the first time I've thought about Jonah's own family, especially his young son and daughter, who will grow up with a father in prison, arrested on murder charges. And for the first time since I've woken up, I start to cry. It's slow at first, just a few percolating tears under each eye, but then the floodgates burst, and I'm suddenly sobbing uncontrollably.

Two decades of pain comes pouring out as I think about Jonah's kids, and while I don't feel a shred of sympathy for their psychotic father, I decide that, after visiting Jess at her oak tree, I'm going to check in with them as soon as I'm out of here. They're going to need support and someone to talk to, or this trauma is going to weigh them down for the rest of their lives too, continuing the cycle of pain, resentment, and unhealthy coping mechanisms. But eventually, the cycle needs to stop. Someone needs to step in and heal that generational wound, or nothing will ever change. Maybe I can be that person for them.

As the tears run down my glass-cut face, I feel the salt burning in every little scrape and wound, but I actually don't mind it. It's nice to let myself feel something, to know that I'm alive and healing and on the road to recovery. And with a deep breath, I force myself to smile.

"What are you thinking about?" Caleb asks.

"Nothing," I tell him. "Everything. I don't know." We fall silent as he holds both of my hands, and then an idea comes to me. "Actually, how do you feel about a vacation?"

"Together?"

"Yes. I realize we barely know each other, and my usual MO would be to ghost you for a few weeks and then complain about you to my therapist. But what if we tried to make this work? Like, a real relationship."

"A real relationship?" he repeats in mock horror, as if only a fool would make such an awful suggestion.

"A real relationship," I say again, really starting to like the sound of it.

"I could get behind that," he tells me. Then his eyes widen with an idea that sends him leaning over me with excitement, like he wants to pull me out of bed and start dancing across the room. "You know, I was invited to this wine festival in France in a couple months. Do you think you'll be able to travel by then?"

My nose wrinkles up in disappointment. "More wine?"

"It's kinda my job."

"Yeah, well right now, if I even *see* another bottle of cabernet, I think I might smash it over someone's head."

"Okay," he says, "that's fair. But this festival happens to be in *Burgundy*."

"So?"

"So . . . that's pinot noir country."

I look up at Caleb's big brown eyes and floppy hair, along with that goofy grin that won me over the moment I first saw it, and I realize it's a face I never want to stop looking at, no matter how hard things get, no matter how much pain I risk in the pursuit of pleasure.

"All right," I tell him with a long, romantic sigh. "I guess it's a date."